Copyright ©2011
James Bernard Frost

Library of Congress
Cataloging-in-Publication Data

Frost, James Bernard.
A very minor prophet / James Bernard Frost.
p. cm.
ISBN 978-0-9833049-8-2
(alk. paper)

1.Bartenders – Fiction.
2.Clergy – Fiction.
3.Male friendship – Fiction.
4.City and town life – Oregon – Portland –
Fiction.
5.Portland (Or.) – Fiction
I.Title

PS3606.R65V47 2012

813'.6 – DC22

2011016070

Hawthorne Books
& Literary Arts

9   2201 Northeast 23rd Avenue
8   3rd Floor
7   Portland, Oregon 97212
6   hawthornebooks.com
5   *Form* :
4   Adam McIsaac, Bklyn, NY
3   generalist.nu
2
1   Printed in China

Set in Paperback

To my parents, Jim & Dodi Frost, who will hate this book but still love me.
And to Portland, Oregon, the city of eternal spring.

Acknowledgements

A RIDICULOUS NUMBER OF PEOPLE AND entities helped me write this, some of whom I will undoubtedly fail to mention. To those I forget, all apologies. You can laugh at me in the afterlife while I burn in hell.

First and foremost, thank you to the wonder-press Hawthorne Books, for opening the fifty-megabyte document that this book originally arrived in. So few dared look at its unusually illustrated pages. Rhonda Hughes, Adam O'Connor Rodriguez, Liz Crain, Adam McIsaac–never has a book entered the world more appropriately dressed.

I would also like to thank the myriad of Portland writing groups with whom I shared pages, laughs, and the occasional Vicodin. Joan Rogers, Magdalen Powers, Gerard Fleck, Bo Yu, Dan Eckhart, Jeff Selin, Luciana Lopez, Kristin Thiel, Monica Drake, Diana Jordan, Lidia Yuknavitch, Erin Leonard, Cheryl Strayed, Mary Wysong-Haeri, Suzy Vitello, Chelsea Cain, and Chuck Palahniuk. Other early readers, and dear friends, were T. J. Firpo, Joe Frost, and Brad Bortnem.

Also vital to the writing of this book were zines, particularly those produced by the bicycling gang, C.H.U.N.K. 666, and by Sean Tejaratchi, the author of the incredible collection of religious iconography found in *Crap Hound*. To these and all others whose work I cut, pasted, taped, Sharpied, co-mingled, over-Xeroxed, and Photoshopped, I claim adoration and fair use.

A Very Minor Prophet is a book about a place, and so it couldn't have been written without many special places. Thanks particularly to the Oregon Writers' Colony, that roughhewn cabin on the coast where words fly off the page; the Writers' Dojo, for providing a lofty escape; and to the many coffee shop owners in Portland who brew the good stuff and let me stay for hours.

I should also mention the book *The Five Gospels*, written by the Jesus Seminar. Your color-coding amuses me. And Ace Typewriter, the last typewriter repair shop in America, for bringing an ancient Underwood typewriter back to life for $4.95.

I'd also like to thank Rosalee Rester, and my two children, Ava Frost and Atticus Frost. Enduring the struggles of a crazy-haired writer in the basement was a difficult cross to bear. Also unforgettable was the talented memoirist, Kerry Cohen. You lifted me up in my darkest hour.

Finally, and most weirdly, I would like to thank that young man who started this novel many years ago—the one who suffered constant misdirection, doubt, self-loathing, shame, and rejection to pursue a calling. I promise never to do it to you again.

– JBF

Portland, Oregon; Summer 2011

A VERY MINOR PROPHET

The Gospel according to Joseph Patrick Booker,

as interpreted by his faithful scribe, Barth Flynn.

a novel JAMES BERNARD FROST

HAWTHORNE BOOKS & LITERARY ARTS
Portland, Oregon
MMXI

The only way to the truth is through blasphemy.
FLANNERY O'CONNOR, *Wise Blood*

A VERY MINOR PROPHET

Preface to this Edition

*Where I Tell You
What You
Already Know*

YOU ALREADY KNOW HOW THIS GOSPEL ends. Safe in your quiet homes, on television, on YouTube, on your respective conservative or liberal blogs, you saw a ragged, bearded crowd of young men, fists in the air, bouncing up and down in bedeviled excitement. You heard them chant, and you watched as the news station cut to an embedded reporter – another young man, bearded himself, but wearing camouflage and clearly distinguishable from the masses by his white skin. Blue-lit, you stared at your screen, bored by a lingering war. The young man spoke, translating the chant from foreign Arabic to familiar English, and what he said jarred you to attention, so that you knocked over a beer, or took a misstep on a Stairmaster, or nearly fell backwards off a pregnancy ball. "They are chanting," announced the reporter, his face a mask, clearly enjoying the drama of a pause, "Behead the midget! Behead the midget!"

It went viral, the clip. The pundits played it and replayed it and replayed it again. They put it in context. He was a cult leader, a pacifist, a freak. He had walked into a war zone. He had gotten what he deserved.

You watched Jay Leno that night, and despite the morbidity of the moment, you laughed when he started his joke, "So a midget preacher walks into Baghdad …" And you laughed even more when he stopped there, a smug look on his jowly face, a twinkle in his buggy eyes, because he'd already delivered the punchline. You were happy then, because what you'd wanted to do, what you'd ached to do when the reporter had

first delivered his line, what you hadn't quite had the courage to do when you first saw the clip, you were now given permission to do by an authoritative source: you had wanted to laugh at the death of another human. And so you did, you laughed. America laughed.

It's a permanent part of our lexicon, this moment in time, like four soldiers planting a flag at Iwo Jima. This small person, this dwarf – hell, as Bill Maher pointed out, let's just say what we're thinking – this midget, he travels to Iraq, some crazed notion of single-handedly bringing peace to a besieged nation, and within hours he is swept up, stock images of mad Arabic masses driven into a killing frenzy, and then, this part deleted by the networks but available on the Web, there is his bloodied head, paraded around Baghdad on a mezza platter.

Successful late night comedy.

After they'd figured out who he was and where he lived, the paparazzi converged upon Portland, Oregon, upon this dreamy-eyed city, and they found us, the midget's friends. They asked us questions, for which we provided long and complicated answers. Then they took the long and complicated answers and cut them out. Film left on the floor. They showed, instead, our faces, our young and frightened and distraught faces, and under our faces they displayed our names, and next to our names were the words CULT MEMBER, black letters over a field of red, white, and blue.

The frenzy let up. The paparazzi tired of the rain and flew back to their big, sprawling, dry cities to the south and east. After they left we laid our friend to rest, head reunited with body, in the ground under a color-filled copse of Northwest maples.

Many months later, I got the stomach to watch the footage. I'll never know for sure what happened, how his head became John the Baptist-ed on a silver disk. But I do know one thing. My friend had been a prophet.

Albeit, a very minor one.

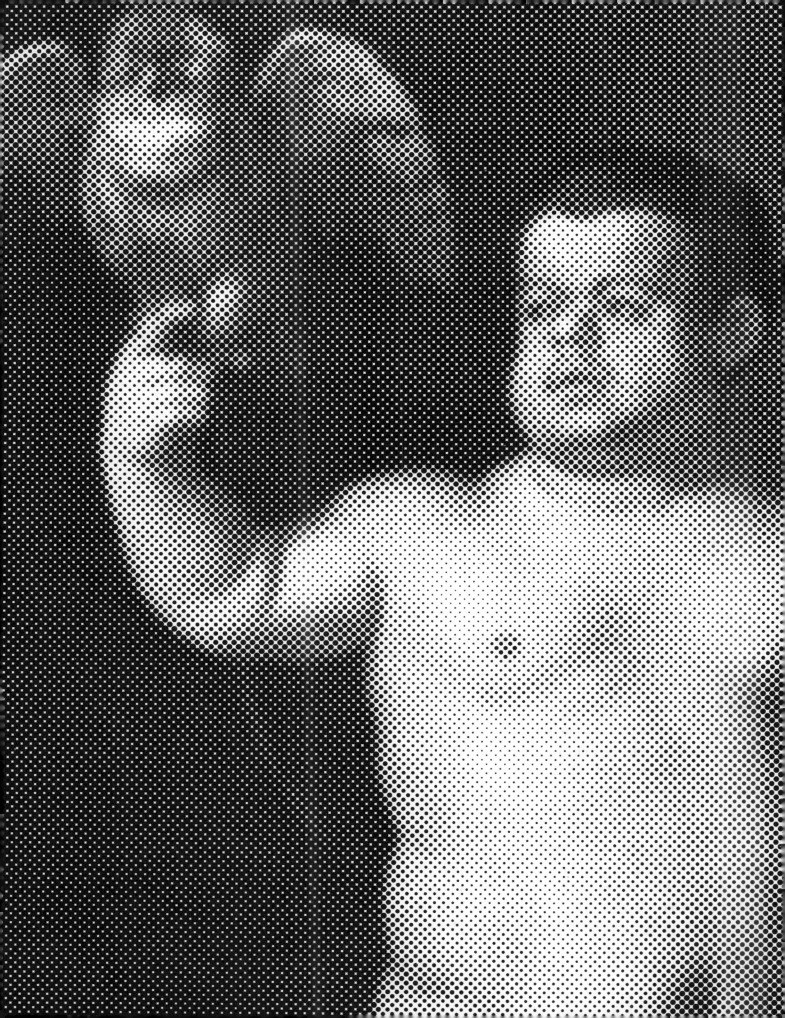

THE FIRST BOOK OF BOOKER TO THE AMERICANS

𝕮𝖍𝖆𝖕𝖙𝖊𝖗 1

Where I, Bartholomew Flynn, First Encounter Joseph Patrick Booker,
and Where He Stands Aloft on His Pulpit for the First Time

THE GOSPEL OF JOSEPH PATRICK BOOKER BEGINS ON A SUNDAY MORNING at the tail end of September, a day when a sandy-haired, green-eyed, twenty-two year-old of average height and weight, a young man named Bartholomew Flynn (that's me!), woke up too early, having nothing to do, having no plans, feeling as I often did those days that life was really quite meaningless. I woke up and did what I often did on mornings where I'd risen in this existential funk – I grabbed my messenger bag, the blue-linen journal I got for ninety-nine cents at Walgreens, and headed out the door on my pink and aqua-colored vintage Bridgestone bicycle, planning to ride to the Mecca Café, where I'd sit with the aforementioned journal and write about how I'd woken up too early, how I had nothing to do, how I had no plans, and how I felt that life was really quite meaningless.

The weather today was what my friend Beale and I called *cith agus dealán*, which in Celtic means sunshine with showers. (We'd memorized all the Celtic words and phrases for rain, which come in quite handy when one lives in Portland, Oregon.)

There was currently more shower than sun, and as I rode down the narrow corridor of Failing Street, getting splashed, despite their dutiful efforts to avoid doing so, by the drivers of Subaru Outbacks and Volvos passing me by, I cursed my overconfidence in the sliver of blue sky I'd seen when leaving my apartment that morning: I'd left my rain gear at home.

I was contemplating whether to turn around or spend the day in soggy jeans when a second misfortune beset me, my tires rode through a field of glass, the detritus of some suburban meth addict's failed attempt to nab a car stereo, and with an emphatic spsssssh, my journey to the local coffee shop to record my daily boredom and angst had become more complex.

Many months later, when I told him about my state of mind on that day, Booker would repeat himself, a smile of serendipity on his somewhat Mongoloid face, *"Ask, and it shall be given you; seek, and ye shall find; knock, and it shall be opened unto you."*

At the moment, though, I wasn't aware that I was asking,

seeking, or knocking. I was simply in desperate need of a quick tire change. I wheeled the bike over the curb, laid it in a pile of wet mulch, slung my helmet into a nest of ferns, then knelt on the sidewalk beside the bicycle, unzippering my wedge bag and spreading out my tools.

The building in front of which this took place was a church, although, as far as I could guess, it hadn't been used as a church for quite some time – it had the stained glass windows, the bell tower, the ubiquitous cross on the side that marked a church – but now it appeared to be some sort of residence, and judging by the look of it, the residence of a disgruntled aging hippie.

A giant Jolly Roger flew from the flagpole where the American flag might have been. There was a letterboard out front, the kind frequently seen in front of churches that usually have on them some sort of believe-and-be-saved hoopla, only rather than a biblical quote, this one had the latest George W. Bush bumble. (That day's read: WE MUST NOT BE DIVIDERS; WE MUST BE UNIFICATORS.)

There was more ephemera on the church's front doors – a whole slew of bumper stickers pasted one over the other (KBOO – Homemade Radio, Keep Portland Weird, What would Jesus Drive?, Praying is Begging, W is for War.) The crème de la crème of the whole concoction was a banner hung over the red brick of the bell tower, which read, in big black letters: IMPEACH BUSH.

The church was one of those local landmarks that made me chuckle, one of the reasons I'd come to live in this strange moss-ridden town.

The rain by then had gone from steady to a true downpour: a *taom fearthainne* – a bucketing down of rain. I sorted through the tools on the sidewalk, and as I did so, a feeling hit my stomach, as if I'd swallowed the pit of some forbidden fruit – I'd forgotten it, the one essential every-cyclist-must-have-it-with-them-at-all-times tool.

It was then he appeared, and it was odd, because although I was genuflecting before him on the sidewalk, his eyes met mine on a level. He presented me something straight-armed, as if it were a sword with which he planned to beknight me.

"Ask, and ye shall receive," he said. "Seek, and ye shall find."

The object in his hand was a bike pump.

I just stared at his face. What else do you do when a midget appears out of nowhere, and in your time of need, when you're minus a bike pump, hands you a bike pump? You stare at his face.

The face could have been black or Asian or Hispanic or Native American, or some combination. It was that wide-eyed half-Asian face that the media outlets show when they're demonstrating world demographics, when they're trying to prove that the average human being isn't white.

In other words, Booker had the face of the everyman.

"Come change it inside," he said. "I've got coffee … it's Stumptown."

Despite the weirdness of the situation, this was not going to be easy to argue against. When offered a dry place to do a bike repair and a cup of Portland's finest brand of coffee to keep you warm, how do you say no?

A yard sign had been hammered into the overgrown garden, with the words, hastily painted in red and now streaking in the rain, CHURCH SERVICE TODAY: ALL WELCOME.

He sensed, as he had an uncanny knack of doing, exactly what I was thinking when I saw it, "I'm not religious," he said, "I'm anti-religious, just like you. That's oversimplifying, of course, because anti-religion is what makes both you and me religious, but let's not get into that."

He walked up the sidewalk and up the stairs to the front doors of his church. I followed without really thinking, wheeling my bike beside me and eyeing the dry stoop. He kept talking, not once making eye-contact to be sure I was listening.

"You see, what I want to start is a retro faith, a sort of a time meld between Galilee and the Summer of Love, minus the patchouli. I want something that challenges authority, you know, something that goes back to the core teachings about how the rich are fucked and how the meek shall inherit the earth and how we should give Caesar back all his coinage, and how … how the Kingdom of God is like a mustard seed, how it starts out small and insignificant – and then grows into this big, twisted, chaotic shrub that grows everywhere, even in the middle of the desert, that cannot be eradicated, no matter how hard you try to kill it. I want – God how do you do this? – how do you start a faith and get followers and all that shit? I mean, it's so … so necessary right now."

Once we reached the stoop, we paused. If anyone else had accosted me like this, rambling on about faith and the Kingdom of God and attempting to convert me, I would have ignored him. Maybe I would have borrowed the bike pump and taken the coffee, but I certainly wouldn't have asked him further questions about the God he was pimping. Booker, though, draped in a black cassock at least three sizes too big for him, was too unreal to simply ignore. It was as if a cut-out cartoon character had been beamed before me. I had to engage him to make sure he was real, "You're really a preacher?"

Booker looked up at me. A flame-red Holy Spirit stole, the kind that Catholic school children wear to their Confirmations,

complete with doves crudely cut and glued on, hung around his neck. There wasn't a hint of irony in his eyes. "Not yet," he said. "But I'm working on it."

"Don't you have to go to divinity school or something?" I asked.

Booker scratched his head as if the question had never occurred to him. "Why? I mean, it doesn't work that way. Like if you're called, if one day you wake up and know you've been called, you have to just listen, you know. Did Paul go to divinity school? Peter?"

I wanted to tell him that two-thousand years had passed, that things worked a little differently now, but he seemed, well, so touched in the head I left it alone.

"That's unusual," I said.

"I guess it is," he replied, "but Jesus was unusual."

It would take a while before my skin stopped crawling when Booker mentioned Jesus. It was such a code amongst Portland hipsters, you couldn't mention Jesus without a snicker. Jesus. Jesus. Jesus. Jesus. See, if you're like me, it's painful.

The bucketing down of rain wasn't stopping. Booker walked into his church and held open the door. I don't remember making the decision, exactly. It was sort of a feeling that this was weird, and weird is good, or at least weird is what I was supposed to be about, and maybe weird was actually bad, but if I didn't want to be a poser I had to accept weird. I mean, KEEP PORTLAND WEIRD, it's like the local religion.

I walked through that held-open door.

The adjective that springs to mind to describe the inside of Booker's church is post-apocalyptic. Rather than traditional wood pews and kneelers, Booker's church was furnished with rows of old theater seats, likely salvaged from one of the many single-screen theaters that multiplexes were running out of town. The rows were all of different lengths – some seats were in pairs, some in threes; others came in much larger sets of eight, ten, or twelve. Booker had bolted these down to the hardwood floors in what appeared to be a hurried and not-so-thoughtful fashion. There was no aisle in the church and the rows were uneven; some seats were cramped up against the row in front of them, while others had abundant space for leg stretching but were slightly askew, angled incorrectly, so that you were facing the front corner of the room rather than the altar. Many of the chairs weren't bolted in all the way, so that when you sat in them and leaned back you ended up facing the ceiling.

Later, I'd come to believe that perhaps this layout wasn't as unplanned as I had originally thought; for I discovered that no matter where I sat in Booker's church something was slightly off, as if Booker were trying to remind us of one of his central tenets: that our lives were intended to be chaotic and imperfect, and that God very much wanted things to be that way. The haphazard layout also caused awkward personal space issues amongst churchgoers, which had the effect of forcing people to talk to one another.

While Booker's church did have an altar, it wasn't of the raised marble or polished wood variety, adorned with a silk altar cloth; it was, instead, a rickety old dining room table extended with a couple of leaves to seat twelve. The table was splotched with house paint, apparently its former incarnation had been that of a giant stepstool for someone painting a ceiling; and it had, around it, twelve mismatched chairs. The chairs were never used during services, except perhaps as a nice visual touch to remind the congregation of the Last Supper, but they did serve, later on, for those of us in his inner circle, as seating for Sunday brunch. Booker was not only a fiery preacher, but also an excellent cook.

I've focused thus far on the altar, the altar chairs, and the theater seating, but these were not, by a long stretch, the only objects in the room. Avalanching down the walls was what Booker termed found art, although most sane people would have simply called it junk. Broken and headless mannequins, yellowed Big Six wheels from old casinos, random segments of 70s kitchen cabinetry, and oodles and oodles of rusty bicycle parts – bent handlebars, loose cranks, stripped frames, and dribbled across the church's floor like loose pebbles, an assortment of useless components.

In the midst of this mess, in a small space conspicuously cleared of debris in front of the altar, was one other furnishing of note, although it's a stretch to call it furnishing. In front of the altar were three stacked milk crates.

It's hard to capture in words the effect the milk crates had on the feng shui of the room. When not in use, they were like the sacred monolith of some decaying civilization.

We stood side-by-side, me surveying the scene, Booker surveying me. It was only after I'd taken in the whole of the church that I noticed the holy water fonts. Two of them flanked the entrance we'd walked through. The fonts themselves weren't all that exceptional, they seemed part and parcel of all the other junk inside the church, but there was something peculiar about them. They were, well, steaming.

There wasn't holy water inside the fonts at all. There was coffee. Blessed coffee.

As I stood contemplating exactly how one is to drink coffee out of a holy water font, Booker strode past me towards

the stacked milk crates. When he arrived at them, he stood behind them for a moment and scratched his head, as if he'd had an idea that sounded good in theory, but as the moment of truth came, didn't seem so good after all. First he tried climbing them, scrabbling at the plastic like a squirrel with its claws removed, before abandoning the attempt. The next thing he tried … well, the minute he started the motions, his eyes on a level with the top of them, you knew it was going to end badly. Booker put his hands together at the top of the milk crate stack, squatted, and jumped.

But it didn't. He landed smack dab on the top of the stack. The stack yielded and tilted, but did not fall. Booker sat there, straddling the stack, and then looked at me as if he'd just performed an accidental miracle.

Rather than applaud or verbally acknowledge his accomplishment, I did what seemed to be equally congratulatory. I hunched over the holy font and lapped up coffee like a kitten. I'd recognized it from the aroma, as any Portland barista would. It was Hairbender, lightly roasted and brewed on a Clover. There was nothing more warm and embracing on a wet, Northwest morning in the world.

Booker, meanwhile, was working his way from sitting to standing. The crates shook. When he reached his full height, he stood perched precariously, like a skinny pre-teen on a high dive. He was nervous. I was nervous for him. As I reared back from my coffee-lapping, I realized what he was about to do, but it was too late for me to back out or protest. He began preaching to me, and I'm not sure whether he stuttered and paused from a fear of falling or a fear of preaching:

"Okay, you see, I have a bunch of them planned out, some really good ones … but I think what I'm going to do, the one … well … I'm going to tell you the story of why I'm doing this, the inspiration, the elementary-dear-Watson moment, I guess I should say the Saul-turning-to-Paul moment, you know, the lightning bolt or whatever knocked me off my horse. I'm sorry … you … just fix your bike, I need to practice."

I must have looked startled, standing there above the steaming holy font watching him. I did as he suggested and went to the back of the church to work on the bike. I tried to tune him out, to just fix the bike and then hightail it out of there, but between the coffee uplift and his odd intonation, Booker's words penetrated my resistance. His voice was somehow both high-pitched and booming, a comic hybrid of Pee-Wee Herman and Martin Luther King.

"It started with Darwin. Or rather, it started with a Darwin sighting. I was on a road trip and, well … I saw one of those

Darwin fish on the back of a car. I'm like you, I kind of think all this Jesus stuff is a joke, and you would have thought that I'd be the type of person to have a Darwin fish on the back of my van. For some reason though the Darwin thing always bothered me: I didn't quite get it, other than the slap at Christianity, what people meant when they stuck a Darwin fish on the back of their car.

"I was driving through Oklahoma, which makes you uncomfortable if you're a midget, so that you pretty much pull in and out of Chevrons as quick as you can, avoiding the cheaper truck stops so you don't run into a rabble of rednecks. I'd been just driving and driving, probably thirteen hours straight, so I could get to Arkansas before dark. When you're riding like that, a lot of thoughts go through your mind. I'd been sort of thinking about my life, about this wanderlust I had. It wasn't a bad life – wandering around bum fuck Egypt, seeing a lot of America, freaking people out when I showed up at their church rummage sales – but it was feeling increasingly purposeless."

Unless you're an artist-type yourself, it's hard to explain what happened to me mentally then, as I sat cross-legged on the floor in the back of the church, wedging levers between my rim and tire, realizing that his sermon was going to be a long and twisted monologue. When he first appeared it was like he was a cut-out cartoon character, somehow both larger and smaller than life. Now, though, it was like everything was a cartoon: his words like blocks hovering in the air; the church and the milk crates and Booker himself narrowing from three to two-dimensions; everything gone black and white and degraded into photocopy.

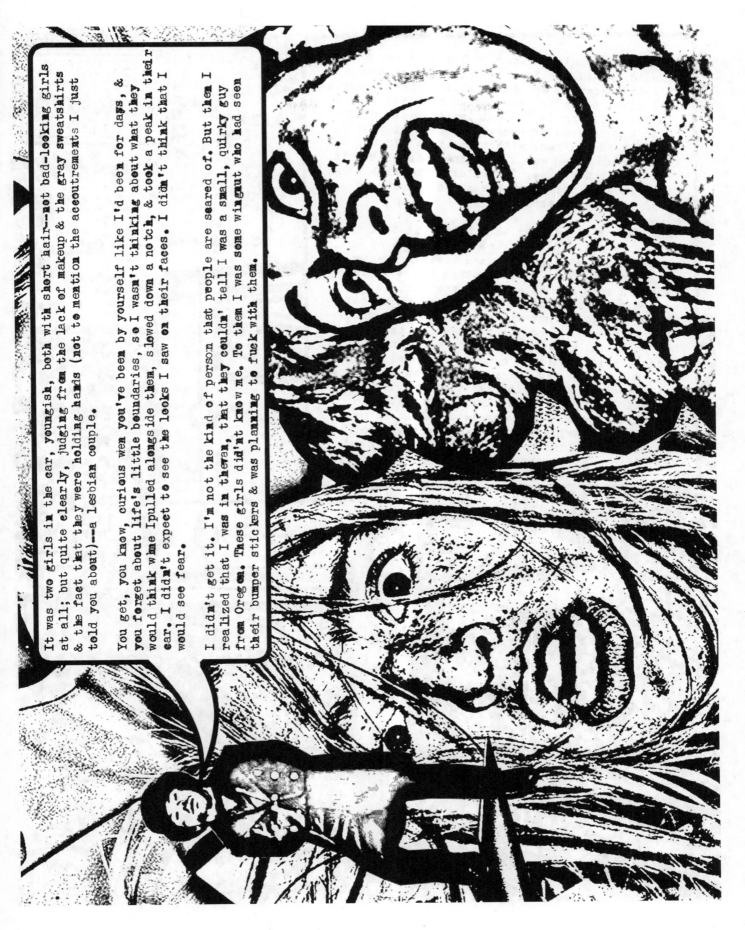

It was two girls in the car, youngish, both with short hair—not bad-looking girls at all; but quite clearly, judging from the lack of makeup & the gray sweatshirts & the fact that they were holding hands (not to mention the accoutrements I just told you about)—a lesbian couple.

You get, you know, curious when you've been by yourself like I'd been for days, & you forget about life's little boundaries, so I wasn't thinking about what they would think when I pulled alongside them, slowed down a notch, & took a peak in their car. I didn't expect to see the looks I saw on their faces. I didn't think that I would see fear.

I didn't get it. I'm not the kind of person that people are scared of. But then I realized that I was in the van, that they couldn' tell I was a small, quirky guy from Oregon. These girls didn't know me. To them I was some wingnut who had seen their bumper stickers & was planning to fuck with them.

As the girls slowed down to let me pass, & as I slid by, taking the lane in front of them, 3 things crossed my mind, in this exact order. The first thing was more of an instinct than a thought--it was the animal instinct the predator has towards its prey. The thought was: maybe I should fuck with them; it would be fun. The second thing was a very human instinct. It was the thought: no, I shouldn't fuckwith them,, they're good people, & I'm a good person, & I'll just leave them be.

New the third thought that I had, it took a while to fully form. By then I'd given my accelerator a bittof a punch & was miles in front of the Geo. I was getting close to the eastern edge of the state, & was anxious to get off the interstate and do some back read before I hit Fayetteville. I'm not sure whether it was the speed that caused my thinking to accelerate, or whether it was the thought acceleration that was causing my speed to go up. But either way I was thinking on a synthesis level--a level I think of now as not an animal level or a human level, but rather a God-like level. I was completely lost in my thoughts, missing the exit to Fayetteville, missing the fluffy pink-tinged clouds & the majestic oaks of the Ozarks.

(While he spoke, I grabbed a tire pump & got down to the job of fixing my flat.)

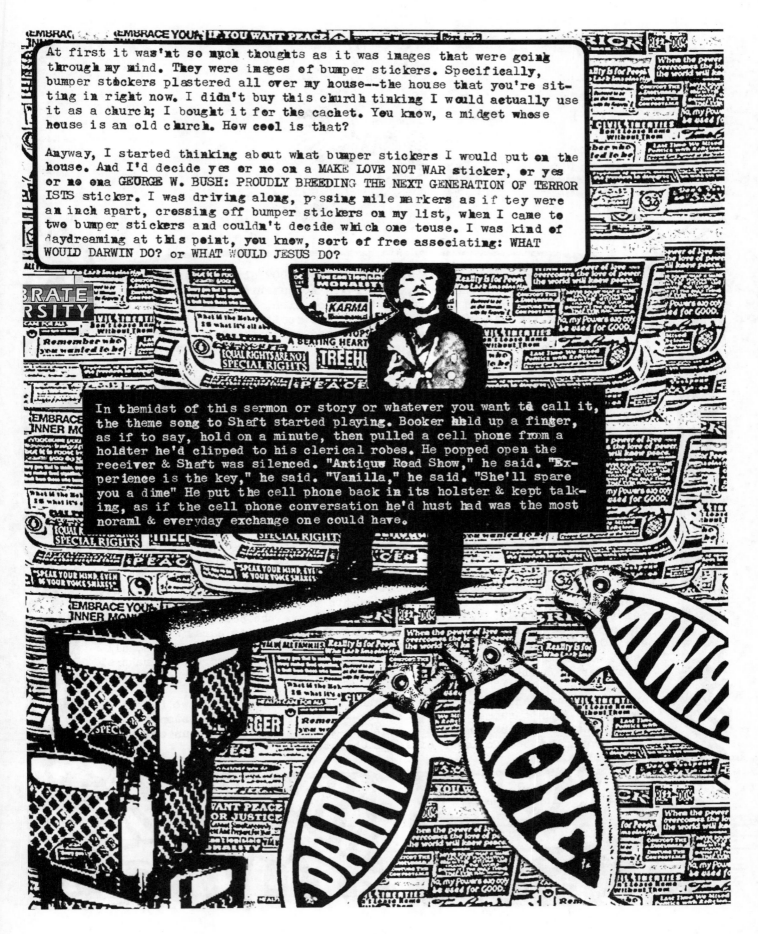

At first it was'nt so much thoughts as it was images that were going through my mind. They were images of bumper stickers. Specifically, bumper stickers plastered all over my house—the house that you're sitting in right now. I didn't buy this church tinking I would actually use it as a church; I bought it for the cachet. You know, a midget whose house is an old church. How cool is that?

Anyway, I started thinking about what bumper stickers I would put on the house. And I'd decide yes or no on a MAKE LOVE NOT WAR sticker, or yes or no on a GEORGE W. BUSH: PROUDLY BREEDING THE NEXT GENERATION OF TERRORISTS sticker. I was driving along, passing mile markers as if tey were an inch apart, crossing off bumper stickers on my list, when I came to two bumper stickers and couldn't decide which one touse. I was kind of daydreaming at this point, you know, sort of free associating: WHAT WOULD DARWIN DO? or WHAT WOULD JESUS DO?

In themidst of this sermon or story or whatever you want to call it, the theme song to Shaft started playing. Booker held up a finger, as if to say, hold on a minute, then pulled a cell phone from a holster he'd clipped to his clerical robes. He popped open the receiver & Shaft was silenced. "Antique Road Show," he said. "Experience is the key," he said. "Vanilla," he said. "She'll spare you a dime" He put the cell phone back in its holster & kept talking, as if the cell phone conversation he'd hust had was the most noraml & everyday exchange one could have.

ll, it was clear to me that the WHAT WOULD JESUS DO? sticker was more ap
propriate, because, the thing is, Darwin was no humanist. I mean, he was
all about survival of the fittest, & in His opinion, people like the lesbians & people like me, midgets, XXXX well, we're the anomolies--we're the
weak ones whose genetic codes won't get passed on to the next generation.
According to Darwin, only the strong survive, & in our society the measure
of strength is money. How strong are you? How much money do you earn?

So here we re these people, these lesbians driving a beat-up old Geo with
a Darwin fish stuck on the back. And they suddenly seemed stupid to me. I
mean, poor lesbian Darwinists? Think about it: non-breeders worshipping the
guy who essentially said our sole purpose in life is to reproduce.

Now I'd never thought of it t is way before, I'd always looked at it from
the other angle; I'd always thought of the other irony--the fact that the
majority of people who are Christians are not Christian at all. I mean, was
Christ a capitalist? Hell no! No one in the annals of history has ever been
a bigger mooch.

Like I said, it had always been obvious to me that the religious right was
full of Darwinists, but I'd never thought about the flipside of hhis: the
fact that all of us supposed left-wing atheists, we weren't atheists at all.
We were, in fact, every single one of us, secret followers of Jesus Christ.
We had completely taking to heart all of his philosophies. We lived the
beatitudes to a T. The beatitudes said blessed are the poor, & here we were
just eeking out a living, riding bikes instead of driving cars. We were
poor! The beatitudes said blessed are the peacemakers, & here we were, all
pissed off about Iraq & going to our useless protests. We were peacemakers!
And hungering & thirsting for justice, we were that. And so on & so forth.

Anyway, that was the third thought I had: the synthesis of my two former
thoughts. I hadn't summed it up just yet--it was all images of bumper stickers & beatitudes--but the bottom line was that, no matter how uncool it is
I was a very devoted follower of Jesus Christ.

Now, like most of the thoughts you have while driving thousands of miles across the country, it is very unlikely that this particular thought would have fluttered away, forgotten forever, had it not b en for a bizarre coincidence. Once I finally cleared my head, & realized that I had missed my turn-off, I retraced my route back to I-540. Once I finallybolte d that last hundred miles to Fayetteville, & get to my favorite BBQ in Arkansas—this little whole-in-the-wall along the main drag with these wooden booths that have been all carved up by university students. Once I got my pitcher of PBR in front of me, & had rubbed a little life into my read-weary eyes, I noticed that in t e very nextbooth, directly in my line of sight, were the lesbians.

THE WAY HE KEEPS REPEATING THE WORD "LESBIANS," IT COULD BE CONSTRUED AS HOMOPHOBIC, BUT IT SEEMS MORE LIKE A METAPHOR, LIKE IT COULD BE SUBSTITUTED FOR "SAMARITANS" OR "SADDUCEES" OR SOME OTHER DOWNCAST BIBLICAL TRIBE THAT THE HOLIER-THAN-THOU LOOK DOWN UPON. PLUS, HE'S A MIDGET WHO REFERS TO HIMSELF AS A MIDGET. IT GIVES HIM SOME LEEWAY.

I don't want to get all Biblical here & talk about fate & shit & how the lesbians were actually angles of the Lord, but the truth is, if it wasn't for the lesbians, I wouldn't be standing on these milk crates right now. You see, when you're on the road for a long time by yourself, what you want more than anything is to talk to some people. It's difficult to do this, because you're a stranger to everyone, so what you do is you look for some sort of in-road into a conversation.

Well, I totally had this in-road with the lesbians. I could walk up to their booth & ask them if they had driven up through Oklahoma today, & tell them that I recognized their Geo in the parking lot, & mention that I like their bumper stickers. It was a slam dunk.

So anyeay, that's what I did. They took it pretty well, like most people do I suppose when I midget interrupts what they're doing & wants to talk to them—an odd mixture of apprehension & curiosity. We engaged in a fairly normal conversation, in which we talked about being minorities, them sexual, me physically & how that sort of freaks us out when we're in Okie country, even though people are mostly as kind as they can be & make pretty good pie too.

We laughed about this, while I finished my first pint of PBR, & was halfway into my second when they asked me what turned out to be the million dollar question, the thing that got me up here on the crates. It wasn't an unusual question, it was just the everyday, "So, what do you do?"

Being younger & adrift, you can probably appreciate the feelings I get when someone asks me that question. I don't like telling people that I buy & resell junk on Ebay. I always want to name some other professions something more interesting & romantic. Now I'd never actually done that. Usually, I'd answer the question with a shrug, a sideways glance, & a vague "antiques". But, I don't know, after being by yourself all day you get kind of loopy & talkative. Plus, I didn't know these people, & I'd never see them again, so I could be anything. So, anyway--it's so fucking weird that I did this, but I did I actually told the lesbians that I was a preacher. And not only that, but I started going off, telling them that I was a minister of a very different kind of Christian church: one that was based on the actual teachings of Jesus Christ--about living simply & not being judgmental & not giving a shit about $$$--& not on all the hogwash about The Resurrection & The Second Coming & all the other made up bull shit that should have gone out with Santa Claus & the Easter Bunny.

It was weird the way it came out of me. All of a sudden I'm saying all these things about Jesus, about what He was all about. I mean, do I look like the kind of guy who spend all his time thinking about Jesus? But all of a sudden all this stuff about the beatitudes & mustard seeds & houses being built on sand is starting to come out of me. I felt like I was speaking in tongues.

IS HE SERIOUS? IS HE TRYING TO CONVERT ME? IS A MIDGET STANDING ON MILK CRATES REALLY CLAIMING TO BE CALLED BY A PAIR OF LESBIANS TO PREACH TO ME? WHEN ARE THE REALITY SHOW GUYS GOING TO COME OUT OF THE SHADOWS WITH CAMERAS, LAUGHING AT ME FOR SITTING HERE LISTENING? WHEN DOES THE PITCH FOR MONEY COME? DAMN, THIS COFFEE IS GOOD.

The strangest thing about it, though, wasn't my own disbelief about what was coming out of my mouth: what was strangest Was the absolute mesmerization job I was doing on the lesbians They were listening to me. They were hanging on desperately to Every word.

I finished the job & sat cross-legged on the floor amazed that he could speak at such length

The feeling that I had then was a feeling I'd never had before, this feeling... this feeling that I have some sort of message to share, that I'm on to something--something vital & important & strong that people really want to hear. No one had ever listened to me like the lesbians were listening to me. They weren't yawning or checking the wall clock or wishing they were somewhere else. They weren't freaking out that some wierdo midget was holding them hostage in a restaurant booth when all they really wanted to do was get to their hotel room so they could carpet munch. They were staring at me. Just like you're staring at me. Like I was a hypnotist dangling a watch in front of them.

Well, it was getting late. And I felt bad because I'd finished my beer & my ribs & the girls had yet to touch their food, so I excused myself. Before I left, though, I put one final nail in the coffin: I gave them this address & told them to come visit the church. They promised they'd come.

They didn't, of course, & I felt really dumb waiting for them today. I bolted all these seats in just for them, so they'd see that I really had a church, that I wasn't making up everything that I'd said.

But then you came, & I got you in here somehow, & now, well... now you're listening to me the same way that they listened to me, like I really am a preacher & really do have something important to say. I feel powerful up here. And called. I feel called. And I don't want to go back to being a junk collector who takes a load of road trips; I want to be a preacher. I want to get up on this stupid stack of milk crates every Sunday & tell it like it is, to tell it like the Bible is. I want to tell people what is bull-shit & what is not, because you don't need to be some sort of Biblical scholar, or know shit about the lost gospel of Thomas, or Q, or the Gnostics, or read Greek, to know what is truth & what is make-believe. All you need is common sense. No temple was destroy-ed in 3 days and no doves fluttered about, & nobody ascended to meet their Father. But some dude named Jesus really didn wander around a lake talking about mustard seeds & how really good things get started that way, how all it takes is a Darwin fish & a rain-bow strip & a couple of lesbians to plant a seed in your head & get something going—something bushy & prickly & twisted & altogether lovely.

That's all it takes. It starts with a rain storm & a flat tire & the need for a dry place to do some repairs. It starts with me gather-ing the courage to invite you in. It starts with whatever the hell we're going to do next, after you walk out of here & get on your bike & go home & mull over this shit.

To be honest, I made up that ending. I'm not really sure how Booker finished his first sermon. I'd gotten it by then, what the extra dimensions were about, what it was I needed to do. By the time he got to the last line about mustard seeds, a mustard seed had been planted in my own head, and after all that Hairbender I was going, as Booker would say, beyond the animal and human and into the God-like.

I wasn't converted by Booker's speech – I wasn't suddenly a follower of either Jesus Christ or this mad midget on milk crates – but it gave me an idea: an idea that would grow and grow and grow.

The idea I had was that Booker was a zine: a zine to type and to draw, to cut and to paste, to staple and to collate. And most importantly, a zine

I left the church and rode my bike to Mecca, my flat tire cured.

Chapter 11

On the Misery of Being Twenty-two

NOT MUCH HAS BEEN WRITTEN, NOT MANY songs have been sung, about the age of twenty-two. All the peaks have been scaled: the driver's license earned at sixteen, the statutory rape law hurdled at eighteen, the drinking age crashed at twenty-one. Hitting the age of twenty-two means nothing, is just a mile marker to pass on the long and frightening road toward thirty. So while John Cougar Mellencamp advised, in his little ditty 'bout Jack & Diane, that we hold on to sixteen as long as we can, he surely wouldn't have done the same for twenty-two.

If anyone would have sung about twenty-two, it would have been someone like Nick Drake, or Kurt Cobain, or Elliott Smith – someone depressed and ultimately suicidal. Twenty-two is the year when reality, when the *all in all is all we are*, sets in. It's when you take your heavily vaunted liberal arts

degree and go work for Starbucks or Noah's Bagels or some other corporate chain store that reminds you you're just as qualified for employment as the elderly greeters at Walmart. If you're lucky (and untattooed) you get a job as an administrative assistant in the corporate office of said chain store instead of a job as a bagel or latte slinger. But either way it's the same: you run into the wall Pink Floyd warned us about, and you discover that it's sticky, that once you've touched it you're attached to it like Super Glue.

At age twenty-two, I lacked the ink that marked my generation of misfits, but I wasn't lucky enough to find a corporate office admin job. I'd salvaged some degree of respectability by working for a local caffeine hawker rather than a national one, but it didn't make the five in the morning opening shifts any easier to wake up to. My snooze button was my greatest enemy. I'd hit it three or four times, red numbers glaring at me in accusation – you're twenty-two; you make coffee; you suck. By the time I made it to work, unshowered, wearing yesterday's T-shirt and mismatched socks, my mood was as black as the Sumatra.

People took it as my shtick, grunting at them when they ordered, but really it was how I felt, all day every day: dark.

There just seemed nothing that I could be. How did one *become* something? I came to Portland after graduating from the University of Iowa with an English degree. I was, I guess, what you'd call a nerd. As such, I avoided football games and fraternities and joined a whole bunch of nerdy student organizations: I was an assistant editor for *The Daily Iowan*, the student newspaper; I was a D rider in the University of Iowa Cycling Club; and on my weekends, dorkiest of all, I volunteered in the acquisitions department at the library, my job there to research and procure small press journals for the university.

I enjoyed my time as a Hawkeye, but then one day I graduated, and everybody was leaving and I hadn't really made any plans. I'd thought about doing something similar to what my peers were doing – I'd considered applying for J-school or getting a master's degree – but in my imagination this was simply prolonging the transition from simply doing some things and learning some things to *becoming* something.

In the end, the "what I was to become" still eluded me, so I chose a "where I would become" instead. I would go to Portland, Oregon, this West Coast city that seemed as in need of defining as me, and once I was there, well, I'd figure it out.

I arrived in Portland with just enough money for a rental deposit. I found a cheap studio above a burrito shop in the run-down Northeast quadrant of the city. And then I did what every recently graduated, non-Peace Corps, non-graduate school, trying-to-find-themselves twenty-two-year-old does– I typed up a résumé and started beating the streets, praying that desperation wouldn't lead me to a Starbucks or a Noah's Bagels.

In the end it wasn't a résumé at all that got me my job slinging espresso at the Mecca Cafe, it was a T-shirt I wore with this image screenprinted on it:

© *Cristy Road. Used with permission*

I was leering at my laptop surfing for jobs when Beale, the counter guy who would soon be my co-worker and good friend, sauntered over to clean the table in front me, saw the shirt, and said, apropos of nothing, "Ironic, huh?"

I glanced up from my computer. The day was odd, eighty degrees and humid on the first day of October, the kind of day that got Portlanders up in arms about global warming. As a general rule, you could tell the local coffee joints from the retail chains by whether they had air conditioning–the Mecca Cafe did not. Despite the ceiling fans, I was hot and irritated. I had $350 in my bank account and a $400 rent check to write in two weeks.

I answered Beale sharply, without looking up from the laptop, "What's ironic?"

Beale was one of those unfortunate guys who's twenty-five and balding. He kept his head shaved, Agassi-style, to cover for it. It gave him a rough edge, which combined with his black The Residents T-shirts and razor-wire tattoos, made him look meaner than he actually was.

"The T-shirt you're wearing," Beale said, "was produced by Microcosm Publishing, its image reminds us of Revolutionary America, when individuals used primitive devices to produce leaflets intended to educate and inspire the masses to revolution. You have a laptop in front of you the screen of which reads Job Builder Corporate Career Center. It's ironic."

At this point, I looked up. Beale's tattoos and the confrontational way he'd approached me, not to mention the annoying fact that he'd been spying on my computer screen, indicated that he was an asshole. Yet there was something in the way he'd delivered his factoids, robotically, that said something different. He wasn't an asshole; he was an awkward nerd. Just like me.

"Philosophy?" he asked.

Beale's leaps of thought were incredibly hard to follow. I looked up at him confused. "Your degree?" he asked.

"English," I said.

"I knew it, a coffee degree," he said.

"Huh?"

"You got a coffee degree. It's cool. I got a coffee degree too. Art."

I wiped a bead of sweat off my brow. Something in the chuckle I replied with must have spoke of desperation.

"If you need something quick, we need a slinger," Beale said. He flipped me a business card. "Give the man a call."

So that's how I'd gotten the job at the Mecca Café (which I will heretofore refer to simply as Mecca, what most of its employees and regulars called it). I'd been making coffee, toasting bagels, and scooping the occasional gelato for almost six months. I had friends, but most of them were in the same boat, baristas doing side projects on a limited budget: artists slopping down acrylic on scraps of cardboard, musicians forming jug bands, zinesters banging out angst on thrift-store Royals. If we had any money left over, we pissed it all out in the form of Pabst Blue Ribbon.

I still thought about *becoming* something, but six months after leaving Iowa I had the sense to know my something was going to be decidedly less mainstream than I'd originally thought. I was more interested in becoming an anti-something, rather than a something. To that end, I spent most of my spare time – spare time I could have spent pursuing a career – working on, reading, and talking about zines.

My particular zine, *Octagonal Table Talk*, was on its eleventh issue, despite as far as I knew not having sold a single copy. This didn't discourage me. If anything it was a point of pride. I didn't pay anything for the production; I had my friends who had the corporate administrative assistant jobs steal materials: paper, photocopies, Sharpies–lots and lots of Sharpies. It was no sweat off my back if the zine didn't sell. In fact, it was good it didn't sell. I was skimming the profits off corporate America, and subverting corporate America was one of the few real purposes of zines, other than giving some outlet for the unfocused passions of twenty-two-year-olds.

Octagonal Table Talk, I suppose, would have been considered more of a comic strip than a zine if I could actually draw.

Much of the zine, however consisted of text, text that was contained in word bubbles such as this. Usually, it was one person delivering some sort of monologue, sometimes about the state of the world, but more often than not about something more meaningless, like how rare it is that a musician can shift styles and still make music good music. Bowie is the only artist I can think of that was able to do this with aplomb, although it could be argued that even as Ziggy Stardust, the changes were mostly cosmetic, (and I mean that literally: eye shadow, lipstick, the works) and thatthe singing, no matter what accompanied it, was always that sort of upper-class English whine he's so famous for. Even more experimental bands with longevity, like Yo La Tengo, they've always got new sounds in their music--a kazoo, whatever--but it's still that slow, careful Yo La Tengo drone that sits in the background. That's the problem with musicians, and actually, people in general, all we've really got is one note: one voice, one instrument, one mes-sage--and when we try to change key it sounds terrible. I mean, did you listen to that last Frank Black album? He got a new producer, and tried to do something different-- oh my God--could you believe that slide guitar?--and it sucked; it really sucked. So then he just said fuck-it and did the Pixies reunion tour and everything was so much better.

I'M SO BORED

Sample of Octagonal Table Talk *page produced for this gospel. Not previously published.*

I couldn't, so I called it a zine. What I would do was draw an octagon, color it in with the Sharpie, and then draw dots around the octagon–sometimes one, sometimes two, sometimes many. The octagon represented an octagonal table, one of those hideous tables made in the sixties that seemed to proliferate in fraternities and other college flophouses; the dots represented people sitting in chairs around the table, having dinner or playing drinking games. All of this was seen, quite obviously, from an aerial view, so that it made sense from a visual perspective–just having everything be dots and octagons.

Octagonal Table Talk was the only zine I'd ever attempted, but the idea I had when I left Booker's church on Sunday, was that I'd start a new series about Booker, he and his church being the perfect backdrop. It wouldn't be a flip book that I did just so I'd be cool enough to hang out with the more talented artists who made up my zine circle–I would put some work

into it. I'd take some digital photos of the outside of Booker's church, then I'd crypt some images of midgets from the internet, then I'd scan some religious imagery out of the clip art zine *Craphound*, and then I'd type up everything Booker had said on my Universal Underwood typewriter. I'd put all this shit together with Photoshop, creating pages, and then I'd photocopy them until the imagery was grainy yet recognizable.

It all came to me like this, too–in a big rush while I was riding my bike back home from Booker's church. I was going to do my first real zine. I even thought of a name for it while I sat on my soggy saddle–*His Church That Sunday*. Anyway, that's how I spent the rest of my day, I bolted out of Booker's church and rode straight home, removed my wet clothes and took a hot shower, then spent the entire rest of that Sunday in front of my computer, doing the cover of *His Church That Sunday #1* :

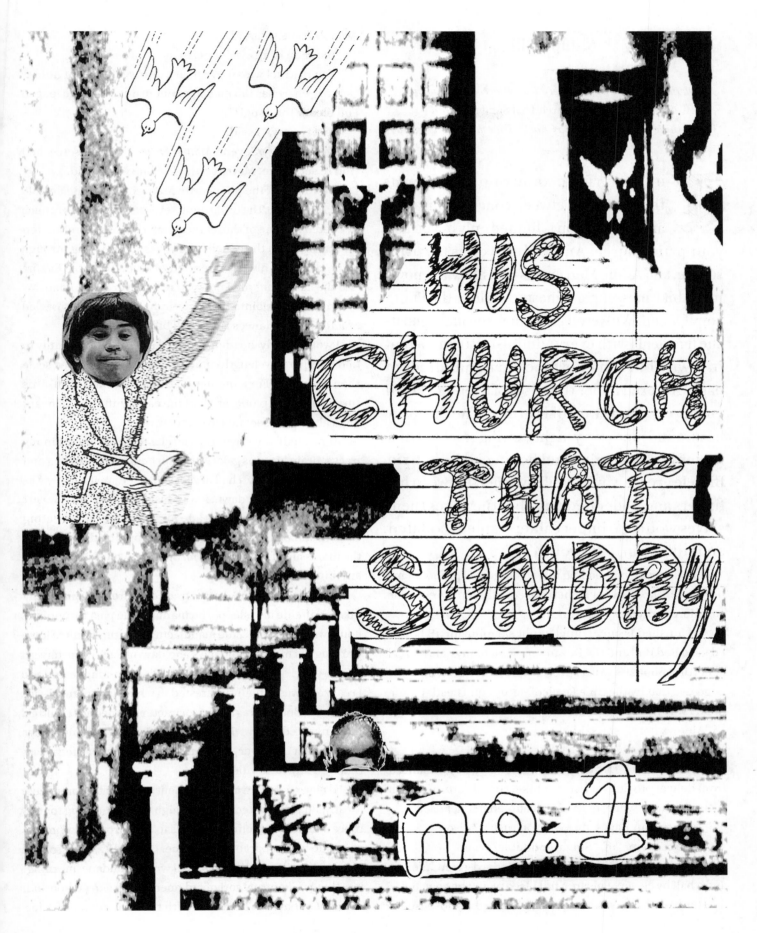

Chapter III

On the Strange Social Anxiety That Proceeded From the
Publication of His Church That Sunday #1 *and*
What Annie Mercyx Had to Say About That the Following Day

THE NICE THING ABOUT DOING A ZINE IS that the time between conceptualization and publication is limited only by you and your print source. Annie Mercyx was my print source, and Annie Mercyx was fast. She was known in the bike messenger/zinester world as the Photocopy Queen. We weren't sure how she managed it – she had deals with every administrative assistant in town – but somehow she did it, hundreds of pages Xeroxed under the noses of deep-pocketed employers. Annie would show up at The Curiosity bar around nine every night, towing stacks of new issues in a trailer behind her decked-out fixie. Bicycle grease would be all over her, between her fingers and under her nails, but the pages themselves would be impeccable: stapled, collated, and still warm to the touch.

Just so you're not reading this whole gospel pronouncing her name *Murks-icks* or something equally damaging to the ear, Mercyx rhymes with Turks.

I'd finished Issue #1 quickly, not sleeping for 48 hours; I'd used Red Bull and No-Doz to supplement my natural zeal at getting Booker's words precise and unfettered onto my pages, so that by the time I called Mercyx on Tuesday afternoon I was wild and frenzied.

"Mercyx here," she said.

"It's Flynn."

"What you got?" Efficiency was Annie's game. She bounced from delivery to delivery on her bike, equally attuned both to traffic and to whoever's voice occupied her headset.

"Twenty-four pages. And can you rush it? Also –"

Mercyx cut me off. "Single or double? Bleed?"

"I think … single. The pages are standard-sized … eight and a half by eleven. I mean, a full bleed would be cool, but–"

Her breathing was heavy. A car honked at close range.

"Asshole!" she shouted.

And then in an even tone, to me:

"You're a lucky man, Flynn. It's deadsville over at Adidas. New org chart has the management in a stew. Single-paged. Full bleed. The usual?"

"Just twenty," I said.

"The Curiosity. Seven. "*Motherfucker!*" Wheels screeched. "You're set, Flynn. Mercyx out." The line went dead.

After I got off the phone with Mercyx, I called Beale, told him to meet us at The Curiosity at seven, and then took a much needed nap – one of those unexpected naps where you momentarily sit on the couch, find yourself browsing through some book you always intended to read, like *Don Quixote*, and the next thing you know you're in Never Never Land. My dreams were disjointed caffeine-induced visions of grizzled Spaniards with lances riding tall bikes.

I woke cloudy-headed. I looked out the window only to find the light wavelengths much further toward the red scale than expected. For a moment, I thought it was dawn. This threw me into a panic, as I had the early shift, which meant I had about two seconds to get to work.

About halfway down the porch steps, I stopped in my tracks, brain hiccups galore, the sun being on the wrong end of the street, the day a hell of a lot warmer than it usually was at this hour. It wasn't dawn; it was dusk. I was late, but I wasn't late to what I thought I was late for. I was only late meeting Mercyx and Beale and the impromptu publication party for the first issue of *His Church That Sunday*, which really wasn't anything to panic about.

I rode slowly down Alberta Street, dizzy from the unhealthy mix of caffeine and sleep. The mania of the past forty-eight hours wasn't like me. Zine manufacturing is the result of long-brewing disaffection and days and days of Pacific Northwest drizzle – not religious inspiration and pseudo-amphetamines. I realized I was actually interested in what Mercyx and Beale would say. Booker was such a character – someone I couldn't have invented in my wildest dreams. I wanted to know how he came out on paper – if I could reinvent him in such a way that he'd still have vitality.

I'd never felt this way before about a zine that I'd produced. Mostly, I'd just wanted a quick laugh and something for my more artistically inclined friends to flip through so I could continue to be a part of their scene. Before *HCTS*, I'd sort of purposely written shit, because if I wrote mundane, meaningless things it kept any sort of judgment of me as a person and an artist at bay. But I realized with this new zine, I had, for the first time, put my ass on the line. The zine was still cheeky, but it had an edge, and the edge wasn't the usual we're-doomed pessimism that marked the artistic inclinations of my generation: it had a dangerous tone of sincerity and optimism to it.

As I approached The Curiosity, I realized that I actually cared what Mercyx and Beale thought. What would they – confirmed nihilists – think of my strange, semi-Christian zine?

Maybe it was the lack of sleep, but when I got to The Curiosity, I suddenly felt like I couldn't go in. I was embarrassed. I'd actually been serious. What kind of person writes a serious zine? That's like someone who writes blue poetry about lilacs and shit. I rode right by The Curiosity, turning my head away lest Mercyx and Beale see me, then I spun the bike around and headed home, where I stayed up until three doing an eight-page issue of *Octagonal Table Talk* #11½:

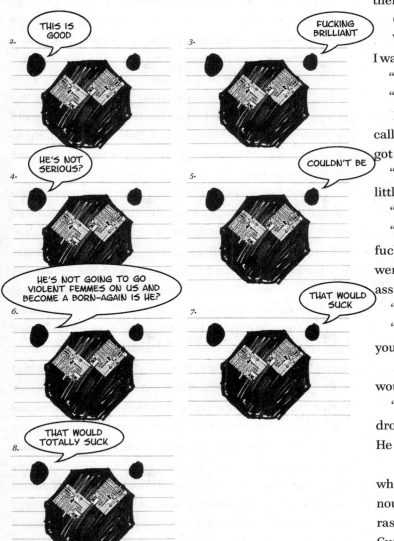

When I made it to work the next day, things did not go well. Double nonfat lattes were coming out mochas, espressos were coming out caps, vegans were getting butter on their bagels. The mistakes came in triplicate: I'd be fine for an hour then I'd screw up three in a row. Beale wasn't much help; he'd disappear into the kitchen for long periods, leaving me to work both the register and the machines. In a lull, he finally pulled me aside and said,

"Dude, this isn't Zombies versus Humans."

I could tell Beale was angry, and that he wanted to ask me why I hadn't shown up last night, but directness wasn't Beale's style. "Sorry, man, I was up all night doing a zine," I replied.

"Write shit down, man. Write down the orders."

I did as Beale commanded. It helped until an hour later when I took three orders in a row, thinking it would be more efficient to take the orders and then go to the back and fill them, and then promptly lost the list on the way to the back.

Curses, foiled again.

While I searched for the list, Mercyx called me on my cell. I was so flabbergasted that I picked it up.

"Hello?"

"Mercyx here."

I couldn't remember Mercyx ever calling me. I always called her. Mercyx didn't make social calls. "Annie, listen, I got a flood of customers up here, can I call you back?"

"What the fuck was that last night?" Mercyx's style was a little different from Beale's.

"Huh?"

"You rush-jobbed me, I bring you your issues, then you fucking ride by without stopping. Beale and I thought you were just fucking with us, so we waited and waited for your ass – "

"Look, Mercyx – "

"I would have tossed the shit, except it was the best thing you've ever done. What the hell inspired that?"

At this point, I was getting seriously glared at, but Mercyx wouldn't drop it.

"I hope you don't mind, but I made more than twenty. I dropped the extras at Ben Dover. Dougie Fresh loved them. He did you an index card. He wants to distro them."

I found myself lost in another threesome: caught somewhere between renewed embarrassment at the biblical pronouncements embedded in *His Church That Sunday*; embarrassment at getting caught bailing on my buddies at The Curiosity; and embarrassment at the fact that I now had a customer raving at me, "Um, is somebody going to make me my triple espresso, or is this some sort of self-service establishment?"

"He wants to distro *me*?"

"Well, he won't touch *OTT*, but he'll help you out with *That Sunday* if you think you have more in you."

"Cool, cool, cool. All right I gotta go."

Mercyx kept right on, as if she didn't hear a word. "I've got to get you these issues. Dinner? Eight at Blowfish?"

Blowfish? Blowfish was an upscale sushi restaurant that I wouldn't think Mercyx would get caught dead in. It was anti-Mercyx, as Mercyx herself would say.

At this point the guy at the front of the line had the rest of the line in stitches berating me. "Hello, mister? A tri–ple espresso. That's three shots. One. Two. Three. Maybe he's deaf. I'll hold up my fingers for him. One finger, two fingers, three fingers."

"Mercyx out," Mercyx said.

Chapter 10

Where an Unusual Dinner with Annie Mercyx Takes Place

J MADE THE MAN HIS TRIPLE ESPRESSO, filled the next two orders, and basically survived my shift. I wasn't really sure what to think about the conversation I'd had with Mercyx. The night before, I'd thought I would throw all issues of *His Church That Sunday* into the Dumpster behind the burrito shop or burn them, but now there were a few more copies to contend with. I was still embarrassed about them, but clearly Mercyx had thought they were worthwhile, so now pride mixed in with the shame.

Then there was this dinner with Mercyx at Blowfish thing. Like I said, Blowfish wasn't a place Mercyx would go – she had a sleeve full of tattoos on her left arm; short, cropped, perpetually bleached hair; and muscled calves harder than Schwarzenegger's biceps. Mercyx was a burrito-and-run kind of gal, and we assumed, Beale and I, that she was a lesbian, although I have to admit that despite all our adolescent con-

versations, we'd never ventured anywhere close to Mercyx's sex life.

It's very strange, when I think back on it, that we hadn't. Beale's comics were all about masturbation and frustrated libido, and mine occasionally dabbled in that direction; so you'd think somewhere in there we would have discussed intimate matters, but it just never happened. Mercyx was one of the guys – a fellow cyclist, pool shark, and zinester.

Don't get me wrong, Mercyx wasn't unattractive. If anything she was hyperattractive – in a small tits, low hips, Suicide Girls kind of way – but we kind of considered her an untouchable. It was like if we'd shown any interest in her, we couldn't have been her friend. We saw the way she fucked with other men in her brash, slick-tongued way, and decided we'd rather be in collusion than on a collision.

Mercyx was tough, and we were soft zine boys. At first, we felt privileged just to be in her presence, and then later, since we'd been hanging out with her for almost a year, we forgot her presence as a sexual being all together. She was gender-neutral Mercyx, the Photocopy Queen and our compadre.

So yeah. I'd finally decided that the whole thing was no big deal, that it was just the raw meat, that she'd chosen Blowfish simply because she had a primal urge to sink her teeth into something fleshy and uncooked. There were better, cheaper sushi joints in town, but it was near my apartment and she knew she'd have to cart the zine stash there afterwards.

I walked down the stairs of my apartment, took in the cooling breeze of an unseasonably warm spring evening, and sauntered down Alberta Street, not thinking anything at all about my unwashed, after-cycling T-shirt, my threadbare black jeans, my half-tied Chuck Taylors. I walked down the street and arrived at Blowfish. And there I saw Annie Mercyx, and Annie Mercyx was the most beautiful thing I'd ever seen.

I am surprised, when I think back on it, that I got words out of my mouth at all. Mercyx was wearing a strapless dress, a kitschy cotton number with ferris wheels on it in pink and yellow pastels. She had on a heavy coat of soft pink lipstick to match, and an ochre-colored eye shadow that extended cat-like to her temples. The contrast between the hard tattoos and the soft colors of her dress was a visual fiasco, making her appear comic and freaky and completely stunning all at once. I suppose the average person would have seen her and just thought she was strange; but for me it was all my fantasies come to life, a beautiful alien from a sci-fi movie.

The words that came out of my mouth – oh, the lovely, stupid words – were, "Annie, do you have a date tonight?"

Zoom of the pattern on Mercyx's kitschy ferris wheel dress.

Now the reality of it is that when I asked Mercyx if she had a date that night, I was being completely sincere. I really thought that she was setting up some office drone to do copies for her. It didn't occur to me that *this* was the date, that Annie had put on a dress and made herself up for *me*. Annie, however, took it as flirting, as if I was up to clever tricks. I had absolutely no idea what I was doing; and yet I was doing all the right things.

Mercyx actually blushed when I asked. I, the embarrassment king; I, Bartholomew Flynn; I was making Annie Mercyx blush. Now it was Annie Mercyx who wanted to just ride right by the store window.

Mercyx responded sarcastically, "Meeting Beale after dinner."

I totally didn't get it. I wasn't gullible enough to think that Mercyx was serious about having a date with Beale – I mean, Beale was the most awkward man on the planet – but I still wasn't making the connect between the makeup and me. "No, seriously, Annie, who are you meeting?"

Mercyx wanted this whole thing to go away. "Why do you call me Annie? Everyone else calls me Mercyx."

I still didn't get it, but I decided to drop the subject of the clothes and answer the question. Mercyx was usually so deadpan, it was strange to see her the way she was, verging on being pissed off. "I don't know, if it bothers you, I'll call you Mercyx. It's just old-fashioned or something. Maybe it's the Little Orphan Annie thing, you know? She had short, orange, funky hair, and your hair, while it's more bleached than orange, is

still funky. But then again, she's so much more wholesome. Maybe it's more the contrast between you and Little Orphan Annie: like it's kind of *ironic* to call you Annie; because you're not an Annie at all, you're much more of a … of a Mercyx … "

Mercyx was looking at me steely-eyed. Between that and the yellow streaks on her eyelids, I couldn't continue my usual ramble. "What?" I asked.

"Why do you do that?"

"Do what?"

"Just go off like that."

"Like what?"

"Like arcane bullshit about Orphan Annie."

I did this all the time. That's what we did, Beale and Mercyx and I, we had long, inane conversations about nothing. And there wasn't conflict. What was going on with Mercyx all of a sudden? "I don't know," I said, "because it's funny? I mean, we all do it."

Mercyx was really making me uncomfortable. I knew she was formidable – I'd seen her in action at The Curiosity absolutely tearing into the well-dressed yuppie types always trying to get into her pants – but I'd never been the target of her ire.

"But it's bullshit," she said, "and you know it's bullshit. All those issues of *OTT*. That was the whole point of those issues, to make fun of yourself for all the rambling you do. And then this new church thing, that was the flipside: you showing how much power you could have if you were only sincere. It was brilliant. The *OTT* stuff was funny, mostly because you took every conversation Beale and you and I ever had and ripped it a new asshole, but *That Sunday* – I mean, dude, you're so right – what if we were all really sincere like that preacher guy. If we were to just tell it like it is. We all know how it is, but we never actually tell it like it is.

"You have to tell me a couple of things, and you have to be serious. First off, you have to tell me how you came up with this guy and what you were thinking, and don't go off on some tangent to avoid the question. And then you have to tell me why you really call me Annie, and I don't want to hear any more of that Little Orphan shit."

I'd never seen Mercyx with such metal in her eyes. They were the gray-blue of a circular saw blade. It suddenly seemed unreal to tell her the truth: that Booker was really a guy who had stood up in his makeshift church that Sunday and talked to me. When it happened, it had been odd but not unreal – if anything, it had been ultra-real, like when you're on your bike and the semi next to you starts to come into your lane, and you know it's going to turn right, and that you're about to be a victim of the dreaded right hook, and that the dual human-sized wheels next to you will crush you, but somehow you slam on your brakes enough to swerve behind him and survive, and then you look around and the world is normal and traffic moves on.

But now it seemed unreal, like I'd made the whole thing up. What was even more unreal was that I hadn't even thought of Booker, the person, since I left his church; in fact, I couldn't even tell you if I'd said anything to him. It was truly as if I'd made him up. But I couldn't have. I'd been at his church, and I could walk over, if I wanted to, the very next Sunday, and I could show Mercyx and Beale the place that inspired *His Church That Sunday*.

It was hard to do, but she was staring at me, and although it wasn't in my nature – as usually when I talk to people my eyes are all over the place, and never actually in the eyes of the person I'm talking to – I looked her back in the eyes, and what I said was, "Okay, there really is a preacher dude, and he really does do a sermon like the one I wrote about in *That Sunday*. As for calling you Annie …"

It's funny how realizations hit you mid-sentence, like it did on that day at Blowfish. We'd made our way into the restaurant and used those little golf pencils to fill out our paper sushi menus, and now I was sitting with Annie Mercyx on the back patio, the late evening blue of the sky tinged a deeper shade of blue; not pink like late evening skies are often described – the air too clean and smog-free for that – but midnight blue: a darker, softer, more romantic blue. There was an umbrella over us, and nigiri in front of us, and cute little bowls to mix our soy sauce and wasabi. Annie was beautiful and she was Annie and not Mercyx. It wasn't the truth what I said, because the truth was probably much closer to what I'd already said before about it sounding ironic: before this evening, Annie Mercyx was always more Mercyx than Annie. But somehow what came out of my mouth was more sincere than the truth – and more importantly it was the right thing to say – because the realization I had mid-sentence was that the reason Annie had dressed up, and put on makeup, and confronted me about my ironic bullshit, was that she liked me in a much different way than as a fellow cyclist and zinester; and perhaps even more importantly it was the right thing to say because I liked her – and if I told her that I hadn't really thought about it, that my calling her Annie instead of Mercyx was nothing more than a quirk; then, although I would be technically telling the truth, I would be implying a lie, which would be

to say that I didn't desire to be something other than her fellow cyclist and zinester.

So the way I finished the sentence was this way, "I guess I just wanted to be different. I wanted … I wanted you and me to be different."

I know, it's such a cheesy moment – it makes me cringe to write it out – it was so disgustingly sincere, but it's really what I said, and you can't change what you say once you've said it.

Mercyx reached a hand across the table, in order to grab mine, and then she said:

Mercyx and I consumed our remaining nigiri in an uncomfortable silence, and then agreed to meet the next Sunday at my apartment for a visit to Booker's church. You would have thought that my statement of affection and Mercyx's reaching across the table for my hand would have led to more intimate conversation, a kiss or two, and if this were an R movie or a porn shoot, the consummation of everyone's desires; but all it did was make us feel really, really weird.

By the time Mercyx mercifully let go of my hand, the union had become clammier than anything we'd eaten that night. I felt stupid. I wanted to be witty and charming but couldn't think of anything to say. I wanted to at least suggest an after-dinner cocktail – or make a date to meet that was a little closer than Sunday morning – but I'd lost all my thunder earlier in the evening, and the plum wine that should have made us feel heady and brave seemed to be lulling us into a stupor.

When we got to the bottom of our rice bowls, we were back on a last-name basis:

I could think of was that of the sushi dinner at Blowfish; and whenever I went to write it, I'd think of Mercyx giving it to some office worker to photocopy and I'd feel like a dumbass. By Friday, I'd resorted to taking long bike rides between shifts, taking the light rail twenty miles out to Gresham and then riding the long, twisting roads of the Old Columbia Gorge Highway past all the waterfalls.

The rides didn't help. I was lovestruck, and it was bad to be lovestruck by someone like Mercyx. Mercyx was cool as granite, like one of the stones submerged underneath Multnomah Falls, rounded and aged by thousands of years of falling glacial melt. There was no getting through to some softer core either – thousands of years of pounding waters had hollowed out whatever softer core there might have been. Mercyx was the kind of person you assumed something horrible had been done to as a child, but who you'd never ask about it.

I was nervous waiting for her to show up. How was I – a soft, skinny, and inkless twenty-two year-old – going to navigate the glacial waters of the Mercyx?

By the time she got there, I'd had too much coffee, so that I couldn't smile but only grit my teeth at her, looking a bit like a soldier digging his heels in for an impact.

"You ready?" Mercyx asked.

"Yeah," I said. I put on my cycling shoes and helmet and we rode over to Booker's church. No other words passed between us.

Chapter v

Where Joseph Patrick Booker Gives His Second Sermon;
and Where His Member Flops About

SUNDAY ARRIVED COOL BUT HOPEFUL. Portland was having an Indian summer, and a thin layer of fog hovered over what I thought would be another unusually bright and sunny October day. I'd made a cup of coffee and was sitting on my balcony in a folding chair, waiting anxiously to see Annie's helmeted head riding up Alberta Street.

I'd spent a hard week sorting out my feelings. Before, Mercyx had just been Mercyx, my friend; but now she was Annie, the object of my desire. I'd wanted to call her, to talk to her, to discuss matters; but she was still Mercyx – and you didn't discuss matters with Mercyx. I'd tried to put together issue #12 of *Octagonal Table Talk*, but the only subject matter

WHEN WE ARRIVED, THERE WAS NO CHURCH SERVICES TODAY: ALL WELCOME sign hammered into the ground. The signboard, with the George W. Bush quote on it, now read WE MUST B EUNICS ON VIDEO. The doors were shut tight. After sitting on the curb feeling stupid for a while, not saying anything to Mercyx, I finally knocked. No one answered. On my way back to the curb, where Mercyx was gnawing on an energy bar, I noted that the thin layer of fog that had seemed so certain to burn off, had gotten thicker rather than thinner, turning a hopeful day into something infinitely more dull.

"Wanna ride?" Mercyx asked, breaking the silence.

I didn't actually want to ride, what I wanted was for Booker to show up – to rub the flint that was Mercyx and Flynn together – but it didn't look like it was going to happen. "Where?"

"The falls."

"Did it Friday."

"Bridge of the Gods."

"Too far."

"You a pussy, Flynn?"

It was dangerous when Mercyx started this – Mercyx's cycling philosophy was that if you didn't feel like doing something, that was the very thing you should do. This wasn't my philosophy. But Mercyx was in charge when it came to matters of cycling, and I knew once she got an idea in her head she wouldn't let it go.

"Yeah, I am a pussy, Annie."

Mercyx and I both sort of flinched when I called her Annie. "You've got to get over that. You know you're going."

The Bridge of the Gods was an eighty-mile ride, no small affair. It was the kind of ride you built up to, not the kind of ride you just did on the spur of the moment when other plans went by the wayside. I pleaded despite knowing that appeals would be denied. "It's eighty miles, Annie."

"At twenty miles an hour, Flynn, that's a four-hour ride. What's the matter, never done a four-hour ride?"

Mercyx knew I couldn't sustain twenty miles an hour up a couple of passes for four hours. "I've never done eighty before."

"Well, you're doing it today."

"Am not."

"Are too."

"Am not."

"There's always got to be a first time, Flynn."

I looked at Mercyx when she said that, wondering if she was thinking what I was thinking. By all appearances, she was not.

I glared at her in not-so-mock consternation. "I've got to pick up some water bottles at home."

That was all Mercyx needed. She hopped on her bike and off we went.

—

O R RATHER OFF WE WOULD HAVE GONE, HAD not the doors of the church creaked open, and a disoriented-looking Joseph Patrick Booker peeked his head out, trying to make us out in the mist. "Hello?" he said tentatively, in that pained way people do when they've tied one on the night before.

"It's Flynn," I said.

"Flynn?" asked Booker.

I was feeling dumb now. "Yeah, you know, I was here last Sunday for your …" I wanted to say *sermon* or *church service*, but it sounded foreign in my head, so I finished my thought with, "…thing."

"Oh yeah." A slight smile came to Booker's face. He opened the door all the way. He was dressed in a gray terry cloth bathrobe, a pair of flip-flops that were at least eight sizes too big for him, and, as we would discover in the not-too-distant future, nothing else. "You didn't say anything when you left, so I didn't think I'd ever see you again."

Neither Booker nor I knew what to say next. It was clear that I was here to attend another church service, and it was equally clear Booker hadn't expected me, much less me and a companion, to show up. Fortunately, Mercyx broke the silence. "Mercyx," she said to Booker, by way of introducing herself.

"Joseph Patrick Booker," he said, "Pleased –"

Mercyx cut him off as she was wont to do. "Charmed," she said.

Booker brightened up a bit at Mercyx's obvious dismissiveness, as if mistreatment was something that fueled him. His voice was a bit gravelly as he spoke. "Why don't you guys come in for a bit? I'll throw on some coffee."

We followed him into the church, which was the same as I'd seen it last week, except that this time around there were people and additional bicycles in it: people passed out on the theater seats and on the misshapen spaces between rows on the floor, their bicycles tossed haphazardly amongst the junk lining the walls. Booker offered no explanation; he simply sidestepped the bikes and tiptoed over the bodies and expected us to do the same.

He led us to the front of the church where the paint-splattered table was, and told us to sit down while he got the coffee. Mercyx and I sat uncomfortably at the table, hoping that none of the skinny, grizzled, wasted-looking young men sprawled like Raggedy Andys over the theater seats would startle and wake.

Mercyx whispered, bewildered, "He really is a dwarf."

"I know."

"How'd you find this place?"

I whispered back, "I just walked in."

"Into this?"

"It wasn't like this before."

That was all Mercyx got as an explanation before Booker came back with the coffee. The last thing I needed was another cup, but I took one anyway.

Booker repeated what he'd said before. He still seemed to be squinting at me, as if he couldn't quite make out the pattern that was Barth Flynn. "I didn't think I'd see you again. You seemed weirded out."

By this time, I'd given it some thought, and had an answer

for Booker about why I'd walked out the way I had, although I didn't know him well enough to actually give it to him. I think when I'd seen him up on that milk crate last Sunday he'd become fiction, like in my head he was already the person on my pages and not Booker; so it hadn't seemed that strange to have walked out, like when you leave a movie before all the credits have rolled.

I didn't offer him this explanation – an explanation that he probably deserved. I also didn't tell him that I'd just assumed he'd be doing it again, getting up on the altar and giving another righteous sermon, something interesting to fill the pages of *His Church That Sunday #2*.

Instead I just said, "Check this out," and tossed him an issue of *His Church That Sunday #1*.

Now that I think about it, *His Church That Sunday #1* had all the explanation that Booker needed, since in its last few pages, it had my thought bubble crowding out Booker's word bubble, showing all my thoughts about how Booker and his church would make a brilliant backdrop for a comic, and also kind of showing in that way how I'd forgotten about Booker, and why it wasn't a normal human interaction that we'd had, but rather two people having their own separate mental processes, completely oblivious of the other.

But whatever Booker was thinking, his reading of *His Church That Sunday* was producing what I can only describe as guffaws. Short, quick bursts of laughter that came out more like hacks. He read it with a prideful smile, the way a father reads a child's report card. When he was done, he slapped the zine down and said in a voice that startled several of the Raggedy Andys, "You're my fucking scribe!"

Mercyx and I exchanged *huh* glances.

A fire shot into Booker's eyes. His voice came out loudly, more gravelly than you would have thought possible on a guy with such a small frame. "Don't you get it? Every preacher, every prophet, every powerful person who has ever held sway over something important – they've had a scribe. And you, I mean, after only one freaking sermon, you … you, Flynn … you show up and you're my fucking scribe! No one gets a scribe in their first go around! No one! And I …" Booker actually stood up and hugged me around the waist when he said this, " …oh my God, do you have any idea how lucky I am? I have to keep going! I thought … I thought you thought I was some sort of freak. I mean, I am a freak, but I thought you thought I was a bad freak and not a good freak. But you see, you didn't think that at all, you were just … you were just *observing*, like … well, like a very good scribe."

"I was going to quit, Flynn. After just one try, I was going to quit. I'd, well … well, fuck, look at this … I'd thrown away all the God stuff and decided that I was going the wrong direction – that I just needed a good night of drinking and the madness would leave me. I'm not saying that there's anything wrong with this. A guy … well, I mean, it's what Jesus suggested you do: let a bunch of lost souls crash out at your pad, and share your wine with them, and, you know, give them what they need without expecting anything in return. But to be honest, that wasn't why I did it. I did it because I was going to give up. But then – I know you think this is such bullshit, and Mercyx you too, I know that you guys are like the believing unbelievers and that all of this is so uncool – but shit, it was God, it was God that made you do this zine. It's all edgy and modern-looking, but ultimately it's also the truth – it's everything that I said and everything that you were thinking and … it's all there.

"You have to do something with this, Flynn. What are you going to do with it?"

Like most questions asked in this manner, I expected Booker's to be rhetorical, but he just stared at me, refusing to go on until I answered it.

Mercyx eventually saved the moment, in typical Mercyx fashion, "I run the copies."

Booker looked confused.

"I'm the runner," said Mercyx.

Booker was getting a quick lesson in Mercyxish. He looked at me for a translation. "Annie already made copies of it. You can pick it up for free at the zine library at the IPRC downtown, or you can buy it at Ben Dover Books, the bookstore downstairs. Annie's the copy runner: people do their zines, and Annie finds a way to get them printed."

Booker was rarely at a loss for words, but here he didn't seem to know what to say. I think he was looking for a biblical equivalent to the term *copy runner*, so that he could go off about having a scribe *and* a copy runner, but he couldn't come up with anything, and so he had to leave it alone. He finally came out with an uninspired, "This is in bookstores?"

"Yeah," said Mercyx.

BEFORE WE COULD CONTINUE WITH OUR EXplanation of *His Church That Sunday*, a woman – Rubenesque, busty and oddly ageless – emerged from a side door at the front of the church, a door that churchgoers would recognize as the door leading to the vestibule. The woman's blonde hair was matted and dreaded, and was askew in a

"A comic? A comic?" said Skye, faking incredulousness. "There's nothing comic about Booker, you know. He's a master and a lord."

There were groans from the peanut gallery. The grizzled, passed-out, sideburned figures were perhaps not as passed-out as they seemed. I could have sworn one of them mumbled, "The master and lord of your pussy," but I wasn't entirely sure.

Booker's coloring was such that if he were blushing you wouldn't have been able to tell. He seemed to take it in stride, as if he were used to being called pussy royalty. "It's a comic about the church I'm starting."

"Joseph Patrick Booker is starting a church?" Skye's sage-colored eyes – bewitched and gleaming – looked up at him from their nest in his lap. "It must be the church of Satan."

Booker looked down at her, still petting her head. "Not at all, not at all, it's a church for the followers of Jesus Christ. Not a church for the so-called Christians – all those misled, mentally and emotionally castrated suburbanites with their white picket fences and one-point-seven children – but for us, the true followers of Jesus Christ, the cyclists and the sex workers, the zinesters and the comic book writers, the gays and lesbians and anarchists – we … we are the ones still doing as he did, growing our hair long and eating grasshoppers and roaming from Galilean town to Galilean town. "Jesus was a freak! That's what no one understands! He was a freak!"

Booker was suddenly animated in the same way he'd been earlier. The way he often got. He had that dangerous look in his eyes people get when they make a hard decision. He stood up rather abruptly, and in the process – as Skye had been clinging to him rather tightly – the belt holding his terry cloth robe loosened, exposing his front side. But Booker didn't seem to notice. He was on a roll. And when Booker went beyond the reflexive and the human and into the realm of the Godlike, nothing could stop the gusher that poured forth. He really was that oblivious. Booker leapfrogged up onto the milk crates in that seamless, impossible way he had and began speaking. As he stood, his member, with oversized length and decent girth, swung to and fro, a pendulum addressing the multitudes:

way that indicated she'd had a hard night. She was wearing Booker's black cassock, which actually fit her much better than it had him. She walked toward us in a straight line, ignoring the MGD bottles that spun and clattered as she kicked her way through them. When she arrived at the table where we were sitting, she threw herself down in a rather theatrical fashion, knelt on the littered, hardwood floor beside Booker's chair, laid her head indecorously in his lap, and oblivious to us, Booker's guests, said, "Joseph, I worship at your temple."

"Good morning, Skye," said Booker, patting her head like you would a sloppy golden retriever. "These are my friends, Flynn and Mercyx."

"From whenceforth do they come?" asked Skye, looking up at us and mangling, with both grammar and accent, a Shakespearean English.

"They're doing a comic about me," said Booker.

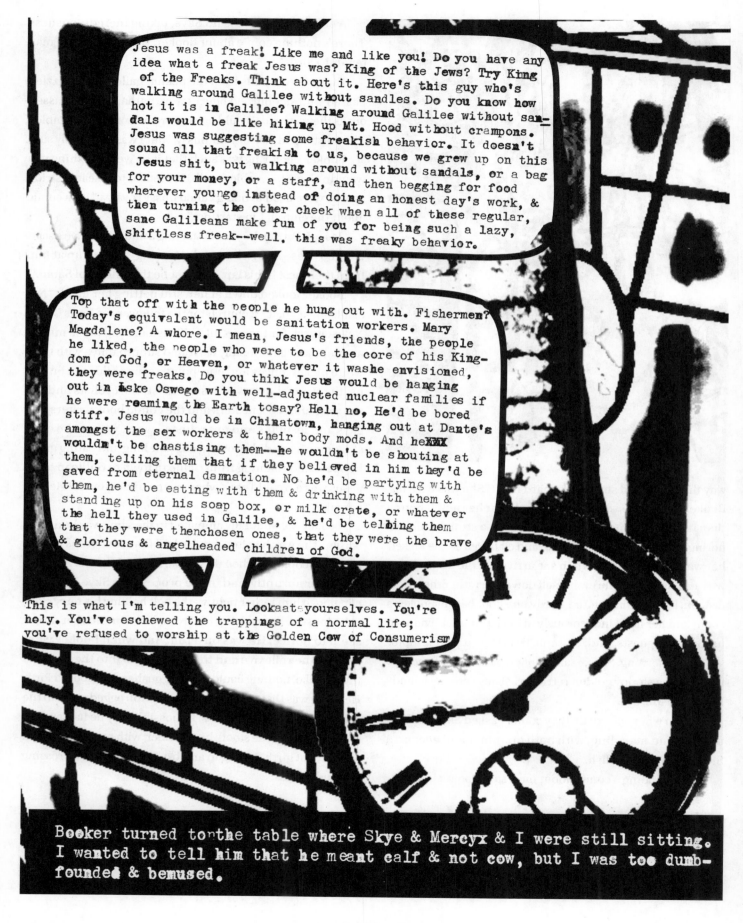

Jesus was a freak! Like me and like you! Do you have any idea what a freak Jesus was? King of the Jews? Try King of the Freaks. Think about it. Here's this guy who's walking around Galilee without sandles. Do you know how hot it is in Galilee? Walking around Galilee without sandals would be like hiking up Mt. Hood without crampons. Jesus was suggesting some freakish behavior. It doesn't sound all that freakish to us, because we grew up on this Jesus shit, but walking around without sandals, or a bag for your money, or a staff, and then begging for food wherever you go instead of doing an honest day's work, & then turning the other cheek when all of these regular, sane Galileans make fun of you for being such a lazy, shiftless freak--well, this was freaky behavior.

Top that off with the people he hung out with. Fishermen? Today's equivalent would be sanitation workers. Mary Magdalene? A whore. I mean, Jesus's friends, the people he liked, the people who were to be the core of his King- dom of God, or Heaven, or whatever it washe envisioned, they were freaks. Do you think Jesus would be hanging out in Aske Oswego with well-adjusted nuclear families if he were reaming the Earth tosay? Hell no, He'd be bored stiff. Jesus would be in Chinatown, hanging out at Dante's amongst the sex workers & their body mods. And he wouldn't be chastising them--he wouldn't be shouting at them, teliing them that if they believed in him they'd be saved from eternal damnation. No he'd be partying with them, he'd be eating with them & drinking with them & standing up on his soap box, or milk crate, or whatever the hell they used in Galilee, & he'd be telling them that they were thenchosen ones, that they were the brave & glorious & angelheaded children of God.

This is what I'm telling you. Look at yourselves. You're holy. You've eschewed the trappings of a normal life; you've refused to worship at the Golden Cow of Consumerism

Booker turned to the table where Skye & Mercyx & I were still sitting. I wanted to tell him that he meant calf & not cow, but I was too dumb- founded & bemused.

Flynn, you were a bright kid, right? You could have been a doctor or a lawyer or a CEO. You hadn the grades & the scores. But you didn't do that; you chucked it & got a liberal arts degree. Do you know why you did that? Did you do it because you were lazy? Maybe you feel that way, maybe you feel like you should have sucked it up so that you weren't slinging coffee to all the lawyers & doctors & CEOs who walk into your cafe & bark out their orders while mumbling into their cell phones. Maybe you don't see yourself for what you are, XXXXXX because you're not a lost soul at all; you're a very healthy & intact one; & you're not a bitter & confused agnostic or atheist either; what you are, whether you want to admit it or not, is a follower of Jesud Christ.

You're not a Christian, because being a Christian implies that you follow some fucked-up rulebook put together by a bunch of sexually frustrated friars; but you are an adherent to the thachings of Jesus Christ, & I8m talking about the true Jesus Christ, the one who was a fucking XX freak--not the one who everyone thinks was the goddamm Savior ofn the World.

You8ve still got your soul, Flynn! How happy you should be! How blessed are you! You barely make your rent. How blessed you are! You can't afford the yuppie-ass restaunts ont the street you live on. How blessed are you! You don't own a Sport Utility Vehicle. How blessed are you! Flynn, you & me & Mercyx & all the rest of the freaks doubled up in the rotting wood bungalows of Portland, Oregon--we're the goddamm light of the world.

At the words "light of the world", the theme song from Shaft sounded from Booker's vestibule. Booker looked at Skye, who--& I noted her familiarity with his ringtone--quickly skirted off to receive his cell phone. When she returned, he took it & answered it the same way he had last week. "Antique Road Show", experience is key", he said. "Vanilla," he said. "GFE", he said. "BBBJ," he said. He slapped the cell phone shut & handed it back to Skye. Then he continued, as if this bizarre & inexplicable phone conversation had never happened.

I'm sick of hiding here in the moss, Flynn. That's why I did what I id last Sunday. I shouldn't have stopped. I shouldn't have given up. I'm so glad you came her, & brought Mercyx, & told me what was up, & showed me this zine you did, because now I'm going to do it again, in fact I'm going to do it every fucking Sunday until I meet my maker--I'm going to take these milk crates & I'm going tostand on them, & I'm going to shout all this stuff off the top of my head because... because it's right, you know? Everything I'm saying is right--& I cna feel it & you can feel it. And the things I'm saying & the way I'm saying it, it isn't really blasphemous at all. Preachers, we can say this shit, we can say fucking and shit & still proclaim the truth, because... because somehow it's more truthful that way, because it's not all high & mighty & thee & thou. It's just the plain fucking truth.

That's what I'm going to do, Flynn. I'm going to keep this up. I'm going to do it because it makes me happy, Because if I don't do it I'll start to think what the world thinks, that I'm just a foolish midget who... sells antiques & rides around with some freaky cycling gang. But that's not true at all, Flynn. We're at the epicenter. We're the pressure building in the bowels of the earth. We're not the fringes, Flynn, we're the it, the middle of everything. Do you see? I've got it, Flynn. And you've got it. And Mercyx has it. And Skye, lovely Skye, she has it. And all t e guys, they've got it. We're the saints, dude. We're not the siiners at all. And, and.;..

Booker stuttered for amoment, giving me a second to look down toward the aisles, where the Raggedy Andies were now sitting up in varying degrees of wakefulness. It was a motley crew. Some held their heads in their hands, some smoked, some spun the beer bottles on the floor, all of them looked towards Booker with irritated expressions, like you would a small child standing on a stool--you were willing to indulge his newfound height, but only for a second or two before you yelled at him to get down.

You see, they're wrong. Theones who have claimed Christianity, they're wrong. The everyday
God-fearing American Christian is actually a
worshipper of the Golden Cow: they're the ones
that Jesus talked about whenbought the farms,
& the oxen, & the wives, & got so fucking involved in the whole life-sucking process of
making money that they didn't have time to
come to His party.

Today's Christians--they're the Pharisees--
they're the ones who horde what they have &
don't share it with others, they're the ones
safe in their suburban homes with their cen-
tralized heating, unwilling to make the con-
nection, when a car runs over a bicycle] when
a bomb drops on a Third world home, when a
drought starves a child, unwilling to think,
my God, that could be me, unwilling to think,
my God, my way of life--it's wrecking everything.

But see, we know differently. Ane we're doing
it--we're living differently. We know Him. We
know Jesus. His core message--it wasn't about
Believing & being Saved; it was about dumping
all your shit, & hanging out with other people
who've dumped all their shit, & figuring out
with those people what you can do to make the
world a better place.

There's no telling what more Booker would have said, surely he would have said more. But at some point in his tirade, one of the slumbering Raggedy Andys had come to life. Smoking a filterless Camel, and wearing large, mirrored cop sunglasses, the Raggedy Andy had decided that this was all too much of a carnival to be dealt with in reverent silence. At the top of his lungs, he yelled "Shut the fuck up!" and after doing so, he leaned over, gripped the neck of a beer bottle, and chucked it toward Booker's head.

Booker saw it coming, and was able to duck out of the way, but doing so caused him to lose his balance, and so the crates slipped out from under him, causing him to fall backwards, now almost entirely disrobed, onto the floor behind.

At this point, there was chaos. Skye let out a yelp, shouted "My Lord!" leapt out of her chair, and threw herself on Booker like some thwarted Ophelia. A couple of the Andys, awoken by the ruckus, began throwing punches at each other, apparently recalling an argument they'd had the night before. Meanwhile the rest of the peanut gallery, observing the scene, started applauding, whether for the fight or Booker's speech or for the Andy who'd thrown the bottle or for Skye or just in approval of the general madness, I couldn't tell.

Whatever the cause, Mercyx and I had seen enough. We slipped out the front door.

Chapter VI

*Where Mercyx and I Go For a Bike Ride
and Where I Ask Myself Many Existential Questions*

THE SENSIBLE THING TO DO WOULD HAVE been to have gone over to Beaterville, and over a long breakfast had a laugh-out-loud conversation about Booker's church of hedonism, but Mercyx had other ideas.

"The cemetery?" she asked, although the way she asked it was more a command than a question.

"The cemetery" meant something different to Mercyx and me than it might mean to you. The cemetery was a route that cyclists took to get from the Willamette River up into Southwest Hills of Portland. You rode up through a grove of maples,

unbelievably colorful in the fall, and after a number of switchbacks, arrived at a graveyard, where a maze of unmarked roads continued to snake upward past oversized granite stones and conifers, the climb getting more and more strenuous, until you finally arrived at the mausoleum near the top.

You could do a number of rides once you'd made it to the mausoleum, and I assumed we'd do one of these after we struggled our way through the maze in the cemetery. So I acquiesced to Mercyx's plan. It was a better idea than the eighty-mile route to the Bridge of the Gods.

Mercyx and I rode. And we rode. Following as close behind her as I possibly could, the outline of her tight glutes through Lycra the only thing spurring me forward, we rode up through the cemetery; but when we got to the top – the place where we could do something more pleasant, like ride around Lake Oswego, or through the tree-lined corridor of Tryon Creek – Mercyx turned around and said, "Reps."

And she sped back down the hill, winding her way downward, with me in not-so-hot pursuit.

Twice, three times, four times, we repeated the strenuous climb, me following less and less closely. The fog finally burned off, and heat rose up almost immediately, reflecting hard off the blacktop. Mercyx would get to the top, wait, and when I got there she'd say, "Again," and then she'd be off, not waiting for my response.

My legs were shot after the fourth ascent, so when I got to the mausoleum and Mercyx said "Again," I just looked at her.

"Again," Mercyx repeated.

"I'm bonked." I said.

"Pffffff," said Mercyx, disdain on her face.

And then she was off, descending perilous curves, her ass a lovely millimeter or two off the saddle.

I watched her go down. I'd hoped seeing the church that inspired me to write *HCTS* stirred whatever emotion had gotten Mercyx into a dress would put us back on intimate speaking terms, but instead it seemed to have pushed her into sadism.

I sat in front of the mausoleum creeped out. It was one thing to ride through a cemetery with your legs cranking; it was another thing to sit in one without a purpose – with no one to visit or mourn. Graveyards make you think about your life and whether you'd feel like you'd accomplished anything if they laid you six feet under. This isn't something you want to be thinking about at twenty-two, because the answer to that question is no.

As I had this existential crisis, it's funny where and to whom my mind drifted. I didn't realize it at the time, my thoughts seemed self-generated – what was I doing with my life? what did I want to do with my life? how long could I go on writing nihilistic zines full of sexual innuendo? was there anything in the world that I cared about? if so, would I ever find the courage to do something about it? – but these thoughts were no doubt driven by Booker's sermons: the purpose he found via lesbian; the courage he conjured via Jesus-as-freak.

In my consciousness, Booker and his words were merely something to fill a zine – a joke to share amongst friends. But in my subconscious, Booker was becoming something different. He was someone with ideals, and whether or not these ideals were something I believed or didn't believe in didn't really matter, what mattered was that he had them and lived by them.

(Jesus is a freak. I'm a freak. You're a freak. Therefore we should all get together and form some sort of freakish Christian church that goes and … well, who knows what Booker had in mind. It certainly wasn't much of a purpose or a philosophy, but it was more than I had at the time.)

Of course, there's likely another reason I was thinking these thoughts then, and she was coming up the hill, panting heavily, though her sunglasses masked any sign on her face of serious strain. She stopped her front tire a few inches from mine. "Get in a good rest, Flynn?"

Shit. "Maybe."

"Again."

"All right."

Mercyx ended up doing the cemetery ten times – four-thousand feet of vertical ascent. I did seven laps myself, and was totally beat. I rode back to my apartment, drank a gallon of Gatorade, and passed out on my couch.

———

I'D REALLY LIKE TO SKIP ALL THIS STUFF ABOUT Mercyx and me. What I'd like to do is just write out all of Booker's teachings in biblical format, complete with chapters and verses: the *Good Book about Booker*. It would be a whole lot more interesting than this stuff about Mercyx and me riding up and down hills without talking to each other.

But I know I can't do it, because Booker would've had a shit fit. He would've wanted, demanded even, that all this context be there. The Bible, he would say, was the most irritating book ever written. Its authors had no foresight. They left out all the context about what Galilee was like, and what the personalities of the apostles were like, and just in general what was going on in Galilee to make Jesus suggest that it

would be a hell of a lot better to throw it all away and wander around the desert than to continue to live with the status quo. The authors of the Bible left things open to interpretation that should have been really damn clear, Booker would say, and it pissed him off that because the context was missing, the majority of Christ's believers believe in a philosophy that's about as un-Christian as a philosophy could be.

So I've got to tell you all this stuff, because if I don't, you won't understand why he said some of the things he said, and then you'll turn around and say that Booker was sending mixed messages, that here he said one thing, and there he said another, and then you'll go off and miss all the finer points, and you'll think that all it's about is holding up signs at Buffalo Bills games that say BOOKER 3:16, and BELIEVE AND BE SAVED, as if the whole damn message was as simple as that, as if believing or not believing was the whole difference between a good person and a bad, as if it wasn't about actions, as if it wasn't about doing what it is you're called to do.

———

SO THIS IS THE SHORT OF WHAT HAPPENED THE week after the second Sunday I spent at Booker's church. That night, trying to get my mind off of Mercyx, I started working on the sequel to *His Church That Sunday #1*, and discovered much to my dismay that I'd reached the extent of my abilities. I could find clippings of midgets and cut and paste them on the page. I could put words in word bubbles. I could do a whole bunch of jiggering in Photoshop. But there was no way in hell that I could draw bikers transformed into rag dolls, dreadlocked girls in priest's cassocks, and accurate portrayals of Booker's pendulous anatomy. I needed someone to collaborate with, a real comic book artist, someone much more talented than me.

The easy choice would have been my friend Beale, but Beale was a two-note artist, and his two notes were big boobs and fiery dragons. I couldn't see him doing the milk crates and the Raggedy Andys and the flying bottles and the priest stuff. Plus, Beale had a thick touch with the pen, and there was no way he could get all the activity of Booker's church in less than fifty pages. The obvious choice, a guy with whom I'd always wanted to collaborate, was a guy named Chester Fields. Chester's comics were super detail-oriented, and his writing was tiny, so he could pull off the whole scene in a relatively small number of pages. But Chester Fields was a hired hand. He worked for Dark Horse and even Marvel occasionally. Chester got paid for projects, and a guy like that wasn't someone I'd dare approach.

This was going to be tough. I wanted to keep pumping out issues, given that Booker was going to preach every Sunday, and that I planned to do an issue on every one, but this would take weeks: getting someone to collaborate with, working with them to get all the details down.

Monday dawned at the coffee shop, followed by an afternoon solo ride up to the flat farm roads around Sauvie Island, an idyllic little island in the Columbia River that's sort of an anti-Manhattan, protected from development by Portland's notorious urban planning Nazis.

Mercyx didn't allow for rides without a vertical challenge, so I had to ride the flat roads alone, unprotected from the capricious Gorge winds. I ended the day at home in bed reading *Don Quixote*. Tuesday looked to be more of the same. I'd put aside *His Church That Sunday* and Mercyx, not at all sure what to do about either. At around noon on Tuesday, in the middle of mixing up a soy milk chai, I got a call:

"Mercyx here."

"What's up?"

"The Curiosity. Eight. Whole gang. Some names too. Be there. Mercyx out."

Chapter vii

On the Unusual Synergy Created by His Church That Sunday #1 *and How I Ended Up with a Deadbeat Roommate*

ON THE SURFACE, WHAT MADE THE CU-riosity curious was that absolutely nothing inside it distinguished it from any other bar. It had stools, a surly bartender, a standard assortment of liquors on lit shelves, six beer taps, booths, a jukebox, and a pool table. There were several bars just like it on Alberta Street alone. If one were to come in from out of town, one might look at the clientele, with their youth and their tattoos and their tight-fitting vintage clothes, and say, "Gee, honey, this sure is a curiosity," but after spending a week or so here in Portland, one would realize The Curiosity's clientele was the same you'd see in every bar in town.

On Tuesday, after getting home from the coffee shop and reading another chapter of *Don Quixote*, I rode over to The Curiosity. If I'd known what crowd was waiting for me, I might have just ridden by again; but I was innocent to this, so I U-locked my bike outside and sauntered on in, still feeling weird about Mercyx, but glad to be hanging out with her in a more relaxed group setting.

I was not the first to arrive. The usuals were there – Mercyx, Beale, Dirk from work, the Dunworthy twins, and a few of Beale's D&D buddies – but there were extras too, the "big names" as Mercyx had called them: Doug Yamhill, owner of Ben Dover Books (the guy we called Dougie Fresh); Dietrich Björnson, this big-time Norwegian comic book artist who'd somehow made his way to Oregon and into Dougie's pants; and Chester Fields, whose presence I felt must have been conjured. He never hung out with lowlifes like us.

When I walked in, Beale was beaming. He got up and bowed to me, hands extended, we're-not-worthy style. Everyone else nodded their heads as if Beale had a quorum. I had no idea what was going on. I just smiled at them shyly.

Chester had a copy of *His Church This Sunday* #1 in one hand and a beer in the other. "This rocks, dude. You want a pint?"

Now you've got to remember that I was twenty-two at the time, and although twenty-two isn't sixteen, it's still young enough to be star-struck. Granted, you tend to be more discerning in who you're star-struck by; you lean away from mainstream pop culture icons and more toward that which is just out of reach. It's Zia, the short, feisty, somewhat robust keyboardist from the Dandy Warhols instead of J. Lo.

So here was Chester. Chester Fields of *The Chesterfields* comic fame offering me a drink.

"Yeah ... sure, I'll have a drink," I said.

"What'll it be?" asked Chester.

I drifted off, dizzy from the unexpected attention.

Chester looked at me quizzically, "What'll you have, dude?"

"Um ... how 'bout a Full Sail."

"The stout? You gotta have the stout," said Chester.

"Sure," I said. I hated stouts.

Chester walked up to the bar and I just sort of stood there, stunned by this turn of events. Beale helped me out a bit. "Have a seat, Flynn."

"Sorry," I said.

I sat down, feeling like fresh meat at a poker table.

Dougie Fresh spoke up. "This is a killer concept. I love

the content. Not everyone can do this – they've got the artistry, you know, but they can't write. You've got the gift of gab, man. This is hot shit."

"Thanks," I said. This was Dougie Fresh. Dougie'd never said a good thing about my work. He'd suddenly gone from Mr. Cynical to Mr. Brown-nose.

Dougie went on, "Mercyx said there's a real Booker."

"Yeah," I said. "He lives in that crazy church on Prescott. You should check him out some time."

Chester came back with my beer, put it on the table, and pushed it in front of me. "Cheers," he said.

"Cheers," I said back.

The Chester Fields was toasting Bartholomew Flynn.

Dougie broke back in, anxious to continue the conversation. "Yeah, yeah, that's great. We'll check him out. We'll do that …"

Dougie looked over at Mercyx, and then at Chester, before changing the subject. "Listen man. This is new. Unique. You've got this voice, man. Or Booker does. Whatever. Mercyx said that you were a fan of Chester's, and I was thinking about it, putting two and two together, and you've got the writing skills, and this octagon stuff that you do with the Sharpie – it's good, in its way, in a primitive way – but, see, it's like you're in a boat, and you can keep rowing with oars, or you can put a motor on it, really jazz it out and go somewhere with it."

Chester chimed in, anxious to get to the point, "Doug wants to move out of distro and into publishing his own stuff, and he was talking to me about producing some of my work, but I'm all tapped out, idea wise, with all the stuff I'm doing for *The Chesterfields*, plus I've got to do something new with Doug, because DC will get pissed off if I publish anything that looks remotely like The Chesterfields somewhere else.

"Anyway, we were talking about all this when Doug came across this new … what are you calling this, a zine? an auto-bio? … this midget preacher thing of yours, and we … it sort of just clicked, what we could do. We weren't sure how to approach it because, you know, we didn't want to step on your toes. But …"

Chester looked over at Doug and Doug looked back at Chester. If either of them had any clue how stoked I was about what they were circuitously getting to, we could have skipped all the canoe versus motorboat analogies. In fact, if I hadn't been so shocked that Chester and Dougie Fresh had been thinking, at the exact same time that I was thinking it, the very thing that seemed utterly impossible to me just the day before, I would have interrupted them myself.

Mercyx, as usual, broke in, cutting to the chase, "Chester and Dougie asked me if you'd be interested in making *His Church* a collaborative effort in exchange for four colors and a wider distribution. I told them you'd do it."

Everyone looked at me. Would I do it? Would I have Chester Fields put my words to art? Would I have Dougie Fresh gloss it up and print it in perfect-bind? I looked at Beale. Beale knew. His eyes were as wide as mine. "Fuck. Sure. Yeah. I can't draw worth shit. I'll work with Chester."

"Right on," said Chester.

Dougie Fresh looked at me like you'd look at someone who's just had the wool pulled over his eyes.

———

SO THIS CONVERSATION HAPPENED AT ABOUT nine p.m. on Tuesday night. By early Wednesday morning, Chester Fields, my hero, had moved into my apartment.

What happened was this. Chester kept dragging me back to the bar and pumping me full of stouts so that my tongue became looser than it would normally be. I filled Chester in on how Booker planned to give a sermon every Sunday, and how I wanted to do a comic a week right along with his sermons. Chester listened, getting me to keep going and tell him everything, all my ideas for the comic coerced by a simple smile and nod; and then, after everyone else had bailed, Chester followed me to my apartment without any sort of discussion, like it was the most normal thing to do in the world, and moved in.

He sat at my desk, asked me questions about Booker, the church, and "this Skye girl," penciling illustrations of them on a scrap of notebook paper with a Number 2 pencil, and at about four in the morning, professing a need for better supplies, he went over to his house, or wherever it was that he was living, encased his drafting table – the only nice thing he owned – in cut-up cardboard, packed an old Samsonite full of drawing supplies, rolled up his futon, slung it all into his late model pickup, and unloaded it into my apartment. I assumed that it was temporary, that we had a lot of work to do together, and that after we were done he'd go back to wherever it was he came from. But Chester never did leave. He just moved in.

I suppose, looking back on it, that Chester was a twenty-eight-year-old loser who was using me, and if I'd been older and more jaded I would have recognized that. Chester never paid rent and I never asked him to. Chester never bought groceries and I never asked him to. Chester just drew. I told him what to draw and he drew it. All night long, all day long, he drew. He had outside interests – strip clubs were his thing – but when he was in the house, he drew.

I was ecstatic. I wrote out the text from Booker's church debacle, and Chester set up in the corner and started drawing. It was a forty-eight hour rush of collaboration – we didn't talk about anything else – by Friday we had a fifty pager ready for Dougie Fresh; and we sent it over to him; and then I went to work and Chester went somewhere else, most likely the Sugar Shack, and when I came back Chester was passed out on his futon in the middle of the living room. I didn't ask him about it and he didn't say anything about it. That was that. By Saturday, Dougie Fresh had the manuscript of *His Church That Sunday* #2 in his hands, ready for publication. And by Sunday, well, by Sunday everyone who'd shown up at The Curiosity was ready for His Church.

Chapter viii

Booker's Third Sermon,
In Which the Most Holy of All Beverages Plays a Vital Role

T HERE WERE TWELVE OF US IN HIS CHURCH that Sunday: Mercyx and me, Beale, Dougie Fresh, Dietrich, Chester Fields, a few D&D dorks, a couple of Raggedy Andys, and Skye. You'd think, given the excitement my zine had generated, there would be a buzz in the air, but instead of anticipating the entrance of my inspiration, everyone stood separately facing the altar, strangely reverent and still, their arms away from their bodies, like hipsters awaiting a band.

Or zombies awaiting commands.

You see, we were all wet.

Some of us, those who had biked over, were drenched. Others who had driven and then walked to the church were merely damp. None of us, however, were entirely dry.

The Celtic word for the rain we had gotten caught in was *níor aimsíodh téarma ar bith*, which, depending on the context, can either be translated as "a soaking mist" or "piss." Portlanders are very familiar with this type of rain, and while all sorts of synthetic microfibers have been invented to combat it, it somehow manages, in its creepy mossy way, to seep through to your skin, creating all kinds of fungal blooms to keep the corporate heads at Tinactin happy.

Into this mildewed silence, Joseph Patrick Booker strode. He came out of his vestibule and crossed the sanctuary to his "altar." His too-big black cassock, the one Skye had been wearing last week, wedding-trained behind him. His red Holy Spirit stole, the one with white doves and peace symbols crudely felted on, dangled like two loose shoelaces.

Unlike the previous week's open robe debacle, Booker looked prepared, although his apparent preparation only served to make him look more foolish. In addition to the clownish vestments, he had parted his hair down the middle and greased it down the sides, a fashion no-no, and the way his dark, curly longish hair fell at the sides reminded me of Tarzan, and Tarzan was not a person that a dwarf should try to emulate.

Whether from the cold and wet or from Booker's appearance, I can't be sure, but we were all slack-jawed when Booker began his striding. He gazed at us, the way we stood there so oddly stoic, and asked, "What the fuck are you guys doing just standing there?"

None of us answered. We wanted to laugh at him – he looked ridiculous. We wanted to laugh at ourselves – what *were* we doing here?

Booker looked us over for a good long while, and then he began talking, his voice jittery:

"This is weird, this doesn't work at all. Talk. Mingle. Do something. I can't just start this way. This isn't right. I mean we're not going to go by the Roman Missal or anything. There's not going to be a grand entrance, and a *Kyrie Eleison*, and a Glory to God in the Highest. You've got to relax me and make this normal somehow so I can get juiced up. Why don't you guys –"

Booker cut himself off and looked us over.

"Christ, what was there – a flood? You're like the corpses of Egyptians caught in the Red Sea. You're like –"

Booker was flapping his arms up and down like a wounded crow, the sound of his own voice doing the juicing for him.

"Wait. I can fix this. See, this is perfect. It'll be like … like a ritual. Like the Israelites, you know, with the unleavened bread and all. You see, it's so us. It's so what we are and what we're about. It's so our place and our time. It's so … Portland.

"Coffee!" Booker was practically foaming at the mouth. "I have coffee!"

"You get it right? You see, we'll have the Kyrie-a-coffee every Sunday, with a glory to coffee in the highest, and a peace to the people who drink it, except of course for the ones who ruin it with skim milk. All right? So everyone up front and at the table. You look terrible. You need to warm up. Come on. Up! Up! Up!"

I for one moved toward the altar to collect my coffee in the highest. Booker was indeed a lunatic, but a cup of java to ward off the chill was just what the doctor ordered. Booker, however, halted me in my tracks:

"Wait! Wait! Wait! Just a minute. I have to do one thing first. We can't just drink it. It has to be blessed. I've got to transub – what's that fucking word – does anyone know it? I know – transubcaffienate. I'm going to transubcaffienate the coffee first. Hold on."

Booker strode back the way he came, opening up the door to the vestibule and disappearing behind it. I looked behind me to where everyone else was standing, awkwardly interspersed between the uneven rows of theater seats. Everyone was speechless. Dougie Fresh caught my eye and mouthed, "Oh, my God."

Booker returned shortly. He had rolled up the sleeves of the cassock to his shoulders. In each hand, he held a French press. He got behind the altar and lifted the French presses into the air, his arms outstretched. For some reason the gesture reminded me of Nixon.

He began again, his head raised in supplication:

"Blessed are you, Lord Jesus Christ, the freakiest of the freaks. Through the goodness of that great whore, our most holy and taken advantage of Mother Earth, we have this coffee to offer. Fruit of the vine and work of human hands, it will become for us a most warming and invigorating drink."

As Booker said these words, he clacked the two French presses together, thus completing the transubcaffienation. When he did so, a splash of the coffee managed to escape one of the presses. It landed on his head and then rivered down his nose. Booker didn't flinch.

"Okay, so get up here people."

Now what happened next was very strange, and how exactly it happened group-think wise is difficult to put together, but clearly there were some ex-Catholics in the crowd, because when I went forward to get the mug of coffee that Booker was offering, one of the Raggedy Andys filed in behind me, inadvertently forming a line, and suddenly what had been created, without any urging or forethought, was a communion procession.

As I approached the altar, Booker took one of the French presses and poured me a full mug.

"The coffee of Christ," he said.

"Amen," I said.

I stood there and took a sip. It was Ethiopian Harrar. Forward and earthy and, yes, holy.

"Step aside, asshole," said the Raggedy Andy.

After pouring each of us a cup of Christ, Booker raised his finger, as if he had a new idea, and exited stage left, without giving us any idea of where he was going or what he had in mind for us next. We were left standing there, oddly congregated near but not at his altar, sipping our respective coffees, which given our wet conditions and the fact that it was Sunday – Hangover Day – seemed universally appreciated.

It was Beale who said it first, but soon afterward there was a sudden chorus of people saying it.

"Holy shit!"

I'd told everyone that Booker was for real, and that I was only doing a caricature of him for the zine, but now that they saw him, and heard him sounding off the way that he sounded off, they all got up and turned to whoever was closest to them, and said "Holy shit." (I wish that the Holy Shit would have turned, like the Coffee of Christ did, into one of the standard rituals of Booker's church. It would have been cool if every Sunday we'd sit down in the theater seats, waiting for him to invite us up for the Coffee of Christ, and then after we'd all received it, we'd all stand up in unison and say "Holy shit!" like we did that day, but unfortunately only the Coffee of Christ worked itself into the standard Booker liturgy.)

It didn't take Booker long to return. When he came out of his vestibule he had a pink box in his hands.

"Sit," he said.

We did as we were told, sitting down in the rickety chairs placed around his altar. That is everyone except Skye, who stood off to the side, folding her arms and sipping her coffee in some mysterious consternation.

Booker set the box on the table. Printed on the top of it was the phrase, "Good Things Come In Pink Boxes." Above the phrase was the image of a Voodoo doll. Because we were Americans we knew what came in pink boxes. Doughnuts. Because we were Portlanders we knew what came in these particular pink boxes. Voodoo.

Booker propped the box open. Inside it were thirteen chocolate doughnuts (a Voodoo dozen). Each doughnut was shaped like a Voodoo doll, complete with a head, arms, and legs. Each doughnut had a pretzel stick pinned through its

belly, with terrified white icing eyes and an O of pain for a mouth.

I'm sure Booker was proud of himself, and had some sort of long speech prepared for the occasion. But Mercyx took one look at the now-open pink box of Voodoo Doughnuts on the table and said what Booker would have spent five minutes roundabouting his way towards.

"The body of Christ," she said.

The implications of Mercyx's statement didn't have much time to sink in, because shortly after, one of the Raggedy Andys yelled "DOOOOOO-NUUUUUUT!," doing his best Homer Simpson, and with that reached across the table, grabbed one of the dolls, and bit off its head. Cherry-filling squirted everywhere.

For a moment, Booker stared at him. Actually, we all stared at him, like when you're stoned and watching the Animal Planet station on cable and a Bengal tiger is ripping through the flesh of a gazelle. And then Booker, he pulled back one of the chairs from his altar, stood on it, and began to speak:

"That was it, you see, Diogenes, he gets it. We don't want to ritualize shit. 'Cuz that's what kills religion. Religion has

to be vital, you know, from the Latin, from vitae, from life. We've got to take the fucking head of Christ and rip it off, not fold our hands together in front of it and take it on our tongues like supplicant lambs.

"Take one, goddamn it!"

Except for the Raggedy Andy, we'd all just sat there, not daring to go for the doughnuts until invited.

"Eat him!" Booker said.

We still didn't move.

"Did you ever think about what Jesus said to his apostles on Good Friday? Did you ever think about how they were all just sitting around drinking – it being Happy Hour and all after the work week – and suddenly Jesus stands up, spreads his arms wide, and says to his buddies, 'Take some of me and swallow it. Take some of me and drink it.' I mean, these guys, they knew Jesus by then, so the freakish shit he said, they were used to it, but still, think about it for a minute. Think about how gay it was. Here's me! Now eat me! Here's me! Now drink me! That's what pisses me off about the supposed Christians and their whole one man one woman thing. Jesus was a *fag*!"

Booker took a breath and looked at us. The doughnuts had become less appetizing. I glanced at Dougie Fresh and Dietrich to see if they'd been offended. Dougie looked bemused. Dietrich looked like his English comprehension wasn't so good.

"All right, look, that was a mistake, I just say things you know, so just enjoy the doughnuts, they're good doughnuts. And fuck the whole Body of Christ thing. Rituals are dangerous. Let's get started, okay, I need to preach."

Booker hiked up his cassock and fumbled around until he'd pulled a pocket King James out of a pair of saggy black 501s. The cassock remained disheveled, the bottom hem getting caught in his back pocket when he took the Bible out, so that his whole outfit ballooned cartoonishly. He looked like a lawn gnome perched on a mushroom. Booker cleared his throat and began reading from the good book.

"Okay. Matthew. Chapter fifteen. Verse twenty-nine. And everyone that hath forsaken houses, or brethren, or sisters, or father, or mother, or wife, or children, or lands, for my name's sake, shall receive a hundredfold, and shall inherit everlasting life."

Booker looked away from the book and back at us.

"Did you catch that? Everyone that hath forsaken wife or children shall receive a hundred-fold! My God, what do the good Christian family values people do with Matthew chap-ter fifteen verse twenty-nine?"

None of us caught him at all. We were all just staring – the Ethiopian not having fired our synapses yet. Booker threw the King James down onto the altar.

"Eat the fucking doughnuts, goddamn it!"

Mercyx and I reached across the table at the same time. Our hands touched. Hers, on a doughnut. Mine, on hers. For a moment, in my own head, it all came together, this talk about marriage and love and bodies eating bodies all mingling with the hand underneath mine. And then Mercyx brushed my hand away, like you would a mosquito. She took the Voodoo doll doughnut and bit off its leg. There was red jelly on her pierced tongue.

"Now the reason I'm telling you this is because I need to set the record straight. I need you to see who you are. Because we can't just lie around here and let these people with their Jesus vision – their very wrong vision of Jesus all ga-ga over their homes and their kids and their wives and their stock portfolios – have all the power. We've got to take him back.

"We godless people. We unfettered people. We unmarried and unmarriageable people. We Mary Magdalenes and we stinky fishmongers. We Mad Max cyclists and we ink-stained zinesters and we underpaid baristas ..."

Booker looked at Beale's D&D buddies, as if noticing them for the first time.

"... and we dorks. And we midgets. We've got to take him back. So don't desire marriage. Spread your love far and wide. Jesus was a bastard, and a blue collar worker, and a faggot, and a whoremonger, and hanging out with all those prim and proper people trying to tie each other down, forever excluding their genitalia from the flea-ridden masses of the scummy human race, this would have bored Jesus stiff.

"So don't try to cling to a person and make them yours. According to Jesus, possessions are bad, and therefore, desiring to possess another for the sake of marriage is bad and ..."

I'd forgotten about her. We'd all sort of forgotten about her. So it's hard for me to describe exactly what she looked like when she did it, or exactly what it was that she did, but I imagine her turning pale, and looking very indignant throughout Booker's speech, and then, when Booker released the word *cling*, her face must have turned rose with rage, driving her to do what she must have done, because although no one witnessed her doing it, it was clearly she who did it, because it was the only angle that it could have been thrown from that would have caused the Coffee of Christ to have come raining down on all of us.

As soon as Booker said "desiring to possess another for the sake of marriage is bad," she threw her coffee mug at Booker, and unlike last week when Booker had narrowly ducked a barrage of MGD bottles, this time the coffee mug hit its target, cracking him square on the right cheekbone.

The blow upset Booker's precarious balance on his chair, and it slipped out from under him, causing him to fall back, adding a second crack to the one that had gone before. Unlike last week, he wasn't rewarded with kisses after his fall. Instead, Skye said, "You deserved that. You're a dick," and then she wheeled, her dreadlocks whipping around like scourges, and marched out the front doors of the church.

Mercyx followed in hot pursuit. I, of course, followed Mercyx. I never did get a doughnut.

———

B EING BARTHOLOMEW FLYNN, I DID NOT RUN after the two women. I strolled. As if coffee mugs flying at anti-monogamist preachers was normal.

When I made it out the doors and to the curb, where Mercyx was standing next to her bike, the *nior aimsíodh téarma ar bith* had changed to a simple *uisge*: rain without nuance. Skye was no longer there, apparently having gone whenceforth from whixever she came. Before I could ask what had happened, Mercyx hopped on her steed.

"Springwater," she shouted over her shoulder.

There was nothing unusual about this exchange – "Springwater" being a Mercyxish code that meant she wanted to ride down the Springwater Trail, a paved, urban bike trail carved out of an old railroad line. It ran the entire length of the Eastside out to the burbs. Once you got to its terminus, you could ride up Powell Butte, an extinct cinder cone vol-

cano with an expansive city view, or you could ride along the Sandy River towards the waterfalls.

There was also nothing unusual about the ride – Mercyx pumped out the high gears while I drafted.

What was unusual was that as we were about to get off the city streets and onto the Springwater, Mercyx stopped. Unless she was at a red, Mercyx never stopped her bike. Even when she was at a red, she often blew it, daring oncoming traffic to flatten her.

But here she was, stopping the Vanilla in the middle of the bike lane at a green traffic signal.

"I don't think I'm going to do this today. It's too wet," she said.

I wasn't about to complain, we were both soaked, but Mercyx never bailed on rides, no matter what the conditions. I mean, we'd ridden through sleet before. I was about to say something to her, but before I could get words out of my mouth, the light turned yellow and she gunned it, leaving me behind at the red. She turned back to me, shouting, knowing that there was no way I could make the light. "The Curiosity. Seven."

Right before she left, I noticed something. At the time I didn't think much of it, but later, as things progressed, it would give me pause. There had been, when she'd turned, what appeared to be a tear rolling down her right cheek. It could easily have been rain, a bead of moisture dripping off an eyelash, but later, after thinking about it, I think it was a teardrop that rolled off her right cheek and splashed on the pavement, a few inches from the toe of my cleats.

COFFEE BREAK #1 ON PORTLAND, OREGON PART ONE

BEFORE I GO ON WITH THIS GOSPEL, I FEEL AS IF YOU SHOULD KNOW A BIT MORE ABOUT THE CITY WHERE ALL THIS TAKES PLACE, THIS VERY UNSUNG LITTLE CITY ON THE WEST COAST OF THE UNITED STATES OF AMERICA, THIS PLACE WHOSE STATE MUST ALWAYS BE NAMED IN REFERENCE TO IT, IN ORDER TO DISTINGUISH IT FROM ITS TWIN ON THE EAST COAST, THIS PLACE CALLED PORTLAND, OREGON.

YOU SEE, DESPITE BEING UNSUNG AND HAVING A VERY GENERIC SOUNDING NAME, PORTLAND, OREGON IS A NEXUS OF SORTS.

PORTLAND, OREGON IS THE END OF THE EARTH.

LET ME EXPLAIN.

ALL OVER THE WORLD, RESTLESS PEOPLE DREAM OF COMING TO AMERICA, AND SOME OF THESE RESTLESS PEOPLE MAKE IT THERE. THOSE THAT MAKE IT, THEY OFTEN HAVE CHILDREN, AND THESE CHILDREN, BEING THE RESTLESS SONS AND DAUGHTERS OF THE RESTLESS PEOPLE WHO CAME HERE TO BEGIN WITH, THEY GO TO THE PLACE IN AMERICA WHERE PEOPLE DREAM OF GOING, THE WEST COAST, CALIFORNIA, AND THEY GO TO HOLLYWOOD TO BECOME ACTORS OR THEY GO TO SAN FRANCISCO TO BE A PART OF THE INTERNET BOOM. WHEN THEY GET THERE, WELL SOME OF THEM MAKE IT, THEY BECOME ACTORS OR CEO'S, BUT SOME OF THEM *DON'T* MAKE IT, AND THEY'RE STILL RESTLESS, AND WHAT THEY DO IS THEY LOOK NORTH, AND WHAT THEY SEE IS THIS SMALL LITTLE CITY, THIS PLACE CALLED PORTLAND, OREGON, AND WHAT THEY HEAR IS THAT IT'S A RELATIVELY CHEAP PLACE TO LIVE, AND THAT IT'S PROGRESSIVE, WHATEVER THAT MEANS, AND ALSO WHAT THEY HEAR IS THIS SILENCE, IT'S THIS PLACE THAT NO ONE REALLY KNOWS THAT MUCH ABOUT.

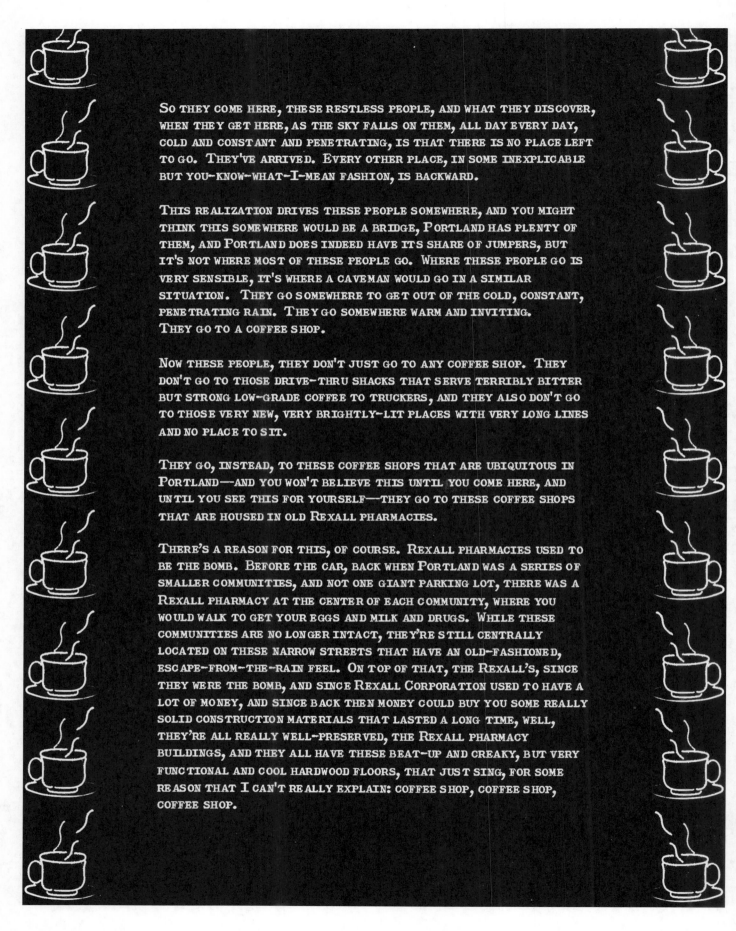

SO THEY COME HERE, THESE RESTLESS PEOPLE, AND WHAT THEY DISCOVER, WHEN THEY GET HERE, AS THE SKY FALLS ON THEM, ALL DAY EVERY DAY, COLD AND CONSTANT AND PENETRATING, IS THAT THERE IS NO PLACE LEFT TO GO. THEY'VE ARRIVED. EVERY OTHER PLACE, IN SOME INEXPLICABLE BUT YOU-KNOW-WHAT-I-MEAN FASHION, IS BACKWARD.

THIS REALIZATION DRIVES THESE PEOPLE SOMEWHERE, AND YOU MIGHT THINK THIS SOMEWHERE WOULD BE A BRIDGE, PORTLAND HAS PLENTY OF THEM, AND PORTLAND DOES INDEED HAVE ITS SHARE OF JUMPERS, BUT IT'S NOT WHERE MOST OF THESE PEOPLE GO. WHERE THESE PEOPLE GO IS VERY SENSIBLE, IT'S WHERE A CAVEMAN WOULD GO IN A SIMILAR SITUATION. THEY GO SOMEWHERE TO GET OUT OF THE COLD, CONSTANT, PENETRATING RAIN. THEY GO SOMEWHERE WARM AND INVITING. THEY GO TO A COFFEE SHOP.

NOW THESE PEOPLE, THEY DON'T JUST GO TO ANY COFFEE SHOP. THEY DON'T GO TO THOSE DRIVE-THRU SHACKS THAT SERVE TERRIBLY BITTER BUT STRONG LOW-GRADE COFFEE TO TRUCKERS, AND THEY ALSO DON'T GO TO THOSE VERY NEW, VERY BRIGHTLY-LIT PLACES WITH VERY LONG LINES AND NO PLACE TO SIT.

THEY GO, INSTEAD, TO THESE COFFEE SHOPS THAT ARE UBIQUITOUS IN PORTLAND—AND YOU WON'T BELIEVE THIS UNTIL YOU COME HERE, AND UNTIL YOU SEE THIS FOR YOURSELF—THEY GO TO THESE COFFEE SHOPS THAT ARE HOUSED IN OLD REXALL PHARMACIES.

THERE'S A REASON FOR THIS, OF COURSE. REXALL PHARMACIES USED TO BE THE BOMB. BEFORE THE CAR, BACK WHEN PORTLAND WAS A SERIES OF SMALLER COMMUNITIES, AND NOT ONE GIANT PARKING LOT, THERE WAS A REXALL PHARMACY AT THE CENTER OF EACH COMMUNITY, WHERE YOU WOULD WALK TO GET YOUR EGGS AND MILK AND DRUGS. WHILE THESE COMMUNITIES ARE NO LONGER INTACT, THEY'RE STILL CENTRALLY LOCATED ON THESE NARROW STREETS THAT HAVE AN OLD-FASHIONED, ESCAPE-FROM-THE-RAIN FEEL. ON TOP OF THAT, THE REXALL'S, SINCE THEY WERE THE BOMB, AND SINCE REXALL CORPORATION USED TO HAVE A LOT OF MONEY, AND SINCE BACK THEN MONEY COULD BUY YOU SOME REALLY SOLID CONSTRUCTION MATERIALS THAT LASTED A LONG TIME, WELL, THEY'RE ALL REALLY WELL-PRESERVED, THE REXALL PHARMACY BUILDINGS, AND THEY ALL HAVE THESE BEAT-UP AND CREAKY, BUT VERY FUNCTIONAL AND COOL HARDWOOD FLOORS, THAT JUST SING, FOR SOME REASON THAT I CAN'T REALLY EXPLAIN: COFFEE SHOP, COFFEE SHOP, COFFEE SHOP.

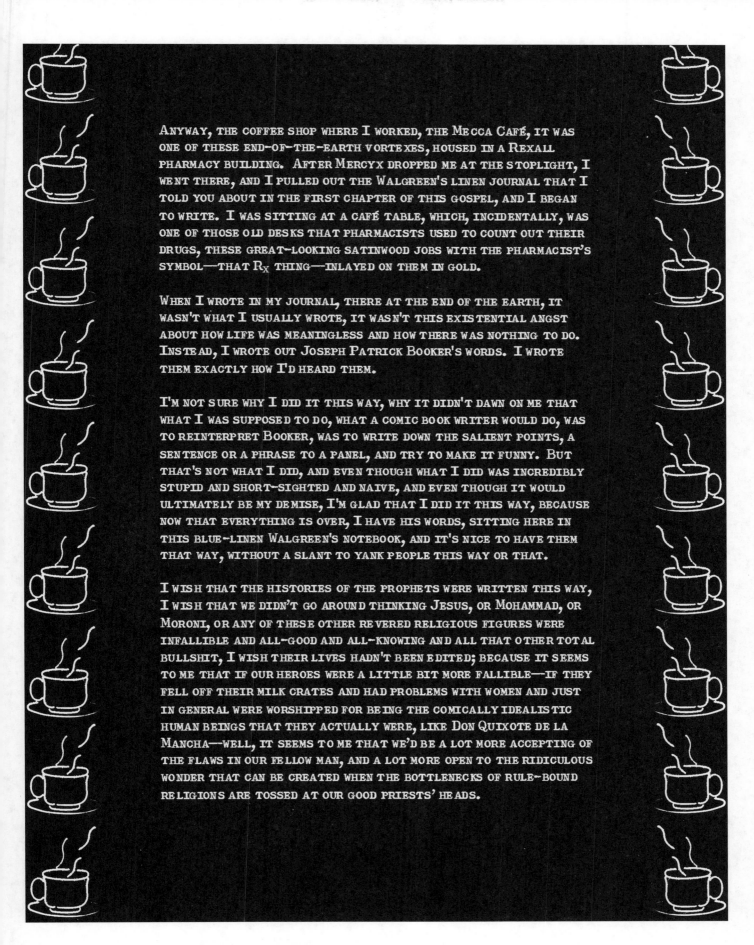

ANYWAY, THE COFFEE SHOP WHERE I WORKED, THE MECCA CAFÉ, IT WAS
ONE OF THESE END-OF-THE-EARTH VORTEXES, HOUSED IN A REXALL
PHARMACY BUILDING. AFTER MERCYX DROPPED ME AT THE STOPLIGHT, I
WENT THERE, AND I PULLED OUT THE WALGREEN'S LINEN JOURNAL THAT I
TOLD YOU ABOUT IN THE FIRST CHAPTER OF THIS GOSPEL, AND I BEGAN
TO WRITE. I WAS SITTING AT A CAFÉ TABLE, WHICH, INCIDENTALLY, WAS
ONE OF THOSE OLD DESKS THAT PHARMACISTS USED TO COUNT OUT THEIR
DRUGS, THESE GREAT-LOOKING SATINWOOD JOBS WITH THE PHARMACIST'S
SYMBOL—THAT R_X THING—INLAYED ON THEM IN GOLD.

WHEN I WROTE IN MY JOURNAL, THERE AT THE END OF THE EARTH, IT
WASN'T WHAT I USUALLY WROTE, IT WASN'T THIS EXISTENTIAL ANGST
ABOUT HOW LIFE WAS MEANINGLESS AND HOW THERE WAS NOTHING TO DO.
INSTEAD, I WROTE OUT JOSEPH PATRICK BOOKER'S WORDS. I WROTE
THEM EXACTLY HOW I'D HEARD THEM.

I'M NOT SURE WHY I DID IT THIS WAY, WHY IT DIDN'T DAWN ON ME THAT
WHAT I WAS SUPPOSED TO DO, WHAT A COMIC BOOK WRITER WOULD DO, WAS
TO REINTERPRET BOOKER, WAS TO WRITE DOWN THE SALIENT POINTS, A
SENTENCE OR A PHRASE TO A PANEL, AND TRY TO MAKE IT FUNNY. BUT
THAT'S NOT WHAT I DID, AND EVEN THOUGH WHAT I DID WAS INCREDIBLY
STUPID AND SHORT-SIGHTED AND NAIVE, AND EVEN THOUGH IT WOULD
ULTIMATELY BE MY DEMISE, I'M GLAD THAT I DID IT THIS WAY, BECAUSE
NOW THAT EVERYTHING IS OVER, I HAVE HIS WORDS, SITTING HERE IN
THIS BLUE-LINEN WALGREEN'S NOTEBOOK, AND IT'S NICE TO HAVE THEM
THAT WAY, WITHOUT A SLANT TO YANK PEOPLE THIS WAY OR THAT.

I WISH THAT THE HISTORIES OF THE PROPHETS WERE WRITTEN THIS WAY,
I WISH THAT WE DIDN'T GO AROUND THINKING JESUS, OR MOHAMMAD, OR
MORONI, OR ANY OF THESE OTHER REVERED RELIGIOUS FIGURES WERE
INFALLIBLE AND ALL-GOOD AND ALL-KNOWING AND ALL THAT OTHER TOTAL
BULLSHIT, I WISH THEIR LIVES HADN'T BEEN EDITED; BECAUSE IT SEEMS
TO ME THAT IF OUR HEROES WERE A LITTLE BIT MORE FALLIBLE—IF THEY
FELL OFF THEIR MILK CRATES AND HAD PROBLEMS WITH WOMEN AND JUST
IN GENERAL WERE WORSHIPPED FOR BEING THE COMICALLY IDEALISTIC
HUMAN BEINGS THAT THEY ACTUALLY WERE, LIKE DON QUIXOTE DE LA
MANCHA—WELL, IT SEEMS TO ME THAT WE'D BE A LOT MORE ACCEPTING OF
THE FLAWS IN OUR FELLOW MAN, AND A LOT MORE OPEN TO THE RIDICULOUS
WONDER THAT CAN BE CREATED WHEN THE BOTTLENECKS OF RULE-BOUND
RELIGIONS ARE TOSSED AT OUR GOOD PRIESTS' HEADS.

So we've had our coffee break. And somehow a short little segment about Portland, Oregon has become a rant about the nature of prophecy. The cause for this tangent, just so you know, is the uncontrollable effect of writing a gospel at the end-of-the-world, in a coffee shop, under the influence of extreme caffeine consumption. I was, and still am, a coffee junkie. It started back then, when I was working at Mecca, and when I met Booker, and when I was driven to find places to work other than my own apartment, and now it's gotten worse—horribly worse.

I wish that I could remove the damning stain of coffee sludge from these pages, for it surely filters my thoughts. But alas, I cannot, for Booker too was a caffeine junkie, and he wouldn't have said the things that he said, in the way he said them, if he hadn't been; and I probably wouldn't have been able to follow him, and been so diligent in recording what he said, if I hadn't been on the same Bat-caffeinated channel.

So again, I apologize for these interludes and the causes behind them. And let's get back to the story, but only after I take one quick pull from the cup, the chalice, the Coffee of Christ.

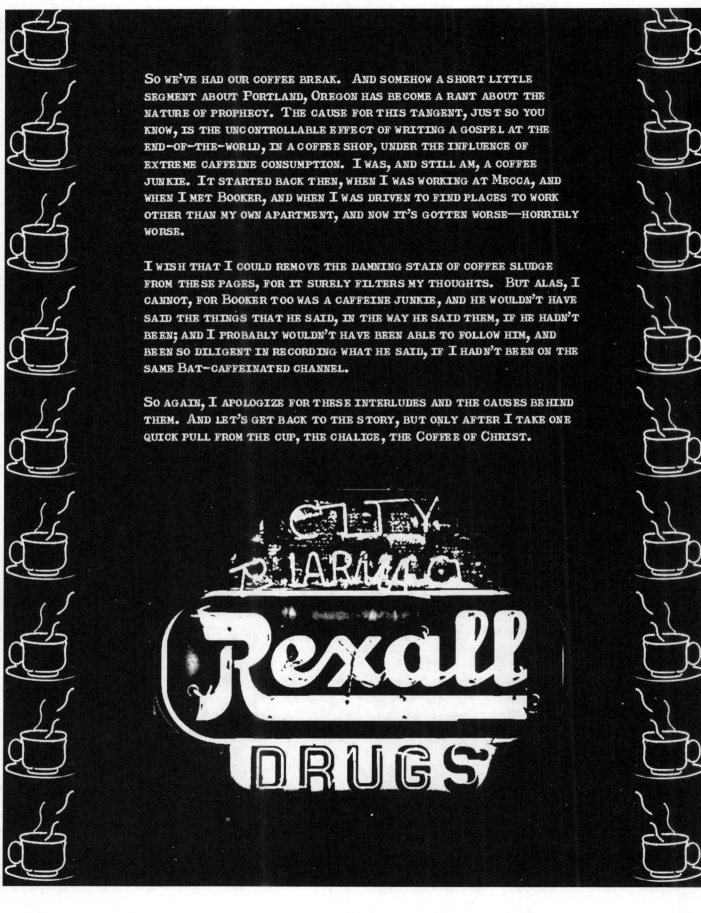

Chapter IX

Where the Fork Runs Away with the Spoon

WHEN I RETURNED TO MY APARTMENT after dictating the sermon into my notebook, Chester Fields was sitting at the drafting table he'd set up in my living room. His right hand simultaneously shredded paper and dangled a limp Taco Bell bean burrito, while his left sloshed black ink all over a sketch pad. He reminded me of a multi-limbed Shiva. While he did all this, he mumbled like a mantra, "We have to change everything."

At Mecca, I'd been contemplating the happenings in Booker's church, and Mercyx's subsequent response to those happenings. I was, after all, a purported atheist – so who the real Jesus was: a fag? an anti-monogamist? – shouldn't have meant anything to me. And yet (although I was far too cool to articulate this out loud), I did care. And not only did I care, but deep below anything I was conscious of at the time, I thought Booker was wrong.

Having a roommate to discuss these things with would have been nice. But Chester's mind was clearly somewhere else: "The milk crates are so crucial, Flynn. They've got to *see* the Alpenrose label, and yet *understand* that Booker's on it at the same time. Okay, so this is it, I'll do a one-frame close-up of his shoes and the crates, draw some quiver lines, you know, to indicate that his balance is precarious, and then fade back to real size. Fucking genius, Flynn, fucking genius."

I wanted to comment on this, to give him my suggestions as his collaborator, but Chester was carrying on both sides of a conversation. Near his feet, a perfect storm of paper strips and shit-colored bean goo pattered into my garbage can.

"Here's the big thing, though. Booker's a midget, and that's funny, but he's got to be a special sort of midget, so what we're going to do – Flynn, picture this – in the comic, we make Booker Tattoo. See, Dougie loves this. It's perfect, Tattoo as the horseman of the post-apocalyptic Mad Max cyclist universe. So what we do, see, we find some old footage of *Fantasy Island*, digitize the face, then bring it to black and white. It's perfect. Absolutely perfect. Every time Booker appears in the comic, he'll have the face of Tattoo, and it'll be that same overly wide grin that Tattoo makes, and it'll be the same face no matter what he's saying, and I'll enlarge and reduce it to the point where it's super grainy, to give it that blurred, sort of punk zine quality. Fucking genius, isn't it?"

While he talked to himself, I tiptoed over the jumble of paper, fast-food wrappers, and strip club advertisements that encircled him. It was slow-going. For some reason, I thought of a moat. When I'd made my way to the drafting table, I opened my journal to the pages I'd just written and placed it to the right of his sketch pad. "Here's the text for number three," I said.

Chester didn't look at it. He took a bite of the burrito. Rust-colored Taco Bell mild sauce hung from his lips. Mouth full, he said, "Image is everything. A gesture, it can imply so many things. If you're good you don't even need text."

Underneath his elbow was a business card with the image of a naked woman on it, red stars censoring her breasts. The card read 999-SKY-SUCK. 36-24-36. Girlfriend experience. 24-7. There was this part of me that was still enamored with Chester the artist, but there was also this part of me that saw how filthy he was, and didn't want him around. These people who you're conflicted about, you tend to invite them to do things with you then wished you hadn't: "Mercyx and I are going over to The Curiosity around seven. Do ... if you'd like to join us, you –"

Chester's left hand stopped sloshing. He interrupted. "The hottie?"

I hesitated in my response. Mercyx was certainly a hottie, but not Chester's hottie.

Chester kept at it. "Short hair and tats. Your friend?

"Yeah," I said. "My ... friend."

"Great face. Amazing ass," Chester said. "She could do with a boob job, but I'd fuck her."

"Great," I said, with a fake smile. "I'm gonna take a shower and change, then we can go."

"Cool," Chester said.

Chester put the remains of his burrito on my open journal. Melted cheese stained its sheets.

WHEN CHESTER AND I WALKED THROUGH THE swinging glass doors into The Curiosity, Mercyx was already there. And I don't mean just there, I mean there. She was dressed to the nines. Not in an all-black, yuppity, Coach handbag kind of way, but in a distinctly Mercyx way. She had on a pink dress with lacy aqua trim that crossed under her smallish breasts. It looked more like a nightie or a slip than a dress. She wore a pair of high-end John Fluevog boots, once again mastering discordance, nothing being sexier than a nightgown combined with a pair of steel-toes. She was playing pool – another sexy thing in a woman, especially one who's good. And Mercyx had always been good. Don't get me wrong, she wasn't a shark – it wasn't like she could sink double banks – she just played it real cool and made her shots when they counted.

Mercyx was also smoking. Now this was particularly weird. I'd seen her play pool before. And I'd seen her – that night at Blowfish – dressed up. But I never thought I'd see her smoke. I mean, Mercyx was an athlete, a cyclist, and it doesn't make sense for a cyclist to fuck up their exhaust system with tobacco. But there she was, leaning over the rail for a shot on the 2-ball with a cigarette between her lips.

While this new Mercyx was undoubtedly more attractive than the Lycra Mercyx I was more familiar with, it felt a little over the top to me, and I immediately had a bad feeling about what was to come.

Mercyx was getting a lot of attention in her new threads, and me, being the shy wallflower, comic book sort, went up to the bar, got a beer, and found a table in the corner, figuring Mercyx would do her usual blow-off-the-yuppie-fuck dance and find her way back to the freaks-and-geeks table. I also kind of assumed Chester would follow me. He didn't. Instead, Chester, who'd dressed for the occasion in a top hat, a black trench coat, a white button down shirt, and a thin, solid-black tie, so that he looked like a character out of Dickens, got his beer plus an extra, made a beeline for Mercyx, whispered something in her ear (a skill I never developed, whispering things into women's ears), and before I knew it was having a heated discussion with her at a separate table in the pool room.

This was strange and awkward, me sitting at one table in the main bar, my friends sitting at another table. I could have easily gone to sit with them, but this was our table, the table we always sat at; and also I guess I felt like I was being schooled, the way Chester had dressed (I was in a red T-shirt that read Pirate's Choice Kombucha, along with my standard holey black jeans), and the way he'd said *damn* when he saw Mercyx, in that chummy guy-to-guy way, and then strode over to her as if he owned her.

So instead of going to them, I sat brooding.

Now there was more going on here than meets the eye, or at least that met my eye. But let's just say for now that Mercyx didn't acknowledge me sitting there, and that her not acknowledging me darkened my mood considerably. I watched them as if it weren't a bar but a theater, and they were a romance being acted out on a screen. I downed my beers quickly, and my waitress brought by new ones with more alacrity than usual, dropping of two dollar PBRs on what seemed like a ten-minute schedule. (Our waitress knew our drinking habits well, although she was too hot and Beale and I too geeky for her to acknowledge that she knew us. Beale, Mercyx, and I had dubbed her Bloodsucker, as Beale and I had both used her in our respective zines and comics. She'd been an unobtainable object of desire in *Octagonal Table Talk #8 & 9*, and done a cameo as a vampire in Beale's *Bloodsuckers with Big Tits #4*.)

After dropping off my beer, the bloodsucker would take the two remaining beers on her tray, two sissy beers with lemon wedges – hefeweizens – a beer Mercyx and I professed to despise, over to the booth where Mercyx and Chester sat. I couldn't see their faces, of course. They had arranged to sit facing the other direction in the booth, so that all I could see was Chester's top hat, and Mercyx's close-cropped hair and her lovely bare neck. Smoke rose over their heads. They were smoking Chester's cigarettes. Chester Fields's *Chesterfield* cigarettes.

It seemed as I watched that the top hat was getting closer to the bare neck. The bloodsucker came over to me with another beer, one I hadn't yet ordered. Chester's costume wasn't Dickens after all, it was Dostoyevsky, and this scene, it wasn't in London or Paris it was Moscow, and the book we were in wasn't fucking *David Copperfield*, it was *Crime and Punishment*, and I was the creepy young man sitting in the corner, concocting conspiracies. I imagined Chester with a new business card. On it was a naked Mercyx, red stars over her tits. 999-SUCK-ANN.

The bloodsucker knew what was going on. I swear she did. She put my beer on the table. She winked at me, then headed pertly over with those sunny, lemony hefeweizens.

The top hat turned. I could see dents in it. Dents from where, at various times, Chester and I had stepped on the hat where it always lay in the living room floor.

The top hat went for the bare neck.

I stood up. My knees hit the edge of the table. The pint tipped over, then semi-circled, making its way to the corner then falling, glass shattering as glass tends to do. I might have saved this moment, made it not such a big deal – just a glass breaking in a bar – if I hadn't done what I did next.

I bared my fangs.

I curled my upper lip, jutted my front teeth out, lifted my two hands up like a bear, and made a noise. "MUA-AH-AH-AH," was the noise. I meant for it to sound sinister, but it sounded goofy, like The Count in the Muppets. After that I shouted, and what I shouted was high-pitched and pathetic: "You're all … vampires!"

It's hard to explain why I did that. It had something to do with life being somewhat fictional for me, and also something to do with that old Morrissey song, How Soon is Now, about the kid with the shyness that was criminally vulgar, the one who goes about things the wrong the way. I was pent up, I guess.

I ran. I ran out the swinging doors and down to the rack where I had U-locked my bike. I inserted my key into the lock and set the bike free. The doors to the bar swung open and it might have been Chester or Mercyx or the bloodsucker waving the tab, but it didn't matter, I hated Mercyx and I hated Chester and I needed velocity. I needed speed.

I set my blinkies and rode off. If anyone was yelling after me, I didn't hear them. Any appeals were drowned out by the *sciorta en aird*, a Celtic phrase for rain that stands for "up-kilt spittle," which isn't actually a form of rain, per se, but a rain after-effect. It rains and then there's a near gale, lifting moisture and God-knows-what-else up from the sidewalk onto your skin and clothes.

I couldn't go home. If I went home, Chester and Mercyx would walk in, giggly, and they would pretend I wasn't there, even though they would know I was there. And they would try to be quiet in the living room while I slept in the bedroom but they wouldn't be quiet, because sex can never be quiet. And so I would hear it, I would hear his hot, smoking, tophatted, Chester Field entering Mercyx's red stars.

999-FUCK-ANN. 24/7.

There were bars. Cheap taverns all over Portland. I rode my bike to them, zigzagging through the wind-swept streets, covered in little black bits of grime, fueled by alcohol and humiliation. Into the corners I went, cold and dripping and miserable, staying just long enough to drink three dollars worth of brew and piss it off in the bathroom. How I did all this without becoming road pizza is beyond me.

The last thing I remember before it's all a blank was a bathroom stall. I sat on a wet porcelain toilet seat, wet jeans and underwear pooled around my ankles. With my key, I etched a vagina into the wall. I etched a pool cue entering the vagina. I added a pair of testicles to the pool cue. I etched a caption:

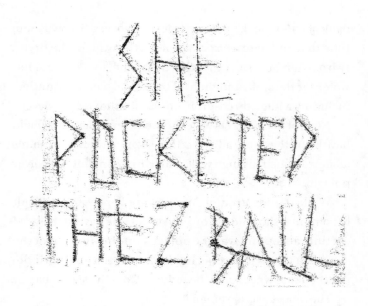

I never did make it home. I did, however, make it to a sanctuary of sorts. And although I would wake up alive, I wouldn't wake up quite the same.

Chapter X

Ouch! Fuck! Amen!

J OPENED AN EYE. NOT BOTH EYES, THAT would have been too painful, but one of them. What I saw wasn't believable – I closed the eye and decided to try again. I waited a few minutes, steeled myself for the effort, then opened both of them. The image was the same, if more three-dimensional. Along the wall I was facing was an array of stainless steel appliances stacked one next to the other. It was all top-of-the-line Jetsons-looking stuff. Next to the refrigerator was a stove, next to the stove was a dishwasher, next to the dishwasher was a sink, and next to the sink was an oversized washer/dryer combo. The wall that all these appliances leaned against was pock-marked with outlets and exhaust mechanisms, an equipment clusterfuck: a rectangular bank of fans to suck up steam from the stove; a silver vacuum tube that ended in a circular hole in the wall for the dryer; two garden hoses, wrapped in duct tape, for cold and hot water for the sink; and then all the actual electrical outlets, including a huge three-pronged 220 for the washer/dryer.

None of these outlets were at ground level like they should have been, they were all *elevated*, at seemingly random points along an unusually high wall, with wires dangling like silver phlegm.

While the odd array of domestic appliances was difficult to compute, the object along the wall I was having the hardest time accepting was the object standing in front of the stove in a terry cloth robe, holding a spatula and a griddle pan, cooking what had to be judging from the sizzle, bacon.

The object was a woman.

She turned to me, bizarrely composed, as if what was taking place was an everyday sort of thing. She asked, "Fried or scrambled?"

The object was not just any woman, but an exceptionally attractive one. She was in her mid-twenties with maroon-dyed hair cut into a bob with perfectly trimmed bangs. Her eyebrows were plucked and tapered. Her lips were rouged the same color as her hair. I don't think I'd ever actually seen a woman this put-together before in real life, much less had one, it appeared, cook me breakfast in bed.

She had hazel eyes, the speckled sort that capture light like an exotic gem. As she looked at me kindly, awaiting my answer, my senses returned to me just enough to realize that I was facing her, on a king-sized bed, completely unclothed.

I was too hungover to be self-conscious.

"Scrambled," I said. "And fried."

The sound of the bacon sizzling had been the first sense triggered, but then came the smell. My stomach turned. I schooched to the edge of the bed. I leaned over. There was a gleaming silver mixing bowl placed on the floor, as if for this very purpose. Next to the mixing bowl was a Glad garbage bag. Inside the Glad garbage bag were wet clothes – my wet clothes – which upon closer inspection were covered with reddish chunks. On top of these clothes was a used condom, expertly knotted. I lurched but nothing came.

"You're a quiet heaver," the object said. "I appreciate that in a man. Some guys it's like a wildcat in a zoo when they go off, but you have a nice silent heave. That's a good quality in a drinker, a silent heave, although in the future you should try to avoid puking on yourself."

I scoured my brain for a scrap of memory, something to explain how I'd gotten here or who this woman was, but the data banks had been picked clean. My head throbbed. I pulled up from the edge of the bed and flopped face-down. The comforter and sheets were black satin. The pillow cover, a cow print. The headboard was covered in black leather and studs, with a couple silver silhouettes of naked ladies like truckers put on their mudflaps. It was like I'd somehow stumbled my way into a private room in the Playboy mansion, only not really like that at all. More like a room in *Shaft*.

The object hollered at the closed door beside the trophy appliance wall, "The dead have risen."

And then, of course, he walked in. Who else would it be?

"Morning, sunshine. I see you and Emerald have become acquainted."

I turned my head towards him. He had a shit-eating grin on his face, like he was greeting a plane on *Fantasy Island*. He really did look like Tattoo. I couldn't figure out which question to ask first. At least I knew her name.

"Where am I?" I asked.

"The church," he said.

Nothing. No recall.

"Coffee?" he asked. In his hand, he had one of his French presses.

Emerald handed Booker a mug. It was like she was an emergency room technician. He poured coffee into it. "Sit up."

I did as I was told.

I felt my nakedness suddenly. Here was Booker standing in front of me, his face eye-level with my loins. He lifted the mug up with two hands. I looked into his eyes inadvertently. It occurred to me they were the same color as the coffee. The grin was so big I thought it might crack his face.

"Coffee of Christ," he said.

I laughed. How could I not laugh? It wasn't funny, any of this, but I laughed. My love interest had gone and slept with my roommate, and I'd gone out on a binge and woken up to a strange woman, who I very well might have spent the night with, and who was cooking me breakfast, and then my friend (Preacher? Muse? What was Booker to me?) strolled in, as if all this was part of some master plan, and then he sacrilegiously proffered me a cup of coffee. The laughter banged around the inside my skull like a pinball. Ding! Ding! Ding!

"Ouch," I said.

I didn't think it was possible, but Booker's grin got wider. "Try a different four-letter word."

"Fuck," I said.

This time, it was Booker who laughed. He tilted the mug

towards my lips. Too frightened to drink the stuff, I stuck my nose in instead. The smell didn't do any damage at all. It was Stumptown. Holler Mountain. Heavenly.

I couldn't help myself. "Amen."

Emerald walked the three steps from the stove to where I was sitting and placed a plate beside me on the bed. On it was one egg scrambled, one egg fried, a heart-shaped chocolate wrapped in red foil, and the bacon organized into a smile. Sneaking a peek into the V of her robe as she bent down confirmed what I'd suspected, underneath the robe, the object, too, was in her birthday suit.

My penis stirred.

Booker, and I believe this was incidental, asked me, "Clothes?"

In any other circumstance, if I'd been sitting naked in front of two people, one of whom was a stranger and the other of whom was a man, I would have instantly squeaked yes, while covering my privates with my hands. This morning, though, I was simply too hungover to be self-conscious. "Sure."

Booker walked around me to the foot of the bed, where lie one of those ladders on a stand with rollers that are used in warehouses. He pushed a button and the ladder began to extend. I looked up. The area above Booker's bed was crisscrossed with clotheslines, and from the clotheslines hung all manner of clothing – leather jackets, priest's cassocks, women's dresses, you name it. The ceiling extended upward of forty feet. It dawned on me, as I looked up, what the room was. The church's bell tower. Converted into an aerial closet. Of course.

Booker climbed the ladder and grabbed an article of clothing off a hanger. It fluttered down to the bed. It was a clown suit.

"This one?" Booker asked.

I looked up at him like he was crazy. A cheerleaders' outfit took flight.

"Or maybe this?"

Before I could say anything, Emerald, who'd just finished washing the griddle in the stainless steel sink, asked, "While you're up there, Joey, could you grab me my day clothes?" She disrobed as she said this.

I stared at her breasts. I wondered if they were fake. It seemed like this should be part of a man's education, being able to tell fake breasts from real breasts. They seemed so firm. They had to be fake.

Emerald was frowning at me. "I'm off the clock," she said.

"He's new to this," Booker retorted.

"Whatever," she said to Booker. And then, to me, "Definitely, cheerleader. They'll admire your spunk."

Emerald got dressed quickly. She seemed an expert at it. She slipped some socks and shoes on that were near the door. It seemed that she was going to leave without saying goodbye. I wanted to say something in response, but I couldn't think of anything. She looked more average now, in a purple blouse and a pair of jeans. Less of an object. What do you say to someone you think you slept with but don't know if you slept with? She opened the door. She hesitated for a moment, then turned. "Don't listen to the mouth here, Bartholomew Flynn. Get her back. You're more of a man than you think you are."

A wig hit me in the face. It was maroon. A perfectly-trimmed bob.

"Cheerleader," she said.

A woman in her late thirties, with tightly-pinned, graying hair, opened a door and was gone.

Chapter XI

Where I, Bartholomew Flynn, Learn About the C.H.V.C.K. Wagon, and Where New Meaning is Given to the Phrase, "You Can Lead a Horse to Water, but You Can't Make Him Drink"

THIS MORNING, WHEN EMERALD HAD thrown me the wig and chosen cheerleader, it had seemed like I should wear it as some sort of scalp won in battle. I'd also still been drunk. Now that I was sober, though, and outside wearing it in public, I couldn't believe I'd put the thing on. I was cross-dressing for Chrissakes. Worse yet, the cheerleaders' outfit was a University of Wisconsin uniform. In college, UW had been our arch-rivals. It was like I'd lost a bet.

We were both on bikes: me, my yellow racer; Booker, a tall bike – a bike that any Portlander is familiar with, but takes far more description for outsiders.

A tall bike is two bikes welded on top of each other in

some backyard operation, the chain ring and pedals of the top bike attached to the rear cassette of the bottom bike via the chain. Each tall bike is different, and Booker's was particularly so. The top half of Booker's tall bike was originally a child's bike, and as such came outfitted with a sparkly purple banana seat, small purple plastic pedals, and tassels. The handlebars of the child's bike were the original cruiser-shaped handlebars, but the front fork was actually a whole stack of forks that had been sawed-off and then fused on top of each other, so that it extended outward like a Harley Davidson chopper, albeit a chopper that was eight feet tall and topped with sparkly purple tassels, pedals and a banana seat.

We were riding through the no man's land of Portland called the Central Eastside Industrial District, a dilapidated warehouse district on the eastside of the river that had somehow escaped urban renewal.

"They're going to initiate you today." Booker was saying, "You remember the two guys that were in church the other Sunday, one of them is Diogenes, the leader."

We were on a hill, and Booker was spidering his way along a fence, his bike having no brakes.

"Who's they?" I asked.

"Chuck," said Booker.

Some kids across the streets were pointing at Booker and me. We were quite the sight: a clown midget on a tall bike and his cheerleader sidekick.

"Stop for a minute and explain this to me, dude," I said. I was getting tired of the one-word answers. Booker was clinging to a yield sign.

"Chuck six-nine six-nine, it's like an anarchist cycling gang. You met them – "

Something came to me all of a sudden. Not something from last night, but something from much earlier, something from my days sorting through zines in the safe and warm confines of the Hardin Library in Des Moines, Iowa. Something I'd ordered and rather deviously placed on the shelves of academia. Sixty-four pages. Eight and a half by seven with two center staples. Technical documentation, crowd-control techniques, cargo haulers, choppers, tall bikes, explosives, and a couple of pages of really bad pornography involving "the brown wrench." Issue One. C.H.V.C.K. 6969. *Bike Off a Lips Now.*

"You *know* those guys?"

"Yep," he said. "and so do you."

Booker pushed himself away from the fence and clung to a yield sign.

"You should have seen yourself. You were like a kid on

Christmas. You kept calling Diogenes a Raggedy Andy, inciting him, and then you challenged him to a duel. It was very entertaining."

My aching head had prevented me, up until that point, of feeling any other part of my body, but the mention of a duel roused a very tender spot just under my left shoulder blade and above my left breast. Diogenes, the self-proclaimed leader of C.H.V.C.K., the guy who'd authored the zine. "I lost," I said.

"For sure."

Booker hesitated for a moment, surveying the road. Attached to the bicycle, with spare brake cables, Booker had attached several framed pictures of religious figures, including, although not limited to, the Sacred Heart of Jesus, Our Lady of Guadalupe, St. Christopher, and the Buddha.

"The C.H.V.C.K. wagon is at the bottom," he said. "Let's bomb it."

I looked down the hill. The street we were on ended at a gated chain link fence topped with razor wire. The gate was currently closed. Behind the chain link fence was a rusting Airstream trailer, converted into – yes – a chuck wagon. In front of the Airstream trailer was a signboard, upon which was drawn, in colored chalk, two cowboys spooning slop into their mouths while flames burst out of their ears. Beneath the cowboys was written, in barely legible text: RED HOT CHILY SERVED HERE.

Booker let go of the yield sign and began his descent. I followed him slowly, wondering how he would stop. It didn't seem likely that he could avoid crashing headlong into the fence on the bottom. I began to follow, more out of concern for a friend than desire to eat RED HOT CHILY from the C.H.V.C.K. wagon. On my way down, I noticed tall bikes similar in design to Booker's, riding towards us on the other side of the fence. As they got closer it became apparent they had no intention of stopping either.

"Tiny!" some of the riders shouted, greeting Booker.

"Ann!" some of the riders shouted, greeting me.

I slowed my bike, fearing what was about to happen. The cyclists, Booker et al, were getting closer and closer to the fence: Booker coasting; the tall bicyclists on the other side pedaling faster and faster. At full speed, they hit it. The chain link jangled, the sound of zoo animals shaking a cage. Most of the riders managed to cling to the fence, while their bikes ricocheted off of it. They hung on it like monkeys. A few of the riders, not as lucky, struck the fence face-first and then bounced, falling into a heap on top of the mass of bikes now strung across the concrete.

One of the riders clinging to the fence was wearing mirrored cop sunglasses. He was the guy who'd thrown the MGD bottle at Booker. I knew at once that this was Diogenes, the leader of the C.H.V.C.K. 6969 anarchist cycling club, and the author of the group's zine. Half a cigarette dangled from his lips, the lit end of which had fallen off upon impact with the fence. Little strips of brown tobacco extended from what remained, like a blown firecracker.

"Popped my cherry," he said.

"Diogenes," Booker said, "Nihilism, as always."

There was a groan from the ground where one of the riders had fallen.

"And you, Tiny, nothing but a clown," Diogenes retorted. "Paramedics!"

Two men came rushing out of the doors of the chuck wagon. They wore chefs' hats, which had black crosses taped on them with electrical tape. Between them, they were hauling a steaming black cauldron.

The rider on the ground was writhing in pain. It was tough to tell just how hurt he was. He had a gas mask over his face.

"IV drip! IV drip!" Diogenes shouted.

One of the other riders clinging to the fence looked down. He was dressed as a pirate. "Gassy got a pedal in the back, me thinks," he said.

The chefs dropped the cauldron and went back to the chuck wagon. They emerged shortly after and came running our way. This time one of them was carrying a six pack of beer, while the other was carrying a beer bong. On the funnel, in the same black electrical tape that formed the crosses on their hats, were the words, "ENTER VENUS SOLUTION."

Diogenes dropped off the fence and walked over to Gassy, tearing off his mask when he arrived. He was gritting his teeth like he was seriously hurt.

"Remember, the pain you feel now will make you stronger after the automotive disruptor field is broken, when our vehicles are revealed to be golden chariots. Even as we speak Detroit collapses," Diogenes said.

Gassy didn't hear a word Diogenes was saying. I thought he was going to go into convulsions. I reached for my cell phone, thinking I should call 911. I felt bare leg. The damn outfit had no pockets. Apparently, I'd left the phone in the vomit bag back at Booker's.

"Drip," said Diogenes.

The chef paramedic holding the bong handed it to him. It was like they'd done this a thousand times. Diogenes held the funnel low and the tube high.

"Solution," said Diogenes.

The other chef paramedic cracked open a can of PBR and poured it into the funnel. After pouring, he hesitated. Diogenes took a hard look at Gassy, as if he were calibrating something.

"Three," said Diogenes.

The chef paramedic nodded, then opened two more beers and poured them into the funnel.

"Can you sit up?" Diogenes asked Gassy.

Gassy was rocking back and forth on the ground, his back arched. He shook his head no.

"Make it four," said Diogenes.

Another beer was poured into the funnel, filling it. Diogenes put the tube to Gassy's lips. Gassy stopped writhing for a moment, his eyes suddenly wide and aware.

"Clear!" Diogenes shouted.

In one motion, the chef paramedic lifted the funnel into the air, while Diogenes held the outlet tube to the Gassy's mouth. Piss-colored liquid went through the transparent tube of the bong then disappeared almost as quickly as it had appeared. Gassy sat bolt upright, as if cured. And then he roared. It wasn't a fake roar either, like some dude trying to imitate a lion, it was a real, actual roar.

"Fuck! Fuck! Fuck! Fuck! Fuck!" Gassy shouted, his hands shooting towards his temples. Diogenes, however, had anticipated the move, pressing his palms as hard as he could into Gassy's head.

"You have been strengthened for the apocalypse!" Diogenes shouted.

"Yes!" Gassy said. His legs shook.

"Your bicycle is a mighty chariot!" Diogenes shouted.

"Yes!" Gassy repeated. His arms shook.

"When I release my hands, the pain shall cease!"

"Yes!" Gassy shouted. His eyes looked skyward.

Diogenes released his hands.

"Ice. Fucking. Cold. Beer," he said, gritting his teeth. He didn't look a whole lot better.

"It won't ever work," Booker said.

"It did work, you clown," said Diogenes to Booker. Then looking up at the chef paramedic. "Clean the wound. Give it some gauze. Then that's a wrap."

———

DISMISSED BY DIOGENES, THE MONKEYS dropped off the fence and rushed over to Gassy, oohing and ahhing over his wound as the chef paramedics lifted off his shirt. Booker was still on his bicycle, pedaling forward and backward in an effort to keep the bike in one place while remaining upright. I'd dismounted, and was looking up at Booker in the hopes of getting an explanation for what had just taken place. None was forthcoming. Meanwhile, Diogenes rolled open the gates so we could enter.

"If it isn't Tiny the clown and his consort Raggedy Ann. So nice of you to join us," Diogenes said. He spread out his arms in an after-you gesture. "Enter the neutron particle field of the chosen."

Booker rode his bike back, gathered momentum, and then rode through the gate, rolling over the pile of fallen bikes in the process. There was the twang of a spoke breaking. How he got over it without falling is yet another Booker mystery.

"Coming, Ann?" Diogenes said to me. I had just been standing there, dumbfounded. Him calling me Ann didn't speed things up. Something had obviously happened last night, something to do with me calling him Raggedy Andy and him subsequently calling me Raggedy Ann, but what was it? And more importantly how did I get him to stop? Being reminded of Annie was the last thing I wanted right now.

"You are right to fear entry, my lovely Ann. Once one has entered the neutronimous particle field of the chosen C.H.V.C.K. wagoneers, you are cowboy hoot donkey dick committed to this whole unstoppable enterprise of Big Bang-accelerated Carmegeddon, through which we will soar unharmed, led by celebrated Pegasi on our transformed chariots, but only after many trials by fire.

"And of course you will be asked to make a sacrifice." Diogenes' eyes shot to my bicycle, leaning innocently against the fence.

I followed his eyes. It dawned on me what he was getting at.

"It will have to be … adjusted," Diogenes continued.

Now while I was not completely enamored with my bike – it being neon yellow and aluminum and geeky and all the other things I've already mentioned – it was still a very practical means of both transportation and exercise, and one that would be difficult to replace, given the cost of racing bikes. More importantly, once "adjusted," the bike would no longer be heading through the cemetery, or out to The Bridge of the Gods, or any of the other places Mercyx deigned to ride. I was still angry and confused about whatever had taken place between us last night, but I wasn't ready to abandon my cycling partner, no matter what she'd done.

I put my hands on my hips. I didn't mean it as a gesture of defiance, it was more like I was trying to figure out what to say or do next. Diogenes, however, didn't take it well.

"You can't resist this! It has been written! Paramedics! Resistance!" he said.

The chef paramedics had been busy dressing Gassy's wounds, and hadn't been paying attention to the exchange between Diogenes and me. At the words paramedics and resistance, though, they snapped to attention. One grabbed the beer bong while the other grabbed the two remaining beers from the six-pack. The chef paramedics were large guys, both over six foot.

Booker, meanwhile, was still on his bike, on the other side of the fallen bicycle stack. Booker's expression was hard to read, but he clearly didn't like where this was heading. "Drop it, Diogenes," he said.

"Paramedics! Paramedics! Mutiny!"

The chef paramedics looked confused, not sure whether they were supposed to go for me or Booker. Diogenes cleared that up fast. In an act of violence I didn't anticipate, he strode over to me, chewing on the cigarette butt in his mouth like it was a cigar, then spun me around so that the back of my head rested in his chest, catching me in a monster headlock.

"The dame! The dame!" he shouted.

I was being manhandled. My arms were locked in by his elbows, made effectively immobile. Behind my wig, I could feel his interlocked fingers. I tried to get my feet under me, but as soon as I did he'd kick them out. I tried moving my hands enough so I could pull his hair, but at this, he laughed. I went limp. I was a Raggedy Ann. I looked down at my hairy, sprawled-out legs. I looked down at my scarlet-colored satin panties.

I could hear Booker screaming, "Stop, you asshole!" He'd lost all the Martin Luther King in his voice and gone 100% Pee Wee Herman. He tried riding his bike back over the pile, but whatever magical cycling skills he'd had before were lost in the heat of the moment. He crashed it.

"Clear!" yelled Diogenes, his voice loud in my ear.

In the scuffle, I'd somehow missed all the preparations, the chef paramedics making their way over, the bong being filled. A gloved hand went under my chin, tilting back my head, a tube went in my mouth, and then, a sword jammed down the gullet.

Ice. Fucking. Cold. Beer.

I'm not sure whether this is a research paper for a physicist or a physician, but the way beer bongs work, the way they circumvent the gulping mechanism, the way they can shoot a large volume of liquid directly to the gut, the way the capillaries, upon surprise contact with the near-freezing, burn then shrivel then die, is worthy of some study. The cell loss must be astounding.

The pain congregates at the temples. Diogenes' palms met it there.

"You must let go of speed!"

I'd say only about half the beer made it to my stomach. When the tube went in my mouth, I'd done some thrashing. If I'd gotten a full-dose I might have been more obedient. Or seriously puked. The rest of the beer had spilled under my blouse, or whatever it is you call the top half of a cheerleader outfit, the part with the megaphone and the big letter W and the badger, and then leaked its way through the elastic waist band and down my legs. A cheerleader drenched in beer from lugs in the stands.

Despite the cold, I was hot. The pressure between my temples and Diogenes' palms could have powered a steam engine. "Fuck you!"

"You must let go of all hard-wired in you by the megahertz, Oracle, American, Steve Jobs microchip!"

"Fuck! You!"

"The phoenix, it burns before it awakens!"

In pressing his palms against my temples, he'd ceded the headlock. I moved before I thought. It was a cheerleader's instinct. I slid out of his grasp and hit pavement. Diogenes looked down at me. The cigarette butt, the one he'd been chewing on, he let it drop out of his mouth. It landed in my eye. It was gooey.

"Fuck you," I said, though more softly then before.

Booker had made his way out from under his bicycle, and now stood beside Diogenes. He'd lost his red rubber nose. A frilly sleeve was torn. Blood bloomed on his forehead. His smile looked spooky. Still sounding like Pee-Wee, he said, "Why do you have to be such an ass to the newbies?"

Diogenes continued to look down. "He's not worthy."

This part is hard to relate. I was laying there. I was looking up at Diogenes, two chef paramedics, a pirate, an ape man, Tiny the clown, and two bearded Mad-Max looking guys with wiffle ball bats taped together to look like Bazookas. In some library in Des Moines, Iowa, I had read about them – read about these guys and laughed at their antics. In some library I had loved this, loved the idea that in some apocalyptic post-industrial world where motorized vehicles were nothing but rusting husks, a bunch of future-thinking guys had been preparing, learning these skills that the rest of the world thought was laughable, learning how to weld, learning how to endure pain, learning how to live as a clan. In the zine, the things they did to outsiders were funny. The stupid manatees, the bulbous lard-addled American masses, the soon-to-be-extinct victims of the coming apocalypse, they deserved everything they got. Waiting for hours at intersections, blocked by gas-masked, tall-bike riding anarchists who shouted insults and hurled beer cans at their windshields. Yes, I thought. In Des Moines, Iowa, huddled amongst the corn-fed, in a galaxy far far away, in a library – YES!

"Lay the fuck off," said Booker.

Diogenes slapped him in the cheek. "Saving the lambs, Tiny? Who do you think you are, Jesus?"

Now that I was here, though, now that I had traveled from the safe and open plains of Iowa to the shaky ground of Portland, Oregon, to the trees and the volcanoes and the uneven tectonics, now that I had found them, my heroes, now that I lay underneath them, prostrate at their feet, a canvas of humiliation, a couple of pages for their zine, now that I finally had my chance, for acceptance, for belonging, for being a part of that which I'd longed to be a part of, now that I looked up at them, comic silhouettes against the grey, ever-present, Portland gloom, now that I had finally arrived, after all the wait, after all the longing, I saw them for who they were.

C.H.V.C.K. was an asshole.

I cried.

It was terrible, the crying. It was a real boo-hoo.

"He's crying," Mad Max said.

I wanted to stop it. I knew how perfect it was, a beer-drenched boy cheerleader, splayed there, crying on the pavement. How precious. What a wet dream.

The pirate snapped a photo.

I couldn't ever join them. I was the Mama bed in the Three Bears house. I was too soft. I got up off the pavement. I brushed off my duo-color skirt. I walked over to my fast, efficient, pre-apocalyptic bicycle. I touched its hard saddle – a racer's saddle, made for riding fast and far in the here and now. Made for escape. Made for spandex.

"Dude," a chef paramedic said.

"We're just fucking around," the other chef paramedic said.

Once I got on it there would be no chasing me down, no headlock, no tubes forced down the throat. My bike wasn't fast, but it was faster than theirs.

I did just that.

"Flynn!" Diogenes shouted, using my real name now, comfort after the fucking, "You can't leave! You're one of us!"

But I wasn't. And I never would be. Anarchy, I didn't have it in me.

COFFEE BREAK #2
ON DWARVES

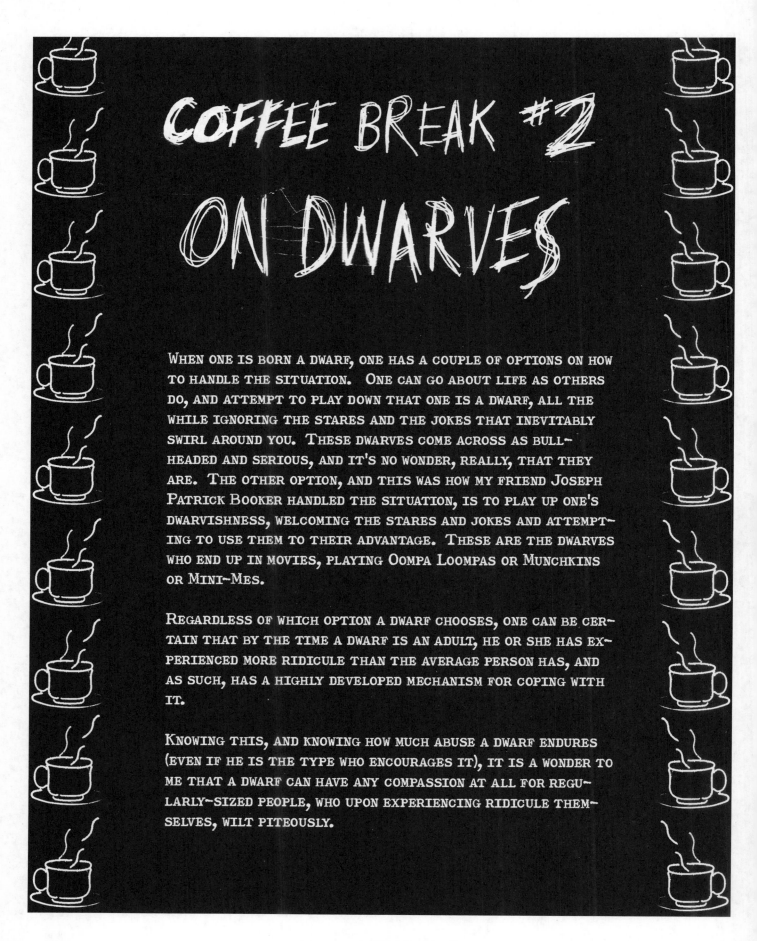

WHEN ONE IS BORN A DWARF, ONE HAS A COUPLE OF OPTIONS ON HOW TO HANDLE THE SITUATION. ONE CAN GO ABOUT LIFE AS OTHERS DO, AND ATTEMPT TO PLAY DOWN THAT ONE IS A DWARF, ALL THE WHILE IGNORING THE STARES AND THE JOKES THAT INEVITABLY SWIRL AROUND YOU. THESE DWARVES COME ACROSS AS BULL-HEADED AND SERIOUS, AND IT'S NO WONDER, REALLY, THAT THEY ARE. THE OTHER OPTION, AND THIS WAS HOW MY FRIEND JOSEPH PATRICK BOOKER HANDLED THE SITUATION, IS TO PLAY UP ONE'S DWARVISHNESS, WELCOMING THE STARES AND JOKES AND ATTEMPTING TO USE THEM TO THEIR ADVANTAGE. THESE ARE THE DWARVES WHO END UP IN MOVIES, PLAYING OOMPA LOOMPAS OR MUNCHKINS OR MINI-MES.

REGARDLESS OF WHICH OPTION A DWARF CHOOSES, ONE CAN BE CERTAIN THAT BY THE TIME A DWARF IS AN ADULT, HE OR SHE HAS EXPERIENCED MORE RIDICULE THAN THE AVERAGE PERSON HAS, AND AS SUCH, HAS A HIGHLY DEVELOPED MECHANISM FOR COPING WITH IT.

KNOWING THIS, AND KNOWING HOW MUCH ABUSE A DWARF ENDURES (EVEN IF HE IS THE TYPE WHO ENCOURAGES IT), IT IS A WONDER TO ME THAT A DWARF CAN HAVE ANY COMPASSION AT ALL FOR REGULARLY-SIZED PEOPLE, WHO UPON EXPERIENCING RIDICULE THEMSELVES, WILT PITEOUSLY.

Chapter XII

*Whereupon Joseph Patrick Booker and His Faithful Scribe
Prepare for What Soon Will Be a Fateful Sunday*

AFTER LEAVING THE C.H.V.C.K. WAGON I'd gone straight back to the church (not wanting to go home on the off chance Mercyx was there with Chester, lounging around in a post-coital stupor), thrown my clothes onto the floor, and gotten under Booker's black satin sheets, naked once again, where I promptly fell asleep. When I awoke my holey black jeans, my Pirate Kombucha T-shirt, my white socks, and a pair of boxers were neatly folded on a bedside stool. Next to the clothes was a bottle of beer – not a PBR, but a 22-oz bottle of a good local microbrew. On the bottle was a sticky note, which had written, in Booker's barely legible scrawl, the pharmaceutical symbol ℞.

Both the clothes and the beer seemed gifts from God. There was certainly nothing more that I wanted than to put on my own clothes and drown both my hangover and my humiliation with a little hair of the dog. I put on the clothes. I drank the beer. While I did this, I couldn't help but notice the loud hissing sounds emanating from behind the closed bedroom door. It sounded like someone was hosing down the floor with a power washer. Afraid that Booker had invited the C.H.V.C.K. guys back, and yet curious what was making the racket, I cracked open the door just a smidge and peeked out.

There, dressed in a silver flame-resistant jacket and heat shield that were of course too large for him, making him look like Neil Armstrong, was Booker, holding a flame torch to what seemed to be a schoolchild's desk. His back was to me, and with the mask on and the torch going, it was clear he could neither see nor hear me. There was no one else in the room.

I stood there for a while, watching him work, before proceeding forward and standing beside him, admiring his handiwork while I finished off my beer. It turned out he was welding the desk to an oversized tricycle, the type used in tourist traps for wheeling lovestruck couples around. He stopped and raised his heat shield.

He could have said a million things here. He could have mentioned the tangerine-sized lump on his forehead, or the shoulder strain – he'd come out of the C.H.V.C.K. hazing in worse shape than me. He could have asked me why I hadn't succumbed, why, if I knew what C.H.V.C.K. was like, I hadn't expected abuse. I mean, at least it hadn't been the brown wrench. He could have gone off on some pseudo-religious Bookeresque tangent. But he didn't say any of those things.

Instead, Booker took a look at my empty bottle, and said, "We need more beer."

It was true, that was exactly what we needed.

"Let's go somewhere Westside, away from the scene."

Also exactly what we needed.

And so we left his church, and worshipped at the temple of beer. We drank that night and we drank the next day. While we drank, Booker told me how he'd met Diogenes, and how he'd got into bikes, and how it had taught him the importance of doing things yourself, in this prefab, Costco world; and while he told me this, I told him about the University of Iowa, and zines, and how it was inspiring to read things that would never make it into mass-manufactured print. We didn't talk about what had taken place at the C.H.V.C.K. wagon, or Mercyx, or who the heck the woman was who I'd woken up next to the other morning. Nor did I ask him why on earth his cell phone never stopped ringing, why he kept naming odd flavors – vanilla, chocolate, yellow curry, mango – and speaking in acronyms; and odder still why he kept rattling off numbers that were either locker combinations or women's measurements – 34-22-36.

We were guys – there's a comfort in avoiding the personal.

The week passed like this, and in the early mornings, when we'd done all the drinking we could possibly do, and when the bars closed, we went back to Booker's. Once there, we welded. All through the night, drunk, we welded. Booker taught me a skill I wouldn't have otherwise learned. The schoolchild's desk became one with tricycle, and fat tires were added for extra support.

On Saturday morning, when we were done, at four maybe five in the morning, Booker looked at me, blurry-eyed and slurring, and with eloquence and a raised hand said, "For my scribe!" There it was, my very own post-apocalyptic rig, of the hauler, not the tall bike category, which seemed appropriate for some reason; a bike on which theoretically one could write and ride at the same time.

So that was that. It happened sort of seamlessly. Booker had been a freak – a comic book midget preacher – and now he was something else: my friend. And when someone becomes your friend, it's hard not to start believing in them.

On Saturday, we slept in. And then we woke up and started drinking. (After coffee, of course.) And after we had drunk and the bars had closed, Booker had a fit of inspiration and spray painted his entire van in gold, adding, as a final touch, in flat black, the words –

– missing, I believe, the Orwellian irony of it.

When he was done, he told me he wanted to do something big tomorrow, something huge, and that he had a really good sermon planned out. He was vague, as usual, but when he said that he made me think of a mountain, about how preachers, when they want to say something elevated, they go up and shout it from a mountaintop.

"Lark Mountain," I said.

"That place above the Gorge," he said. "Perfect."

When I suggested it, I thought of Mercyx. Lark Mountain was an epic ride we'd always imagined doing. It wasn't as far as The Bridge of the Gods – eighty miles round trip instead of a hundred – but in some ways it was more brutal: Lark

Mountain was four-thousand feet above sea level, and involved a steep, twisting, and often windy and freezing ascent. I didn't voice my plan to Booker at the time. I'm not even sure I fully realized what I was thinking myself. But somehow I knew I wouldn't be in the church van heading up the mountain – I'd be on Old Yellow.

As I thought this, Booker brushed his way through the overgrown ferns in his front lawn and moved the letters around on the church's letterboard:

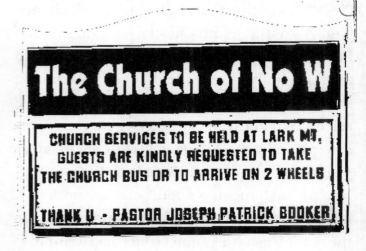

When he returned from his walk through the overgrowth, he said, "I think we're ready," and both of us knew it was time to get a bit of shut-eye before tomorrow morning, before C.H.V.C.K. and Mercyx and Chester and a long, twisty ride/drive and whatever other madness Sunday would bring.

COFFEE BREAK #3
ON THE CATHOLIC UPBRINGING OF BARTHOLOMEW FLYNN

So we're getting near this big culminating scene, the Sermon on the Mount, and it's starting to get a little strange, us being this far into the story, and you not knowing all that much about me, except that I went to college at the University of Iowa, and that I like zines and bikes and don't have much money.

If you were paying attention, you might have guessed that I grew up with some religion, and that the religion I grew up with was Catholic, given my knowledge and fascination with Booker and churches, and just in general how oddly easy I'm shamed.

My parents were, indeed, devout Catholics, and as such sent me to Catholic schools. The schools were exactly as stereotyped: there were uniforms—white shirts and navy blue pants for boys, white blouse and plaid skirt for girls; there were nuns, who insulted you and wore funny habits; and there were priests, who showed an irregular interest in boys.

I survived this, for the most part, without serious psychic injury, until about the fourth grade, when something happened to me that happens to most kids at that age, but which—and it's so bizarre to me that this doesn't happen the same way with every kid—made the rest of my stay in Catholic schools difficult. When I was in fourth grade, I stopped believing in Santa Claus.

It's interesting to me that Booker alluded to this in that very first sermon he gave, standing up on his milk crates while I repaired my bike. Why on earth, when you stop believing that Santa Claus can fit through four-billion plus chimneys in one evening, and that the Easter Bunny can drop off ten billion eggs, don't you also stop believing in walking on water, exorcising demons, and raising the dead?

When I was in the fourth grade, not only did I stop believing in Santa Claus, but I also stopped believing in Jesus Christ. This is a tough thing, when one goes to a Catholic school, to be ten and to lose your faith. There's not much you can do with it. You can't go up to one of those mean nuns, and say, "Sister Mary Joseph, I'm an atheist, don't make me take communion please." So what you do is, you hide it. You go up to the priest, and you stick your tongue out at him, and when he places the wafer on it, it's not God that you're taking, but a weird, glue-like, doughy disk that you'd never eat in a million years if all your classmates weren't in a line behind you.

HIDING SOMETHING LIKE THAT WHEN YOU'RE TEN KIND OF SCREWS YOU UP. YOU'RE SUDDENLY DIFFERENT FROM YOUR PEERS. YOU FIND YOURSELF TAKING YOUR LUNCH ONTO THE PLAYGROUND AND EATING ALONE ON THE CURB. TO BE GOOD, IN A CATHOLIC SCHOOL, YOU MUST BELIEVE. BUT IT WAS A HOAX, MIRACLES COULDN'T BE DONE, SO HOW COULD I BELIEVE? NO MATTER WHAT MENTAL TRICKERY I TRIED, I COULDN'T BELIEVE. SO I WAS BAD—A DARK CLOUD ON THE PLAYGROUND. AND WHAT WAS WORSE—AND THIS WAS SOMETHING I TOTALLY COULDN'T CONTROL—WHENEVER I WAS IN A CHURCH, I WOULD LAUGH. I WAS AN ALTAR BOY, AND I'D BE BRINGING THE HOLY WATER, IN THESE ORNATE CRYSTAL CRUETS, TO THE PASTOR AT THE ALTAR, AND HE'D HAVE HIS ARMS OUTSTRETCHED, BESEECHING GOD TO TURN THE WATER I WAS BRINGING HIM INTO THE LIVING BLOOD OF JESUS CHRIST, AND ALL OF A SUDDEN I'D JUST START LAUGHING, RIGHT THERE IN FRONT OF AN ENTIRE CONGREGATION. I'D BITE MY LIP, MY TONGUE, MY CHEEK—ANYTHING TO MAKE IT STOP—BUT I COULDN'T STOP LAUGHING, IT WAS UNCONTROLLABLE, AND THEN I WOULD PEE.

IT WAS SO OVERBLOWN AND RIDICULOUS—"THE BLOOD OF THE EVERLASTING COVENANT, YOUR ETERNAL DRINK..." I'D HOLD THE CRUETS UP TO THE PASTOR PIOUSLY, TEARS OF LAUGHTER STREAMING DOWN MY EYES AND PEE DRIPPING DOWN THE INSIDE OF MY LEG. THANK GOODNESS NO ONE COULD SEE THE PEE—CASSOCKS ARE GOOD FOR THAT SORT OF MY THING—BUT THERE I WOULD BE AT THE ALTAR, DESECRATING ITS SANCTITY WITH URINE, AND ALTHOUGH I DIDN'T BELIEVE I'D BE GOING TO A HELL THAT INVOLVES FIRE AND PITCHFORKS FOR LAUGHING ON THE ALTAR DURING MASS, I DID BELIEVE IN THE HELL OF A SWIFT FUTURE BEATING IN THE SACRISTY.

MY PARENTS SAID IT WAS A MONEY DECISION, ALTHOUGH PARENT/TEACHER CONFERENCES WITH PRIESTS AND NUNS MIGHT HAVE CONTRIBUTED, BUT AFTER THE FIFTH GRADE, MY PARENTS PULLED ME OUT OF THE CATHOLIC SCHOOL AND SENT ME TO A PUBLIC ONE. THE MOMENT I LEFT, THE WORLD OPENED UP TO ME—TO BELIEVE OR NOT BELIEVE WAS NOT A PRIMARY CONCERN IN PUBLIC SCHOOL ACADEMICS—MATH AND SCIENCE WERE. AND FROM THAT POINT ON, QUESTIONS OF FAITH DIDN'T PARTICULARLY CONCERN ME.

UNTIL I MET JOSEPH PATRICK BOOKER.

Chapter XIII

*Where Another Sunday Arrives, and Where Annie Mercyx
and Bartholomew Flynn Ascend a Grueling Incline
on a Very Paintable Day*

THE SKY WAS WHITE. NOT GRAY OR BLUE, but white – a low-level fog thick enough to keep the day from being bright but thin enough to keep it from being dark. It was neutral – like a blank canvas – a day very clearly in need of painting, a day for which there were no Celtic words.

"Needs painting," Booker said. And when he said it, I knew exactly what he was talking about.

Below us along Prescott Street, Diogenes paced atop Booker's van, directing his minions with his megaphone: bikes Bungeed to the top of the van and duffels thrown into the back. Chester Fields had shown up early – sans Mercyx I might add – and was being harangued by Diogenes with taunts about his small anatomy and current state of bikelessness.

Meanwhile, more of our "gang" showed up: Beale, Dirk from work, the Dunworthy sisters. They piled into the van at Diogenes command, looking bewildered. Dougie and Dietrich showed up too, but despite Booker's sign, they decided – rather wisely – to drive up the hill by themselves in Dougie's biodiesel-powered black Mercedes Benz.

In a remarkably short amount of time, given the chaos of fitting some twenty-odd humans into one van, everyone except Booker and I was inside. Diogenes had installed himself in the driver's seat. He was trying to get out of it, shaking the interior handle and shouting something we couldn't hear because the window was rolled up.

"Childproofed," Booker said.

It took me a minute to realize it was a joke, that driver's doors aren't childproofed, that it was likely just a broken lock.

Booker walked down the steps from our perch, and released Diogenes from the van. Freed, he took a quick jog around Booker's church, returned – with a gasoline can – situated himself back in the driver's seat (tossing the pillows that Booker's used as elevation into the back, assumedly hitting one of the twenty people huddled together in the process), and started the engine, the van emitting a puff of black smoke. By then, Booker had gotten in on the passenger side, leaving me alone on the stoop.

We leered at each other. Me at Diogenes. Diogenes at me. I expected him to insult me, and then command me into the van, but he didn't. Instead, as he drove away from the church, the wide-ass grin on his face so like Booker's and yet so not like Booker's – Booker's being innocent; Diogenes' being evil – he issued me a challenge, "Still yellow, Ann? Or will we see you at the top?"

With that he floored it, leaving me in a cloud of his exhaust. I watched it go.

I sat on the stoop with the thermos and the mugs. I drank more coffee. Everyone was off to the mountain. Everyone but me. The coffee was strong. It had high acidity. There were hints of hazelnut. I ground my teeth. My stomach burned when all that coffee struck a whole week's worth of beer. I calculated, ever so briefly, the odds of me getting to the top of Lark Mountain minus the sight of her glutes spurring me on. (Five-hundred to one.) And then, suddenly, there she was, racing up the street, looking sleek and sea otter-like in her Lycra jersey and shorts.

My love.

My nemesis.

My cycling partner.

Annie.

"WHERE THE FUCK HAVE YOU BEEN?" SHE SAID. Seeing as that was supposed to be my line, I didn't answer. Instead I asked,

"Ready to ride?"

"Ride?"

"Church is up at the top of Lark Mountain today."

It didn't even register for her – how hard that would be. "Where the fuck have you been?" she repeated. "Everyone's been worried about you."

"If everyone was worried about me, then why didn't everyone call me at the coffeeshop on Friday," I said.

Mercyx hesitated. "You haven't been at home."

That one got me. "And how the fuck would you know that?"

Mercyx stared me down. "Do you have a question for me?"

I didn't meet her gaze. "Listen, are you riding or not? We've gotta haul ass if we want to get to the top by one."

"I'm riding."

And having exchanged those pleasantries we started our ride.

Despite the brutal climb ahead, I rode hard through the

city streets, actually staying in front of Mercyx, who was probably more than happy to draft so she could sprint by me as soon as we got to the real climb. There was really no reason for me to be hauling ass in town, before we hit any hills, but I was wired, and more importantly I wanted to stay in front of Mercyx–viewing her ass while imagining her with Chester wasn't good for my psyche. The speedometer read a fairly consistent twenty-one.

We didn't talk; we rode. And after about fifteen miles of stop and go traffic, we hit the beginnings of the climb–not the thirteen miles of direct ascent, but just a taste of the hills–a climb up to Vista Point, where you could look out over the Columbia River Gorge. I was out of my saddle and riding hard. Tapping into my lactate threshold, my thighs totally burning, my calves contorted, Mercyx keeping pace all the while without difficulty. There was nothing I could do about it.

We rode like this for another eight miles, mostly uphill, for about half an hour. After all the morning's coffee and all the week's drinking, I could feel myself getting dehydrated; I'd polished off the contents of my water bottles well before we'd even started up the hill. I knew what I was in for, but I was going to stay in front of Mercyx for as long as possible, at whatever cost.

I kept waiting for her to pass, to watch her make her move, effortlessly gliding by me as she so often did. It didn't happen, though. The only thing I ever heard from behind me was the occasional cough. It surprised me when I saw it. I'd ridden to this point so many times that I'd knew it was coming, and yet, there it was, just ahead, that funky round tower hanging precariously over the Gorge. There was one quick downhill before you got there, a couple of hairpins through a patch of Douglas firs, the Old Gorge Highway sided with moss-covered stones, and I'd make it to Vista Point before Mercyx, because she wouldn't pass me on a downhill–it was one of our unspoken riding rules, that it was lame to pass someone on a downhill–and somehow this seemed a victory, although I was completely aware that Mercyx wasn't racing.

She'd said nothing to me the entire ride, but as we descended I heard her shout, "You need to stop!"

All the potential metaphorical meanings of this went through my head before resting on what Mercyx meant: *Was I going to stop at the viewpoint?* I didn't want to slow down and answer her. I didn't want to pull aside and discuss. I wanted to beat her. And I wanted to do it before I …

And so I kept going. And we got to Vista Point. And I won. Whatever that meant. And I pulled off into the parking lot

and lay the bike against the old stone railing and leaned over it and I puked. I puked coffee. I puked a week's worth of barley, malt and hops. I puked jealously and hatred and humiliation.

I watched it fall. It was just like Multnomah or LaTourelle or Oneonta, cascades of it racing down at different speeds, bouncing and spinning and tumbling and finally bottoming out in a thicket of Oregon ash trees.

It felt good: puking.

And then something really weird happened, because next to me Mercyx was puking too, and her puke was mixing with my puke, and our puke was spinning and tumbling down together, her Chesterfields and Hefeweisen puke mixing with my Stumptown and PBR puke, roiling together amongst the rocks, granite and vomit becoming one. And for a few minutes neither of us spoke, we just stood there, one beside the other, staring hard at the recently purged contents of our insides.

And somehow the cascade of vomit, it wasn't gross but lovely. And Mercyx said it, and even though she said it with sarcasm it was the thing that cracked the glacial ice. "I love you, Flynn."

"What the fuck does that mean?" I asked.

"You rode 'til you puked."

"Special, isn't it?"

And then suddenly, Mercyx softened. I hadn't thought this possible. Booker had hinted at this, and I'd seen it myself in the is-that-sweat-or-tears incident, but all of a sudden I was witnessing it myself, those gray-blue eyes, the circular saw, blunted.

"Why did you leave me with Chester?"

I gazed into her clouded eyes. She was upset. And yet how could this be? She'd been laughing with Chester, smoking his cigarettes, drinking the beers he bought her. She'd left me, not the other way around.

"I kept fucking winning!" she said.

I continued to gaze.

"I kept clearing the table!" she said

The pool table. My God. She'd been on a streak.

"You left me with Kling Wrap!" she said.

Mercyx caught the fear in my expression. "You thought? Oh, fuck. I wondered what that vampire thing was about. Thank God, Chester had that stupid top hat on. He was about to tongue me."

I did it before I could think about it. It was such a relief. She didn't have any feelings for him. She hadn't kissed him, she hadn't slept with him, she hadn't done anything with Chester Fields at all. I'd just been insecure – yellow Flynn. And I'd … that was an accident, it wasn't my fault, who knows if it had really happened. Emerald was just a wig.

I hugged her. And after I hugged her, I realized I was hugging her – I was hugging Annie Mercyx, and we stayed like that, longer than was appropriate, sweat-moistened cheek against sweat-moistened cheek, sports-bra restrained chest against non-restrained chest, Lycra-ed warmth of upper thigh against Lycra-ed warmth of upper thigh. I wanted Annie Mercyx. And our faces, they began to rotate then: hers towards mine, and mine towards hers. And we were getting close. Close to a kiss.

We sniffed it simultaneously.

Vomit.

Mercyx pulled away from me before our lips touched. "Fuck," she said.

And then Mercyx turned and remounted her bike. And I did the same. And then the two of us, we started riding again. We didn't race; we paced ourselves. We didn't talk, we rode side by side. And Mercyx, she shared her water and Power Bars with me, and despite the difficulty of the climb, we made it up the grueling incline on that very paintable day.

Chapter xiv

Where Joseph Patrick Booker Gives His Infamous
Sermon on the Mount and Where Bartholomew Flynn
Does Something Inexplicably Heroic

EFORE MERCYX AND I REACHED THE summit, the color of the sky changed from white to blue. It was a sugary blue you only get when you've ascended above the cloud line, blue like a bright and glowing maraschino cherry on top of whipped cream, only instead of red, the cherry is blue.

Despite our slow pace, we hurt from the long climb, so when we passed through the open entry gates and saw the parking lot, we weren't really capable of the fist-in-the-air type stuff you normally do when crossing a finish line. I think

we were delirious. We got off the bikes, locked them, and walked across the parking lot. We held hands as we walked. In any other circumstance this would have been a big deal – holding hands with Mercyx – but I was exhausted and mindless, and I suspect that she was too, and it just seemed a natural thing to do under that cherry blue sky.

As we walked, we passed Booker's golden van, a Barbie parked amongst G.I. Joes. Mercyx, having never seen it before, caught a glimpse of the FOUR WHEELS BAD, TWO WHEELS GOOD spray-painted on the side and shook her head. It could only be Booker's.

I'd never been up here before, and after all the hype, I'd expected something more spectacular. The parking lot itself was huge and level, covering almost the entire summit so that you felt that you'd arrived at an industrial park in Des Moines rather than a viewpoint overlooking one of the world's most scenic waterways. On one side of the parking lot, the side where you could assumedly see the Columbia Gorge, if there hadn't been a white low-laying haze, there was a short strip of grassy lawn with picnic tables. Beyond the picnic tables, the ground gave way to a steep slope, at the bottom of which lie a shallow, abandoned gravel pit, complete with the requisite rusted vehicles that seem to appear wherever you find abandoned gravel pits. On the other side of the parking lot were trees – nice symmetrical conifers, for sure, but the very same trees you can see anywhere in Portland.

As Mercyx and I walked, Booker and company came into sight. They were sitting on part of the grassy strip on the far side of the parking lot, distanced a ways from the families inhabiting the picnic tables. They sat in a sort of ragged oval – Booker with his back to the gravel pit behind him and the rest of the group splayed out facing him. Diogenes saw us first. He put his megaphone to his lips and spoke, the speaking coming out shouting, "The warriors approacheth. Stand and applaud, lesser beings." The C.H.V.C.K. guys immediately obeyed. The rest of the group – Beale, Chester, Dirk from work, the Dunworthy twins – did so more slowly, as if something was wrong with them. They all looked ill – red in the face and unsteady on their feet. Chester Fields had the word ART in permanent marker on his forehead.

For some reason, the applause was more humiliating to Mercyx and me than if we'd been ribbed with catcalls. We suddenly became aware we were holding hands, like Adam and Eve caught with the apple. We jerked our hands apart.

After applauding, everyone sat back down, cross-legged. Mercyx and I stepped over the curb that circumnavigated the parking lot and onto the grass. The group made a spot for us. It wasn't long before the source of everyone's illness became clear to me. The chef paramedics were trudging over to us carrying a large, white plastic bucket between the two of them. On the white of the bucket was hand-drawn the same words I'd seen on the food cart at the C.H.V.C.K. wagon: RED HOT CHILY. As they laid the bucket in front of us, two bowls and spoons made their way around the oval to us.

I knew, of course, what we were in for, and it wasn't going to sit well after a twisty bike ride to the summit. Mercyx took one of the bowls enthusiastically, not knowing what I did. I took one too, knowing where resistance got you in the world of C.H.V.C.K. A chef paramedic pried the top off of the white plastic bucket with a flathead (the plastic bucket was a twenty gallon latex paint bucket, and had clearly been used as such at some time in the near past), dipped a ladle into the steaming mixture, and poured both Mercyx and me a bowl-full. When he poured it in he guffawed, in that low dark way that people who smoke and drink too much do, and said, "The bile of Christ." Neither Mercyx nor I said amen.

They hadn't even bothered to slice the jalapeños in it. They were floating in the broth whole. The steam of it burned my eyes.

Next to me, Mercyx was taking a bite. Having Diogenes say something to me, call me Ann in front of the real Ann, I just couldn't stand for it. I took a bite too.

Have you ever poured salt on a slug? Have you ever witnessed the way it makes their bodies recoil and shrivel, the way they instantaneously dehydrate and die? That's what happened to my tongue. I wanted to scream but I didn't want it to sound like the whistle of a kettle, so I held it in. It took all the will I could muster. All the blood that had congregated in my thighs after the long ride, it shot up to my temples and eyes.

Next to me, Mercyx was taking another spoonful. Her face was at least as red as mine, but aside from that she didn't seem the least bit affected. "Thanks," she said to the chef paramedic, as if he were a sweet grandmother, "you'll have to give me the recipe sometime."

Fortunately, I'd taken my water bottle out of the cage. I popped the top off and gulped down the water. I wasn't going to scream like a girl, but I couldn't be as cool as Mercyx.

You could tell the chef paramedic was impressed. "The secret ingredient," he said, "it's love."

Everyone was just staring at her, seeing how many spoonfuls she could take without cracking. It would have been an interesting experiment, but Booker, despite missing his milk crates, stood up to speak, determined not to let C.H.V.C.K. steal the show. I don't think it would have worked – we would have all just stared slack-jawed at Mercyx – if it weren't for the woman who had stood up next to him. It wasn't Skye or Emerald, but someone new, a woman who had the same coloration as Booker, minus the wide-eyed creepiness. She had brown, opaque eyes, a long but slender nose, and a thin-lipped, yet pliant mouth, the sort that dazzles with its wideness when given its fullest expression. Her body was large-breasted and voluminous, as was the case with all the mysterious women who appeared around Booker. She also seemed ageless – another Booker-woman trait.

In short, she was beautiful. She was dressed in some sort of Middle Eastern hoodie thing (an Islamic prayer shawl, it turned out, but I only know that after looking it up). On most women it would have seemed conservative, but on her it came across as kinky. It occurred to me that this woman was like his milk crates – some strange magic that he conjured around him when he started speaking:

"The Bible," Booker said.

"THE HOLY BIBLE!" Mad Max stood up and shouted.

Ape Man booed. Gassy hissed.

"I've been thinking about what you must think," Booker continued, ignoring the derision, "how every time I say something, like last week when I claimed that Jesus was against marriage, how you must go and find your Bibles, and flip through them, and find a passage to counteract what I'm saying."

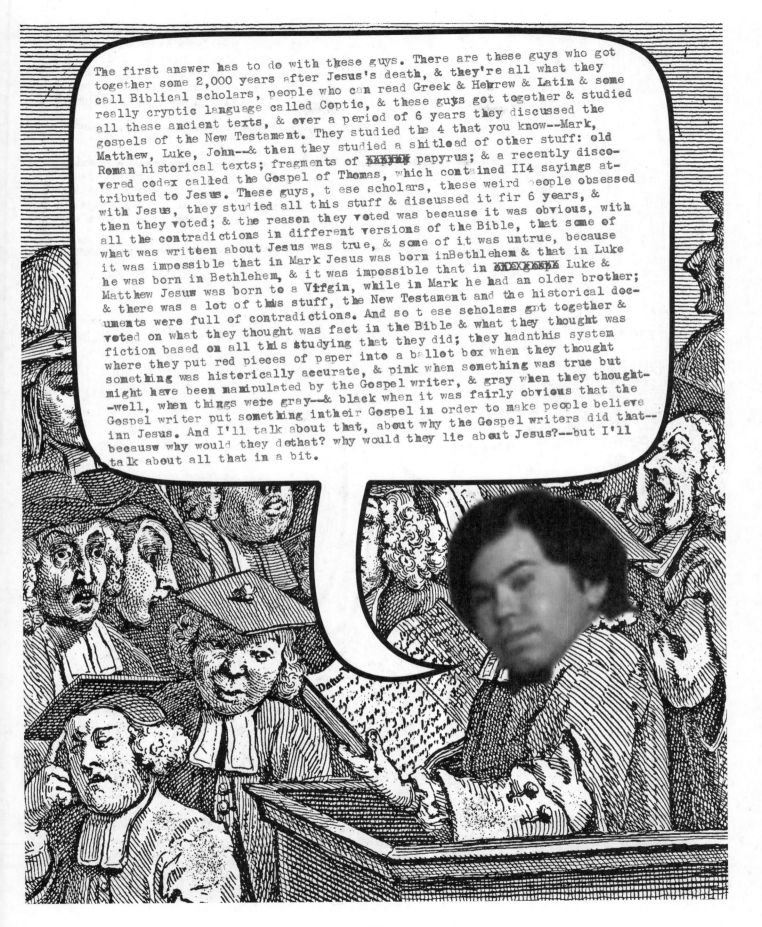

The first answer has to do with these guys. There are these guys who got together some 2,000 years after Jesus's death, & they're all what they call Biblical scholars, people who can read Greek & Hebrew & Latin & some really cryptic language called Coptic, & these guys got together & studied all these ancient texts, & over a period of 6 years they discussed the gospels of the New Testament. They studied the 4 that you know--Mark, Matthew, Luke, John--& then they studied a shitload of other stuff: old Roman historical texts; fragments of ~~papyrus~~ papyrus; & a recently disco-vered codex called the Gospel of Thomas, which contained 114 sayings at-tributed to Jesus. These guys, t ese scholars, these weird people obsessed with Jesus, they studied all this stuff & discussed it fir 6 years, & then they voted; & the reason they voted was because it was obvious, with all the contradictions in different versions of the Bible, that some of what was written about Jesus was true, & some of it was untrue, because it was impossible that in Mark Jesus was born inBethlehem & that in Luke he was born in Bethlehem, & it was impossible that in ~~Matthew~~ Luke & Matthew Jesus was born to a Virgin, while in Mark he had an older brother; & there was a lot of this stuff, the New Testament and the historical doc-uments were full of contradictions. And so t ese scholars got together & voted on what they thought was fact in the Bible & what they thought was fiction based on all this studying that they did; they hadnthis system where they put red pieces of paper into a ballot box when they thought something was historically accurate, & pink when something was true but might have been manipulated by the Gospel writer, & gray when they thought--well, when things were gray--& black when it was fairly obvious that the Gospel writer put something intheir Gospel in order to make people believe inn Jesus. And I'll talk about that, about why the Gospel writers did that--because why would they dothat? why would they lie about Jesus?--but I'll talk about all that in a bit.

So anyway, what I'm saying is that these scholars created a brand new Bible--a Bible that is colored red & pink & gray & black. And you can buy this if you want. And it will tell you what these 70 or 80 scholars--these people who have devoted their lives to studying who Jesus really was--it will tell you what they think Jesus did & didn't say.

That's the first thing you can do. You can go out & buy the red & pink & gray & black Bible. And it will help you determine whether Jesus said anything about cleaving men & women together. And when you do you'll find that Matthew chapter 19, verse 13 & 14 are marked black-- Jesus never said that at all.

OH SHIT

Diogenes had left the cliff's edge & hadnwalked behind me into the parking lot. From my vantage, facing outwards, I could't see what we was up to. Dougie Fresh, however, was sitting next to Booker & could see what was going on. It appeared to me that he was mumbling, "Oh shit."

But really, you shouldn't just go out & buy the red & pink & gray & black Bible if you want to know what Jesus said or did. All you've really go to do is use your common fucking sense.

I mean, if it smells like bullshit, it is bullshit, Was Mary a virgin? No! Did Jesus change water into wine? No! Did he walk on water? No! Did he raise the dead? No! Did he ascend into heav n after being dead for 3 days? No! No! No!

Did any of this shit happen? No, none of this shit happened.

So now you're asking, well if it's all bullshit, why did they do it? Why did Mark & Matthew & Luke & John make all of it up? I'll tell you why. They made it up because there was this man named Jesus, & the things he said & the way that he live his life were so fucking cool that they wanted other people to live their lives like he did. And the way that they could get other people to do t at was to make make him larger than life, was to have him perform miracles & be visited by wise men & float uo to heaven after being dead for 3 days.

Now the thing is, if you think about it, this is a bigger miracle than everything else. These guys, they so like what Jesus had to say—this ordinary bastard carpenter- -that they started to see him as God. Now that's amazing--that's the fucking miracle. It's a miracle that this homeless man who spent his life among migrant workers & pros. titutes is the most revered man who ever lived.

The size Dougie's eyes were--I just had to turn around. Diogenes had opened the suicide doors on the back of Booker's van & was yanking everything out of it. And I do mean everything. The bikes, of course, but also seats, the spare tire, the jack--it was if he were stripping it forparts. Booker had to be aware of this, & yet he went on, determinednto get as far into what he was saying as possible. It was clear he wasnjust warming up.

I lost track, a little bit, of what I wanted to say. I wanted
to tell you who Jesus was, minus the gray & black. He's this
blue-collar dude born out of wedlock, who made oars or
canoes or somet ing for fishermen in Galilee. His job seems
pointless, because the Romans take all his money for taxes
to fight their stupid wars; and one day, he thinks to himself
<u>fuck-it-all</u>, & so he stops working & wanders out into the
desert, & what he discovers there sort of blows him away:
he doesn't die--His Father provides for him; & not only that
but for the first time in as long as he can remember, he's
happier--happier than he's ever been in his life.

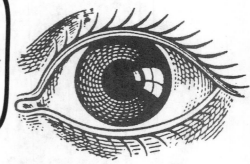

Well, this is a true revelation to Jesus, & he's so
inspired by it that h decides to go out & preach
his fuck-it-all philosophy to the masses. People are
pretty resistant, & who wouldn't be--quit your job;
join the homeless--but Jesus tells them to have faith,
to try it out, & when they do they discover the same
thing he does: they dont' die; they're happier.

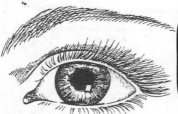

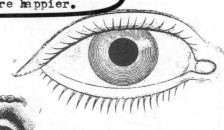

Before anybody knows it, his philosophy is spreading like wildfire, & the Roman & Jewish elite
have to string him up from a tree before all of
Galilee stops working.

In a nutshell, this i Jesus's whole message, once you black out
those pesky miracles: If you don't like the way the world is being
run, quit your job--the Father will provide--& in the process the
coffers of the establish ment will run dry. Oh, & while you're at
it, pick up some milk crates, ot whatever object is handy forstand-
ing on, & tell the world why you're doing it, what's happening to
make you want to fuck*it-all.

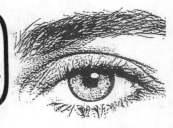

This is why I like you guys so much, what you
are all doing, in your different ways. But see,
unless we band together & clarify our message,
unless we---

There was a loud shriek as Diogenes peeled out from the parking space.
He sped through his parking row--all eyes, including the eyes of thefam-
ilies picknicking beside us, turned towards Booker's van.

The c.h.v.c.k. guys sprang to life. Ape Man lifted a twig, holding it in both hands above his head. Gassy slipped his gas mask over his face. The chef paramedics moved their paint buckets full of chili. Mercyx and I, who had been sitting directly in the van's path, skittered out of its way.

Booker, however, stood on the grassy lawn, defiant before it. Next to him, stood the Middle Eastern hoodie woman, bewildered. The window of the van rolled down. Diogenes leaned his head out the window, his megaphone an extension of his lips. "SAAAAC-RIIII-FIIIIICE!" he shouted, his voice transmogrified, so that it sounded like the public address system at a Monster Truck rally.

The look Booker gave Diogenes was oddly philosophical. "Why?" Booker asked.

"THE EEEEEND IS NIIIIIIGH!" shouted Diogenes. He gave the van a rev. The golden cow glistened, sun-dappled against the dreamy sky. On the dash lay a cigarette, its smoke misting up the windshield.

"But it's mine," Booker said. The c.h.v.c.k. guys were all chanting now. *Sac-ri-fice. Sac-ri-fice. Sac-ri-fice.* Ape Man was jumping up and down. Yes, like a chimpanzee.

"CLEAR!" Diogenes shouted.

Diogenes revved the engine yet again, dropped his megaphone out the window, plucked the cigarette off the dash, pinched it like a joint between his forefinger and thumb, took a puff, removed it from his mouth, glanced thoughtfully for a moment at its lit end, and then tossed it into the back of the van.

There was a woof.

Not a dog's woof but the woof of gas igniting.

Diogenes' face broke into its Bookeresque grin. Black smoke filled the van. The families who'd come up for the view and the fresh air and not for a sacrifice all looked our way from their picnic tables in horror. Mid-rev, he put it in drive. The van leapt the curb separating the parking lot from the grassy flat, its muffler scraping against pavement. It lurched directly towards our ragged oval, bouncing dangerously like a dune buggy, sounding loud and sick and mufflerless.

Booker, who had still been standing there in defiance, leapt out of the way. Everyone else who hadn't already, did as well. Everyone, that is, except the Middle Eastern hoodie girl. She just stood there – stunned, perhaps; sick from the chili, perhaps; unaware that someone would actually do such a stupid and destructive thing, perhaps – a second deer in the headlights.

Through the windshield, I could see Diogenes' jaw drop. Just before the black smoke completely obscured him, he made a swimming motion, with his hands, as if to say, get out of the way.

There was too much momentum, though. She hit the grill, then went under.

Not the sacrifice we'd expected.

People remain in awe of what happened next, and I can't really explain why, at that moment, under those circumstances, I did what I did. I had never been a doer. I was an observer, the kind of person who sits in the back row and watches the world make an ass of itself. But I was being called upon, and what I was being called to do was extremely dangerous, and furthermore, what I was being called to do involved saving someone who by all measures I should have let die. And yet I did it, of course. I suppose, really, anyone would have done it. Why are we like this, by the way? Why in these moments when higher thought has no time to intervene are we so willing to sacrifice ourselves for the sake of another, for an enemy, as the case may be?

As the van rolled over an innocent woman, I remembered Booker's door. It was childproofed. Diogenes couldn't get out.

I ran for it. The van was no longer going fast, its accelerator no longer pressed, but it was still moving forward, approaching the edge. Behind the windshield, Diogenes was invisible, shrouded in smoke. I grabbed the driver's door handle. As I did so, Diogenes, and I'd like to think that he was thinking of the rest of us, that if the van was going to blow up with him in it, it was better if the van didn't also blow up his friends, floored the accelerator.

My feet left the planet earth. I dangled from the door handle sideways, unable to get the leverage to open it. The van, with this sudden acceleration, was only seconds from the edge.

At the last moment, he swerved. I don't know how he did it. He couldn't see. But just as he was about to go over he swerved hard right. He must have timed the distance in his head somehow, I don't know, how or why he did it is anybody's guess, but he swerved just in time, and this hard swerving to the right, while it had a fortuitous consequence for him, it did not have a fortuitous consequence for me. Via laws of centrifugal force I can't really comprehend, I was flung away from the van, and since I still had the handle in my hand, and since I still had the lock depressed with my thumb, the door flung open with me, springing Diogenes from Booker's golden flaming sacrificial van.

Now anyone who has ever been in a car wreck will probably vouch for me: in these split-seconds when disaster strikes, time comes to this bizarre standstill, where we are suddenly allowed more time to think and feel than the actual time available. Some have suggested that this mutability of time is spiritually-driven, that it's like the beginning stages of the afterlife, of eternity, when time ceases to matter. But whatever the case, during a ridiculously short period, I had experienced a full range of emotion, a range I can't remember having ever felt before: from utter despair during the moment when Diogenes ran over Booker's beautiful muse to utter terror when I realized Diogenes was going to immolate himself; to sheer joy in the moment when Diogenes had swerved, and when I had managed to unlatch the door, and when, it seemed, that all was saved.

I still felt this joy while the door, having achieved its full range of motion, jarred my hand loose from the handle, sending me sailing through the air at a very high velocity. This joy, surprisingly, did not leave me when I realized, sailing as I was, that not all had actually been saved, that the swerve, although it had spared Diogenes, wasn't going to spare everyone, that I, Bartholomew Flynn, sailing feet first through the air on that bright and glowing blue-maraschino cherry sky day, my momentum defying gravity, carrying me outward rather than downward, was going to clear the edge of the summit plateau.

It is strange to think that at age twenty-two, I would be downright gleeful as I sailed through the air to my doom. But gleeful I was. I felt no fear. Instead, I saw myself falling, as if I was not the one falling but the one watching from above, and as I was falling I arched my back and I reached skyward towards the sun, and as I fell I wasn't me, I was one of my friends, a zinester or a punk cyclist or a raving preacher or Mercyx, and my falling, though horrible to watch, horrible to see a friend go like this, it also seemed to sum everything up, it was something that Flynn finally did, he fell, like a cascading waterfall, like cascading spew, from a worthy, though not so great height, to his death. And why did he do it? He did it as a sacrifice, he did it because in the act of falling he was actually lifting, because in going down they went up. He did it because when he did it, there they would be, these Portlanders with their outlandish ideas, these goddamn freaks, or anarchists, or hipsters, or urban terrorists, or whatever the next derogatory term for them will be, looking down at him as he fell, looking at him in his final moments, and they would see as they watched him with his arms outstretched that he harbored them no ill will, that he, in fact, loved them for what they had done, because in their hearts, underneath the drinking and the pyromania and the recklessness, there

was this notion that if we could, somehow, through some drastic act, through a new tablet tumbling down Mount Sinai, make everyone see what we saw, make everyone, for a year or two or ten, follow some eleventh commandment – stop driving! Stop working! Stop your reckless, busy, mindless consumption – well then we might in fact be able to prevent the floods, and the storms, and the famine, that the prophets, the scientists, and God himself was storing up for us.

Like I said, it was strange that I was able to think all of this as I sailed through the air, and it was equally strange that I believed it, that in that moment right before death, my mind (soul?) had somehow been stripped of all pretension, that I saw in this split-second what all my motivations were: why I worked at a coffee shop, why I was interested in zines, why I was following Booker around, why I rode a bike. Booker wasn't a clown. He wasn't spouting nonsense. He was speaking what no one else had the courage to speak. He was speaking the truth.

This red and pink Jesus that Booker saw – this Jesus without the miracles; this penniless Jesus who would scribble zines and ride bikes and hang out with prostitutes – this was a Jesus I could believe in. Sure, Jesus was uncool, but it was time to end the soul-crushing desire to be cool and do something absolutely foolish instead.

The world needed changing. This flight I was taking, even if it ended in my demise, it was a way to make them see that. How could I make them see! My God, how does one make people see!

I had never actually thought of any of this before, it all came to me in this rush, and then I hit the gravel and began tumbling down the slope, curled up like a doodle bug, and as I spun I could see Booker's van, tumbling down as well, repeating itself over and over again, like a flipbook, gold on a background of blue, smoke coming out its two front windows like ears, the words spray-painted on it, FOUR WHEELS BAD, TWO WHEELS GOOD, crystal clear, and then, just as a Buddha smile appeared on my face, having achieved total sublimity at the beauty of what I was seeing, my body unraveled, having been flattened by a rock slab, and I lay there, pain replacing joy, oxygen expunged from my lungs in one great burst, and then there was an explosion, and not long after:

darkness.

COFFEE BREAK #3½

ON BOOKS AND PARENTS

The epicenter of Portland, Oregon is not a giant penis-shaped edifice, named for some wealthy corporation or exec, like it is in most cities—the epicenter of Portland, Oregon is a somewhat squat and run-down former car dealership, which has been converted, in a typically Portlandesque ramshackle style, into a bookstore. Powell's Books is where Portlanders bring their out-of-town guests, who always walk in sort of bewildered, as if they would have preferred instead to have been brought somewhere with drinks, hors d'oeuvres, and a view, but now are forced to wander around pretending to be intellectual.

Like most bookstores, Powell's has a foyer: the front of the bookstore where the latest and most likely to be purchased books lay. Tables are there, with books stacked on them, their covers face-up and getting far more play than the covers of books stacked upright on the shelves. Now over the generations, it is interesting to see what sort of books appear on those tables, what the current obsessions of the literary are. Once you would find fiction there, or books on feminism, or politics, but these days you find something else: memoir.

Now these memoirs, they're all basically the same: they involve parents who did something horrible to them; a period of time in which the author did a whole bunch of drugs and had a whole bunch of sex; and then some sort of redemption, in which the narrator got their shit together enough to write the book that's there at the table, and presumably become a contributing citizen of the world.

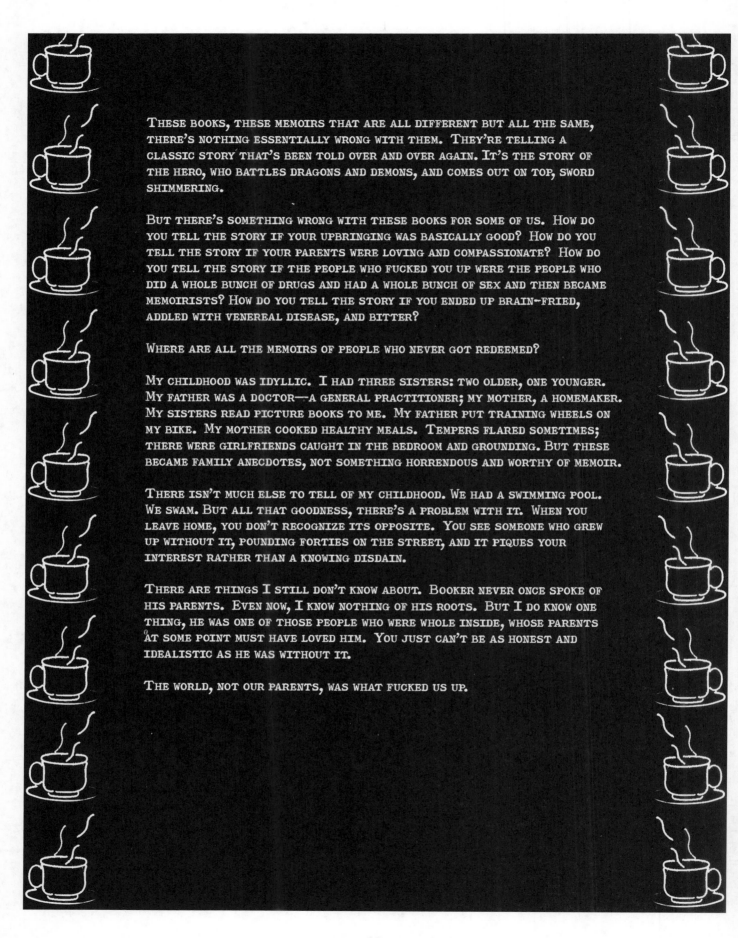

THESE BOOKS, THESE MEMOIRS THAT ARE ALL DIFFERENT BUT ALL THE SAME, THERE'S NOTHING ESSENTIALLY WRONG WITH THEM. THEY'RE TELLING A CLASSIC STORY THAT'S BEEN TOLD OVER AND OVER AGAIN. IT'S THE STORY OF THE HERO, WHO BATTLES DRAGONS AND DEMONS, AND COMES OUT ON TOP, SWORD SHIMMERING.

BUT THERE'S SOMETHING WRONG WITH THESE BOOKS FOR SOME OF US. HOW DO YOU TELL THE STORY IF YOUR UPBRINGING WAS BASICALLY GOOD? HOW DO YOU TELL THE STORY IF YOUR PARENTS WERE LOVING AND COMPASSIONATE? HOW DO YOU TELL THE STORY IF THE PEOPLE WHO FUCKED YOU UP WERE THE PEOPLE WHO DID A WHOLE BUNCH OF DRUGS AND HAD A WHOLE BUNCH OF SEX AND THEN BECAME MEMOIRISTS? HOW DO YOU TELL THE STORY IF YOU ENDED UP BRAIN-FRIED, ADDLED WITH VENEREAL DISEASE, AND BITTER?

WHERE ARE ALL THE MEMOIRS OF PEOPLE WHO NEVER GOT REDEEMED?

MY CHILDHOOD WAS IDYLLIC. I HAD THREE SISTERS: TWO OLDER, ONE YOUNGER. MY FATHER WAS A DOCTOR—A GENERAL PRACTITIONER; MY MOTHER, A HOMEMAKER. MY SISTERS READ PICTURE BOOKS TO ME. MY FATHER PUT TRAINING WHEELS ON MY BIKE. MY MOTHER COOKED HEALTHY MEALS. TEMPERS FLARED SOMETIMES; THERE WERE GIRLFRIENDS CAUGHT IN THE BEDROOM AND GROUNDING. BUT THESE BECAME FAMILY ANECDOTES, NOT SOMETHING HORRENDOUS AND WORTHY OF MEMOIR.

THERE ISN'T MUCH ELSE TO TELL OF MY CHILDHOOD. WE HAD A SWIMMING POOL. WE SWAM. BUT ALL THAT GOODNESS, THERE'S A PROBLEM WITH IT. WHEN YOU LEAVE HOME, YOU DON'T RECOGNIZE ITS OPPOSITE. YOU SEE SOMEONE WHO GREW UP WITHOUT IT, POUNDING FORTIES ON THE STREET, AND IT PIQUES YOUR INTEREST RATHER THAN A KNOWING DISDAIN.

THERE ARE THINGS I STILL DON'T KNOW ABOUT. BOOKER NEVER ONCE SPOKE OF HIS PARENTS. EVEN NOW, I KNOW NOTHING OF HIS ROOTS. BUT I DO KNOW ONE THING, HE WAS ONE OF THOSE PEOPLE WHO WERE WHOLE INSIDE, WHOSE PARENTS AT SOME POINT MUST HAVE LOVED HIM. YOU JUST CAN'T BE AS HONEST AND IDEALISTIC AS HE WAS WITHOUT IT.

THE WORLD, NOT OUR PARENTS, WAS WHAT FUCKED US UP.

Chapter XV

Where Bartholomew Flynn is Led to the Bug Cave,
and Where He Encounters Bears

I WAS WOOZY. I SHIVERED ON A BENCH at the MAX train station, my head pulsating. Blood caked the right side of my face, a shoulder of my cycling jersey, and the Lycra of my shorts. Mercyx paced back and forth in front of me, battering me with exclamatory statements.

"He ran over that girl! He set it on fire! He blew up his van! On purpose! Fuck!"

It wasn't like her to be rattled.

"You got up, crawled up the hill, all fucking bloody, and then took off! We're accessories! You didn't even pull aside for the emergency vehicles! She could be dead! You could have been …"

She turned her back to me, facing the tracks.

"Was it worth it? Do you have something good for your *zine*?"

I could hear what Mercyx was saying, but I couldn't really think about it. I wasn't sure why I'd done any of those things either. They'd all sort of just happened. I'd gotten up from my fall, woozy and shaken and amazed that I was alive, and then panicked. There were all these people up there, once Booker and Mercyx had helped me out of the gravel pit, and they were all concerned about me and wanted me to wait for an ambulance, and with all that crash-induced adrenaline coursing through my body, I'd just had this uncontrollable urge to escape, like a dog who's been hit by a car and who limps off to die in some suburban alley.

Mercyx covered her eyes with her hands. "I mean, you're a pussy, Flynn. Not a … *hero*."

I knew Mercyx was furious, and that I should do something about it, get up and hug her, but I was, literally, glued to the bench. Once we'd gotten off the Old Columbia Gorge Highway and onto the level roads of town, and once the adrenaline rush had subsided, and once I was no longer numb from the cold, all the pain from my fall had rushed in on me at once, and my muscles basically seized up, making pedaling impossible. We'd managed to coast to the MAX station in Gresham, but getting the rest of the way without public transportation was no longer feasible.

"When you get home, tell Chester to wake you up on the hour. Brains hemorrhage. You had a serious concussion."

Mercyx had a point. I was feeling clammy. The side of my head throbbed. What's more, *Ave Maria* was playing in my head. Not a good sign.

She pulled my cellphone out of my wedge bag. Jesus, I was zonked. Ave Maria was Booker's ring tone.

Mercyx battered Booker in the same way she'd battered me. I only caught one side of the conversation. "Is she okay? Fuck! The rest of them? Fuck! Did they get him? Fuck! He's a moron, but he's okay. No. Would cost him two grand. Will do. Your friend is a douchebag. Mercyx out."

She snapped the phone shut. My eyes pleaded for the answers.

"Alive," she said, "six broken ribs and a collapsed lung. Saved from being crushed by a missing muffler. Gassy broke his collarbone in the descent. Mad Max separated a shoulder. Douche Knees, or whatever his name is, ran off into the woods. There's a manhunt. Did you help plan that?"

Before I could answer the MAX train was in front of us. Portland's light rail is notoriously quiet. Good for noise pollution. Bad for pedestrians. Mercyx got her bike, put it in the train, and then held open the doors. I was still sitting there.

"Get your bike!"

I got my bike. I was hunched over at the waist, my lower back locked into a downhill cycling position. As I wheeled the bike through the doors of the awaiting car, I noticed a slash in my cycling shoe. My feet had been so frozen from the cold ride down that I hadn't felt anything. I'd been cut. It was a nasty one. And when feeling returned, it was going to really hurt.

The other passengers on the train took one look at me then quickly stared out the window. I shambled into the seat next to Mercyx. I looked like a zombie. Mercyx turned her head out the window and wouldn't look at me either.

"So you saved your gang leader. How does it feel to be a hero?"

The train lurched forward. A wave of nausea rose up from my chest. I leaned my head against the seat in front of me. *Like shit* was the easy answer, but the thing was, Mercyx had it wrong. "I hate that guy," I said.

Mercyx turned away from the window and looked at me. She winced. She was facing my bloody side.

"I didn't save Diogenes because I like him. He's an asshole. I just saved him because … I don't know, people save people."

Those twin electric saw blades of Mercyx's, they were boring through me. "You didn't join the gang?"

I scoffed. "I wasn't–*worthy*."

Something happened to her eyes then. The blades in them, they stopped spinning.

"We'll get off at Overlook Park. Chester can't be trusted to wake you up every hour."

I looked into Mercyx's eyes and Mercyx into mine. Her eyes weren't solid steel at all. They were liquid.

It occurred to me that Mercyx had just asked me to spend the night.

<hr/>

MERCYX LIVED IN NORTH PORTLAND, A NEIGHborhood of old rotting bungalows perched perilously above a Superfund site, not too far from my apartment on Alberta Street, a couple of miles. She lived in what the local real estate agents call an old-PDX, a unique to Portland, turn-of-the-century hybrid between a Victorian and a farmhouse. Real estate agents tend to make things sound more charming than they actually are, and Mercyx's old-PDX was no exception to this rule. It was pretty much just a flophouse for housing service-industry, poverty-wage, recent graduates with some waterstained crown moldings to give it character.

Eight people lived in what was officially only a two-bedroom, one-bath house, although with a little creativity it had been converted into a five/two. They (and when I say they, I mean some unknown entity, because so many people had revolved in and out of the house that no one knew anymore who the person was who'd done all the renovations) had turned the attic and basement into living space. All the insulation had been ripped out of the attic, and a stairway built by dismantling a downstairs closet. The wood beams were exposed, and the attic still felt like an attic, with bare bulbs and everything, except instead of musty old boxes the attic had in it a double-sized futon; a couple of large wood dowels screwed into the wall to hold clothes; pairs of shoes, underwear, and some rolled up socks stuffed into a corner; and beside the futon, a drum set. The basement contained more bedrooms, and the additional bath.

The only nice thing about the house was the lighting. Someone who had once lived there had either been an artist or good friends with one, and had either made or traded for (clearly, since no one who ever lived in the house had any money) these very cool lamps. The shades to these lamps were constructed similarly to Chinese lanterns: the wire structure was formed using old, reshaped clothes hangers while its "skin" was formed using scraps of cellophane. Rather than dragons, though, the lamps were in the shape of giant flowers and bugs: lilies, wasps, and spiders hung from the ceiling and crawled along the walls.

The lamps explained the name of the house, although no one remembered whether it was called The Bug Cave first, and then someone made the lamps to match the theme or whether the lamps themselves dictated the theme. Either way it was one of those houses in Portland everyone seemed to know about.

I had spent very little time at The Bug Cave, just going over to pick up Mercyx before rides. When I came I waited for Mercyx outside, although I'd been introduced to the others who lived there tons of times, and could have easily gone in and made myself comfortable.

To be honest, they intimidated me. I felt about the people who lived there the way most people feel about film actors–they were sort of just too cool for me, like if I tried to hang out with them they'd find out how lame I was. The tattoos didn't help either. Everyone in the house had tattoos. Being inked felt like a prerequisite for entry–when I went inside it was as if I'd shown up for a battle with my troop and forgotten all my armor. I always imagined, despite never hearing Mercyx or anyone else mention them, that decadent parties occurred there on a regular basis. The house, more so than its inhabitants, seemed responsible for this.

That she lived in this house was part of Mercyx's murky mystique. Despite her sometimes coquettish behavior, I assumed–because she was an inhabitant of The Bug Cave–that she was a regular participant in mandatory house orgies, and that the trouble I was having consummating things was due to my lack of primitive markings and my general geekiness, not any prudishness on Mercyx's part.

She was gone for a short while, before she returned and said, "The coast is clear."

I stood for a minute, hesitating. Part of it was the house, and part of it was that Mercyx was inviting me to sleep at her house, meaning there was a possibility, however miniscule, that I would also be sleeping with her.

Mercyx had never been a patient person. Hesitation was just another way of saying no. "Just go home," she said.

Oh no, I'd blown it. "No, I'll–"

"Go. Home," she insisted.

I blurted, "I'll come."

Mercyx shook her head in mock disgust. "Well, come then," and she was up the steps before I could get my shoes unclipped from my pedals.

<hr/>

MERCYX DIDN'T SAY ANYTHING ELSE AS WE tiptoed through the house. Given that we were wheeling our bikes behind us, and that the detritus of eight very busy and active twenty-something individuals was strewn about, tiptoeing was difficult. I managed to clip a coffee table with a pedal and knock over two ashtrays, causing them to clatter loudly on the hardwood floors. Mercyx turned around and glared.

I didn't think to wonder why we were being so secretive, which is surprising considering the kinds of jealousy I felt towards Mercyx's orgy participants. I guess I was too busy concentrating on not making any noise.

We made our way through the living room, the dining room, and the kitchen, then wheeled the bikes out the back door and locked them to a bike rack in the backyard. Still silent, we went back into the house and walked down a flight of stairs. It was pitch black.

Like I said, I hadn't seen the basement of The Bug Cave yet, and so, when we got to the bottom, and Mercyx flipped on enough of the lamps so we could see our way around, I was kind of freaked out. It was the same feeling you get when you've been invited to the private rooms at a party – simultaneously nervous and electrified. The bugs and the flowers seemed sinister in the dim light. Drywall, never painted or primed, was nailed to the basement's wood supports to divide it into rooms. The whole thing had been done in such a crude and hurried way that it felt like a set in *Silence of the Lambs*.

I paused to look around, but Mercyx shot me another glance and beckoned me to continue. We walked around the maze of a basement, going down a long hallway and passing a couple of doors. Behind one of the doors came a creepy metallic buzzing sound.

Despite all my longing for Mercyx, all I could think about was getting the fuck out of there. This was weird – really, really weird – and though Mercyx had never given me any indication that she was into whipping or nipple clamps or some sort of erotic electrocution, I was thinking I'd entered some sort of S&M parlor.

We passed the room with the buzzing sound, and arrived beside the second door. Mercyx pulled out her keys and went to open it.

By then, I was no longer right beside Mercyx, but a little way down the hall, bug-eyed, trying to figure out my next move. I'd decided I wasn't going to go in there: I mean, it had been a long day, and I'd just go home and relax, because this was weird. What was the buzzing sound? What was Mercyx into?

Shit. Mercyx had the door open. Shit. Mercyx was addressing me.

"What?" Mercyx asked.

I wish I could go back in time with a mirror and see the look I gave her. It must have been priceless.

Mercyx, though, decided she'd had enough. There were no more choices. She took my arm. She tugged me in.

———

MERCYX FLIPPED THE LIGHTSWITCH. HER LAIR wasn't what I expected. It was, well, pink. Whereas all the outside walls in the basement were just drywall, Mercyx's room was finished and painted. The room had the same flowers and bugs as the rest of the basement, but scattered around the pink room the lilies and butterflies and ladybugs looked much more innocuous. It was a girl's room – not an adult girl's room, a little girl's room.

Placed on a shelf about a foot away from the ceiling was a very large collection of teddy bears – forty, fifty, maybe sixty teddy bears. There were teddy bears on the bed as well, a whole family tucked under the covers. There was a teddy bear comforter to match, and a wagon, an old, red, rusted Radio Flyer filled with, you guessed it, teddy bears.

At first, the pink and the teddy bears had eased my nervousness a little, but then I got even more freaked out. Hundreds of teddy bears in a room is freaky.

Mercyx saw me looking at the teddy bears, and suddenly, just as forcefully as she'd strong-armed me into the room, she shoved me out. "Just forget it."

"Forget what?"

"Go home." Mercyx said this loudly, then caught herself speaking loudly, then covered her face, the way people do when they're really frustrated, then she said, "Fuck."

She shoved me again.

"Ouch," I said. Her pushing me sent a twinge down my spine.

"Shit," she said. We were standing in the doorway now, neither in nor out of the room. Mercyx was staring at the floor. "They're my friends," she said.

"Who are your friends?"

Mercyx was red-faced. "The bears, goddamn it, the bears are my friends."

"Oh."

"I've had them a long time, and I have to tuck them in every night. It's … they're innocent."

Mercyx was trying so hard to explain. Explaining wasn't her strong point. I tried to help her. "Like *The Catcher in the Rye*," I said.

"Like what?"

"Like Holden Caulfield in *The Catcher in the Rye*, how he didn't want his sister Phoebe to be exposed to all these bad things –"

Mercyx looked up from the spot on the floor she'd been staring at. Like I'd mentioned before, Mercyx had a habit of getting in people's personal space and sort of intimidating them that way. She was right up next to me. Only this time, it wasn't like that at all, it wasn't like she was trying to back me up. Her eyes locked on mine, like what I'd said was of vital importance. "Everyone else … well, they all think it's just kitschy."

There's this gravitational force when someone gets in your space. You either have to back off or you have to go forward and meet it. "It's like they're real," I offered.

"They're not *real*. It's just that if I don't tuck them in, they'll die, or maybe I'll die or someone I love will die. I've tried to stop; my roommate in college, she freaked out. I got a studio and lived alone. I tried to see a shrink. I even didn't do it a few times. I didn't tuck them in. It was horrible. I …"

And then it came out, what she wanted to tell me, what her toughness, her persona, had meant all along. Mercyx wasn't rounded and hollowed out at all. She hadn't had sex with her cousin at fourteen, or been gang raped on a beach, or run off with a ponytailed, forty-year-old drug dealer, or any of the other things I'd suspected. She wasn't into S&M. In fact, the something that had happened to Mercyx was much more common. It was a something that happens to a lot of us, a something that's sort of difficult to talk about because of what it is. The something that had happened to Mercyx: it was a nothing.

It didn't have anything to do with the teddy bears, as far as I could tell, but here it was, the kicker, "I'm a virgin."

So here I was. I mean, this was Mercyx. Mercyx was, well, Mercyx was most definitely not a virgin. I mean, Mercyx was one tough bitch – she was short with people, and when she needed to be, full of backtalk. She had a sleeve full of tattoos. She rode her bicycle faster and further and more dangerously than Cipollini. She wasn't … she couldn't be … a virgin. And she couldn't have a pink room with teddy bears. This was impossible.

I kissed her. What else could I do? I kissed her. It was full-mouth-to-mouth with sufficient pressing together of lips. And a tongue slipped in, tentatively at first, then a bit more exploratory.

It tasted of the morning's vomit.

Mercyx pulled back faster than I did. "I need to brush my teeth."

"Me too."

"I'm going first," Mercyx said. Suddenly she was behaving much more like a schoolgirl than Mercyx.

"Okay."

"I'm going to take a shower, too."

"Okay."

"Okay, well, I'll be right back."

"Okay."

Mercyx walked out her door.

WHEN MERCYX LEFT THE ROOM, I HEARD THE metallic buzzing again. I'd sort of forgotten it, for understandable reasons. I'd ascertained by then that it was coming from the room next door. I couldn't for the life of me figure out what it was. A really ancient ultra-noisy washer and dryer? Someone welding at one in the morning? A part of me still held on to the possibility that Mercyx had brought me here to be tortured by her sadistic roommates.

I didn't know what to do. I was stuck in this pink room full of teddy bears with nothing to do but wait for Mercyx-she-can't-really-be-a-virgin to come back. Mercyx had left me a packet of blue ice to put on my wounds. I shook it. I snapped it. I put in on my forehead. And then I played with the bears. What else was I going to do? The bears talked to each other.

"Hi, I'm Annie Mercyx."

"Hi, I'm Bartholomew Flynn."

"I'm a virgin."

"No, you're not, you can't be a virgin."

"I am."

"What the hell is that noise?"

"It's my roommate."

"What's he doing?"

"He's captured a woman. She's strapped to a chair. He's zapping her with progressively stronger electrical charges. You can't hear her anymore because she's passed out. Sometimes they die; sometimes they live."

"Oh."

"Want some rose-colored glasses?"

"Sure."

"They'll bring world peace."

This went on for a while. I was thinking that this would make a good comic, a new take on *Octagonal Table Talk*, like Matt Groening's *Life in Hell* comic only with teddy bears instead of gay men with fezzes. It was good therapy talking with the teddy bears, maybe it wasn't too weird, tucking teddy bears in every night.

Mercyx walked back in wearing nothing but a towel. I was sitting on her bed with two teddy bears on my lap.

"What are you doing?" she said.

Mercyx was wearing nothing but a towel.

"Don't touch the bears," she said.

Mercyx was wearing nothing but a towel.

"Hello? Flynn?" Mercyx took the bears out of my hands. "The shower's down the hall. Oh, and the blue toothbrush, you can use that one."

Mercyx was wearing nothing but a towel. Some part of me got up and left the room.

I REALIZE THAT THIS NARRATIVE HAS GOTTEN convoluted, but all this really happened: the buzzing, the pink room, the virgin declaration. It was as schizophrenic to me as it is to you. So please bear with me (pardon the pun) for a while. It only gets weirder. In order for lives to change, though, things have to get weird. Remember that. Don't be afraid of weird.

IT TOOK ME A WHILE TO FIND THE BATHROOM. Mercyx failed to mention the hallway was not straight, but sort of wrapped around in a U on the outside of the basement. I was nervous about walking into bedrooms or orgies or whatever, so I didn't peek in any of the doors to find out which one was the bathroom until I'd gone all the way around and had no other choice. Coming back around the U, I found a laundry room, a storage locker, and finally, right before the room with the strange buzzing sound, the bathroom.

I opened the door. The bathroom was like something you'd find in an Eastern European hostel. The showerhead was directly over the sink and the toilet, so when you took a shower everything got wet. I went to the sink, found the blue toothbrush, brushed my teeth, then stripped off my clothes, tossing them onto a low bench, and took my shower. The hot water stung my wounds a little so I adjusted the temperature. Despite all the oddness going on, the shower felt darn good. Water, no matter how strange the circumstances, has a tendency to relax.

Could Mercyx be a virgin? I guess she could. She never talked about guys; she was purposefully cold; she dressed like a jock most of the time. We'd always joked about Mercyx being a lesbian, but never a virgin. She had plenty of opportunities.

Was she secretly religious? *Was* she a closet lesbian? Had she thought she was a lesbian and changed her mind. Maybe …

I turned off the shower. Thinking about it seemed stupid, since all I had to do was turn off the shower and ask. That was clearly the step that needed to be taken. I looked for a towel. There wasn't one. There weren't any towels. I went over to my clothes. They were soaked. Fuck.

I SAID IT WOULD GET WEIRDER. IF I WAS SOME sort of trained writer, and this was all fiction, I would definitely separate all these events: the Sermon on the Mount from the Ambulance Ride from The Bug Cave from the Virgin Declaration from the-thing-that-happened-after-I-got-out-of-the-shower; but this isn't fiction, this is real life; and real life happens all at once, not in neat little narrative segments. For the most part our lives are boring and predictable and then something happens that changes everything. It happens so quickly – a car hits us; a plane takes out a building – and suddenly everything is different. I don't know why it's that way, but it is, and it sure does make it hard to tell a true story.

YOU'RE IN A STRANGE HOUSE. YOU'VE JUST taken a shower and find that there are no towels. You've placed your clothes in a not-so-smart place and they're now soaking wet. The girl who brought you here just told you that she is a virgin. The girl who brought you here does not want anyone else to know, for unknown reasons, that you are here. Between you and the room that you need to go into to get a towel and some clothes is a door behind which is coming an unpleasant and unidentified metallic buzzing sound. In the room with the towel in it is the girl who has just told you that she's a virgin. That girl may or may not want to see you naked.

Knowing these parameters, you consider your options. You can *a*) put on the wet clothes, thus voiding the point of the shower and making a mess of the basement hallway and the girl's bedroom or *b*) leave the wet clothes in the bathroom and make a run for it, potentially shocking the newly-discovered virgin – not to mention any roommates or serial killers who might be lurking about.

I chose, not very sensibly, a hybrid of the two paths, taking my shoes, and using them to cover my front; and taking my shirt and pants, and attempting to use them to cover my back. Fear, at this point, had taken control of my senses, and I didn't consider the ramifications; that doing this would both make a mess of the hallway *and* shock virgins and roommates and serial killers.

You can see where this is heading. It was inevitable, of course. The minute I stepped out into the hallway, the dreaded door opened; and I saw what I saw and the two people who opened the dreaded door saw what they saw, and there was really no way of telling who was more frightened.

"OH MY GOD," CAME OUT OF A MOUTH. I was speechless, I could feel the cold metal of my biking clips against my privates. My member hid between its twin barrels.

"Oh my God," the mouth said again. The mouth was attached to the head of a man with a shaved head. On his head was tattooed brains. I wanted to shriek *Oh my god* too. I didn't. I stood there slack-jawed.

"Mercyx?" the mouth on the head queried, speaking in the direction of Mercyx's door.

I said nothing.

"Mercyx?"

Mercyx opened her door and peeked out. "Oh my God," she said.

"Is this … *yours*, Ms. Chastity?" asked the mouth.

Imperturbable Mercyx was red as a beet. "Yes, he's mine."

"Would you get him dressed?"

Mercyx came out, dressed in a negligee, grabbed me by the arm, and pulled me into the bedroom. It was the second time she'd had to do it that night. I suspected it wouldn't happen a third.

"What the …?" Mercyx was thoroughly flustered. "Here, take this towel." Mercyx flung her wet towel at me. "Jesus."

I dropped my wet shoes to catch the towel, then thought better of it since her carpet was white. I picked the shoes back up and stood there dumbly, "Is there somewhere I can put my clothes? They're wet."

At this point Mercyx must have figured out what had happened. What I did was dumb, but then again, she hadn't explained the European-style hostel bathroom to me either. "Just … here." Mercyx pulled out the plastic liner bag from a small wastebasket, dumped the contents of the liner bag into the now-unlined wastebasket, and handed me the bag. I put my wet clothes in it and started to dry off. I was conscious that Mercyx was there, watching me (and that she was a virgin, and wearing a negligee, and that she was Mercyx), so I kind of just dried off my mid-section and skipped drying off my hair, until I became aware that I was just drying off my mid-section, and thought that that was strange, and so mentally said fuck-it and went ahead and dried off my hair.

When I was done drying my hair, and could thus see again, Mercyx was smiling at me.

"What?" I said defensively.

"Nice," she said, looking at my penis.

"Fuck," I said.

Mercyx kept looking at me.

"Can I get some clothes?" I said.

I wrapped the towel around my waist.

"Don't do that," she said.

"Don't do what?" I said.

"Don't put the towel on," she said.

"It's cold," I said.

"Get in the bed."

This was the first reasonable thing she'd said all day.

I moved towards where she was sitting on the edge of the mattress, wrapping an arm around her as I did so, "So who was the guy with the brains tattooed on his head?"

"That was David," she said. "What are you doing?"

"I'm getting in the bed."

"Not *my* bed," she said.

Lord.

"The bears sleep in my bed. There's no room for you."

My head was spinning. First, Mercyx was a virgin, then she was admiring my penis, then she wanted me in the bed, then she didn't.

"There's a Thermarest and a sleeping bag under my bed. Hold on and I'll set it up."

"So you want me to sleep naked and alone in the sleeping bag on the Thermarest."

Mercyx had already started to pull the stuff from under the bed when I said this. She paused. I should, I suppose, describe what Mercyx was wearing and what she looked like when she said this. When I say she was wearing negligee, I don't mean some sort shimmery sheer wrap with a bra and a thong, I mean a more Mercyx sort of negligee, a low-cut brown and turquoise lace top with thin straps and a pair of matching panties. Sexy, but not bimbo sexy, if you know what I mean.

Mercyx turned around. "It's not what you think, okay?"

I had no idea what I thought. I'd nearly died about four hours ago. All these things Mercyx was throwing at me, it was like the flipbook golden cow all over again. I stared at her with an eyebrow raised, tucking in the towel at my waist.

"I mean … it's not like my parents … you see, I was raised the opposite. My parents didn't believe anything. It was sex and drugs and blah, blah, blah."

Mercyx wasn't making any sense, and as she talked I had

this amazing revelation. She wasn't short with people because she was tough, she was short with people because she didn't really know how to speak, because what she wanted to say was too complex for people to comprehend. She was, well … she was like me. I chuckled.

"What?" Mercyx asked.

"Nothing," I said.

"I'm trying to tell you something and you laugh?"

I didn't want to share the revelation I had just had with her. Something told me it wouldn't go my way. I looked for a way to change the subject. A framed photograph in her room caught my eye. "Is that you?"

"Yeah," she said.

In the photograph was an eight year-old version of Mercyx, still lithe, her body tight and tiny for her head. She was sitting on the back of a man with a mustache, who was on his hands and knees. The girl was wearing a suede riding helmet and had in her hands a horse crop.

"Is that your dad?" I asked, referring to the man in the mustache.

"Yeah," Mercyx said.

"It's kind of creepy," I said.

I sensed something snap in Mercyx when I said that, something cold and chemical, like the blue ice I'd be needing soon for my bruises. She didn't say anything. I didn't say anything either. I remembered that I was standing up in front of Mercyx with nothing but a towel around my waist; I fiddled with the knot I'd made where I'd tucked the towel in. I started to mumble something about pajamas. Mercyx interrupted me.

"Why do you think it's creepy?" she asked.

I didn't want to answer this. It was creepy because there was something sexual about it: the way it had been set and stylized; the fact that it was in black and white.

"My dad was a photographer," Mercyx said. She said *photographer* like she'd wanted to use a different, but similar, word.

"He …" Mercyx was clearly upset. "Do you want to know?" she asked.

I don't know, did I? "Yes," I said.

"Sit down," Mercyx said. Mercyx had pulled the Thermarest out from under the bed and sat to blow it up, but now she gave it up, patting the bed next to her and indicating where I should sit. I obliged.

"My dad, for a living, he shot porn. I just … when your dad does that and you start to learn about it and figure it all out, it makes things, well, *squeechie*, you know. I mean, you're a kid, and your Dad's *photography* – some submissive hung by her

ankles in a *noirish* Motel 6 – it's in *Penthouse* and shit, and all you can think about is your Dad, this nice guy who cares about you, leering all slobber-mouthed behind a lens.

"After all the weird sex I was forced to grow up with, I took a personal vow of chastity. It's not religious in nature – it just sort of … *is*. But withholding, all this time, just on principle, after a while, that gets hard too. And it makes you angry – what you've been made, you know."

Those now liquid gray eyes of hers. The ocean on a cloudy day.

I kissed her, again. It was different this time. It was a kiss that wanted to go deeper. She had said chastity, and she had said hard, and she had said that stuff about her dad being a pornographer, and she had on this negligee, and I had on nothing but a towel, now tenting. It was too much. I knew she needed to go on, to get it all out, but it had been too long of a day, and I had nearly died, and I couldn't listen anymore. I needed action. I pushed her onto the bed. I pressed my full lips onto her thin lips and I gave her deep tongue. She responded in kind. She wrapped her arms around me, then her legs. The words of Captain Kirk entered my mind: *to boldly go where no man has gone before*.

So there I was, about to enter virgin territory, when out of the blue and contrary to every masculine instinct I had, contrary to what my entire being desperately craved, contrary – and I didn't think about this at the time, but it would become very important later – to what Mercyx's entire being craved, I made the fatal decision, a decision that simultaneously haunts me and defines who I am today.

I rolled off of Mercyx. And then I said something, I said, "Let's not do this. Let's wait."

It all sounded so beautiful when it left my mouth, so noble. "I mean, why spoil it?" I said. "You've waited this long – we'll just – we'll just fucking get married. It's so backassward, it's cool. It's like post-post-modern. It's, well, it's totally like part of your vintage virgin plan. I mean, if we were normal people, high-school sweethearts, or religious freaks, it would be lame; but the fact that we're not, that we're like these weird urban people who are supposed to have like hundreds of partners before they ever get hitched, and then when they do they get divorced three or four times, I mean it makes it sort of cool, because we're not doing the normal thing for our, like, peer group. I mean, how many bike messengers marry comic book artists at the age of twenty-two? It's like some sort of hybrid between being hard core and being domestic. It's like … it's like … domesticore. We'll like create our own subculture. It –"

"Flynn," Mercyx flipped me over. I'd been hovering over her, propped up by my arms, going off the rails on my idea train, my hard-on receding. Mercyx sat bolt upright, her arms crossed over her breasts. "I don't–"

"But I'm serious." I don't know if I was actually serious; I was too inspired by this sudden idea to be serious.

Mercyx looked at me sharply, her brows knotted. I couldn't read her expression. "Shouldn't you be more cautious? It sounds perfect, this little dream of yours, but it's also, well, kind of a fantasy. You don't know me. I'm just starting to tell you what I'm about. Maybe I don't want. Maybe I want–"

I was looking at the ceiling while she spoke. I wasn't really listening. I was happy. Mercyx and I were having this conversation. It was a breakthrough. We'd never had a conversation like this. We were like a couple now, and it was only a matter of time before Mercyx was mine. I interrupted her again. I didn't want to talk anymore.

"Let's do The Bridge of the Gods next Sunday, after Booker does his thing," I said.

Mercyx looked at me–the smile on my face, the palms behind my head, the way I was staring at the ceiling. I can still see myself lying like that, so smug, so unaware of what I was missing. Mercyx must have seen the smugness then too.

"Okay," Mercyx said curtly, stopping her confessional and settling back into typical Mercyxish.

"So where's the Thermarest?" I asked

Mercyx didn't answer that. The Thermarest was in plain sight at my feet. She began pulling the teddy bears from the shelf instead. Tucking them into her bed one by one. It was clearly a ritual she had–it was very OCD and cute. I blew up the Thermarest while she was tucking in the bears. I loved Mercyx. Mercyx was so mine.

"Will you tuck me when you're done?" I asked

"Sure," Mercyx said.

I missed the coldness in her voice.

"I NEED TEXT, MAN," SAID CHESTER. "WE CAN'T blow this. You need to talk to Dougie."

It was Monday. I'd ridden my bike back from the Bug Cave, wearing Sunday's bloodied, soggy cycling clothes. One would think Chester would've commented on this when he saw me in the doorway. Given his vantage point, however, he couldn't see me. Sometime in the week when I was away, Chester had placed a cubicle in the middle of my living room. Trash was piled up around it. From inside its walls, Chester was speaking to me. "You have no idea, do you?"

I didn't. I walked around the fortress to find its entrance. A path had been cleared in the garbage so you could get through, like shoveled snow.

"#2 sold out."

I tried to catch up. "*His Church That Sunday*?"

"Two hundred copies. One of the buyers at Powell's got a copy at Doug's shop, and when he read it he flipped. They put the issues on the center rack at the front of the store, and the small press guy–you know, Sampson or whatever his name is–wrote up a kick-ass review of it, and by the time the weekend was over they were gone. Doug went over twice to refill the racks."

"That's crazy," I said.

"Yeah, no shit. This is huge, man. It's at Powell's! And it's not hidden in the zine section behind the café so the grandmas won't see it, it's fucking front and center. Dougie's got to get more of the other two on the shelves. This is crazy."

The circumstance wasn't the only thing that was crazy. Chester was crazy. He clearly hadn't showered in about a week. He reeked. His hands, his T-shirt, his jeans, they were all blackened with ink. His face was smudged. The word ART was still permanent markered on his forehead. He looked like a madman. I didn't say anything.

"So you don't have the text yet?"

"Maybe tonight." To be honest, the comic had been the last thing on my mind.

"No, no, no," Chester said, "that's good. Don't write it out yet. We need to make some operational changes, and Dougie thinks it's best if he talks to you about it first, you know, before you start writing. Plus, well, he's got some money for you."

I didn't see. Operational changes didn't sound good. I looked at Chester warily.

Chester picked up on my look. "Don't worry, it's not bad. You … well, you'll understand when you see Number Three."

He fumbled through a pile of garbage at the feet of his drafting table. The comic was so smudged it looked like it was twenty years old, not brand new. He handed it to me. I cringed from his stench.

"Look, man, I'm going to go out – I've got some money to spend," and then, as some sort of afterthought, he said, "that Mercyx friend of yours is a total tease. You guys, never, you know?"

I left Chester's question hanging. I had this sudden very unbidden vision of Chester banging Mercyx on the dirty brown shag carpet of the living room, surrounded by bean-stained Taco Bell wrappers. I know it didn't happen but I had the vision nonetheless. Mercifully, Chester didn't linger. He opened the apartment door and stepped out. As he was going, he said, "That girl doesn't have a clue about what she wants."

C HESTER'S COMMENT ABOUT MERCYX THREW me. And when I am thrown, my natural inclination is to go somewhere to think, and the place where I do my best thinking is the shower.

I have this theory that all good decisions are made in the shower. I think this is why Booker and Mercyx had weird showers in the houses they lived in, and why the decisions they made were both good and weird. Me, I was more into the small, low-key, sliding-glass door and lots of privacy shower. My decisions required deeper thought and less spontaneity. Not that my decisions weren't weird – but they required a little more slow-brewing to come out right.

I quickly forgot about Chester's comment and began thinking about what had passed between Mercyx and me last night, and about how a door that shouldn't have been opened was open. All it would take was a laugh, a chuckle, and the door would shut. It would be easy to do, easy to call Mercyx and say what a great lark the whole thing was. Of course I didn't want to get married! I was twenty-two. Marriage at twenty-two is for happy people who live in Iowa and get too much sun. I was a zinester. Zinesters don't get married! They exist to bring the median family size down, not up. How silly I had been last night.

There were so many easy ways out, so many easy ways to shut that door. And yet – well there it was – a very different world on the other side of the door. The possibilities of it coursed through me, warm and comforting and happy – really fucking happy. A wife – me, Flynn, just a boring old shoe with a really sexy wife. And we could have sex, whenever we wanted, sex without condoms and pills and worrying about STDs. These things, these things that couldn't possibly be for me, they could be for me! There it was, an open door! A beautiful, unbelievable open door!

Who knows how Mercyx would react. I didn't know her head. I still didn't know her masks, didn't know that the shortness and coolness was just a cover for nervousness. How would she react? What would rejection feel like? I didn't know. But then again, what difference did it make? So she said no? Did I care? I'd been dressed up in a cheerleader's outfit and had beer poured all over me. How could I care?

As I sat there in the steam, with the water pounding me in the chest, I experienced what can only be labeled an epiphany, not unlike the wavy onrush of an ecstasy high, or the flush of the Holy Spirit in a revival tent. I knew, then, that I was about to enter into my true existence, my true life – whatever the heck that was. And I was happy. And content. All the teenage angst, all the post-college depression, it all fell from me.

This sounds really corny when I write about it. And I suppose we have a lot of these moments in our lives, these sort of fake epiphanies in the shower that don't amount to much. But this one, this epiphany, it ended up leading to a lot. And ever since that day – well, I've been a more peaceful person. So if it should ever happen that you have one of these epiphanies, and it doesn't have to be about getting married at twenty-two, it can be about something entirely different, like quitting your day job and becoming a writer, or like quitting trying to be a writer and getting a day job, or whatever; you'll know it's an epiphany because it'll happen in some alone moment and your hair, despite the cliché, really will stand on end and you'll sob uncontrollably.

If ever you should have an epiphany – and I think you know what I'm talking about – latch onto it, no matter how small or large the epiphany, and try your best to make it happen. You might make a fool of yourself, but better to make a fool of yourself than to spend your life jealous of the fools.

T HE EPIPHANY THAT I HAD IN THE SHOWER gave me direction. It was getting late in the day, but I still had time. I put on my bike clothes, carried by bike from its perch on my balcony down the front stairs and rode it west down Alberta Street. My destination was Jantzen Beach, which isn't a beach at all, but rather a huge shopping mall, designed like all the outlet malls these days, acres of giant cinder block warehouses with miles of parking lot in between.

I rode west and then north up to Jantzen Beach, which lies very conveniently on the Washington/Oregon border, so that all the Washingtonians can take advantage of Oregon's lack of a sales tax; and what I did, parking my humble little bicycle amongst those miles of metal, was walk into a Toys "R" Us, one of those toy stores stuffed to the gills with the latest super-skinny girl dolls and the latest heavily-armed boy dolls, and poke around until near the front of the store, actually in one of the check-out lines, I found a six-pack of fake plastic rings for ninety-nine cents, the ones that end up in Christmas stockings or Halloween bags; and I purchased this; and I went outside; and I opened the bag and dumped out the five rings with colored fake gems and kept the one ring with a white fake gem; and then I rode home, inhaling the diesel fumes and exhaust of thousands of metal boxes on wheels, people driving from Washington to Oregon and back to Washington again, people entering giant warehouses and buying lots and lots of plastic items made with petroleum byproducts, people driving thirty miles to work and thirty miles back to home; and for the first time in my short life I pitied, rather than envied, the people in their Lexuses. I had a bike. I had a comic. I had a ring. What else did I need? I was so glad I wasn't driving back and forth from Washington to Oregon every day.

When it all collapsed, when we finally sucked every last ounce of petroleum product from the soil, when the people were no longer able to shuttle across bridges and states so easily – I'd still have my bike, I'd still have my comic, I'd still have this ring, and if things progressed as I wanted them to progress, I'd still have my woman.

Next Sunday, after Booker's sermon, we'd be riding to The Bridge of the Gods.

COFFEE BREAK #4 ON PORTLAND, OREGON PART TWO

THIS HAS BEEN A HARD GOSPEL TO WRITE, AND THE REASON IT HAS BEEN HARD IS BECAUSE THE WHOLE TIME I'VE BEEN WRITING IT, I'VE BEEN AWARE OF HOW PASSIONATE PEOPLE ARE ABOUT RELIGION. EVERY TIME BOOKER SWEARS, OR SAYS SOMETHING BLASPHEMOUS, OR GETS SOME POINT OF CHRISTIAN THEORY WRONG, I CAN FEEL SOMEONE TAKING THIS BOOK AND DROPKICKING IT ACROSS THEIR ROOM.

WHAT HAPPENS NEXT IN THIS GOSPEL IS EVEN HARDER TO WRITE, BECAUSE WHILE PEOPLE GET PASSIONATE ABOUT RELIGION, THEY SEEM TO GET EVEN MORE PASSIONATE ABOUT POLITICS, ESPECIALLY IN THE UNITED STATES OF AMERICA, WHERE POLITICS HAS GOTTEN SO DEEPLY DIVIDED.

UNFORTUNATELY FOR YOUR SCRIBE, THOUGH, THE SHORT MINISTRY OF JOSEPH PATRICK BOOKER TAKES PLACE IN A VERY POLITICAL TIME, AS WELL AS A VERY POLITICAL PLACE, AND ALTHOUGH THE ZINESTERS AND CYCLISTS AND, ERR, WOMEN WHO BOOKER HUNG AROUND WITH WEREN'T NATURALLY POLITICAL, AT LEAST IN THE SENSE THAT DIDN'T NORMALLY WEAR ELEPHANT OR DONKEY PINS AND SOLICIT STRANGERS IN FRONT OF GROCERY STORES, PRETTY MUCH EVERY HUMAN BEING IN PORTLAND, OREGON HAD AN OPINION ABOUT THE ELECTION THAT WAS GETTING READY TO TAKE PLACE IN THE FALL OF 2004.

THE OPINION WHICH PRETTY MUCH EVERY HUMAN BEING IN PORTLAND, OREGON HAD, I SHOULD MENTION, WAS EXACTLY THE SAME—GEORGE W. BUSH WAS A FUCKING IDIOT, AND JOHN KERRY, HIS OPPONENT, SHOULD BE SUPPORTED WITH ALL THE ENERGY ONE COULD MUSTER, DESPITE THE FACT THAT HE SEEMED A BIT OF A WUSS. BOOKER, OF COURSE, HAD A LOT OF ENERGY, SO I SUPPOSE IT COMES AS NO SURPRISE THAT HE MUSTERED IT.

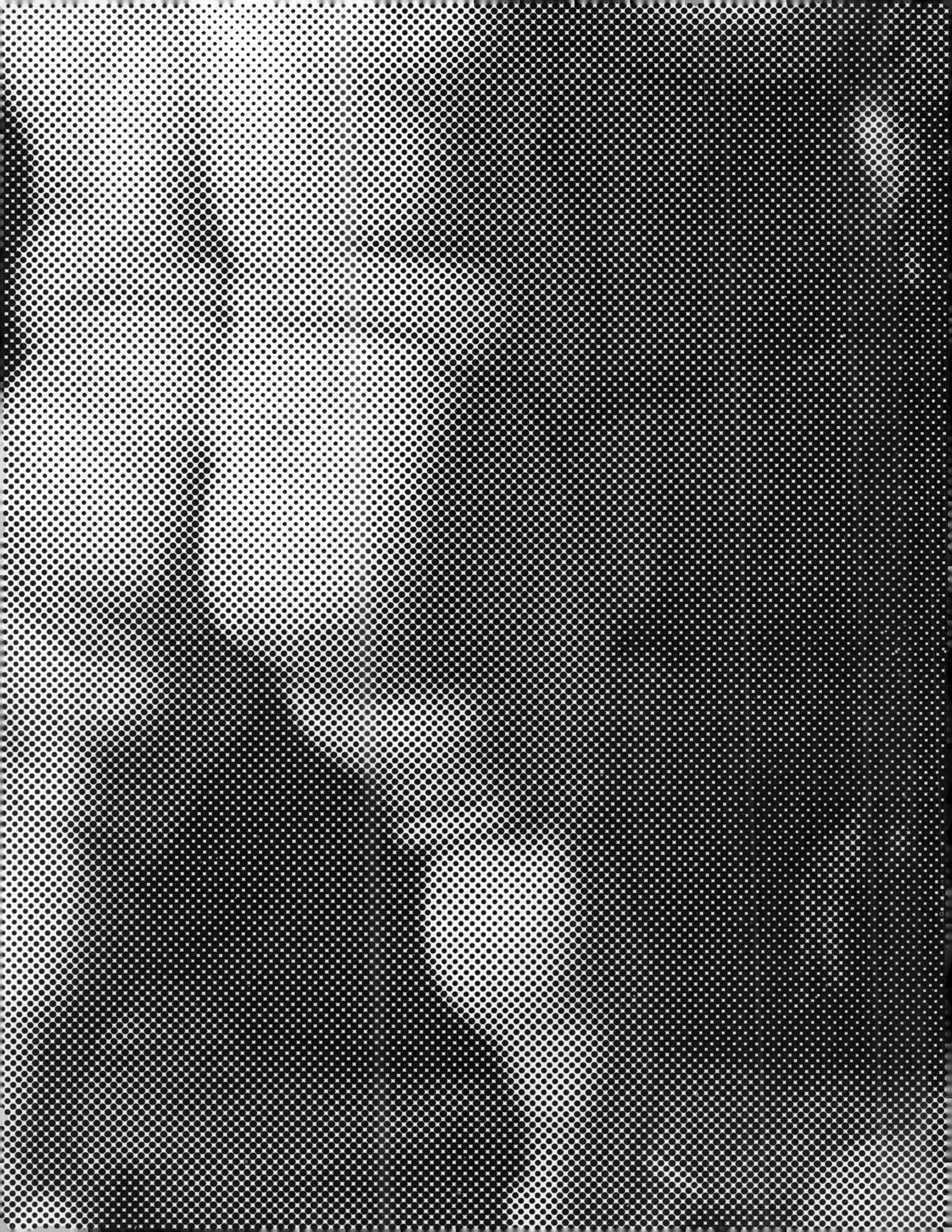

THE SECOND BOOK OF BOOKER TO THE AMERICANS

Chapter XVII

Where Two Lesbians and a Guy with a Skull Tattooed on His Head Found a New Religion

and Where the Rest of Us Are Quite Surprised by the Proceedings

THEY LAY IN THEIR PINK COFFIN, TWELVE OF THEM, PRICKED BY PRETzels, an O of pain frosted on their faces: voodoo dolls from Voodoo Doughnuts. I could relate. ¶ For the last few days – the supply of Vicodin one of Mercyx's roommates provided wearing thin – I'd avoided movement as much as possible, but no matter what I did, whether I stood or sat or lay down, some bruised part of my body recoiled in protest. ¶ This, of course, was only a small part of the reason my enthusiasm for Booker's enterprise had waned. Half the people who showed up the previous Sunday

were absent, and those of us who remained, with few exceptions, were all either physically bruised, emotionally bruised, or both. A human could handle only so much foolishness.

I chose a doughnut from the box, removed a pretzel, and with my finger, spread chocolate over the hole the pretzel had left. It was ten o'clock, time for coffee and doughnuts, and I was the only person in attendance. I wondered if Booker would have to hit the streets again, waiting for some unsuspecting cyclist to suffer a flat.

There was a knock on the door. Doughnut in hand, I answered it. Two women were standing there, petite with mousy brown hair. I knew who they were without asking.

The lesbians.

I gawked. Raspberry filling dribbled down my chin. I wanted to hug them.

"Is this the church of Joseph Patrick Booker?" one of them asked.

I had to know. "Are you the l …" I caught myself. They were certainly the lesbians, but I couldn't call them the lesbians. "…ladies he met in Arkansas?"

"Yes," the other said. They looked at me skeptically, as if bailing was an attractive option.

"He gave a sermon about meeting you once," I said.

This didn't seem to alleviate the skepticism. I tried to wipe the jelly off my chin. I smeared it.

"Is there a service today?" one of them asked.

The way she asked it threw me off. She was so formal and serious, like she didn't get it at all. "Sure, yeah," I stammered.

There was no reason for me to stammer. They must have thought I was mentally challenged.

"Can we come in?" the other asked.

It dawned on me what was happening: the lesbians thought this was a real church. They were expecting a greeter, or whatever they call the people who hand out bulletins and hymnals at church front doors. "Oh yes, sure, come in. He's … there's doughnuts and coffee. You can have some now. Our church …" The way I said our church, as if were really a church, and as if I was really a member, sounded odd coming out of my mouth. " … it's a little different."

They seemed to relax at that. "That's what he told us," they said.

———

CHESTER ARRIVED AFTER THE LESBIANS, A piece of duct tape covering the ART on his forehead. Mercyx came next, towing David. She surprised me with a peck on the cheek. Beale popped in after that, bleary-eyed from a Dungeons & Dragon all-nighter. Finally, and rather tentatively, I noticed a guy slipped in who it took me a while to recognize. It was Ape Man. He'd shaved. That was the extent of the gathering. On a relative scale, it was rather sedate. Diogenes was the most notable absence. (He had yet to turn up after disappearing into the Lark Mountain Wilderness. After Sophia had survived the accident and not pressed charges, the Portland P.D. had called off the hunt.) Also missing was Booker's standard accompaniment, the unexplained female companion he always seemed to have draped around him.

Booker came out of his vestibule dressed entirely in white. The cassock he wore – an altar boy's cassock – actually fit him. The smile that always owned his face was notably absent. He looked something that, surprisingly, he'd never looked to me before. He looked small.

He stopped the minute he spotted them at the table.

"Maggie? Lizzie?" he asked.

They smiled at the mention of their names. They seemed tickled that he'd remembered them.

"You … you're here." The smile returned to Booker's face. He looked at them in amazement, like you'd look at a lover resurrected from the grave.

"This is so …," he was stammering as been as I'd been stammering, " … perfect."

The girls looked awkward. You could tell they weren't used to celebrity.

"I …" And his gaze dropped from the lesbians and latched onto the rest of us. "I'm humbled."

He looked humbled, too. He wasn't his ebullient self. Something had changed.

"This is what we do, at this church. There is no priest up here." He held a hand up high. "And congregation, down here." He held a hand down low. "There's just the people." He put his hands together, interlocked his fingers, and wiggled them.

None of us was sure how to take this new Zen Booker. It was like he was Yoda.

"It's the way all Christian churches should be, and the way they were, back before three thirteen anno Domini, back before Jesus was Christ and Messiah and King, back before Matthew, Mark, Luke, and John became the indisputable gospel truth."

He'd started to go off, but checked himself. The lesbians were looking at him curiously, not like he was crazy, like the rest of us looked at him, but like he was saying things that made sense.

"You see …" *You see* was always trouble with Booker, it meant he was starting what was sure to be a long and convoluted story. We were all just standing around the "altar," which he'd covered in a white altar cloth, matching the white theme he'd concocted for today's occasion. Knowing what was coming, I took a seat. Mercyx and the others followed. *You see* was just as effective as *be seated*.

Booker continued. "Three thirteen after death was when the great cover-up occurred."

"The edict," Maggie said.

Booker raised an eyebrow as if he'd suddenly discovered someone formidable.

"That's right, the Edict of Milan. So everybody follow me here, and don't forget to have plenty of coffee and doughnuts while I'm at it."

He had quite the spread in the pink box today. Besides the Voodoo dolls, there were all kinds of sprinkled wonders. Doughnut varieties with names like Grape Ape and Tangerine Dream. Those who hadn't yet partook did so. One was about all I could take. I stuck with my coffee.

VS.

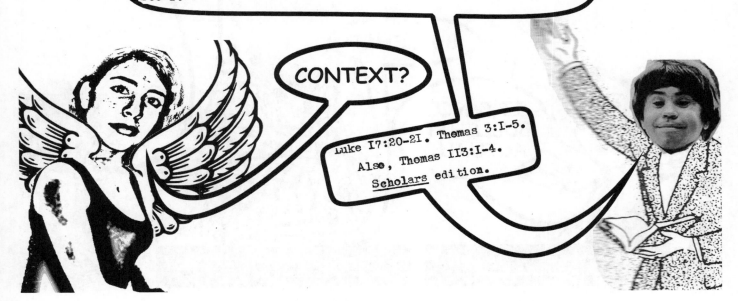

Before the year 313, there wasn't any sort of unified Christian thought. There were Christians, who were walking around without sandals like Jesus, living lives of voluntary poverty, & who carried around the sayings of Jesus on various scrolls, some of which contradicted each other. There were also, strangely, followers of John the Baptist still wandering around. John the Baptist had preached that the end was near, & that when the end came the good were going to go to a happy place in the clouds. This was very much the opposite of what Jesus had taught--Jesus suggested that the Kingdom of God was something that existed here, on the planet Earth, right now, if only people had the vision to see it--

CONTEXT?

Luke 17:20-21. Thomas 3:1-5. Also, Thomas 113:1-4. Scholars edition.

So here's where we get to the Edict of Milan in 313. Christianity is running rampant throughout the Roman Empire, despite frequent feedings of Christians to the lions. No one's doing any work, & Constantine, the Roman Emperor at the time, has to come up with a solution fast. So what he does is--& this is brilliant, Constantine should probably be considered the founder of modern Christianity over everybody else--he invites all the Christian leaders over to visit him in Constantinople, & in a process over which he presides, he decides to accept Christianity in the Roman Empier, but only after he makes all the rules.

BULLSHIT

IT'S NOT BULLSHIT, ACTUALLY.

Ape Man wasn' sure how to respond to earnestness. He looked around as if he wished his C.H.V.C.K. buddies were here to back him up.

Constantine places the Kingdom of God in heaven, where
John the Baptist wanted it, thinking that people looking
to the skies for the good life are going to be a whole
lot less trouble than people trying to create one here.
He turns Jesus into a king, a savior, & a miracle worker—
someone to be in awe of.

He tops off the conference by making it a heresy to think
otherwise. He declares Matthew, Mark, Luke & John the
only gospels, & orders any scrolls where Jesus is an ordinary dude who doesn't perform miracles destroyed.

Fifty years ago, though, something funny happened. One of the scrolls that Constantine ordered destroyed turned up. Apparently, some early Christians who didn't like what was happening sealed one of the gospels into a bottle & buried it in theearth. In 1950, some farmer is out hoeing his fields in Palestine, & lo & behold his hoe—

HO? WHERE'S HIS HO?

WHAT"S YOUR DEAL, APEMAN?

His digging turned up a scroll supposedly written by Thomas. It's interesting that Thomas is the maligned apostle named in Luke as being the doubter, because in Thomas's gospel, there isn't anything doubtful. The Gospel of Thomas is simply a book of quotes. No miracles, just quotes. It was simply a book which told t e early Christians how they could live their lives in a way that was compatible with his teachings.

THE POINT?

IT'S TRUE, THOUGH. NOT MANY PEOPLE KNOW THIS STUFF.

Mercyx interrupted this time. She'd been swinging her legs under the table for some time now, impatiently. Without anyone here to physically assault him or blow up his vehicle, it was clear that Booker might never stop, that he might preach the morning away.

Booker had been standing while the rest of us were sitting, regaling us from the head of the table, although his stature put everyone at eye level. He scooted a chair out and sat. There were pillows on the chair, so he looked like a toddler in a booster seat. He grabbed a doughnut out of the box – a maple bar topped with bacon. Those of us used to some sort of dramatic ending, or a tirade about marriage, or at least some good swearing were a bit disappointed. What was this sudden sincerity? According to Booker, wasn't Jesus supposed to be a clown?

Booker looked up for a moment. It was clear he had at least one – if not a hundred – more things to say. It seemed a bit disconnected from everything he'd said before, but it wasn't, once I'd thought about it.

"Do you know what faith is? Do you know what it really is? Faith isn't belief in nonsense. Faith is believing that you can stare down the barrel of a gun without having anything in yours and still win."

He took a bite out of the maple bar. Crème filling squirted out the end.

———

THE DOUGHNUTS WERE MANGLED. THE COFFEE cold. We sat there, not sure what to say or do. This is where there was supposed to be chaos, and where Mercyx and I were supposed to leave and go for a bike ride.

"So what are we going to do?" Maggie asked. She reminded me of a squirrel.

"They're not going to do anything," Lizzie said. If Maggie was yin, Lizzie was yang. "Pearls before swine."

Booker was still in the middle of his doughnut. The crème filling oozing out the end of it made him impossible to watch. "We're just starting," he said.

The lesbians looked us over to confirm Booker's statement. We all looked away.

"Does your church have a name?" Maggie asked.

I cringed when Maggie asked this question, I thought Booker would have a long-winded answer, but he didn't, he simply said, "No."

Beale lifted his head off the table. We all thought he'd been asleep. There was a dark spot where he'd drooled on the white altar cloth. "The first order of any clan is to construct a banner to fly under," he said. He laid his head back down when he was finished.

"So why don't we name it?" Maggie suggested.

"Okay," Booker said. It was unusual for him to let someone else take over. He seemed bemused by this turn of events.

"I'll start," Maggie said. Really she was more like a chipmunk then a squirrel. Spunky is the word that comes to mind. "How about the Living Church?"

I wanted to gag. Mercyx grunted in revulsion. Chester drew.

"How 'bout Snow Dwarf and the Seven Hipsters?" said Lizzie, in retaliation for Mercyx's grunt.

"Hold on," said Booker. "Let's just brainstorm. Throw anything out that comes to mind. No comments. We'll discuss all the ideas after we've got some solid ones."

David, Mercyx's roommate, spoke this time, and when he spoke, he spoke in his special pot-addled way, not answering the question at all, "It's like you're a band, only there isn't any music."

Everyone looked at David like he was being weird, which he was. Booker still didn't know what David's name was. He asked him, "What's your name?"

"David," David said, and then he went on, off on his own mental tangent, "I was thinking, you're like a band, so you should have a name that sounds like a band. Why don't you name it after that new gospel? Thomas. You could call yourself The Thomas Sect."

"Sexy," said Mercyx.

"Totally." I had to admit, it was sexy.

"It's perfect!" Booker said.

Chester drew.

Booker reached over the table. He grabbed David by the shoulders, and kissed him on the top of his head, or rather, to complete the visual image, he kissed the top of the brains tattooed on David's head. Maple glaze handprints remained on David's shoulders. "David, this is so fucking brilliant. You deserve that name. You deserve the name of a king. King David. That's what I'm going to call you from now on, King David. Shit. It's so –"

"Ding!" It was Lizzie. "Times up, Booker."

Booker was not to be deterred. "But don't you see, it's the name. We're like, the doubters, like Thomas, and we have this gospel that can turn the doubters into believers, and also, well it's like Mercyx said, the word sect is sexy, and kind of old-school, it has a slight feel of edginess and blasphemy to –"

"Ding," it was Mercyx this time. She seemed to like Lizzie's attitude.

"What?" asked Booker.

"Times up," said Mercyx.

"So we should vote," said Booker.

"But there's only been two suggestions," said Maggie.

"Any more suggestions?" asked Booker.

No one responded. It seemed settled. The Thomas Sect was a decent name. You'd think, being a scribe and all, that I'd have a suggestion, but I wasn't particularly good at on-the-spot decision making. I'd probably come up with something two weeks from now.

"Great. Now we're going to vote," Booker said. We'll make it a show of hands. "Who votes for The Living Church?"

Chester was no longer drawing. He'd pushed his papers into a neat stack. He got up from his chair and walked behind us. Starting at the head of the table, where Mad Max sat across from Booker, he placed the first page of his stack face-up on the table. On the page was a meticulously illustrated initial C.

Maggie and Lizzie raised their hands.

"Who votes for The Thomas Sect?" said Booker.

The pages continued to come down. There was an H. And a V. And an R.

Booker and David raised their hands. The rest of us watched Chester. He laid down a C. Then an H. Then a 3.

"It's even, I guess," said Booker.

Chester placed a 1 next to three. Then, in front of Booker, laying it over Booker's éclair drippings, one final 3.

Booker stood up when he realized what it was. His mouth open. The remainder of his doughnut, crème and cake alike, visible in his jaws. The look was akin to horror.

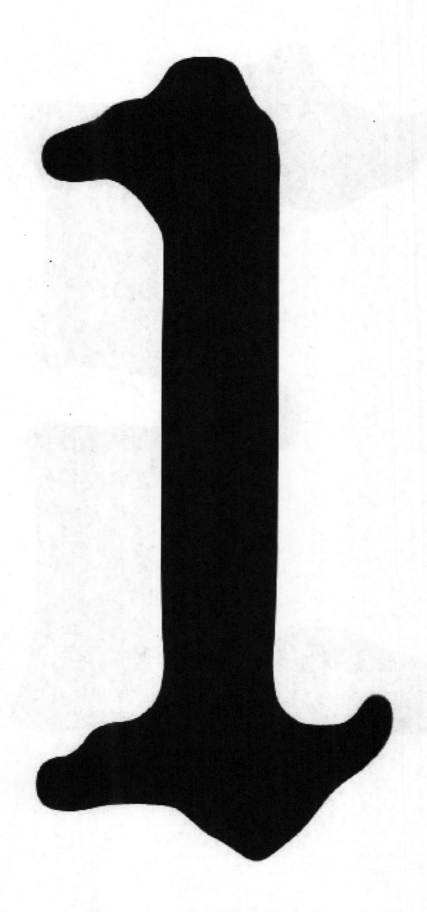

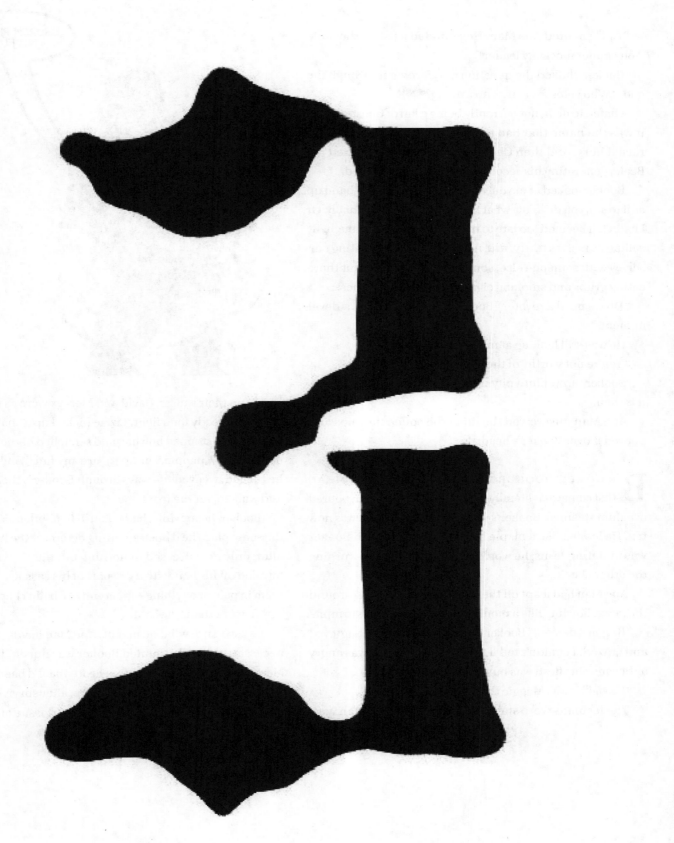

"No!" shouted Ape Man. He pounded a fist on the table. "You cannot mock my leader!"

Booker choked the question out, forcing it through the goo. "Who votes for c.h.v.r.c.h. 313?"

I hated to do it, not currently being a fan of Chester's, but it was the name that had to be. I raised my hand. Mercyx raised hers. And then Chester, with a flourish, raised his. Beale, generating his second pool of droll, abstained.

Booker looked at me quizzically while I held my hand up, as if to say, you do know what this means. I didn't actually. Or I hadn't. It seemed too late to put my hand down, though. By calling ourselves c.h.v.r.c.h. 313 we were associating ourselves with someone else, someone who was still out there, eating grubs and smoking cigarettes in the wilderness.

"Do we need a revote?" Booker said. "Given the ... development."

He was still looking at me. I shook my head.

"You're not worthy of the title!" shouted Ape Man.

Booker threw him a pitying look. "Church three thirteen," it is then.

Ape Man unscrewed the lid of the coffee thermos and poured it over Booker's head.

———

"B E GONE!" BOOKER WAS STEAMING, AND I MEAN that somewhat literally. The coffee that had been poured over him steamed. Booker's white altar boy cassock was now tan. He looked like a maple bar. It struck me that if Booker was imitating Jesus, he wouldn't be yelling, he'd be turning the other cheek.

Ape Man had leapt off the altar and was dancing around the pews, howling like a monkey and scratching his armpits.

"Be gone, demon!" Booker continued. He looked bug-eyed and crazed. I couldn't tell if this was because he was angry or because his flesh was burning.

"Leave!" it was Maggie this time.

The lesbians were standing now, facing Ape Man with hands on their waists. David and Mercyx were as well. They all looked ready for a fight. Lizzie picked up a chair.

Ape Man stopped howling and scratched his head. "None of you *church* people," he spat, "are any fun." And with that he turned, weaved his way through Booker's theater seats, and walked out the front door.

Booker, meanwhile, had taken of his clothes. He stood in the same place he'd been standing before, at the head of the altar, only now dressed in nothing but tightie whities. He toweled off his hair with a dry part of his cassock. He didn't seem in pain or anything–apparently he hadn't been scalded.

"To work then," he said.

I wasn't sure what he meant. Ape Man having made the necessary scene, I assumed Booker was finished, and that Mercyx and I would now be free to do what I'd been thinking all week about doing. The day before, after surviving another shift at Muddy's, I'd created a Word Art issue of *OTT*:

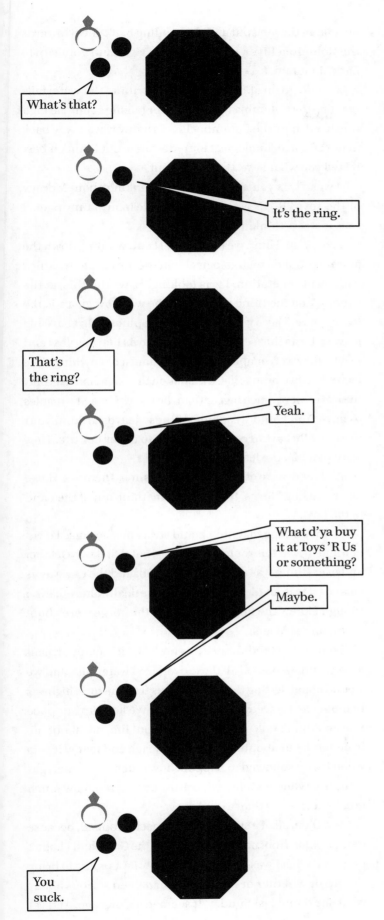

Maggie, however, seemed to be on Booker's page. "We should do something for the elections."

Like I mentioned before, we lived in Portland, Oregon, in the Fall of 2004, and therefore when elections were mentioned, there was no need to discuss which elections or which side we were on. The only question to any of us was: What should we do about it?

My answer to that, at this stage in my life, was nothing. I hated George W. Bush as much as the next guy, but working on an election campaign – getting signatures and soliciting voters and all that – was for earnest people. I mean, you had to have long hair and listen to Phish and be slightly starry-eyed. Or an old lady. You had to be one of the two.

"I'm so glad you're here," said Booker. It looked like he was, too. As mentioned in *His Church That Sunday #2*, Booker had some significant equipment, and bundled up in those tightie whities, he looked quite happy. No one else noticed, or said anything, though. Without C.H.V.C.K. there, everyone was serious.

"I work for the Democratic National Committee already," Maggie continued, "and this space would be perfect for a call center, and all you guys … I mean, you're the people we need. There's certain people who vote all the time, but you guys can get the new voters … you're cool, you know."

It was weird being called cool. I always thought of myself as sort of a dork, but I knew what she was saying. It wasn't so much that I was cool as it was that I was aloof. There's kind of a whole generation of us come to think of it.

It suddenly dawned on me that we were being recruited.

Booker's woody seemed to grow. "This is exactly want I wanted," he said. "To be an active church, to be …" he used Maggie's word here, and it made me cringe " …a living church, a church that acts on its beliefs. Let's … can you talk to them? Can you tell them that we're up for it? We're all up for it, right?"

Up for it. I started to laugh. It was like … well, it was like church. There was Booker, in nothing but a coffee-stained pair of Fruit of Looms, recruiting us all for a political campaign. Everyone was staring at me.

"What?" Lizzie asked, directing the question to me.

"It's …" This was one of those times when the truth just wasn't what I wanted to say. Booker was so oblivious to his own comedy. He wanted to be serious, and yet looking at him, how could you take him seriously? I liked him, though. There was no reason to make a dick joke. Besides, I really wanted to take the ring that was burning a hole in my fanny pack and find a way to get it on Mercyx's finger. At this point, I'd agree to anything.

"... just funny, how quickly this is all moving. It's a great idea," I said. "Ask them what they need from us, Maggie. We all want to volunteer."

It was strange that I spoke for the entire group like that. It wasn't like me. No one objected, though. Booker, Mercyx, David, Lizzie, Beale, all nodded in agreement. It was like we had a new leader.

"So next Sunday," I said. I was finding a way to wrap this up. "Maggie, you'll talk to the DNC, right? And when you come you'll tell us how we can move forward." (I actually used that phrase – move forward.)

When I got up, my heart nearly dropped out of my chest and knees nearly buckled. It wasn't nerves about going door-to-door with a clipboard. It was that in about three hours, in the time it would take for Mercyx and me to ride to The Bridge of the Gods, I had planned to ask for Mercyx's hand in marriage.

Chapter XVIII

After Much Ado, The Bridge of the Gods

AFTER LEAVING BOOKER'S CHURCH, WE rode away wordlessly, as was our custom. The day was perfectly clear: a rare, crisp autumn day. Our route started the same as the ride to Lark Mountain: flat at the beginning, a smooth multi-use path along the shore of the Columbia, then a tuck inland to a narrow, curvy strip of pavement that skirted the wide, mellow Sandy River, then upwards, towards Vista Point and Lark Mountain.

We rode steadily. There was a little bit of a headwind, so we took turns in front, keeping up the pace for a few minutes, then pulling aside to let the other one pass, then kicking it in the back, letting the other one carry forward the momentum.

We stopped at Vista Point, at the exact spot that we'd stopped at ten days ago. We looked down. It was still there, our conjoined chunks. We shared a couple Clif Bars and rode

on, taking the left split and descending back down towards the Columbia River, rather than the right and going up to Lark Mountain.

I could go on about the ride, describing the waterfalls that line the Columbia River Gorge, or talking about the highway itself, how the Columbia River Highway was, way back in the 20s, a technological tour-de-force, but I think it best if I tell you what I was thinking about.

I wasn't, as you might imagine, thinking about Mercyx, or the Toys "R" Us ring burning a hole in my fanny pack. I was, instead, thinking about leaves.

After Vista Point, we began a descent, winding down the aforementioned technological tour-de-force under a thick canopy of vegetation. I was looking, as we did this, at the canopy, and the thing that struck me was how gigantic the leaves were. There were pines, but the pines didn't have big leaves; it was those trees that have leaves like maples (and maybe they were maples, I'm not a botanist or anything). The leaves had five prongs like the ones on the Canadian flag, only the leaves were much bigger than the leaves I imagine maples to have. You could wrap one of these leaves around your torso. Dolly Parton could use them to cover her tits. They were that big, the leaves.

And there were other gigantic leaves, too. There were huge leaves on huge ferns. It was like something out of the Land of the Lost.

It was strange that this should strike me, because I'd ridden and driven this route many times, but that it was October, and everything was at its most colorful, and the day was as clear as it was, made things seem genetically altered, even though I knew the flora and fauna of the gorge were about as organic as it gets.

Mercyx and I rode under this prehistoric canopy of giant leaves, and we passed all these oversized waterfalls, and we wound about, letting the route take us from historic highway to modern-day freeway to bike path. We kept up our pace line and didn't talk. And I thought about life, not about life in general, but about plant life – how rich and loamy it gets when it's just allowed to happen, how much wilder and glorious it is when it's allowed to grow unfettered, how much greater a forest is than a garden.

And then, all of a sudden, my stomach dropped, because it was right in front of us, The Bridge of the Gods, and I hadn't prepared what I was going to say or how I was going to bring this up or whether or not Mercyx had been serious about what she'd said last Sunday. It seemed so long ago. And yet we were there at the place I'd planned to say all the things I hadn't planned to say, and so of course I had to get on with it, even though I didn't know how to proceed.

The bike path ended and dropped us into a town called Cascade Locks, and then we rode around a vehicle-choked curlicue until we arrived at the foot of the bridge. By now, my heart was sort of fluttering. Mercyx and I hadn't said a word to each other for two hours, and all of a sudden I was supposed to break into *will you marry me?* How was that going to happen?

And then there was the bridge itself. It sounds romantic and all, The Bridge of the Gods, and you imagine some high span with glorious archways like the Golden Gate, but The Bridge of the Gods is nothing like that. It's gray steel, and it looks more like it's constructed with rickety roller coaster scaffolding than the thick, elegant piping on the Golden Gate. It's also quite a bit narrower, and it doesn't have a separate bike or pedestrian lane, and there's no cement or blacktop or pavement on it – the whole base is a steel grate.

Like I said, I'd been over the bridge before, but I'd remembered it differently. In my mind it was quite a bit more graceful and romantic. I'd imagined us standing together looking over the edge and gazing into each other's eyes, and then me popping the question. Quite clearly, this wasn't going to work at all. There was nowhere to stop – we'd get run over. I mean, it would actually be dangerous to stop on The Bridge of the Gods.

Mercyx and I circled around the curlicue and got behind a line of cars to pay our fifty cent toll. The tollbooth, I might add, was (and still is) the nicest feature of The Bridge of the Gods. It sits underneath this awesome covered bridge, the quaint ones you read about in tour guides or see in chick flicks like *The Bridges of Madison County*. Whether the covered bridge was part of the design of The Bridge of the Gods or whether it was packed up from somewhere else and brought in to cover the tollbooth is a mystery to me, but it makes a nice contrast, this wooden structure, with all the gray steel girders above it.

I paid the toll for both of us, and we started over the bridge. I felt panicked as we rode over. This was my chance, this was my moment, and yet here I was, just barely maintaining control of my bike as we rode uncomfortably over the steel girders. We made it up the upslope and then started down, and then passed the Welcome to Washington sign, and then under the low-key, old-fashioned archway that says The Bridge of the Gods, and then it was over, I hadn't stopped on the bridge to ask Mercyx if she'd spend the rest of my life with me. It was the end. If I couldn't ask her now, after all this planning, how would I ever find the courage to ask her.

After the bridge we hit the big highway, Highway 14, that runs along the Washington side of the Columbia. To head back towards Portland, you turned left. I wasn't at all ready to head back toward Portland, because I hadn't done what I'd set out to do, but then I couldn't go back to the bridge, because I couldn't do on the bridge what I'd planned to do.

There was, to the right, a little turn off, and one of those brown signs that say Historic Marker that usually lead to some bronze plaque proclaiming that a cattle drive or Indian massacre had taken place on the spot three-hundred years ago.

I was so weirdly wound up, and yet I got it out of my mouth, "Let's stop over there."

Mercyx nodded. And then we did it. We rode to the turn off on the right with the Historical Marker, got off the bikes, and then walked a short ways onto a ridge. I continued with my plan. I'd brought my backpack. I pulled a blanket out of it and laid it over a patch of bare dirt, then grabbed a pair of Zip-locked peanut butter and jelly sandwiches. Mercyx sat on it and gazed across the gorge at what we'd just ridden. I sat next to her.

I couldn't believe this was happening. I knew as I sat there, dry-mouthed, having a hard time getting through the peanut butter and jelly, that this was it. It was speak now or forever hold your peace. It wasn't perfect. It wasn't a castle looming over the Mediterranean or a lonesome crag looking over the Pacific or a Venetian gondola. It was much more subtle and personal than those things, and what made it that way was how easily it could be overlooked. No one, in my estimation, had ever come to this little spot, this lonely dirt pullout on a long stretch of freeway, and walked up to this hidden ridge, and looked over a cheap steel-grated bridge, and asked the person they wanted to marry to marry them. This was our spot, Mercyx and my spot, and it would always be our spot, and it wouldn't be anyone else's.

I pondered the panorama. A wall of the deepest green, the Oregon side of the gorge, rose up from the waters of the Columbia. The Columbia itself was deep in color too, darkened from the forest shadow. The bridge we'd just crossed cut diagonally across these two features, the forest and the river, and the bridge suddenly looked more silvered than gray, brightened a bit from the sun.

It was beautiful – not grandiose – but beautiful.

I pulled my fanny pack around, unzipped it, and pulled out the ring. I didn't say anything. I just twirled it around, gazing at its cheap zirconium gem, or whatever the hell a Toys "R" Us ring is made out of. The gem seemed to catch facets of light and gleam despite itself. The silence between us, a silence that had been a calm, quiet silence before, was gone. Replacing it was a loud silence, a silence rising like a fever pitch.

I just did it, still looking at the ring, knowing that she was looking at the ring. I did it despite the fact that I didn't really know Mercyx, and that Mercyx didn't really know me. I did it despite cultural influence to the contrary and common sense. I just did it. I really said it, "Annie, will you marry me?"

I looked up into her eyes.

Mercyx's eyes weren't looking at the ring after all. They were looking at my backpack. Hanging from the zipper was another item gleaming in the sunlight. An item that was ruby red.

A wig.

Mercyx looked at me. Then at the wig. Then, back at me. She stared into my eyes for a while. The silence became uncomfortable, then unbearable. Mercyx turned away. She took a bite out of her sandwich. It must have been like five minutes before she spoke.

"You slept with one of them?"

There were many correct responses to this question. *What the hell are you talking about* would have been good. *I wore it to a c.h.v.c.k. function* would have sufficed. Even *it's like a talisman, I just carry it around* would have been acceptable. None of these would have been a complete lie either.

Stammering "One of who?" however, was not a correct response.

Mercyx's eyes narrowed. "One of his whores."

If I'd swung and missed before, the next one was a line drive right back to the pitcher. "They're not whores."

"You did."

It was my turn to be silent. I stared out at the deep green water that had seemed so perfect to me a moment before. Now it just looked like something convenient to drown in. I had slept with one of them. I didn't remember sleeping with her. I don't know if I enjoyed sleeping with her. I wasn't even sure she was a whore, although based on all the innuendo flying around, it was probably safe to assume she was. But I had slept with one of them. How did I explain this?

Mercyx didn't wait for the answer. My silence was answer enough. "I'm the virgin, so you want to marry me. She's the whore, so you'll screw her on a dime. Fucking typical."

What she was saying, it wasn't true, or at least it wasn't that simple. I'd been inspired by her whole story–the story of her dad being a pornographer and her wanting something deeper, something intimate, something the opposite of what she'd gotten. And I had been taken up by it, and I wanted, well, I wanted something deeper to believe in, too. It had nothing to do with virgins and whores. Fuck, I'd been so drunk. This wasn't fair.

"Cat got your tongue? Or was she a … *kitty*." Mercyx did not say this with mirth. She was up in my face. Her eyes reflected the ruby red of the wig. I know it's a cliché, but if any look could kill, it was the one Mercyx gave me.

I blurted it out. "I don't know."

"You don't know …?"

"I don't know what I did," I said. "That night I ditched you at The Curiosity, I thought something was going on between you and Chester, and I got hammered, and I ended up at Booker's, and the next morning when I woke up this chick was making me breakfast. I think I might have slept with her, yes." I didn't have a right to be mad. But I was. "I really don't–"

"Shut up!" Mercyx'd had enough. She put her hand over my mouth and shoved me, like my head was a shot put. I fell backwards on my ass. My hands landed on thorns.

"You didn't mean to sleep with her, but you're carrying her wig around like a trophy? That's fucked *up*!"

"I–"

"Shut up!"

I shut up. Mercyx hovered over me. She laid the saw blades of her eyes down and began cutting. "I wanted to *sleep* with you, Flynn. And maybe someday, after I slept with you, after many moons had passed, I'd want to marry you. You're normal and you're good and you're not weird. But then you have to go and–"

Mercyx picked a rock up from the ground. She turned towards the river and threw it. I watched its arc, watched it somersault end over end, watched it hang in the air for a moment, seemingly suspended, as if it weren't sure what would happen next, and then I watched it sink fast. There was a kerplunk, a definite splash. Mercyx didn't throw like a girl.

"I don't think we should see each other for a while," Mercyx said.

And then she went for her bike, leaving her half-eaten sandwich on the blanket. I got up to follow, not really knowing what I would say to stop her, but knowing that I needed to. It wasn't like she was saying. The wig wasn't a trophy. It was more, well, like a crucifix. I carried it around with me because with it I'd been humbled, just like Jesus had been humbled. I carried it around with me to remind me that it's better to be honest then cool. I carried it around with me for all sorts of reasons, none of which involved being proud of sleeping with a whore.

I moved too slow. Mercyx hopped into her saddle. She pedaled down the freeway, heading back to Portland on the Washington side. I knew I wasn't man enough to catch her.

I sat back down in that perfect place, the ridge overlooking a bridge dubbed The Bridge of the Gods. On one side of me lay a wig, and on the other lay a Toys "R" Us ring. If the gods were indeed here, here by the silvered bridge and the deep green river, I had a feeling I knew what they were doing.

They were laughing.

I put the ring and wig back in my pocket – more reminders of humility. Then I rode back the way I'd come, across The Bridge of the Gods, along the Oregon side of the Columbia Gorge.

And that's how we returned to Portland: parallel paths, a chasm between us.

Chapter XIX

A Deceptively Uneventful Chapter, In Which Bartholomew Flynn Reads Comic Books and Signs Paperwork

MY LEGS WERE JELLY. THE CAPRICIOUS Columbia Gorge winds swung around in the afternoon, and I was faced with a repeat of the morning's headwind, without Mercyx to draft behind. I arrived home after dark, circumvented Chester's fortress, and fell asleep in my bed. One benefit, I suppose, of being exhausted was that I didn't stay up all night pining after Mercyx.

The next morning when I awoke, lying atop Don Quixote on my nightstand, was an inked but not colored draft copy of *His Church That Sunday* #3: *The Sermon on the Mount*. Not having ever given Chester any text for the comic, I was surprised to see it sitting there. Eager to forget what had taken place yesterday, I picked it up and began flipping through.

It wasn't at all what I expected. Chester had cut out the entirety of Booker's speech, had turned Booker into Diogenes, had replaced Diogenes with Tattoo, had Tattoo dressed as the devil, and had the devil driving Booker's van over the side of the cliff, which wasn't a van anymore but one of those Mexican chicken buses. The only thing true to life was that the bus still had FOUR WHEELS BAD, TWO WHEELS GOOD printed on the side.

The majority of the comic did not take place on the mountain, as it should have, but rather on the drive to it. Inside the bus was drawn a skinny and frightened boy, who was wearing a beret and had the facial features of Chester Fields. Pages of the comic were devoted to imps beating up beret boy, the force of their punches exaggerated with text boxes reading BAM! and KAPOW! and ZOWIE! There were also several pages of Tattoo driving the bus without watching the road, shouting with bloodshot eyes at the passengers from the drivers' seat.

One page explained something I'd wondered about for a while. The top panel had Tattoo yelling, "Paper has no utility in post-carbon transition!" The middle panel showed beret boy bloodied and beaten, his shirt torn and missing its buttons, the imps pinning down his arms and legs. Off-scene, Tattoo was still yelling, "Our scars the only art! Our bicycles the only design!" In the bottom panel an imp snapped a finger. A Sharpie appeared out of thin air. While the other imps held him down, the imp with the Sharpie wrote ART on beret boy's forehead.

(I apologize for not including these comic pages. The reason for their omission will be clear very soon.)

I found myself chuckling at Chester's comic despite myself. It was really funny and imaginative. On the other hand, especially when it got to Booker's actual Sermon on the Mount, it wasn't anything close to what had actually happened. (Chester had Tattoo spouting off about floods and storms and fire destroying all of the world's SUVs while winged horses appeared out of the sky to rescue all those pedaling tall bikes.)

I was surprised at my own reaction to this. What bothered me about it wasn't that Chester had done it without consulting me, what bothered me was that it wasn't historically accurate. I'd taken Booker's designation of me as his scribe to heart.

I wasn't sure yet what to do with this realization, whether to tamp it down and be more realistic or whether to fight Chester over it. I did know one thing, though. It was time for me to visit Dougie Fresh at Ben Dover Books to find out what Chester had meant by "operational changes." I'd been dreading it before, but anything was better than sitting in my bedroom thinking about the fact that I'd blundered a wedding proposal.

PORTLAND IS A CITY WITH A HABIT OF MAKING small things bigger than they actually are, and Ben Dover Books is one of these small things. Everyone in Portland knows about Douglas Yamhill's little downtown bookstore. They gossip about it. They even use it as an example of why this city is better than other cities. Yet for all the hype, Ben Dover Books is housed in a tiny, renovated old barbershop (the antique barber pole outside still runs), has a collection of less than five-hundred titles, and other than regulars like Beale and me, seemingly only gets visited by foreign tourists armed with *Lonely Planet* guidebooks.

Don't get me wrong. Ben Dover Books is a great thing, and Portlanders are right to throw it accolades, but its greatness lies more in its concept than in its actuality, and what makes its concept great is its proprietor, Douglas Yamhill.

Dougie wanted to run a bookstore that was a throwback to Paris in the 30s, when booksellers sold books by people they knew, who were writing books that they liked. He disdained the giant chain bookstores sprouting all over America, with their six-digit inventories and their bored, on-the-clock, staff workers. He hated the abundance of choice. These bookstores didn't *discern* anything. I can hear Dougie arguing now, "How do you know what to buy in a store like that? You don't. There's no direction. My bookstore has an opinion. Everything that's in it is there because I valued it. You can ask me why I put the book in my store and I'll tell you."

That opinion is harder to describe, although I could walk into almost any bookstore in America, and look at any tome, and tell you in about fifteen seconds whether or not it was something Dougie would put in is bookstore. It has a lot to do with aesthetics. Dougie carried every book printed by a small press called McFeeley's, which published only hardcover originals, sans flashy throwaway dust jackets. McFeeley's books trend towards the absurd: a murder mystery set in Alaska in which the characters are all mute Inuits or the autobiography of a yellowtail tuna turned hunk of sushi. He carried other books too, an assortment of small-run, contemporary fiction that often involved homosexuality in some way, as well as ridiculously dated Victorian volumes with laughably long titles. Things like *How Heroes of Fiction Propose and How Heroines Reply: Familiar Quotations in Poetry and Prose*. The majority of Dougie's collection, though, wasn't in books at all, it was in comics and zines.

These weren't the comics you think about when you hear the word comics. None of Dougie's comics involved superheroes. There is this whole genre of comics the general public doesn't know about that's largely about regular people (or in some cases about regular people who have morphed into felines, for the sake of visual panache, but who are otherwise indistinguishable from regular people). As a general rule, the characters in these comics are depressed, alienated, and live sordid lives, and the comics are only actually comic in a dark, uncomfortable way.

As a whole, if you put Dougie's comics and books together and tried to come up with a word to describe them, the word I would come up with is "ironic," although the way I use ironic encompasses a lot of other things: fatalism, nihilism, and a sense that the world has gone hopelessly mad. In fact, ironic, the way I use it, is more like the way other people use Postmodern or Modern or Victorian to describe the feel of a certain age. We live in the Age of Irony, and Dougie's little bookstore was ground zero for its artistic expression.

The long and short of this is that Ben Dover Books was holy ground to me. I'd visit the place just to be there, would browse its shelving even though I had no money and no intention of buying anything. I'd hope that Dougie was in a talkative mood, or that some other comic book artist or zinester would stroll in, and that Dougie, who particularly liked the role of connector, would introduce me. Sometimes this happened, but sometimes the trip would be completely wasted. If anything, that I often came and left Ben Dover Books dissatisfied heightened the sense of reverence I had for the place, like a slot machine player who craves slots not for the occasional big win but for the slow quarter-sapping loss.

This was the spirit in which I rode my bike over the Broadway Bridge towards downtown. I could have called first to see if Dougie was there, but that ran counter to Ben Dover Books magic. I locked my bike to the rack across the store and walked in.

Dougie sat behind the cashier stand as he was always did, his feet propped up next to an old-fashioned analog cash register and his handwritten sales and acquisitions notebook. He had a comic opened and the standard Dougie look of bemusement on his face. When I open the front door, the cowbell strung from it rang.

"Barth," he greeted me.

"What's up, Doug?"

I've referred to Doug as Dougie or Dougie Fresh throughout this gospel, but you have to remember that neither Mercyx nor Beale nor me ever called him this to his face. It was just our secret little nickname for him. Dougie, which for some reason made calling him Dougie Fresh funny, although I can't really explain why, since as far as we knew the real Doug E. Fresh – the beatboxer – wasn't particularly persnickety. The truth is that although we talked smack about him behind his back we all had a great deal of respect for him. Dougie was one of the few adults we could look up to and say, *Hey, this guy's over thirty and he never sold out.*

The other reason I called him Dougie was to get back at him in a passive-aggressive way for calling me "Barth." No one called me Barth. My father called me Bart, which bugged the hell out of me, and my mother called me Bartholomew, which over the years I'd grown to like, but Barth? Sure, I used it as my pen name – Barth Flynn – but people called me Flynn, and most of them just assumed it was my first name. No one called me Barth. It was way too close to "barf."

"I've got a fat check for you," Dougie said.

Now this was strange. I had never, in my long history of hanging out at Ben Dover Books, heard Dougie offer to pay anyone. There was a lot of talk about zines – what was selling, what wasn't; who was doing what, who wasn't – and then, eventually, you asked Dougie if he had anything for you. You said it just like that too, as if you didn't give a shit (and generally you didn't, since it rarely came to over ten or twenty bucks), "You got anything for me?"

And Dougie certainly didn't prepare checks in advance. He didn't operate like a traditional bookseller. He didn't have some giant database that tracked sales for him; he had his ledger and that was it. He'd hem and haw and continue to gossip, while flipping through his little notebook, which didn't appear to be alphabetized or anything, and eventually he'd find the entry where your sales were. Once found, he'd punch a few numbers on a small calculator, cross your listing out of his book, then handwrite you a check. Upfront, Dougie told you that it was fifty-fifty, but in reality it came to something more akin to sixty-forty in his favor. If you complained, Dougie would just say, "sorry, lost books," meaning, and he probably had a point here, that some of the zines had been stolen. I'm sure Dougie never counted his stock, so he actually had no idea whether any of the zines had walked off or not, but it was very hard to argue with the guy who owned the only shop in Portland where you could exhibit your stuff.

So like I said, this was strange, Dougie having a check prepared for me. And as is typical of me when confronted with something out of the ordinary, I just stood there, and also as is typical, the party who I'm supposedly having a conversation with begins talking, rather than waiting for me to come to terms with what has just been said.

"Sales are really amazing, Flynn. We're getting requests from both comic stores and independent bookstores, many of them simply due to Chester's reputation and some word-of-mouth buzz. They want to know how many we're going to do, if the dots are all going to connect, you know, what the overall scope of this is. Anyway, there's … see … there are possibilities here. It's not just a zine – it's a potentially lucrative enterprise. It's, well, I'm the publisher and Chester's the artist and you're …"

"So look, I'm beating around the bush here."

Dougie had a terrible habit of overusing clichés and mixing his metaphors. I continued staring stupidly; Dougie continued talking.

"Chester pointed out something that's bothering me about this whole thing. You see, you're not … you haven't been … well, *interpreting* Booker. What you've written is *ipsissimus verbis*, word for word and letter for letter what Booker says. That's problematic. I mean, you're sort of a fly on the wall, you know, sort of … just a bug, you know, like the FBI kind. Chester wants the narrative to be more … controlled. You can't just have words, words, and more words, you know? The words have to go into panels, into neat little boxes, you can't think outside the box too much, you'll –"

Since I wasn't going to interrupt him, Dougie interrupted himself. "You understand what I'm trying to say, right?"

I understood perfectly well what Dougie was saying. And the way Dougie's circuitous monologue affected me, it was like when the class bully kicks out the backs of your legs and causes you to tumble to the ground. Or when some guy puts you in a headlock and puts a beer bong down your throat. I was devastated. And given that this was taking place less than twenty-four hours after my ridiculous marriage proposal, my ego had submerged below the earth into some Crustacean era substrata.

I hadn't seen this coming, and yet now that Dougie was saying it, I couldn't believe I hadn't thought of it before.

I really needed to say something, if only to get him to stop, but I didn't.

"I mean, you should … well I mean, writers write scripts,

you know? You're … you're. I know you're smart. You have an English degree or something like that right? But you know, you just gave him the text, you didn't break into panels or anything. If … well, I mean, there's books you know, you can pick it up pretty fast I imagine. But I can't mince words anymore, Flynn. Chester's … well, Chester is a professional, you know, and he's used to working with professionals."

Dougie was right. Chester had thought I'd made up this fictional preacher character who was saying these outlandish and blasphemous but with a-hint-of-truth-to-them things. Then he shows up at this church, and he realizes that this "writer" is actually just mimeographing what a real preacher is saying.

Now if I'd been thinking, and if I didn't have a fairly low self-image, I might have defended myself. For one, Chester was my friggin' roommate, and if he had wanted something other than pure text it wouldn't have been too hard to ask me for it. He'd never given me an inkling what he wanted. For two, when Chester took the project on, he knew my experience was limited, and he should have expected to tutor me a little. And for three, I really hadn't thought – and still don't think – Booker needed any embellishing. The things he said and the way he said them were everything they needed to be. If anything, recording them verbatim was genius.

Unfortunately, I didn't see any of this while Dougie was talking. And I certainly didn't smell the rat. Dougie was such a God to me. It didn't occur to me that he was just like the rest of us – that given the chance, even Dougie Fresh would sell out.

"Anyway, I'm not trying to bring you down or anything. Really, you're awesome. I mean, you discovered him. I just think … well, it's hard for Chester, understand? So what I proposed, have you heard of this? A kill fee. Or a finder's fee. Or however you want to think about it. It's significant. It includes the royalties for the first two, plus a huge bonus."

Dougie opened the drawer beneath the cashier's stand where he kept his calculator and his check ledger. In a normal Ben Dover Books transaction, he would take them both out and in a grandiose manner write you a check in his large looping penmanship. Today, though, he pulled something else out, placing it in front of me and then turning it so it faced me. It was a money order made out to Barth Flynn. It was for five-hundred dollars. After I saw the amount, he pulled it back and put it in the drawer.

"If you need to think about it, that's cool," Dougie said. "Chester and I really want to hook you up to the drip, you know."

Money is a relative thing. You might be reading this and thinking five-hundred dollars is a lot of money. You might be reading this thinking its chump change. To me, it was four-hundred ninety-three dollars and fifteen cents more than I'd ever made on an artistic pursuit in my life. Plus, after Dougie's little speech, and after the whole fiasco with Mercyx, I felt like it was five-hundred dollars I didn't deserve. I could pay a month's *rent* with that money.

"I never look a gift horse in the mouth," I said. "Hand me that check."

Dougie hadn't really looked up at me until then. He'd been standing there, looking down at and carelessly spinning his sales notebook. When he did look up, I thought I saw a twinge. Whether of guilt or mockery I'll never know. "Great then. I just need to make this official, you know? Just a sheet or two of legal *ease*. We could do this with a handshake, but you … I think it would help you if you got into the habit of it, you know – being professional."

Dougie opened his drawer again, pulling out a sheet of paper with a lot of small print on it, and a pen with a feather taped on the end. He turned the paper towards me. There was an X on the bottom and a line. Above the X and the line was another X and a line. That X and line held Chester Fields' signature. Whatever the small print said, Dougie's hand covered it.

I SIGNED IT. DOUGIE PULLED OUT ANOTHER sheet. I signed that. Dougie pulled out a third sheet. I signed that. And a fourth. There were eight sheets. I didn't look up at Dougie while I signed them. He didn't, I don't imagine, look at me.

When he was done obtaining all those signatures, and had placed all those sheets back in the desk, Dougie held out the money order. He didn't pass it to me, with a flourish, like he normally did, instead he sort of just let it hang there. I took it from him fast, like it was hot. A cowbell rang as I walked out the door.

The saddest thing about selling out is just how cheaply most of us do it for.

COFFEE BREAK #5
ON BRIDGES

THERE ARE MANY BRIDGES IN THIS NOVEL. THIS WAS NOT MEANT AS A METAPHOR. I LIVE IN PORTLAND, OREGON, AND PORTLAND, OREGON IS A CITY SPLIT IN TWO BY A RIVER, AND SO IT NATURALLY HAS A GREAT MANY BRIDGES THAT MUST BE CROSSED AND RECROSSED IN ORDER TO GET FROM ONE SIDE TO THE OTHER.

AND YET I CANNOT DUCK UNDER THE DEEPER MEANINGS OF BRIDGES, UNDER THE TIMES WHEN A BRIDGE IS STOPPED ON AND NOT GONE OVER, OR THE TIMES WHEN ONE RIDES OVER A BRIDGE WITHOUT REALLY THINKING ABOUT IT, OR THE TIMES WHEN ONE STANDS ON THE BRIDGE AND REALIZES HOW FLIMSY IT IS, HOW THERE IS SAFE LAND ON ONE SIDE OF A BRIDGE, AND SAFE LAND ON THE OTHER SIDE OF A BRIDGE, BUT HOW THIS MIDDLE GROUND, THESE TIMES WHEN YOU'RE CROSSING FROM ONE SIDE TO OTHER ARE FAR MORE FLIMSY AND PRECARIOUS.

I SUPPOSE IF I WERE A REAL WRITER, I WOULD JUST LET THE BRIDGES COME, AND LET YOU DIVINE THE DEEPER MEANINGS BEHIND THESE BRIDGES, BUT I'M NOT A WRITER, I'M A SCRIBE, AND A SCRIBE'S JOB IS TO MAKE SURE YOU DON'T MISINTERPRET THINGS.

SO THIS IS THE DEEPER MEANING BEHIND THE BRIDGES: BOOKER WAS A BRIDGE FOR ME TO WALK OVER, AND I WAS A BRIDGE FOR DOUGIE TO WALK OVER, AND WELL, THIS GOSPEL, IT'S A BRIDGE FOR YOU TO WALK OVER, YOU WHO ARE AN AMERICAN, YOU WHO SO DESPERATELY NEED TO LEAVE THE SAFE LAND YOU ARE STANDING ON, AND WALK OVER A BRIDGE, AND SEE WHAT'S ON THE OTHER SIDE.

THERE ARE OTHER THINGS THAT BRIDGES ARE GOOD FOR TOO. AND AFTER I LEFT BEN DOVER BOOKS I THOUGHT ABOUT THIS, SERIOUSLY, FOR THE FIRST TIME. I WAS CROSSING THE BROADWAY BRIDGE, THE ORANGE-TINTED BRIDGE WHOSE DISTINCTIVE FEATURE IS THE ALBERS MILL GRAIN SILO THAT IT PASSES JUST FEET AWAY FROM, GIVING THE BRIDGE A CLAUSTROPHOBIC GOTHAM CITY SORT OF FEEL, AND THERE WERE THESE HISPANIC PAINTERS THERE, HANGING ON A NARROW BOARDS ON THE SIDE OF THE SILO, REPAINTING THE SIGNATURE CROOKED UPPER-CASE "S" AT THE END OF THE ALBERS LOGO, KEEPING IT HISTORICALLY ACCURATE, FOR THE BEAUTIFICATION OF THE CITY, AND FOR SOME REASON THAT MADE ME REALLY DEPRESSED, THAT MY COUNTRY WAS SIMULTANEOUSLY CRACKING DOWN ON ILLEGAL IMMIGRATION WHILE HIRING THE ILLEGAL IMMIGRANTS TO DO DANGEROUS JOBS, AND THIS DEPRESSING THOUGHT SOMEHOW MINGLED WITH THE DEPRESSING AND PAINFUL MEMORY OF HAVING MADE AN ASS OF MYSELF ON THE BRIDGE OF THE GODS, AND NOW HAVING STUPIDLY AND CAVALIERLY SIGNED AWAY ALL RIGHTS TO THE COMIC ABOUT BOOKER THAT I HAD AUTHORED. AND AS I RODE TOWARDS THE APEX OF THE BRIDGE IT OCCURRED TO ME THAT I COULD KILL MYSELF, AND THAT IF I KILLED MYSELF I WOULD NO LONGER HAVE TO FEEL ASHAMED FOR BOTH MYSELF AND MY COUNTRY.

I DIDN'T GET MUCH FURTHER THAN THIS IN MY THOUGHT PROCESS ON THIS CROSSING.

BUT THE SEEDS WERE PLANTED.

Chapter xx

Where Bartholomew Flynn's Brief Flirtation with Suicide is
Averted by the Arrival of a Pair of Buckets

IT SEEMS STRANGE THAT WE'RE THIS FAR into this story, and I've yet to tell you about my post office box, it being such an important feature of a zinester's life. But I never had any reason to bring it up before, because, quite frankly, visiting my P.O. box was a pretty blasé affair.

Way back when I started *Octagonal Table Talk*, I did what zinesters do when they start a zine, they get a post office box. Certainly, I could have used my home address on my zine, because no one actually purchased *OTT*, but the thing was, you didn't really feel like a zinester until you had a P.O. box.

Besides, every once in a while another zinester would see *OTT* at Ben Dover Books, and not wanting to pay a dollar to buy it, they would send a note in the mail asking if I would trade them a copy of *OTT* for a copy of their zine. It felt very twentieth century and Thomas Pynchon, sending and receiving zines via P.O. boxes, and when Beale and Mercyx and I would meet at The Curiosity, we often brought with us the notes and the zines that we received in our little bronze boxes and spent most of our evening pouring through them and laughing at our booty. (Beale, with his big boobs collegiate humor zine, tended to get the most mail.)

The post office where I had my P.O. box was just on my side of the Broadway Bridge, and so I stopped there, as was my habit when heading that way. I walked through its twin doors, full of posted security alerts, and to that sacred back room that most post offices have, where the solemn rows of numbered, gold-plated P.O. boxes are.

It was nice to be doing something normal, something I did before I discovered Booker and before I'd gotten the idiotic notion to try and bag Mercyx. I found my number, took out my keychain, and placed it in my box. I turned the lock. I pulled. It was jammed. I pulled harder. Mail poured out.

I jumped back as it fell, overwhelmed by the bounty. I'd never gotten that much mail before. I hadn't visited in a while, a whole month come to think of it, but still. I picked up the mail that had fallen on the floor – mostly letter-sized envelopes – then pulled out several magazine-sized packages stuffed into my box, sorting through them as I did so to surmise what might be inside. What shocked me were the return addresses. I'd usually see Portland, Oregon, or Des Moines, Iowa, but this mail was from all over the place: California, New York City, even a package from Tokyo. Among the letters and packages there was also a yellow slip – a note directing me to the counter to pick up yet another package.

It wasn't unusual for me to receive a slip like this, since I, like every other impoverished zinester, rented the smallest and cheapest box one could rent, and since an 8½×11 zine wouldn't fit in one.

I closed my box and removed the key, left the postal box room, and got in line to await my turn at the counter. While I waited, I tore open an oversized manila envelope with a finger, and took out the letter inside:

Dear Mr. Flynn,
OMFG this killed me. It's so nice to read an irreverent zine about religion that isn't the typical song and dance about a priest diddling you when you were in high school. Could you send us 10 more copies? We own a comic shop in Boulder and we'd love to carry this.
Loved it!
Loved it!
Loved it!

Madeline Summers
Proprietress, Subterranean Comix
123 Bugle Street
Boulder, CO 80320

I read the letter again: *Loved it! Loved it! Loved it!* Then, a third time. Someone liked *His Church That Sunday*. And not just anybody, but a comic book store owner – a comic book store owner who I didn't know, who'd just picked the zine up randomly and liked it. (Not liked it. Loved it! Loved it! Loved it!)

"Next!"

I'd been just standing there, reading my mail, not moving forward. Everyone was staring at me. The postal lady was chewing gum.

I handed her the slip. She disappeared into the mailroom. Usually the postal worker would return with two or three large zines curled-up in a rubber band. Instead, when she returned, she was carrying a bucket. She grunted, then slammed it on the counter.

"One more," she said, then disappeared again.

I looked in the bucket – more letters and more manila envelopes, hundreds of them. Inside the letters and manila envelopes would be more words like the words of Madeline Summers of Boulder, Colorado.

The postal lady came back with the other bucket. She slammed it on the counter, grunting, once again. The second bucket was just as full.

I crumbled. I sobbed. Right there, in the post office, I sobbed. It seemed to be happening to me quite a bit these days, sobbing and crumbling. I was Flynn, the wannabe gang member, the poser illustrator, the humiliated lover, and here were love letters. Most people would simply call it fan mail, but to me, at least in my current state of mind, they were love letters. And they were addressed to me, not Chester, not Dougie, but me, Bartholomew Flynn. And being who I was, a zinester, I knew what to do with all this fan mail. I'd read it. Every single letter. And after I read it I knew what I'd do next. Answer it. How could I not? That's what zinesters did, that's what made zinesters better than the rest of the population. They didn't mass produce. They didn't take all this shit for granted. They answered their fan mail. And anyway, what else would I do now, now that I'd lost my cycling partner, and the rights to do my zine, I'd address my fans. Bartholomew Flynn's fans. The fans of Bartholomew Flynn. Flynn fans!

"Woohoo!" I threw some of the mail up in the air, an envelope landing in the curly white hair of the octogenarian behind me.

The postal lady had a look of revulsion on her face that was easy to interpret. The look said *freak.*

The octogenarian didn't move.

The postal lady said, "Next!"

Chapter xxi

A Deceptively Uneventful Chapter, In Which Bartholomew Flynn Reads Comic Books and Signs Paperwork

HEN I SET OUT TO WRITE THIS GOSPEL, I promised myself that I would never summarize anything, that I would include even the boring parts of the story. I wanted Booker to be a real person, and real people stumble and are at times inarticulate, and I was determined to include everything, even if you got bored.

But now I've gotten to this odd point where the scribbles in my blue-linen notebook, the one I used to write down all of Booker's words, suddenly end. Having been dropped as the writer for *His Church That Sunday*, I no longer had the need to transcribe all of Booker's harangues, and not envisioning ever wanting them for posterity, I ceased writing them down.

Though tragic for historians, for you, my faithful reader, this is probably for the best. Had I transcribed them all, one sermon after another, this gospel would have stretched out, five hundred, six hundred, perhaps a thousand pages, and while some of the things Booker said were insightful, and some funny, and some ludicrous, all of it – at least it seems to me – was being said by many other people.

You see, it was autumn of 2004 in the United States, election season, a time at which an overweight nation sat on the far right side of its ever-tilting political seesaw, while Portland, Oregon, sat hopelessly on the left, thin and flailing its arms about like a small child desperate to be set down. Booker was at the forefront of this movement. On Sundays, when he got up on his milk crates, flailing his arms about like, well, like a small child on a seesaw, he had a ready audience. "They're the Pharisees," I can hear him ranting, "and we Portlanders, rotting in the cold and drizzle, we're the Samaritans!"

During this time, Booker's church became a real church. It was still strange, complete with Voodoo Doughnut and Stumptown Coffee transubstantiations, but the congregation no longer saw Booker through a performance art lens – Booker wasn't an imitation of a preacher anymore.

The change was gradual. The new people – the lesbians, David, the people they brought in, the people brought in after that – they didn't know the Booker I'd seen, the one half-exposed, surrounded by drunks and dubious women, soiling the institution of marriage in both word and action. They didn't know the Booker whose sermons always ended in a spectacularly humiliating fashion. They saw this new Booker, this somehow both intellectual and plebian little person – his dips into Biblical scholarship, juxtaposed with slips into profanity – and they saw an unorthodox holy man.

It was weird. Booker had no divinity degree (did he? Maybe he did. I'll never know) and given how it had all started, as a joke, I would often turn around, swiveling in those improperly bolted down theater chairs and gape in awe at the piety I beheld in the faces of his audience. Where was the insolence? Where were the haters? Booker wasn't a *little person*. He was a midget! It had been so much of his charm, to me anyway, the way he proffered himself for ridicule.

It was a bit like that book I was taking so long to get through, the one I fell asleep to at night. Booker was a modern-day manifestation of *Don Quixote*. When one plays the hero in a particularly unheroic way, and when one fails and fails and fails and fails again to be an actual hero, one somehow becomes a hero.

Or maybe even a messiah.

It was during this time that Maggie's suggestion became a reality. Booker's church turned into a sort of impromptu headquarters for the Democratic National Committee. People met at his church for one of his sermons, then afterwards they gathered around Booker's altar, which was covered with maps of Portland and city voter registration rolls, and they'd subdivide everything into neighborhoods, and then they'd head out into the streets, bands of inarticulate and annoying young twenty-somethings showing up on porches with Vote Early flyers and clipboards with checklists, trying to get the faithful to the voting booths.

You've noticed here that I've said "bands of twenty-somethings," and indeed, as the weeks passed, Maggie and Lizzie, born organizers, had brought in all kinds of outsiders. It started with a group of Unitarians who they'd attended services with before joining Booker, then extended into some contacts they had at the local public university.

Meanwhile, I worked. It was excruciatingly painful at first – working the phones; going door-to-door with flyers and clipboards – it was embarrassing, and I was bad at it. But after everything I had been through – the c.h.v.c.k. humiliations; Mercyx's rejection – I was just thick-skinned enough to knock on the next door or make the next phone call. And then, something surprising happened: I got decent at it. Not great – I've never been very good at holding my own in an argument – but decent. The occasional person who didn't make some excuse up about dinner and shut the door, and who'd talk my ear off about medical marijuana or whatever their pet concern was, well, it was sort of fun.

While this good for me – finding a touch of inner-strength – I couldn't stop thinking about Mercyx. All day and all night – Mercyx, Mercyx, Mercyx. Despite the courage I summoned to knock on the doors of strangers, I couldn't summon the courage to call an old friend. I couldn't call her to get answers to my omnipresent ruminations: Who are you running zines for? Who are you cycling with? When can I

have you back, as a friend? I didn't even talk to David, her roommate, who'd become a fixture in Booker's church, and who, I'm sure, would have been more than happy to keep me abreast of Mercyxish happenings.

Of course, if I had called her, or if I had talked to David, I might not have liked all the answers.

To distract myself, when I wasn't slinging coffee, canvassing neighborhoods for John Kerry, biking all over Portland, or going to church on Sunday, I read my fan mail.

It's funny, when I look back on that day in the post office. You hear people talking about "rebounds," the act of dating someone because you've been rejected by the person you really wanted to date or dating someone because you've been with someone else for a really long time and you need a light-hearted, somewhat meaningless relationship (usually sexual in nature) to help you forget.

The fan mail was my rebound, and except for the lack of sex, my fan mail was the perfect one. My fan mail was at my beck and call. When I needed alone time, I could ignore it. When I needed it to spend the night with me, it would do that, it would spend the night entertaining me – complimenting me, telling me stories, pleading with me to give it something back (but only if I wanted too! And only when I wanted too!). I sat at my desk, listening to rain beating against my window (I felt so much like myself with my fan mail) and wrote my fan mail back – sometimes long blue letters, sometimes short notes, sometimes an issue of *OTT* – a personal gift to a faceless fan.

Don't get me wrong, once every ten minutes or so, I'd flash back to myself on that bluff over The Bridge of the Gods (if I could bomb that place with a small nuclear device, oh how quickly I would) and my whole being would be filled with unspeakable shame. But despite the horror my apartment had become, the smell of meat from Mexican carniceria mixed with the offensiveness of Chester mixed with my own floor full of unlaundered clothes, it was still a safe place to rendez-vous with my lover – my fan mail – and there my fan mail comforted me and told me how brilliant I was and never said anything about what an ass I'd made of myself.

So there goes the summarizing I had promised not to do, and looking back on how George W. Bush somehow won re-election anyway, it all seems for the best. There's one other thing I should mention, though, before we go on. Booker wouldn't have become the new Booker if it hadn't been for a certain circumstance. c.h.v.c.k. had disappeared.

Somewhere, though, east of Portland, in the thicket-choked depths of a Northwest forest, a voice shouted out from the wilderness.

Chapter XXII

All Hallow's Eve

T WAS A SUNDAY, A CHRISTIAN DAY OF worship, and it was also Halloween, the original Pagan harvest holiday, a celebration of the worldly, and finally it was the last Sunday before an election, which meant that all over America, the heart rates of pastors and rabbis and mullahs and witches were up. It's hard to imagine, though, a heart rate higher than Booker's.

I rode my bike down Prescott Street, sans spandex, in rain gear layered over a T-shirt and a pair of rolled-up jeans. The day was *ramhar pléascadh*, which translates roughly into English as exploding Zeppelin, which is to say that the clouds were so gray and full that it seemed impossible that it wasn't raining. When a day in Portland starts out *ramhar pléascadh*, it generally ends up *taom fearthainne* or *uisge*, which was why I put on the rain gear, not wanting to end up wet and wearing someone else's clothes yet again.

When I arrived at Booker's church, I did not stop, but rather rode past it, observing the church's letter board, which read:

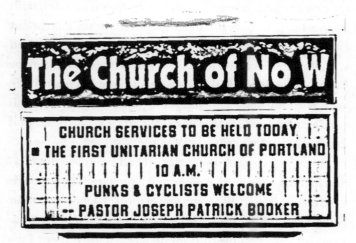

The First Unitarian Church of Portland had been Lizzie and Maggie's church before they had ditched it for Booker's.

They'd kept up with the church's pastor, Reverend Nool, and after describing to her what Booker was doing, and how he managed to draw young people to his church, the Reverend Nool had asked Booker to preach at her church.

So here I was, Bartholomew Flynn, atheist, riding my bike over the Steel Bridge from the down home East Side of Portland, to the downtown West Side in order to attend a real church service. This morning, when I woke up, I had actually taken a moment to decide how to dress. If I was going to real church, shouldn't I wear a button-down shirt? Shouldn't I iron it? Shouldn't I wear slacks? That I had to think about this was annoying, so I wore the same clothes I'd wear to Booker's church, and even this felt weird, because now I was wearing what I was wearing in protest rather than because it was what I normally wore.

Because it was Sunday, the downtown streets were deserted, so I rode up the incline of Salmon Street freely, taking up an entire automobile lane, and I passed the elk statue that sits in the Park Blocks, like a portal to Portland, significant because it's a statue of a wild animal and not of a human, which I always felt a fitting symbol of this place.

By the time I made it up the hill to 12th Street where the church was located, the rain had begun, although it was *éadrom agus soineanta*, a light and innocuous rain, still too light for the weight of the clouds. There was a parking attendant on the other side of the street from the church flagging cars into a lot. Families walked down the sidewalk, the men wearing button-down shirts and slacks, dressed up but not too dressed up, as is the Portland formal style, the women also wearing button-down shirts and slacks, which is also the Portland formal style, while the children were more dressed up than their parents, wearing suits and dresses – also the Portland formal style.

I wasn't sure what to do with this, mentally. It seemed wrong. I didn't belong here. Booker didn't belong here. I parked my bike in front of the church on a bike rack devoid of other bikes, which considering the masses of people pouring into the church, was surprising; one would think at least a small percentage of these Portland churchgoers would attend church on a bike.

In front of the church were three incredibly well-trimmed hawthorne trees – a hawthorne tree being a tree ubiquitous to Portland that only bears flowers and leaves and berries for about a month in May, before it drops all its flowers and leaves and berries and sits there bare and gangly for the rest of the year. How these terribly ugly trees became popular in

Portland I'll never know, but the way they flower, so briefly, seems symbolic of something insignificant that has a shining moment. Like a prophet. Or a small, independent press.

I U-locked the bike to the rack and walked to the front doors of the church. The nylon of my rain pants rubbed together as I strode, making me sound like a human windshield wiper. The other churchgoers were carrying umbrellas. It dawned on me that when I got in the church there would be nothing to do with all my rain gear, that I'd be stuck wearing it – sweating in a pew next to some wiggly, sniveling little boy.

The walls of the church were elegant red brick. There was a plaque outside declaring it a national landmark. There were stone archways with Biblical sayings engraved on them in Latin script:

LOVE THY NEIGHBOR AS THYSELF

It was wrong. We were not formal. We were anti-formal. What was Booker becoming?

I walked through the propped-open grand doors of the church. A man – this time wearing a suit and tie – handed me a bulletin. I took it. On its cover was this:

ca ca ca SERMON ಬಿಬಿಬಿ

today's topic

ca ca ca JUDGMENT DAY ಬಿಬಿಬಿ

as spoken by

ca ca ca JOSEPH PATRICK BOOKER, MINISTER OF

ಬಿಬಿಬಿ

ca ca ca C.H.V.R.C.H. 313 ಬಿಬಿಬಿ

By now the rain had started, and the umbrellas had all come up. Upon receiving the bulletin, I did my usual brain fart thing where I just stand there. The man who'd handed it to me cocked an eyebrow as I did this, blocking the entrance and causing a train wreck of umbrellas on the steps behind me. "Flynn?" the man asked. "The scribe?"

"Yes," I said.

He grinned at me. It was as if he knew me. It was as if, well, it was as if he were my fan. How did he know me? It wasn't like my face was plastered all over the Internet. "You biked here," the man said, kind of asking it as a question and kind of not.

I nodded.

"There's a coat check, over there," he pointed. "You can check your helmet and rain gear. Tell the usher who you are, and they will show you to your seat."

It was so *established*, this church. I made my way into the foyer, was handed two separate numbers for my helmet and rain gear by the coat checker, and then walked through one of the four entrances into the entry hall of the church. There was, indeed, an usher there, a middle-aged woman dressed in a maroon suit. There was a badge on the suit, or a crest or something – the crest had some sort of genie lamp on it. As I looked, I realized that all of the ushers had the same colored suit with the same genie crest. The ushers had uniforms! I was in a church where the ushers had uniforms.

"Flynn?" the usher asked.

This was too much. It was making me paranoid. It was as if I were a contestant on some reality show, only I didn't know I was a contestant on a reality show, so everybody knew me but I didn't know why.

"Yes," I said.

"This way," the usher said.

I walked down the aisle. As I walked, I realized that my pant leg was still rolled up just below the knee, and that my calf had a big black grease smudge on it. If I stopped to pull it up, I'd call more attention to it, so I didn't, I just kept following the usher. He walked me all the way to the front row. I could feel the eyeballs behind me, all staring at the grease spot on my leg. A velvet rope blocked access to the front pew with a little sign on it that read Reserved. When we got there, I saw everybody, at least everybody who hadn't jumped ship. Maggie and Lizzie were there, and David and Beale, and then all the other people who the lesbians had brought in. I was pleased to note I wasn't the only one in street clothes, and when I saw them, their faces all with the *holy shit* look they'd had the first time they'd encountered Booker, I relaxed. This was going to be just like all the other times. It was going to be good.

The service started, and it went along much as I remember services being back when I was a boy: lots of standing and sitting; hymns. I was very fidgety during this, as it was slow and boring. I also had a headache – I'd grown so accustomed to services starting with the consecration of coffee, that I hadn't had a cup before I'd left.

Finally, the minister, the Reverend Nool, walked up to the podium and began to speak, talking about our church and describing its mismatched pews and talking about how it was founded by young Christians (I was not a young Christian! How little she knew!), who wanted to start a truly activist church. (I was not an activist! How little she knew!) She said nothing about midgets, or tall bikes, or exploding vans, or wigged women. And then she introduced him, and when she did so, she used the word reverend. When had he become a reverend? He wasn't a reverend. You have to be ordained to be a reverend. "I introduce to you the Reverend Joseph Patrick Booker," she said.

He appeared, stage left, as was his custom. He did not have coffee, which was a disappointment, but he did have his Alpenrose milk crates. He carried them in a triangle, pressing the bottom two together to support the top one. You couldn't make out his face. In fact, at this point, he looked like three milk crates walking on a pair of really short legs.

There was laughter–children's laughter. It sounded twinkly, in that solemn churchy place, the laughter. It was quickly suppressed. I couldn't see them, being in the front row, but I could sense parental hands going quickly over the mouths of offspring.

He put the crates down, stacked them, and did his leap-frog thing. He was so good at it now. It looked like a magician's trick. Most of the laugher remained suppressed, but a couple of squeals snuck out just the same.

And then they saw his face. We all saw his face. It was George W. Bush. A very, very, short George W. Bush. George W. Bush with a red cloak, a pair of horns, and, yes, a pitchfork.

There was a communal gasp. Men, women, children, the entirety of congregation simultaneously gasped. If you can't imagine what a communal gasp sounds like, go to a sporting event. Even if you don't like sports do it. Hockey is great for this, as is women's roller derby, a perennial Portland favorite, but any violent sport will do. Keep your eyes closed. At some point, a player will get crushed against the boards, two bodies colliding in a sickening way, and everybody in the stadium will gasp simultaneously. There is nothing quite as deliciously celestial as a communal gasp. It's the sound of suns smashing.

My love of Booker grew a thousand-fold.

Reverend Nool's face was sheet white, as if Satan himself had invaded her altar.

"Banish me!" Booker said. His voice magnified by the wireless microphone clipped to his devilish cloak.

Silence.

"Banish me!" Booker said again.

More silence.

It looked like Reverend Nool was about to get up from her chair and do just that, but before she got the opportunity, Booker starting speaking, and once Booker starts speaking, as we all know, he's hard to stop. "Banish me!" Booker repeated for a third time. "The devil has appropriated your precious pulpit. Rub your genie lamps, or whatever it is you

Unitarians do to exorcise demons, and banish me.

"This congregation that you have," Booker continued, "it's one of the oldest in Portland, it's been here over a hundred years, how much power it must have by now! You can move mountains. When the Reverend George Eliot came to Portland way back 1888, he had to preach in theaters and homeless shelters, just so he could get people to listen, but now look at you, look at these stained glass windows, this polished marble, all these additions, with classrooms and meeting spaces and whatnot, what awe all this imparts, how much power you must have."

There was some grumbling coming from the back of the church. I assumed that someone wasn't very happy with Booker, for a whole host of potential reasons. I didn't turn around.

"You don't have the power, though, do you?" Booker went on. "Hundreds of you here, amongst all this grandeur, how little you've done. Do you know why you can't banish me? Do you know why the election that's being held next week is so close? This is why."

Booker dropped the pitchfork and began fooling around with his red cloak. I knew what he was doing, he was trying to pull the red and pink and gray and black Bible out of his pants, but it wasn't working. He pulled off the George W. Bush mask. His horns went askew. He found the Bible eventually. I can't imagine how surreal this whole thing must have been for the Unitarians. Booker's real face was as bizarre an apparition as the masked one.

The color had returned to Reverend Nool's face. It was now as red as it had formerly been white. Booker flipped the Bible to a dog-eared page.

"Be passersby! The core and crux of the entire New Testament, here in two words, here in the Gospel of Thomas, discovered in modern times specifically because we need to hear it so bad. Chapter forty-two, verse one, the smallest verse in the entire Bible. Be passersby!"

The George W. Bush mask dangled from the corner of a milk crate like a Dali watch.

"Do you think this is what Jesus envisioned, a bunch of people sitting stiff-backed in pews listening to a good reverend, praying in silence for salvation? No. Jesus envisioned a church without a home, a church that wandered around and visited with people around a lake, a church much like your church originally was, when Reverend Eliot brought his faith and opinions to the homeless shelters and theaters and brothels of Portland, Oregon. He envisioned a people and a religion on the move and responsive to the times.

"Did Jesus spend all his time sitting in a church lecturing his apostles? He didn't. The one time he hung out in a church, he ripped the Pharisees a new asshole –"

Reverend Nool got up at this one. Booker, normally oblivious to his audience, sensed her rise. He turned and looked at her sheepishly.

"Sorry," he said.

He suddenly looked like a kid standing on milk crates and not a reverend preaching in a church. "I'm really, really sorry. I swore to Reverend Nool that I wouldn't swear up here … but I … damn …"

Reverend Nool glared.

"I'm still new at this … can you forgive me? Please? I mean, there are children here. I mean, it's okay that I swear in my church but it's not okay that I swear in your church, can you all …"

Booker turned away from the reverend and looked out to the audience. He took a deep breath, recovering himself. "I need you all to say something, in unison. To participate, you know, like, as if we were friends and fellow Christians and somebody did something wrong that they needed forgiving for. So say this, say, "We forgive you Joseph Booker for swearing in our church." It will take some doing, I know, but these guys in the front can get you going. Okay, so I'm going to stop, and then I'm going to point at you all, and then you're going to say 'We forgive you Joseph Booker for swearing in our church.' Okay."

Now swearing to give people a feel for him and his church and then immediately apologizing for it and then immediately insisting that the audience have empathy for him by forgiving him; I really don't know whether to talk about how incredibly genius this was or how terribly manipulative or how weirdly Booker. The truth is that it was just him. It was just the way he was, but the way he was, it was sort of accidently powerful. When he stopped there and pointed at us, Lizzie and Maggie and David and Beale and me and all the rest, we all said it as loud as we could, on cue, "We forgive you Joseph Booker for swearing in our church." And Booker, he said it wasn't loud enough, and he asked us to forgive him again, and again he pointed at the crowd, and this time, in chorus – this stiff, this very white, this church of regular churchgoers, these Unitarians – they joined us, "We forgive you Joseph Booker for swearing in our church."

It was gorgeous, this moment, we were suddenly all one, c.h.v.r.c.h. 313 and the Unitarians. How did Booker do this stuff?

"Thank you, for that," Booker said, and he was on a roll once again, "that was important to me. See that was something unexpected, doing something in the moment."

All the great religions, when they started, were started by people living in the moment. Jesus, he was not speaking to us, he was speaking to t e Galileans who were struggling under the weight of the heavy taxation imposed onthem by Caesar. Muhammed, he was not speaking to the Muslims of today, he was speaking to a bunch of Arab leaders on the best ways to conduct battle. The prophets of Judaism were not speaking to Jews today, but to the Israelites who had, for the first time, found themselves in power & were having a hard time with the transition from oppressed to oppresser.

These great religions were certainly great in their beginnings, but now they are not so great, they are incredibly lifeless & lame. And the reason they are lifeless & lame is because t ey no longer live in the moment.

Religion must speak to the moment. Every sermon that is given by every reverend of every faith should speak to the immediacy & importance of the time in which that sermon takes place, otherwise that religion is pointlesw & that religion is false. A religion that talks about an afterlife instead of talking about a now, that religion is nothing but a death cult, We are alive & we are alive in this moment & this moment IS the Kingdom of Heaven, there IS no afterlife & there IS no beforelife--there IS only now. This moment is all we have & this moment is electric & this moment is infinite.

I thought Booker had them pretty roped in, after that forgiv ness thing, but what had started out as grumblings from the back row, had turned into active arguing. I was afraid to look. The Unitarians were in general a pretty liberal lot, but it wasn't hard to imagine an offended Republican or two in the audience.

I know I'm preaching to the choir here.
The Unitarians do things right. I've
heard you have a basement, & after all
the sitting & standing & kneeling, you go
downstairs & have your real service,
where you drink coffee & eat doughnuts
like the original Christians, sharing a
meal, & where people get together & decide what they're going to do about everything that was preached about.

But sometimes if you need to get people to do something
daring & dangerous, if you need, like Martin Luther King
to get people to go out into the streets without weapons
& arms, & to walk in front of people who do have weapons
& arms, if youwant to get people to stand as lambs before lions, to have faith that people will come forth
& see the rightness of your message, you've got to repeat to people things that they already know.

It seemed to me that there was a great deal of squirming in the pews.
Booker's sermon was getting long-winded, as they tended to be, but the
squirming seemed out-of-proportion to the long-windedness. Reverend Re-
newl wasn't watching Booker anymore either, she was looking to the back
of the church, where there had been arguing earlier, but from which now
exuded an uncomfortable silence.

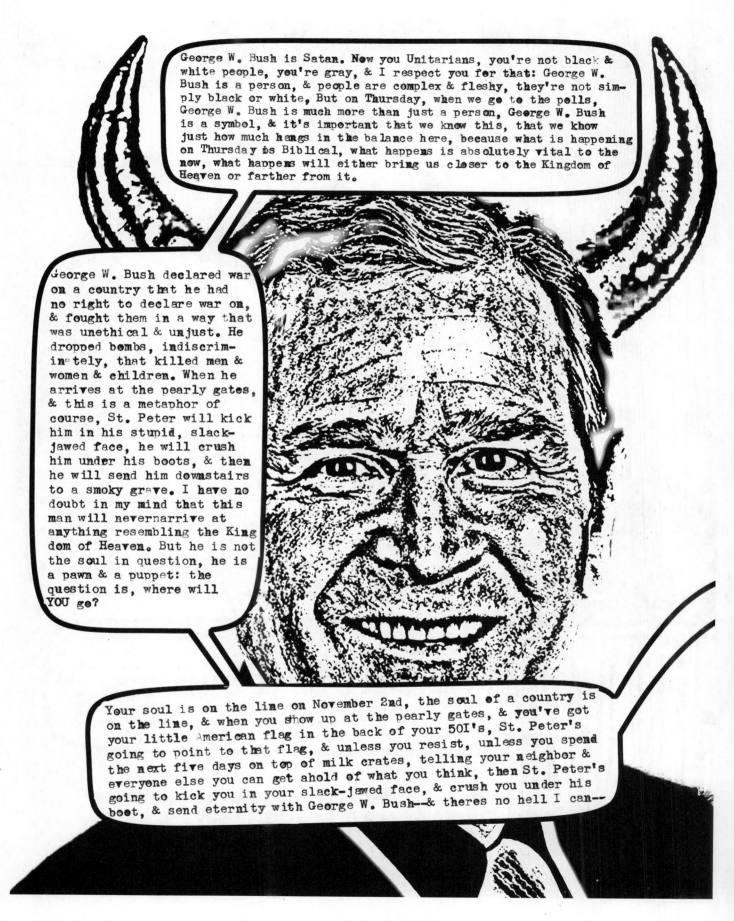

There was a thwock. Then a whoosh. Then a dnnnnnn. What amazes me is how long Booker saw it coming and how long he went on anyway, desperately trying to deliver his message in the face of what was to come.

In the lectern next to Booker, in the Unitarian banner, in the middle of the symbol of a lamp, an arrow vibrated. A scroll hung from the arrow.

Every head in the church turned. It was c.h.v.c.k.

They were standing in the back pew while everyone else was seated. The chef paramedics and the pirate and Mad Max and Ape Man and Gassy. And of course, he was there. You could see no flesh in his face. His cop sunglasses covered the only bare spots on his skin, while a full, dirt-matted beard covered the rest. He was wearing the same clothes he'd been wearing on Lark Mountain, over two months ago, only they didn't look the same, they were a monotone brown, the same color as his beard, the color of the bark of a Douglas fir. He didn't look homeless, though. There weren't tears and there weren't shit-stains. He looked like woods.

A second arrow was notched. It was aimed at Booker.

The celestial gasp was heard again.

"Tiny," Diogenes said, "so high and mighty. Have you lost your whores?"

A girl screamed. A man stood up.

"Heads down!" Diogenes shouted, as if this were bank robbery.

The bow was crude, as if he'd fashioned it himself. The arrow, the same, with a stone head and carved shaft. I have no idea what he might have formed the bow string from. It seemed sinewy.

Thwock. Whoosh. Dnnnnnn.

George W. Bush leapt off the edge of the top milk crate. He reappeared on the crucifix in the back of the church, pinned to Jesus's bicep, an arrow through his eye.

"Missed," said Diogenes. He notched a third.

"We duel. Tomorrow night. Dante's. All Saints Day. Bring your disciples. There's a flyer on that arrow. THE END IS NIIIIIIGH!"

Thwock. Whoosh. Pop. Clatter.

Booker went down. The First Unitarian Church broke out in bedlam, the screams of gray-haired church ladies louder than those of the children. Reverend Nool ran to the lectern, grabbed the microphone, and shouted, "Order! Order!" the familiar voice preventing what easily could have become a very ugly church trampling incident. Having a front row seat, and being somewhat used to this sort of thing, I wasn't nearly

as panicked. The arrow wasn't embedded in Booker, but lying rather harmlessly on the floor, having taken out a milk crate.

Booker picked himself up off the floor and walked to the lectern. I got out of my pew and did the same. The three of us met at the arrow – Reverend Nool, Booker, and me. Booker yanked the scroll off, then unrolled it. He read it first, then handed it to me.

It was a handbill, artistically produced with an old-fashioned letterpress. Battle of the Bookers, it read, Dante's Inferno, All Saints Day @ 9 P.M., c.h.v.r.c.h. vs. c.h.v.c.k.

Chapter XXIII

Where Chester Fields Departs in a Golden Chariot and Where Bartholomew Flynn Takes out the Garbage

ESPITE THE BIBLICAL INJUNCTION TO share food and drink with strangers, I chose not to partake in the coffee and doughnuts in the basement of the First Unitarian Church. I was pretty sure they wouldn't have Stumptown and Voodoo, and after going for hours without, I needed the strong stuff.

With frantic discussions taking place all around me, I managed to retrieve my rain gear and helmet from the coat check without having to exchange too many pleasantries, and slip out the door. Judging by the amount of water on the streets, the clouds had discharged their full grayness during church services, and I'd have a reprieve until the next set rolled in.

I rode my bike to the downtown Stumptown outlet first, settling down with my fix and a copy of the *New York Times* that had been left around. Then to Voodoo, where I settled on an ordinary vegan applesauce cake doughnut. Finally, I rode over the Broadway Bridge to rendezvous with my fan mail at the post office, forgetting it was Sunday, and bumming out when I opened my box only to find it empty, remembering that I'd checked it on Saturday, so naturally nothing was there.

There was nothing for it then but to ride home.

I had always liked my apartment. Its location was perfect,

along Alberta Street, full of street life and eccentricity; its size also perfect – tiny, easy for a bachelor to keep clean. But now, with Chester in it, it was neither. Every time I entered or exited I'd see Chester's cubicle, with his moat of trash around it like a shrine to my stupidity in letting him live there for free.

I was riding down Alberta Street, a few blocks from the apartment. In front of it, half-blocking the bike lane, was a bright yellow Hummer. This wasn't a car you see too often in Portland, much less in my neighborhood. I considered giving it a kick, or at least screwing with its mirrors.

I was just about to pass it, when the door flung open. I slammed on the brakes. A man stepped out. The front tire of my bike stopped mere inches from his waist.

It was Chester Fields. If I hadn't recognized him, I would have gone off on him for almost dooring me. "Dude," I said.

Chester looked mysteriously dapper. His hair was not only cut, but styled, all spiky like some boho hairdresser had taken to it with a razor. All the ink stains on his clothes and skin were gone, and he smelled of what I imagined to be expensive cologne, although I wouldn't have any idea what expensive cologne smells like. He was wearing a leather jacket with European styling and what appeared to be – yes, was – a pair of Diesel jeans, which unless he'd got them on closeout were currently selling for $200 a pop.

"Dude," I said again.

Chester closed the door of the Hummer and locked it. The keychain was a statuette of a stripper on a pole.

"Flynn!" Chester said. "I thought it was about time I got out of your hair. I'm just about finished packing. Mind helping get the drafting table into my … into this car."

I might be slow, but obvious is obvious. "Come into some money?" I asked. We were in the middle of Alberta Street, a dangerous spot, and so I wheeled the bike to the curb. On the way, I noticed the license plate. It read COMIX.

"No man," he said. "Time is time. I hope I've been helpful with your career."

He walked swiftly to the iron gate that guarded the entrance to our complex. He held the door open, letting me in, then sped ahead, taking the steps in twos as I carried my bike over my shoulder to the apartment door. After locking my bike on the balcony, I walked in. All the big stuff was gone: the cubicle walls, his clothes, the shredder. His drafting board was carefully cased in cardboard. The trash, however, remained.

"Plan to clean this up?" I asked.

The look on his face indicated he hadn't planned on it. "Man, I'm kind of in a hurry. Do you mind?"

"Yeah, I mind." I didn't know what was happening exactly, but I was pretty sure whatever was happening involved me getting screwed. I'd never seen anyone so itchy to leave a place.

"Maybe you can hire a cleaner." He pulled out his wallet. The wallet was brand new. It looked Italian. It was stuffed. He opened it and pulled out a hundred. "Can you break this?"

"No," I said, which was true, but if I had been able to break it, I doubt I would've. With the mess he'd made of my carpet, I'd likely have to rent a steam cleaner.

"No worries," he said. "A token of my appreciation. You were a great roommate." He patted me on the back, then handed me the hundred.

I stiffened. If I could get a do-over, I would have had him hand me over a few more of those hundreds. In fact, if I'd known then what I found out later that evening, I would have taken his entire Italian wallet, his new leather jacket, his Diesel jeans, and his goddamn brand-new Hummer. I took the hundred from him, and stuffed it in my front pocket. I really was too soft.

"I think I can get this out myself," Chester said, it becoming increasingly apparent I wasn't budging from my dumbfounded spot on the floor. He dragged it down the stairs. Thump. Thump. Thump. I heard the gate open and then close. I heard scratching as the table made its way along the concrete. I heard conversation. I heard a heave. And then I heard the engine of a Hummer guzzling its way to life like an overweight baby suckling.

I ran out to the balcony to yell for the apartment key, but Chester Fields was already gone. I hope he at least chipped a corner off that drafting table.

I KEPT THE HUNDRED FOR MYSELF, OF COURSE, and spent the rest of the day cleaning the apartment. Chester's garbage filled a total of fourteen garbage bags, which is quite impressive considering it was contained in a 10 × 10 space. He'd left a few decent things, including his black trenchcoat and dented top hat, abandoned apparently for the European-styled leather jacket and the spiky hair cut. I put them both in my closet. While I was at it, I cleaned my bedroom too, something I hadn't done in weeks. It took the entire day just to pick up and vacuum. The steam cleaning would have to wait.

I resolved to spend Halloween evening alone, which is

depressing when you're single and twenty-two, and when you live in a town like Portland, Oregon, where just about every bar and club in town has a Halloween event involving scantily-dressed women in the mood to do something wicked.

If I'd called around earlier, I could have found somewhere to go – Beale was always up for something – but I'd been so preoccupied with cleaning, and in the preoccupation of cleaning, ignoring all the potential implications of Chester's newfound wealth, that I hadn't picked up the phone.

I went to my room and started writing fans, telling them about the First Unitarian Church episode. It wasn't as fulfilling as it usually was. I gave up after an hour or so.

By ten o'clock, I deemed it dark enough to do what needed to be done. I could only fit about two of the garbage bags in the apartment waste receptacle, which meant I needed to find happy homes for the other twelve. With all the bars and restaurants on Alberta Street, I didn't think finding a Dumpster would be much of a problem.

I took the first two down to my basement, then grabbed two more, walking down the street with them. I was wearing the same clothes I'd been wearing all day, a holey T-shirt and a pair of old sweats, which, given what I'd been picking up, were covered in food stains. The first restaurant I came to had locked its Dumpster. So had the first café. This was a bit harder than I thought.

A group of about four people, costumed, walked my way. It hadn't dawned on me to be self-conscious, which was unusual.

"Flynn!" one of them exclaimed. Oh God, I'd been recognized. They surrounded me on the sidewalk.

"Dude, awesome costume," he said.

The guy talking was dressed as the Joker. I had no idea who he was. Some comics dork I'd met at a convention, I supposed. He smelled like mojitos.

"I heard about the movie rights, man," he continued. "Five hundred Gs. Holy shit. And you're out here dressed as a garbage man. Fucking righteous. Don't ever change, Flynn. Come get a drink with us. This is Chloe, and Petra –"

I cut him off. I couldn't listen to another word. "I'm not a garbage man," I said. "I'm just … trash."

The Joker thought I was joking. He laughed. They all laughed. I had to get out of here. I walked right at Chloe, who was dressed as Bat Girl, and Petra, dressed as Wonder Woman. They stepped aside gingerly, not fast enough, and the garbage rubbed against their brightly-hosed legs, the smell of month-old Taco Bell lettuce and tomatoes, rotten despite all the human effort put into making them unrottable, sneaking through the twist tie.

They laughed even harder as I stormed off. It was like all of DC Comics was out to make a fool of me.

I got off Alberta Street, walked up a side street, left the two bags on the sidewalk, and then returned to my apartment via side streets. At around two in the morning, still raging, I took the other ten garbage bags, walked out to my balcony, and tossed them, one-at-a-time, into the middle of the road.

When they landed, they burst, shredded paper poofing out like bottled confetti.

Chapter XXIV

The Battle of the Bookers

ON MONDAY, I WOKE UP LATE, GOT A CUP of coffee at Mecca, then rode straight to Booker's church. Distraction is good, and there's nothing more distracting than spending an entire day on phone banks, calling elderly Democratic voters in Florida, reading a script reminding them to vote and arranging transportation for them, if necessary, to the polls.

Booker was there as well, and at seven o'clock, when we closed shop for the night, breathless and exhausted, tongues sore from all the exercise, he asked me if I was going to be at Dante's that night. In the mental space I was in, I neither wanted to be alone nor talking to people, which meant the best place to be was somewhere where I could be with people but not have to talk. An entertainment venue, like Dante's Inferno, sounded like just the ticket.

Now you might think I'd want to avoid Dante's, given the challenge C.H.V.C.K. had presented, not to mention the humiliation Diogenes and company was apt to dish out. But I'd sort of thought this out. Dante's was a notorious club in the heart of everything that is seedy in downtown Portland. It had started its life as a brothel, then become a gambling den, then a speakeasy, then a flophouse, then a punk venue, then a strip club, then a Mongolian noodlehouse, before its current incarnation, as … well, it's hard to describe what Dante's had become, except to say that it sort of contained all the elements of what it was formerly, including the noodlehouse.

It was kind of an anything goes club, with burlesque shows, and sex worker nights, and fireeaters, and bands, and even a philosopher or two.

Clubs like this, with this level of potential chaos, needed the best of something that all clubs need in order to survive, and that something was this:

Bouncers.

Dante's bouncers were huge. They were six foot six bald guys with bull rings through their septums. They had arms and thighs that could have fed the Donner party for weeks. They had so many tribal tattoos they looked like zebras. They had ice blue, opaque eyes that didn't so much see as they absorbed. They were circus strongmen minus the handlebar mustaches. No one did anything untoward at Dante's and got away with it. Brush a tasseled tit and Dante's bouncers would have your arms behind your back, a hand over your mouth, and your ass on the street before you could put your drink down. You just vanished. Your friends couldn't even find you. You'd wake up three hours later in the drunk tank with a broken rib and wouldn't remember anything. They erased memory, Dante's bouncers. Not a single lawsuit had ever been filed against the club.

I was pretty sure Diogenes hadn't thought things all the way through.

I told Booker I'd come, went home to my clean and Chester-less apartment, took a shower, got dressed, and resolved to take a bus downtown so I wouldn't arrive smelling like body odor for once. As an afterthought, before I walked out the door, I put on Chester's black trenchcoat and top hat and looked in the mirror. They fit me well. I looked like he had, like a character in a Dickens novel. I thought it would feel weird dressing like Chester while I was angry at Chester, but it didn't at all, it made me feel older and wily.

Either way, it was a hell of a lot better than dressing up as a cheerleader.

I decided to keep them on and headed out the door. There was a great deal of garbage in the block or two of Alberta near my apartment, much of which I recognized. It was a long stroll to the bus stop, but even though it was chilly and *éadrom agus soineanta*, it seemed that something good would happen tonight for a change. It was All Saints Day, and to be honest, I felt more comfortable with the saints than the sinners.

The bus was long in coming, and when it did come, it zigzagged around the East Side before making its way down-

town. I arrived a half hour late. I assumed it was a doors open at nine, show starts at nine-thirty thing, but it was a Monday night, so one never knew.

One of the bouncers I've already described took my identification, shone his flashlight at it, tilted it a few times to see the hologram, turned the light into my eyes, holding it there longer than necessary (as a good bouncer always does, just so you know who's boss), then pressed a stamp to the underside of my wrist and let me pass.

I strode in. There was a cashier behind a bulletproof banker's window taking money. When I took my wallet out there were six Ben Franklins in it, plus a couple of Lincolns. The five hundred I'd cashed from Dougie's check plus the hundred Chester had given me yesterday plus some chump change from Mecca's tip jar. The show was only three bucks, but for some reason I pulled out the hundred.

"All I got," I said. The cashier's eyes narrowed a smidge, she got out one of those markers for checking bills, and after it stayed whatever color marked bills are supposed to stay when marked, she counted out the change and let me pass. As I walked into Dante's, my trench coat flared.

Booker was already on the stage.

The stage was red with red velvet curtains. On tables, throughout the place, were recessed coal burners, full of glowing red coals, and red flames bursting forth an unbelievable insurance liability. The bar to the right of the stage was backlit, with red lights. I couldn't tell if all this red was some aftereffect from the bouncer burning out my retinas with his flashlight, or if it all really was this red, but either way the whole place screamed SATAN, SATAN, SATAN.

Booker was up on his milk crates. He looked shell-shocked, like things weren't going well. A woman stood behind him on the stage holding a mallet. She was dressed in a gold sequined bikini and a hat with peacock feathers, like a Vegas showgirl. There was an amazingly large brass gong beside her.

Booker was in the middle of one of his standard anti-Bush soliloquies. "George W. Bush is a modern-day Constantine," he said. "He takes the facts and twists them to his needs. George W. Bush."

GOOOOOONNNNNNNNG!

Not only was it an unnaturally large gong, but it had also been wired to an amplifier. The sound of the gong made my face stretch. Flames flickered. Booker, being only feet from it, must have been rendered deaf. It wasn't that he looked shell-shocked. He was shell-shocked. The crates shook.

The audience chanted, "NO POLITICS, NO POLITICS, NO POLITICS."

Apparently some ground rules had been established, and Booker was breaking them. He was sweating.

He started again. He was back to stuttering, the way he used to when it was just him preaching to me about lesbians and Darwin fish. "Okay, all right, no politics, that's okay, but it's important, we must participate in the times, you ought to, well … okay."

He was stuck. Politics was all he could think about. We'd been on the phones to Florida all day, and the election was the next day, of course, he wanted to talk about politics.

"I'm not, well, this church of mine, it's not what you think, it's not just a theater act, we're not just a bunch of clowns. We really do believe in Jesus, but"

GOOOOOONNNNNNNNG!

I nearly hit the ceiling. I'd been watching Booker, and not the showgirl, and hadn't seen it coming.

"NO JESUS! NO JESUS! NO JESUS!" the audience chanted.

Booker's eyes looked like they were going to pop out of their sockets. He held his hands to his ears. He was shaky. The crowd was frenzied and laughing wildly, as if this weren't a show but a lynching. I looked over to a table near the bar, from where the chanting seemed to originate. Sure enough, it was C.H.V.C.K. The waitress taking their drink order looked startled, like she'd never served such a motley crew. A couple of the bouncers were swiveled their way as well. Diogenes had out the megaphone, with which he'd started the chanting.

He wasn't going to get bounced, though. The crowd was on his side. Booker wasn't the entertainment, Diogenes was.

Through all this, I'd just been standing in the back, staring at the stage. Booker caught my eye and I his. It seemed to relax him some. He got down off the crates and sat on them, a much safer position.

"Nietzsche," he said.

The Vegas showgirl swung the mallet back and raised her eyebrow, taking cues from Diogenes whether to use it. Maybe there weren't ground rules, maybe the ground rules were Diogenes. It looked like a set-up. He waved her off. Apparently, one could safely speak about Nietzsche at Dante's, but not Jesus or politics.

Booker was squinting, looking at me for cues as to whether or not he was going to get gonged. I gave him a thumbs-up. Nietzsche seemed pretty safe.

"When Nietzsche proclaimed that …" Booker was speak-ing slowly, annunciating each word to make sure it wasn't gongable. "… dog …was dead, and every non-atheist freaked out, they kind of missed his whole point."

"You see, dog being dead, it was only half the line. The second half of the line was the most important, 'And we have killed him!'"

"Nietzsche wasn't saying that dog didn't exist. In fact, dog did exist, at least in the past. Nietzsche was saying that dog had become old and useless and irrelevant."

"BORING!" It was Diogenes shouting through the megaphone.

"Boring!" It was Gassy.

The showgirl pulled the mallet back as if to strike. I brought my finger across my throat to warn Booker to cut back on the philosophizing. It didn't deter him.

"Back when dog was young and present in people's lives, dog's people would think about dog before they did anything, they would consider their communal dogliness, and they would only do things as a society if it were a just and compassionate thing to do."

A new chant was starting. It wasn't originating from Diogenes, though, it was just some random people in a corner booth. Without the megaphone, it started out faint, but it seemed to be building.

"Dog is god. Dog is god. Dog is god."

"But modern Chr …"

The Vegas showgirl waved the mallet around in a circle, egging on the crowd for a strike. I cut my finger across my throat over and over, in an effort to prevent the gonging. He wouldn't stop:

"But dog's people today, they act like dog is dead, and they ignore politics and …"

The showgirl had thrown the mallet in the air, in a baton move, and so couldn't strike when he mentioned politics. It seemed to hang in the air longer than possible.

The whole crowd was chanting it, "DOG IS GOD! DOG IS GOD! DOG IS GOD!"

" … social movements and all the things that make dog useful and relevant and even potentially fun, and they just sit around and wait until it's over so they can lie down for all eternity with their dead dog."

GOOOOOOONNNNG!

GOOOOOOONNNNG!

GOOOOOOONNNNG!

It was like Big Ben the way she was gonging it. Like it was Big Ben and you were inside the clockworks. The whole bar was vibrating. Cocktail glasses slid off tables. A bottle of Ketel One shattered.

Despite the sound-induced earthquake, Booker did not become unmoored. He continued to speak despite no one being able to hear. He was like a monk, mouthing holy words under his breath. Maybe it was because I'd studied him in college, or maybe it was because I'd seen so many of Booker's sermons before, but I could read his lips. He was quoting Nietzsche. I understood what he was mouthing:

> *Whither do we move?*
> *Away from all suns?*
> *Do we not dash on unceasingly?*
> *Backwards, sideways, forwards, in all directions?*
> *Is there still an above and below?*
> *Do we not stray, as through infinite nothingness?*
> *Does not empty space breathe upon us?*
> *Shall we not ourselves have to become Gods?*

The red velvet curtains closed.

I WAS SHAKEN BY THIS SERMON OF BOOKER'S, and what shook me about it wasn't what he said, but what he wasn't allowed to say. Whither had we gone? When had the search for meaning become so uncouth? Since when had seriousness been so disavowed? It was so normal we didn't even think about it anymore, this death of earnestness. If you wanted to sell a product on television, you didn't talk about the product itself, about what a good product it was, you got horses and ducks to tell dirty jokes.

It was like an entire country had turned into *Animal House*.

I was further shaken by my shakenness. It dawned on me, as I stood there in Dante's, trenchcoated and top-hatted, that I didn't think about what he had to say too often, that I didn't really consider his words.

That vision of him as the curtains closed, quoting Nietzsche, his smile, that ever-present glowing smile, defeated and downturned. I'll never forget it.

I needed a drink.

There was a bit of a backup at the bar, the end of Booker's speech having brought about intermission. Being Flynn, this usually meant a long wait. I normally didn't strike much of a figure. The top hat caught the bartender's eye, though. She picked me out from the masses in front of me, skipping lord knows how many customers who'd been waiting longer.

"Two double bourbons," I said. "Straight up. Maker's Mark." I said it with authority, like I knew what I was ordering when in fact I'd never ordered double bourbons in my life.

She set them up and I left her a twenty.

I assumed, given that c.h.v.c.k. was sitting at a table on the left, that c.h.v.r.c.h. would be somewhere on the right, near the front of the stage. I sauntered in that direction. There wasn't anybody there. Befuddled, I turned to the c.h.v.c.k. table. Mad Max waved me over. Ape Man held his hands under his chest, mocking tits. Gassy stood up and said, "Ann!" Diogenes, mercifully, was backstage preparing for his act.

I turned away. Where was everybody? There were some booths against the wall. I spotted brains, David. And next to him, shit, it was Mercyx. She was looking unusually butch, wearing some sort of black velvety thrift-store dinner jacket that flattened her already small breasts. It was adorable, of course.

I spun again. I was going to get dizzy, spinning.

There.

He was against the wall, next to the men's room. He wasn't waiting for the men's room, just standing next to it, in the worst possible place in a bar, a place where you'd only stand if you didn't really want to be there, if you'd been obliged to be there by your partner or something. It was the place in a bar to where odors escaped. It was the place for drunks.

I went to him. He smiled a half-smile, not a Booker smile. I handed him the double bourbon. He held it out, toasting me, and we tapped them together and we shot them, quickly, wordlessly, hopelessly, like conscripted men leaving in the morning for basic training. I leaned against the wall next to him. From our vantage, we could see Mercyx's booth, and the back of c.h.v.c.k.s' heads, and the stage. I wanted to ask him where everyone else was but thought better of it. We awaited our destiny.

The gong was tapped lightly, like you would a cymbal. The curtains opened. There he was.

Diogenes was glorious. He was wearing only Booker's gray terry cloth robe, but it didn't look oversized and silly on him like it had on Booker; it looked like it was a part of him, like there wasn't that much of a difference between the robe and his body hair. He was still bearded and matted and dreaded from his time in the wilderness, and the mattedness and dreadedness spread from his face down his neck down his chest down his navel and below, where the V finally met at a loosely tied knot. It was unclear whether or not he'd showered. It might have explained his waitresses' expressions. He had his trademark glasses and his trademark cigarette and his arms were spread wide open and he faced the ceiling. There were no shoes on his feet. They were earth-colored.

"Man!" he wailed. His cigarette fell off his lips and dropped to the floor. He put it out with a bare foot. "Or midget!"

The crowd went wild. "MAN! MAN! MAN!"

Booker and I shrunk. We were one with the wall.

"Jesus!" Diogenes said. The showgirl had been leaning the mallet against the floor, like she hadn't been planning to use it. She picked it up.

"Was a cyclist!"

The crowd applauded, although the applause wasn't as universal as the man or midget chant.

"He wasn't a fisherman, or an Englishman, he was a cyclist! And he didn't say thee and thou, he said fucking and shit!"

I recognized the line. Diogenes was mocking Booker, the sermon he had given the day I'd characterized the C.H.V.C.K. guys as Raggedy Andys.

"Fucking!" yelled Ape Man.

"Shit!" yelled Mad Max.

"And furthermore!" Diogenes wagged his finger at the audience. "it's been two-thousand years since our Lord and Savior was buried in that tomb, and His true message, yes I say, His true message, well, what was that true message?"

"Tell us!" yelled Gassy.

"Tell us!" yelled someone random in the crowd.

"Jesus's true message. Yes, the true message of our Savior Jesus Christ. Did I say Jesus Christ." Diogenes turned at glared at the gold-sequined bikini girl. "Yes, I said Jesus Christ. *Jesus Christ. Jesus Christ.*"

It took her a while to get the hint. But eventually, she did it. GOOOOOOONNNNG!

Diogenes nodded his head and strutted while the sound of the gong died down. It was hard to tell whether the leftover ringing was actual ringing or just the after-ringing in my ears.

When the decibel level returned to reasonable, he finished his sentence. "His true message, it was turn the other cheek."

Diogenes turned his back to the audience, bent over, and lifted up the back of his robe, mooning us all. It was one skanky ass.

The audience groaned. The bouncers, I noted, had moved closer to the stage, arms crossed and muscles taut. Public nudity wasn't enough for dismissal from Dante's. Oregon laws were odd like that, you can pretty much expose anything anywhere, so long as nobody touches anybody else's goods.

A bottle shattering, however, was a different matter.

It landed near Diogenes' bare feet. Shards of glass show-ered him. He stood from his prone position, but didn't move from his spot. "Get off the stage!" Surprisingly, the person yelling and apparently throwing the bottle was one of the chef paramedics, standing with his hands on his waist look-ing farcically indignant. Another bottle hit him on the shoul-der blade, ricocheting off of him then plunking down on the stage lights. "Asshole!" It was the second chef paramedic, mimicking the first.

A lot of things happened at once. Flames flickered. A couple bouncers and the chef paramedics simultaneously disappeared. Under the lights, Diogenes staggered, in what seemed a very staged and theatrical fashion, fell to one knee, let his robe fall off his shoulders and onto the stage floor, and then, once again overdramatizing, flopped over, his legs splayed and his feet facing the audience, which, given the fact that he was, at this point, entirely disrobed, forced every pair of eyes in Dante's to follow the V of his legs to their van-ishing point, a mass of tangled and matted pubic hair and an astonishingly erect penis.

I confess that this is confusing, why and how this hap-pened, but what was even more bizarre was what happened next. From the back of the stage, from behind the gong, ap-peared the Vegas showgirl, who had slipped off for a moment in the midst of the mayhem. Her gold sequined bikini top was now missing, or rather it had slid down to her navel, a mass of undercup and shimmer and nude-colored nylon hosiery. She ran forward, on her tiptoes, like a ballerina, her hand over her mouth in mock horror, and as she arrived beside Diogenes' prone and immobile body, in a voice that seemed to match his prior overdramatizing, she screeched, "Booker, my Lord!"

I was staring at her now-bare tits. I probably would have been staring at them anyway, being a guy and all, but I wasn't staring at them out of lust or desire or even because a great pair of tits is simply a wonder to stare at. I was staring be-cause I recognized them.

They were Emerald's tits. My whore's tits. They were at least D's. They were more raisined then I'd seen them before shy, apparently, in the spotlight but they were definitely her tits. And now that I'd studied up a bit on tits on the Internet, just so I wouldn't be in the dark next time I was confronted with tits like these, I knew whether they were fake or real. They were taut and ball-like and fake. They weren't Mercyx's tits at all.

Emerald got down on her hands and knees beside Dio-genes. She put her thumb and forefinger to her mouth. She made a ring with her now wet fingers on the base of Diogenes' cock. And then, brushing her feathered hat aside, she lunged for the head of that which eagerly awaited her arrival.

Diogenes was still miked.

You could hear the squash as she went down on him.

The curtains weren't rolled shut or even snapped shut, they were just suddenly and completely *there*. There was a whoosh of air as if wraiths had entered the room. Flames went out, leaving nothing but the dim light of the glowing coals and the backlit bar. There was neither the faintest muffle, nor the faintest jiggle from the behind the curtains.

When Dante's bouncers took care of things, they did so in silence.

Chapter xxv

The Last Supper

BOOKER WAS GONE. HE'D DEFINITELY been there, right up until Emerald had appeared topless beside the gong, but now he was gone. I was instantly concerned – he'd done nothing wrong, but as part of the "act," it was entirely plausible the wraiths had gotten him too.

I checked the men's room. Not there. I looked over at Mercyx and David's booth, a place I'd been avoiding looking. No sign of him there; in fact, they were gone, too. Dante's was a huge venue, with three other bars besides the main stage lounge. I could have looked in the other bars, but I had a hunch. I walked past the entranceway with the bulletproofed banker's booth and out the club doors. If he was upset, and he surely was, there was one place he might stop before he went home, and it happened to be right across the street from Dante's: Voodoo Doughnuts.

I walked across broad 3rd Street, the fresh blacktop glistening from the *éadrom agus soineanta*, a soft drizzle, to the queue. Any night of the week, in any weather, including a Monday after a big party night, a queue waited outside Voodoo Doughnuts. It wasn't too long, just a few hooded figures, the wetness soaking through cotton, true Portlanders never fighting it, but just letting the moisture penetrate.

I got in line next to him. I didn't say anything, men knowing better than to bring up something emotional with other men. We were inside the doors shortly, not too wet, the drizzle mere pinpricks, and we made our way around the U-shaped line inside Voodoo's bedroom-sized interior, looking at the wall of Polaroids, the glazed faces of former patrons drunk and sugared. There was a buzz in the air as there always is in Voodoo, as if you're not in a doughnut shop but a shrine. Groups in fours, fives, and sixes, speaking in low, excited voices, Booker and me an unusually subdued exception.

Finally, we were up at the front, all the different Voodoo Doughnut options spinning around a glass-encased motorized Lazy Susan, a cacophony of misshapen hand-formed creations, dolls and dicks and bright orange suns, a middle finger to the turnkey American fried dough industry, the Dunkins and the Krispy Kremes and even the strip-mall doughnut shops run by recent immigrants, still inspired by the American dream, all with the same perfectly rounded and shaped rows of glazed and caked and old-fashioned and frittered. They weren't even that good, Voodoo Doughnuts. They made you feel terribly sick. But when you put a Nyquil-flavored doughnut to your lips and you bit down, and you tasted its syrupy wrongness, you were aware that what you were putting inside your mouth was a rebellion, and when the carbohydrates and proteins and fats of that doughnut became your fuel, and in some cases even your being, an extra inch of fat above your belt line, you couldn't help but feeling that in a nation bound by chains, you were somehow more free.

"Two Voodoo dolls," Booker ordered. We'd gotten to the front while my brain had gone off on its reverie. He looked up at me to make sure he'd ordered what I wanted. The cashier was staring at Booker as if he was a figment of his imagination. This kind of staring was common, I'm sure, for Booker, but the cashier's stare was unusually long and confused.

"Are you … real?" the cashier asked.

Now in order to fully understand this question, you have to understand something about Voodoo Doughnut employees. They're all on acid. This isn't something I know for a fact, so if you work for the DEA or something don't go in and bust them, it's just deduction, mixed in with odd questions such as the one the cashier asked. If you own a doughnut shop that runs twenty-four hours, seven days a week, and if you employ young, attractive twenty-somethings with absolutely no work ethic, but whose youth and attractiveness makes them employable just about anywhere, there is only one way to keep them at your shop and focused and working into the wee hours, and that way is acid.

Booker's eyes were just about level with the counter top. He'd put a five on it, anticipating the cost. His response to the cashier's question was unusually thoughtful. "No," he said.

The cashier looked away from Booker and up at me. You could tell he was making a super-human effort to control his shit. "What can I get for you?" he asked.

I'm pretty sure it was the top hat that made me say it. "Your face is melting."

He gulped. He blinked. He put a hand to his face and rubbed. "What can I get for you?" he repeated. He said it like he wasn't sure whether or not he'd said it the first time.

I knew I could do more to him, but I didn't have it me. Booker and I had already doomed the guy to an entire shift of midget appearances and face meltings.

"Two Voodoo dolls," I said. "He's not real, but his money is." I took the fiver off the counter and handed it the cashier.

He held it up to the light, not so much to check for its hidden plastic thread, but more to verify its existence, then he walked to the chrome shelving behind him, where the trays of magical doughnuts waited, pulled two Voodoo dolls off sticky wax paper, put them in a brown paper bag, and handed the bag to me.

Waiting for change seemed too complicated. I handed the bag to Booker, and the two of us left Voodoo Doughnuts, the cashier's melting eyes burning the back of Booker's head.

After we stepped through the threshold and out of holy ground, I looked over at Booker, expecting to see a smile of humored recognition about what had just been said. His face, instead, was grim. His eyes white, like fish gone belly-up.

He's not real, but his money is.

THE *ÉADROM AGUS SOINEANTA* HAD UPGRADED to a *uisge*, but Booker and I sat back against the red brick wall in front of the doughnut shop anyway, letting the hard rain fall. I was glad for the trenchcoat. A hipster walked by smoking a cigarette, and Booker asked him for one. The hipster obliged. I'd never seen Booker smoke. He seemed unhappy.

From our vantage point, we could see the entrance to Dante's. There was a lot of impressive leg coming into the club. After our show, at ten o'clock, it was sex workers night.

"Magdalene wasn't a prostitute," Booker said.

I had expected Booker to lament what had taken place at Dante's. Not this, whatever it was.

"What?" I asked.

Booker blew smoke out his nostrils. "In the Scholar's Edition, it's black."

Neither one of us had touched the doughnuts yet. Booker only exhaled through his nose. The way he did that, through his flat broad nose, he reminded me of one of those Chinese dragons you see on Chinese New Year.

Booker continued, "I'm just like all of them really. Like Constantine and George W. Bush and Jerry Falwell. I just use the Bible for my own ends –"

"Can I have a drag?" I asked.

"You don't smoke," he replied.

"Neither do you," I said.

"That woman Diogenes ran over on Lark Mountain," Booker went on, ignoring my request, "she was a refugee. Her real name was Zaina. They're easy prey in my line of work. They come here. They don't speak the language. They don't have any skills. They don't have papers. But they have something, you can see that right away. I mean, you flatter them, you respect them, they like the money…"

He handed me the cigarette. It was true, I didn't smoke. I'd tried smoking, of course. And being an alternative zine boy, smoking was sort of my demographic, but honestly, coffee provided a far superior and longer lasting buzz, tasted good, and didn't cause wheezing and lung cancer.

"The INS caught her. They flew her to Jordan. There's no telling what will happen to her when she arrives. If someone in a Muslim country finds out she's a prostitute, it won't bode well."

I looked at the logo. There was an F crossed by a C. It was a Chesterfield.

"I run a service," he said.

I tried being cool about this conversation and took a drag. It got all caught up in my lungs and produced a coughing fit. Booker didn't let the fit stop him.

"The girls liked me, the midget thing plays out well in the porn industry. I found a nice niche, older girls with a little experience. Antique Road Show, it was a cover."

I'd taken a few more drags while he'd been talking. He took it out of my hands.

"I wanted out, Flynn," Booker continued. "I met the C.H.V.C.K. guys, and they thought I was the funniest thing they'd ever seen, 'Tiny, the midget pimp!' And they got me involved in their whole guerilla cycling thing, and Diogenes, I mean, behind all that nonsense, he sort of had a good idea. Moving people. Getting people to do things they wouldn't otherwise do. Taking them out of their comfort zone. It was attractive."

"But the thing was, I wanted to do it differently – I wanted to be sincere. And that's when … you know. It's impossible. I'm a midget, for one, and a pimp, for another, and even if I wasn't a midget or a pimp, people just won't stand for sincerity. It's become culturally impossible to do anything other than entertain."

He had stopped blowing the smoke out of his nostrils and was blowing rings. I knew he was telling me all this stuff because it bothered him, but all I could think about was how brave he was, how wildly he had lived his life. Here I was, a normal-sized Flynn, and I'd never have the guts to be a preacher, much less a pimp. Hell, I couldn't even sleep with a whore unless I was passed out. Booker had no fear.

"I can't just leave her, Flynn. They really will …"

He went on about what was going to happen to this girl, Zaina, but I wasn't really listening. Mercyx was walking out of Dante's, alone. I knew what I needed to do. I'd known what I needed to do for months. And yet my ass stayed on the sidewalk.

Booker followed my eyes and changed the subject. "You're lucky," he said.

While watching her, I'd absently picked a Voodoo doll out of the brown paper bag, and was randomly pulling pretzels out and pushing them back in. "How exactly am I lucky?"

"She loves you," he said.

He'd taken his own doll out, and was turning it over, figuring out whether he wanted to eat it or not. Mercyx was trying to hail a cab. I tore off a leg off the doll, and popped it into my mouth. For a moment, I recalled Mercyx doing the same thing. The sexy way the red jelly had hung off her pierced tongue. "And you know this because …"

"People talk." His cigarette was in one hand, the doughnut in the other. "I wish I could have something like that, something real. Have you thought about … pursuing her?"

I didn't respond. I tore off the other leg. Popped that in my mouth. I bent my knees. I was going to do it. I was going to go to Mercyx, and ask her how she was, then I was going to get in the cab with her and …

Diogenes and Emerald stepped out of the club.

I tore off the head.

The minute Diogenes saw Mercyx, he abandoned Emerald. He took long, sly strides.

The minute Emerald saw Booker, she abandoned Diogenes. Her strides were just as long, but seemed angry. Her hair was different from what it had been in Dante's, it was now in a perfect Betty Page. She had a mink coat draped around her, or what could have been any kind of furry coat, real or synthetic, but was mink in my head because it spoke of money. It covered her in such a way that it hinted there might be nothing underneath. She wore heels.

She stepped off the curb and began crossing 3rd Avenue. She didn't look both ways.

"Shit," Booker said. She was upon on us before we could get our backs off the wall.

In the distance, Diogenes had reached Mercyx. They were chatting.

"Five hundred dollars," Emerald said. "Dish."

"It wasn't my –" Booker started to speak, but was quickly cut off.

"I'll never be able to step foot in that club again. He wasn't … washed." Her eyes smoldered.

It didn't look like the bouncers had damaged her, but then again, it was hard to tell with all the fur she had on. Maybe they didn't go after girls.

"Susan, I'm out of the –"

The toe of her high heel jumped to his crotch. She held it there, threatening to crush it like a bug. "You'll either pay me now, or you get me a gig. Freelancing sucks, and you know I can't work for anybody else."

Booker was looking up at her. What I saw in his eyes wasn't fear but pity.

"And don't ever, ever, use my real name." She pressed down. He squirmed, but didn't move. He was willing himself to be at her mercy.

I wish I could say I did what I did to save him, but that wasn't it at all. A cab had stopped in front of Mercyx and Diogenes.

I stood up from the wall. She wasn't quite as imposing at eye level. I pulled my wallet out of my back pocket and began plucking them out. One hundred, two hundred, three, four, five. It was the money I had earned from the comic – all of it. I could feel her eyes watching the bills as I counted them. I put them back in my wallet. Put the wallet back in my pants. I looked into Emerald's eyes. "They're yours," I said, "but you have to finish the job."

She started to speak, but I cut her off before any words came out of her mouth.

"My apartment, one hour, full service."

I expected her to balk, or knee me in the balls, or just flat out laugh. She didn't. Emerald was a professional. The hardened expression, the anger, in an instant, it was gone. "Flynn, right?"

I nodded.

"You were sweet? I left you my wig?"

I didn't nod this time. Sweet wasn't something I wanted to be known for. Emerald slipped her spidery hands inside my trench coat, pressed her fake tits against my chest, and whispered in my ear, "two hundred up front, the rest when you're done."

I pulled my wallet back out and handed her the two hundreds. I thought she was going to kiss me but she didn't.

I WISH I'D GIVEN MORE THOUGHT TO HOW BOOKer wanted to be me – normal; and how I wanted to be him – weird. It would have saved us both a lot of grief.

Emerald and I stepped arm and arm to the curb. Mercyx and Diogenes were arguing. The cab driver, losing his patience, spotted us and peeled out, taking a right off of Burnside and pulling in front of us at Voodoo. She saw us then, Mercyx did, and I know what I should have done.

I didn't, though.

Emerald and I got in the cab. The cabbie drove us over the Broadway Bridge, back to the East Side and home.

Chapter XXVI

Election Day

IT WAS TEN THIRTY. I'D PLANNED TO WAKE up early, vote, then ride to Mecca for my eleven to close shift. I wouldn't have time for any of that now. I got up, tussled my hair into an acceptable shape, found a reasonably clean T-shirt, hoodie, and pair of jeans, checked the weather – rain – added my rain pants and rain jacket to the mix, made sure my tires were full enough for safe riding, and then headed to work, hoping I wouldn't sweat enough to mix with the previous night's sex.

When I barged through the door at ten fifty-nine, Beale stared at me like he had a huge question to ask. As he was friends with Mercyx, and was still in contact with her, I imag-ine he did. Typical of Beale, though, he asked something else, "Voted?"

I wiped the grounds off the counter top underneath the espresso maker, then cleaned the steam wand. If you were having an I-don't-want-to-deal-with-customers day, you'd work the espresso machine rather than the counter. By wiping it down, I was marking my territory.

"Not yet," I said.

"Double split-shot Americano, to go," he said, passing along an order. "You're closing tonight, right."

"Yeah."

"So when are you going to vote?"

I clicked two shots into the double filter basket, then tamped it smooth.

"I guess I'm not," I said.

Beale and I had spent the last two months training people on how to cope with this very situation, how to gently remind friends and associates to go to the voter's booth with kind, encouraging words.

"Hazelnut latte, extra foam," he said.

I put a demitasse under the filter basket. I poured the contents of the demitasse into a sixteen ounce Styrofoam cup. I heated up some water under the steam wand.

"You're a fuck-up," he said.

I poured the hot water into the Styrofoam cup, placed it on the counter next to Beale, then clicked another shot of espresso into the filter basket for the latte. *You're a fuck-up* wasn't part of the training.

"I get off at two," he said, "but I'm going to stay until three. Between two and three, you're going to go to your polling place – you do know where it is, don't you? – and you're going to vote. When you come back you're going to give me a ten-spot. Depth charge."

I nodded. Kind and encouraging is often overrated.

I HAD A BIT OF A PREMONITION WHAT WAS GOING to happen. As a Portlander it was difficult to understand George W. Bush's attraction. To us, George W. Bush was so obviously an imbecile that you wondered if Republicans were brainwashed. We looked to the sky for alien spaceships. We wondered if all that stuff about chem-trails was true. And yet, when you turned on FIXED news, and you saw all those red, angry white faces, and you saw those words FAIR and BALANCED, and you heard all that stuff that wasn't, you couldn't help but feel like the machine had us. That despite an errant war, the torture of innocents, imprisonment without trials, and all of this stuff you were sure had been permanently squashed by democracy, we were going to lose.

Of course, there were other reasons, too, why I didn't want to go to Booker's.

I asked Beale if he'd go to a bar with me rather than to Booker's church, where there was a party and free booze and all the people we'd worked with for the past two months. Beale eyed me skeptically, but Beale being Beale, and Beale being a good friend, and Beale thinking what I was thinking, that we were probably going to lose, and that it would suck to be at the church if we lost, he agreed. So on the night of November second, Beale and I went to a bar, and the bar was selling pints of beer for two dollars, so we got good and sloshed, and at first the evening was quite jovial, but then, as the evening progressed, and as a map of the United States was splashed on a screen, half of it red and half of it blue, the evening took on an air of doom. We were in a bar in Portland, Oregon, and the people in the bar, were overwhelmingly, if not one-hundred percent, Kerry supporters, and the fact that it was even close, that so many Americans could vote for this man who had led us so astray, was depressing. Finally, sometime around one, Florida, that state we'd spent so much time calling, that state that had stayed gray for so long, it turned red. And then Beale and I knew. We knew all the numbers, and without Florida, all was lost.

George W. Bush was going to be the president for another four years. The bar went silent. That silence was the sound of people looking down at the dregs of their pint glasses. It was the sound of people wanting to jump in.

❧

Chapter XXVII

Where Bartholomew Flynn is Struck By Lightning and Knocked Off His Horse

O HERE WE ARE AT THIS BIG MOMENT in the gospel, and the problem is, I don't want to write about it. I've been stuck on this page for days, not wanting to tell you what happened. There's a saying that time cures all, but there isn't an equal saying that says memory rips open the scab.

There should be.

It was the day after the election, and it seemed like I should help Booker take the place down, it being somewhat cathartic to rip cords out of phone jacks. There were a host of other reasons why I should have wanted to see Booker, too. Reasons I was only subconsciously aware of: I was embarrassed about what I'd done with Emerald and for not showing up for the party. I wanted to explain it to him, and I knew, being who he was, that he'd tell me it was okay, that he'd put it in perspective.

I thought I'd go cycling afterward, so I put on my cycling gear – shorts, jersey, arms, legs, gloves, jacket, cap – it being cold and rainy, belted my fanny pack around my waist, then biked over to the church. A *sciorta en aird* had gone through in the night, and Prescott Street was littered with tree limbs and garbage can lids and other debris, making riding down it extremely hazardous, given its narrow width and lack of a bike lane.

I arrived at Booker's a bit road-shaky. The storm had ripped one side of the IMPEACH BUSH banner from the bell tower so that it hung down vertically, wet and clinging to the side of the church. The letterboard out front was missing letters. Instead of VOTE EARLY!, it read T EAR Y! The Jolly Roger still hung from its flagpole, a tad more tattered.

I U-locked my bike and knocked on the door. No one answered. Being headquarters, the lack of an answer was no longer a detriment to simply walking in, and so I did.

The place was trashed. Despite losing, the party, it appeared, had raged on. A keg sat on the altar – the bank of phones, askew and off-the-hook, having been shoved aside to make way for it. Beer cups littered the aisles between the pews. The American flag, which had been hung behind the altar where a crucifix would be in a normal church, had come unpinned. Red, white, and blue waste was everywhere: yard signs and door knob flyers and mailers. We'd tried to outpatriotize Bush and lost.

I called out rather timidly, got no reply, and finally walked up to the altar. Paperwork was scattered all over it, underneath the keg and the phones, all those voter rolls and call lists and memos that had seemed so crucial just a couple of days before, now useful only as a means for soaking up spillage.

The low sound of Bob Dylan's *Like a Rolling Stone* was coming from the vestibule, where Booker's bedroom was. The door was cracked.

I don't know what made me do it. I had this image of Booker, in his gray terry cloth bath robe, cooking bacon and eggs while a whore lolled naked in his bed, pleased as punch to see his good ol' buddy Flynn poking his head into the room. "Come on in, Flynn. Here's a condom, have at it!"

I walked over to the vestibule door and peeked through the crack. It wasn't who I was expecting in the bed. He was lying under his black satin sheets and his cow print comforter facing me, sound asleep, his face more peaceful than I've ever seen it, his mouth full and upturned, as if nothing at all disappointing had happened the evening before. Behind him, with the exact same expression on her face was indeed his whore. Only the whore wasn't one of the usual whores, it wasn't Skye or Emerald or Sophia, or some other girl with a name that wasn't really her name.

The whore was Mercyx.

They were spooned.

One of his eyes opened.

I wonder how he would describe the expression he must have seen on my face. Crestfallen? Horrified? Devastated? Crushed? Whatever expression is all of those feelings combined and worse, like that drawing that's used to represent the horror of Nazi Germany. The one that looks sort of like this:

I fled.

Shouting, "What the fuck!" would have been the more appropriate action, but as usual, when faced with a fight or flight option, I fled. I leapt off the altar and onto the hardwood floor of the nave, slipping on sludge – the mixture of beer and paperwork like ice – and sliding into a pile of bike frames that had been covered with a red, white, and blue banister.

The bike frames fell on me and I tossed them onto the theater seats and I slipped trying to get up, and another bike from the stack fell on top of me. It would have been funny, if you had a YouTube video of this, me trying to flee and me falling over and all these bikes falling on me.

I could hear Mercyx behind the door, saying no, no, no, and I could hear Booker shuffling, likely getting clothes on, and I'd banged my chin on a bicycle fender and was bleeding, having opened up a good-sized, stitch-ready gash, but I couldn't stay, I had to escape, I had to run from this vision branded into my head:

Post-coital midget smile.

Post-coital Mercyx smile.

I slowed it to a safe, sludge-proof gallop and I limped and I was the hunchback and this was Notre Dame and I'd never make it through this fucking maze of theater seats to the doors in the back of his church.

He'd opened the door to the vestibule and I knew without looking that he had that damn Hugh Hefner grey terry cloth robe on and he shouted "Flynn!" and his voice was midget cock in Mercyx vagina, midget cock in Mercyx mouth, midget cock in Mercyx ass.

It was steeplechase. I was over the seats. I opened the back doors and leapt the three steps of the stoop and getting out of that church was like being blown out of a cannon. Or an ass. Or a vagina. Like some Thai number girl shooting ping pong balls.

My ankle gave and they were entwined and fucking. I soldiered to the bike and they were entwined and fucking. I removed the U-lock (I was good at this one thing, no amount of fear or anger or hurry or pain or fucking being able to slow this one thing that I was good at, removing a U-lock.)

They were entwined and fucking and I was on the bike, jangly, and when I went to click my shoe into the pedal I missed, and my shin scraped the back of the pedal and if you're a cyclist you're wincing, because you've done it before and you can see the skin peeling. I was all pain. I tried to click in a second time and succeeded. My bike was on the sidewalk and I jumped the curb into the street in front of the church in which midget and Mercyx were one.

I turned. Midget cock was in the doorway. It wasn't the terry cloth robe. It was a cassock. Somehow worse. His arms were crossed. He looked forlorn. I shot him the finger. If he had looked down from where he'd stood he would have seen spots of my blood. He didn't flinch.

ONE CAN NEVER ASK THOSE WHO HAVE COMmitted suicide what exactly it was at that very last second, that point of action, that made their brain send the message to override human survival instinct and jump off a bridge. I suspect, though, it's not so much the laundry list of shame, the weight of all the stuff that got them on the bridge in the first place, but more of a dare. Like kind of a you've fucked up before, I dare you to really fuck up thing.

Despite the shame of it all – the original proposal on The Bridge of the Gods, the selling out of the comic, the spending all my money on a fake-boobed whore, to the culmination,

Booker (a midget!) screwing Mercyx instead of me – I knew I couldn't do it, I didn't have the strength of character to jump.

I'd ridden the bike straight to the Broadway Bridge. With my various injuries, I couldn't put much weight on the pedals, so I'd spun the chain in a low gear, frantic and bandy-legged. Passersby would have thought me mentally ill, which I suppose at the time I was. I rode past the midpoint of the bridge, where most sensible suicides would have stopped, jumping into the Superfund sewage of the Willamette, and slowed instead at the span's two-thirds point, where it passed right next to the Albers grain silo. I didn't know whether one could actually die on the Broadway Bridge, whether the distance to the water would actually kill you, so I determined to jump onto pavement.

I parked the bike and leaned it against the orange railing. Looking down at the railroad tracks a good five stories below, I was pretty sure if I jumped death would happen. It would suck for whoever had to clean it up, but some things you had to be sure of.

I wouldn't do it, of course; I didn't have the courage. I hadn't had the courage, for two months, to tell Mercyx the truth: to tell her about the sex worker and tell her that the marriage proposal had been a mistake and tell her that I cared about her and wanted to be with her. I hadn't had the courage to tell Chester to get out of my apartment. I hadn't had the courage to tell Dougie I wasn't ready to sign his contract. Hell, I hadn't even had the courage to yell, to scream in rage, to punch Booker in the face when I'd found him with my girl (even if she wasn't my girl).

I was such a coward that I'd run. Like a little girl dressed in a cheerleader outfit and started awake by a nightmare, I'd run. For all I knew they were just cuddling under the sheets, chaste as nuns, but I was too much of a coward to even find out the truth.

I picked up the bike – my swift efficient neon-yellow machine – and I threw it over the railing. I watched it spin, like a high diver doing reverse somersaults with a couple of twists. I watched it shatter, its chain rings popping off and rolling down the gravel banks of the tracks. I'd thrown it before I'd even thought about throwing it. It seemed to me I'd just destroyed the only thing I had left to live for.

I just kept going. I unstrapped my bike helmet and tossed that, and my cleats, I un-Velcroed them, and tossed them too, and my cap, and my legs, and my arms, and my socks, and my jersey, and my shorts. There was only one thing left wrapped around me, my fanny pack.

A cyclist rode by me on a cruiser. She had one of those Amsterdam bells. Ching, ching, it went. Cars drove by honking. Someone yelled WOO-HOO! out their window.

I knew why I'd done all this. I'd turned the tables on myself. I was buck naked on a bridge with no way to get home. It wouldn't take courage to die. It would take courage to live.

I spun the fanny pack around so the zipper was in front. I unzipped it. I pulled out my cellphone. It was the last thing really, the last thing that could save me. I tossed that too.

Someone threw a milkshake. It hit me in the calf and burst, bovine lactation splattering everywhere.

I unstrapped the fanny pack and was about to twirl it around and toss that too, when something stopped me. Something red was hanging out of it. Something gem-like.

The wig.

I was going to die. There was no way that I could not die. There was no way that I could walk back across the span of this bridge, naked, with nothing but this whore's wig. I would have to jump.

I pulled the wig out of the fanny pack and held it, just looking at its glowing rubescence. I thought about wearing it, about Diogenes making such an ass of me, of me laying there dressed in a Wisconsin Badgers cheerleader's uniform, in a headlock with a beer bong tube going down my throat.

It started out small, on my tongue, and then it took over my mouth, and then it filled my head, and then it sunk into my chest, and then it was all of me. It was a laugh. I laughed. It was funny. I was funny.

I was standing on the Broadway Bridge, my favorite bridge in Portland, buck naked, the day after Bush got reelected, with nothing but a whore's wig. This wasn't sad. This wasn't tragic. This was the funniest thing ever.

What does not kill me only makes me stronger.

I put the wig on. I turned to the road. I gave traffic a full frontal. I shook my arms and hips. I puffed out my chest. I danced. I was one of Booker's prostitutes, one of Jesus's prostitutes, a prostitute of the world. I'd been fucked. Oh, how I'd been fucked.

"Fuck me!" I yelled. "Fuck me!" I shouted. "FUCK ME!"

I wasn't a coward. Why had I ever thought I was a coward? I could take all of this and then some. I was a funnel for everybody else's bullshit. Hell, I was Jesus. Bartholomew Flynn equals Jesus fucking Christ.

This time it was a soda. An ice cold Vanilla Coke. It hit me square in the chest. I could almost see it in slo-mo, the way it turned oval upon impact, the way the plastic lid popped off, the way the corn syrup and cubes forked up and ricocheted off the underside of my neck. It hurt. I'd have a bruise. The sweetness stung the cut on my chin. I didn't give a shit. I really didn't give a shit. I was impervious. I laughed even harder.

That's when it happened. With sticky, overflavored, Vanilla Coke dripping off of me, it happened. What happened was way more than a laugh, although for anyone who's experienced it, a laugh is a huge part of it. My whole body was filled with what can only be described as lightness. I tingled. I instantaneously understood everything. I understood Booker and Diogenes and Nietzsche and Jesus. In order to reach the Kingdom of Heaven, or whatever you want to call it – your higher calling, your fullest potential – you have to make an ass of yourself. Over and over and over again.

It wasn't a lightning bolt knocking me off a donkey that converted me to Christianity.

It was Vanilla Coke and a whore's wig.

Chapter XXVIII

Where King David Passes Some Time at 24-Hour Fitness
& Where Bartholomew Flynn
Considers Life in the Trunk of a Toyota Tercel

I HAD MY WIG ON AND WAS LAUGHING AND WAVing my arms around and tears and blood and Vanilla Coke was streaming down my face and I was brainless – my ticket punched for the loony bin – when a late model car screeched to a halt beside me on the bridge. The driver had brains tattooed on the outside of his head. I'd always thought David was crazy. I was pretty sure now that I was crazier than he.

"Get in!" he shouted. "Get in!"

There was a whole lot of honking going on, David blocking a lane quite illegally, a naked man dancing on the bridge.

The minute I saw him I came to my senses. It was freezing. I jumped in his car.

"Jesus Christ," David said. "Would you cover it?"

I put the wig over my cock, embarrassingly shrunken from the cold. The wig looked like an earmuff. A cock muff.

"Is this some sort of catharsis thing for you, running around naked? I mean, it's attractive, but you're going to get yourself killed."

I crossed my arms across my chest and shivered.

David cranked the heat to max and started driving, looking rather worriedly behind him in the rearview mirror for cops. They were sure to come. His brows were furrowed, but there was something else in his face as well – amusement. He drove off the bridge and onto Lovejoy, quickly turning off that onto 8th, into the chichi of the Pearl.

"She loves you, you know," David said.

I didn't reply. Now that I was in the car I was kind of in shock.

David continued, "She saw you walk off with that sex worker and … Why did you do that? Everyone knows what you really wanted."

My instinct was to unlock the door and jump out as David was telling me this, but I was done with running. There were things you already knew but didn't need to hear. I let him talk.

"A lot of things went wrong for the two of them – your little fling, the election – sometimes with too much booze people just take comfort in each other," David said.

The Vanilla Coke was beginning to dry. My crossed arms stuck to my chest.

"You don't have to let this destroy you," David said. "None of you do."

David's cellphone rang. He answered it.

"I found him," he said. "He's okay. Yeah, you really did fuck up." He clapped the cellphone shut.

David was taking lefts and then rights and then lefts as we drove through the Pearl. We could hear a siren off in the distance. He pulled into a U-Park parking lot and stopped the car.

"Get out and get into the trunk. I'm going to pull into the 24-Hour Fitness Club parking lot – it's covered so the fuzz can't see it from the street. I'm going to stay there for maybe ten minutes, just until your trail gets cold and they give up, and then I'm going to go in and get my gym clothes and a towel from inside and bring it out to you.

"You're not going to freak out, are you?"

"No," I replied. Ten minutes in a trunk naked and covered in Vanilla Coke was going to suck, but I understood David's logic.

The siren was getting closer. David popped the trunk latch. "Go!" he said.

I put the wig back on. I went. Being naked and wearing a wig, I ran around an extra time for good luck, as if this were a Chinese fire drill. David had his hands over his face like he couldn't believe what he was seeing. I jumped in the trunk. It was pretty nasty in there. My ass cheek was pressed up against the hubcap of the spare, my head on the jack. There was other shit back there as well, a banana peel for one, but the trunk door slammed before I had a chance to suss it all out. David put the car into drive and did a quick U-ee. A few more turns and a polite conversation between David and what must have been the parking lot attendant. Then the car was parked and there was silence.

I was cold. The heat from the car's interior hadn't seeped into the trunk. I curled up into a fetal position. A siren came near then quickly whizzed away. I'd been saved, but here, in the darkness, things slowed down a bit. It wasn't so neat and easy after all. There were still consequences. I was broke. I was bikeless. Booker and Mercyx had still slept together, and even if I wasn't going to kill myself over it, I'd still have to deal with the awkwardness of it.

In addition to the wig I'd put on my head, I'd brought the fanny pack into the trunk. I suddenly had the urge to make sure I had the keys to my apartment, a safe hideaway where I could lounge about in pajamas and read fan mail for a week. I shook it, they were in there, for sure, but still. I unzipped the pouch where the keys were. I reached my hand in. My fingers curled around the keys instantly, but my thumb felt something else, something circular with a bump.

I was shivering there in the trunk. The metal of the hub-cap and car jack against my bare skin was cold. There was creepiness, banana peels and other rotting objects. It was like a grave. In the midst of what David had said was the gem – *what you offered was exactly what she wanted*. I hadn't been that wrong after all. It was just too much, too soon, at too unstable a time.

I could still have it if I wanted it, if I was willing to forgive.

The circular thing with a bump was the Toys "R" Us ring. I put it on. It was strange, these talismans of my humiliation, a wig and a Toys "R" Us ring. They were like crucifixes. They were comforting. It felt a bit warmer in that trunk with it on.

The trunk popped open. "Coast is clear. Hurry, hurry, hurry!" A sweatshirt and sweatpants landed on me. The fluorescent lights of the fitness club garage weren't normally very bright, but after the darkness of the car they seemed blinding. I put the sweatshirt and pants on as quickly as I could, squinting in the light. There was a noticeable lack of sirens.

"Okay, into the car, then I drive you home."

COFFEE BREAK #6
ON BEALE

BEALE IS SORT OF A FORGOTTEN CHARACTER IN THIS GOSPEL, AND WHEN HE DOES APPEAR, IT'S MOSTLY ABOUT HIS GEEKY OBSESSION WITH DUNGEONS & DRAGONS AND HIS PENCHANT FOR DRAWING WOMEN WITH BIG TITS. I FEEL BAD ABOUT THIS, BECAUSE BEALE IS MY FRIEND, AND BECAUSE BEALE WILL BE ONE OF THE FIRST PEOPLE TO READ THIS, JUST AS HE HAS ALWAYS BEEN ONE OF THE FIRST PEOPLE TO READ MY STUFF. ON THE SURFACE, BEALE APPEARS TO BE SHALLOW, BUT THERE WAS SOMETHING ABOUT THE WAY HE FOLLOWED MY WORK, AND THE WAY HE VIGILANTLY ATTENDED BOOKER'S EVENTS, THAT HINTED AT MORE COMPLEXITY.

I GUESS WHAT I'M TRYING TO SAY IS THAT HE HAD A SORT OF KEANU REEVES QUALITY—A TENDENCY TO PLAY DUMB (ALTHOUGH WITH KEANU IT'S REALLY HARD TO TELL...)—AND IT'S HARD TO EXPLAIN TO AN OUTSIDER THAT THERE WAS MORE TO IT. HE ALSO DID THIS DEVO THING WHERE HE DRESSED PURPOSEFULLY NERDY. HE HAD SQUARE-FRAMED GLASSES—DESPITE THE FACT THAT HIS PRESCRIPTION LENSES WEREN'T PARTICULARLY THICK—AND HE WOULD WEAR POLO SHIRTS WITH THE TOP-BUTTON BUTTONED. WHEN YOU LOOKED AT BEALE YOU WANTED TO PUNCH HIM, AND PEOPLE DID PUNCH HIM: FRIENDLY STUFF, LIKE PUNCHING HIM IN THE SHOULDER OR TACKLING HIM WHILE HE SAT INNOCENTLY IN A CHAIR; BUT ALSO NOT SO FRIENDLY STUFF, BEALE ATTRACTED RANDOM VIOLENCE FROM STRANGERS LIKE NO ONE ELSE I'D EVER MET—I'D SEE HIM ONE DAY WITH TWO BLACK-EYES AND A NOSE THAT HAD OBVIOUSLY DONE A GREAT DEAL OF BLEEDING: HE'D JUST SAY, 'SHIT HAPPENS' AND YOU'D KNOW THAT IT HAD.

After I'd destroyed my bicycle and could no longer go on mind-clearing rides, I'd gone to Beale and begged for a seat at his D&D table. Beale knew that I was flaky, and wouldn't last a whole campaign, but he found a non-player character I could inhabit for a while, and for a couple of days I wasted long hours in the dim, single-bulbed light of his basement, killing off giant spiders and zombies and the occasional dwarf, when I was fortunate enough to stumble upon one. Beale seemed to put a lot of dwarves in my path, and I enjoyed finding particular gruesome ways to kill them.

He saved me, in a way that Booker and Diogenes and Nietzsche and Jesus, despite themselves, couldn't quite do. He saved me in the way a good friend does, by taking up time you're trying to get rid of and by finding creative ways to let you blow off steam.

Anyway, that's all I have to say about Beale. He's a good guy—an underrated guy—and I wanted you to know a little bit about him. But there's no narrative arc to him. He doesn't change or do very much. He just sort of hangs out and pays witness to what's happening: important in real life, but not so important when you're telling a tale.

So anyway, here's your page, dude. You've always been there. Thanks. (Oh, Beale's first name is Joe, just like Booker's. Not an important detail—I just thought you should know.)

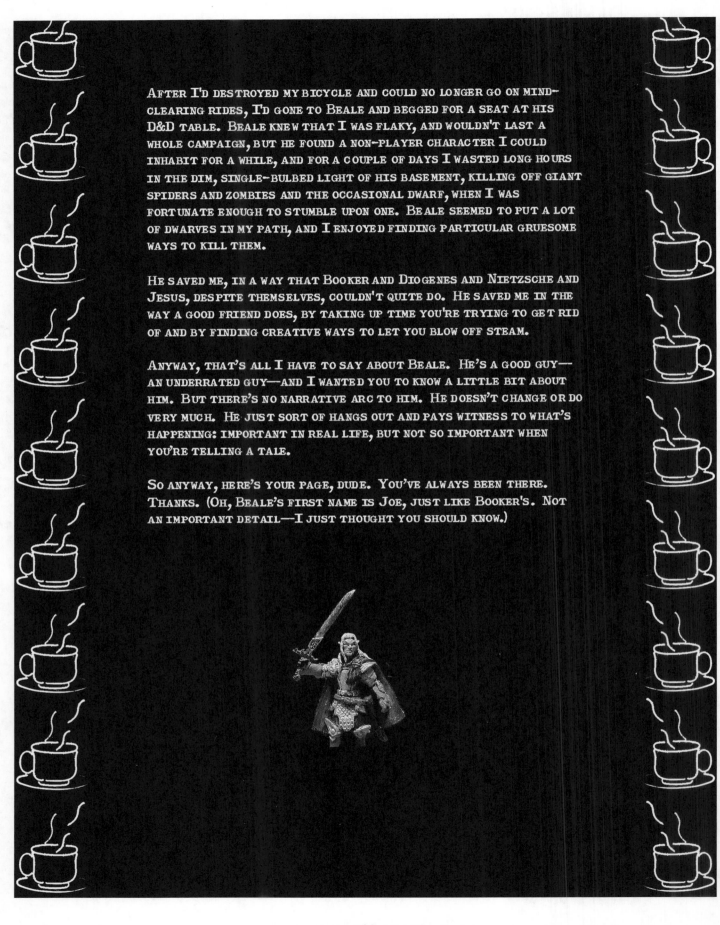

Chapter XXIX

Where Joe Beale and Bartholomew Flynn Sit on a Couch,
and Where Joseph Patrick Booker Confesses His Transgressions
to the Entire City of Portland, Oregon,
and Also Where He Apologizes for a Nation

A FEATURE OF END-OF-THE-EARTH COFFEE shops in Portland, Oregon, is "the couch." "The couch" is designed for group hangouts – for students pretending to work on a project together or twenty-somethings planning a music gig. "The couch," in order to distinguish it from the spotless couches at second-tier coffee shops must be shabby, unique, and vintage, preferably without an odor. Muddy's couch was large and pea green. Its fabric was frayed to a cozy fuzziness, and its cushions, though devoid of cush, allowed one to slouch deep into its coils. It held a faint odor of smoke, breaking the odorless rule, but the odor was the odor of clove cigarettes. The couch was clearly a couch for hanging out. And it could (and I can personally attest to this) hold you in for hours.

In short, there wasn't a better coffee shop couch in the nation. It was ideal.

Beale and I sank into it side by side.

It was Sunday, a difficult day for me, given that I'd normally be attending Booker's church. Rather than sit at home brooding, I had taken the bus (it was painful, riding the bus everywhere) to Mecca, and I'd spent the last hour or so drinking coffee and perusing the *Players Manual* that Beale had lent me to brush up on my rusty Dungeons & Dragons knowledge.

Beale was on a fifteen minute break, so he sat next to me and turned the pages of the Players Manual to poisons, where he pointed out some poisons for purchase that caused dwarfish brains to explode. I'm not sure how he'd found out about Booker and Mercyx, but it was easier that he knew without me having to tell him.

As was Beale's custom, the radio at Mecca was set to KBOO, Portland's community radio station. Normally, the voices on the radio provided a sort of background wa, wa, wah, like the teacher speaking in the comic strip Peanuts, but when the broadcaster mentioned a certain name, both Beale and I looked up at the speakers.

"Today we are live from the church of the Reverend Joseph Patrick Booker, where he is speaking about the Christian reaction to the reelection of George W. Bush."

Beale looked at me, to confirm that I had just heard what he had, and then he slumped back into the coils of Mecca. Reluctantly, I followed suit. Before we knew it, Booker was speaking:

I needed to figure out what I was going to say today, because Thursday's election, it changed things for me. So what I did was, I hopped a Greyhound to the coast. It poured down rain the entire ride down the coastline. I got off around five in the evening at a small town called Yachats, where all these small hotels with names like the Seadrift Inn advertize small condos with kitchenettes & a fireplaces for cheap, winter rates. I got onw of these, then walked, through the incessant rain, to a smallcorner store, where I planned to buy firewood, beer, & some grub.

This is where something amazing happened. You see, when I walked out of the corner store the rain had suddenly cleared, & there was, close to the horizon, a dim & orangish sun. Seeing as the rain had cleared, & seeing as I hadn't actually seen the odean, except as a gray, looming shadow, despite the fact that I'd been riding next to it all day, I walked back to the condo, dumped the provisions on the counter, stripped off my wet clothes & put on dry ones, then made a beeline, or as much of a beeline as possible, seeing as there was much private property & sea grass & sea walls to maneuver around, to the ocean.

Now what you would expect me to say was how amazing the sunset was, but by the time I got to the ocean, a cloud on the horizon had mangled my view of the sun, & although I could make out its outline, it just wasn't all that dramatic; no, it wasn't the sun that was amazing, nor was it the sky. I'm not sure whether it's the latitude up here, or the lack of particulates in the atmosphere, but Oregon sunsets just aren't that vibrant; the orange of the sky is more like a Creamsicle that's been left in the freezer too long than a mango or tangerine or any of the other exotic, tropical fruits used to describe sunsets.

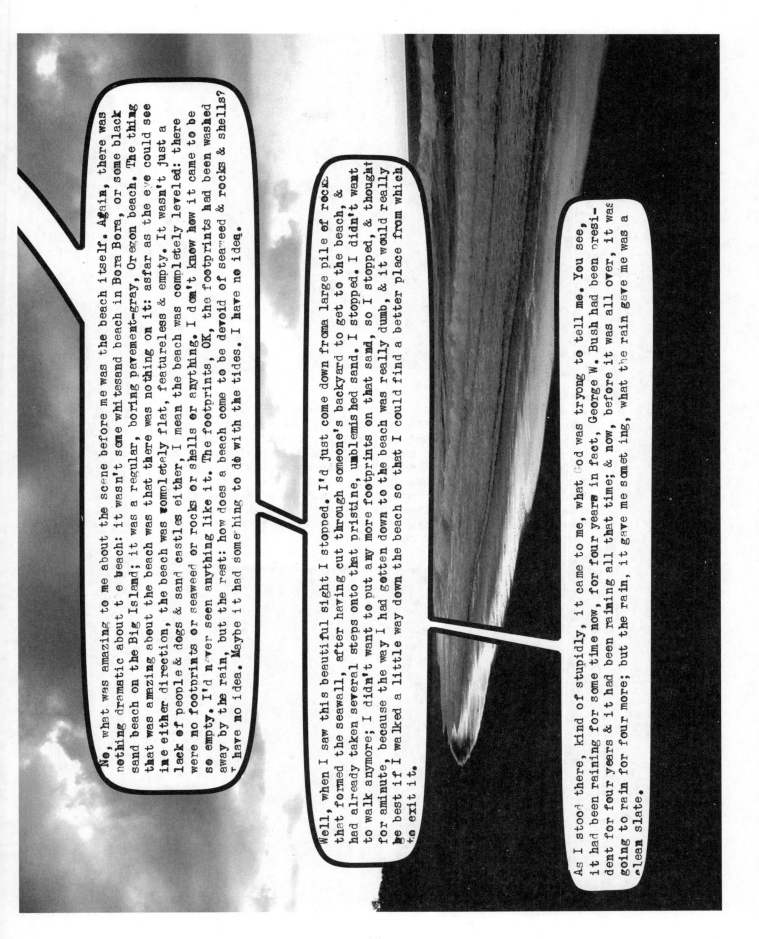

No, what was amazing to me about the scene before me was the beach itself. Again, there was nothing dramatic about the beach: it wasn't some white sand beach in Bora Bora, or some black sand beach on the Big Island; it was a regular, boring pavement-gray, Oregon beach. The thing that was amazing about the beach was that there was nothing on it: as far as the eye could see in either direction, the beach was completely flat, featureless & empty. It wasn't just a lack of people & dogs & sand castles either, I mean the beach was completely leveled: there were no footprints or seaweed or rocks or shells or anything. I don't know how it came to be so empty. I'd never seen anything like it. The footprints, OK, the footprints had been washed away by the rain, but the rest: how does a beach come to be devoid of seaweed & rocks & shells? I have no idea. Maybe it had something to do with the tides. I have no idea.

Well, when I saw this beautiful sight I stopped. I'd just come down from a large pile of rocks that formed the seawall, after having cut through someone's backyard to get to the beach, & had already taken several steps onto that pristine, unblemished sand. I stopped. I didn't want to walk anymore; I didn't want to put any more footprints on that sand, so I stopped, & thought for a minute, because the way I had gotten down to the beach was really dumb, & it would really be best if I walked a little way down the beach so that I could find a better place from which to exit it.

As I stood there, kind of stupidly, it came to me, what God was trying to tell me. You see, it had been raining for some time now, for four years in fact, George W. Bush had been president for four years & it had been raining all that time; & now, before it was all over, it was going to rain for four more; but the rain, it gave me something, what the rain gave me was a clean slate.

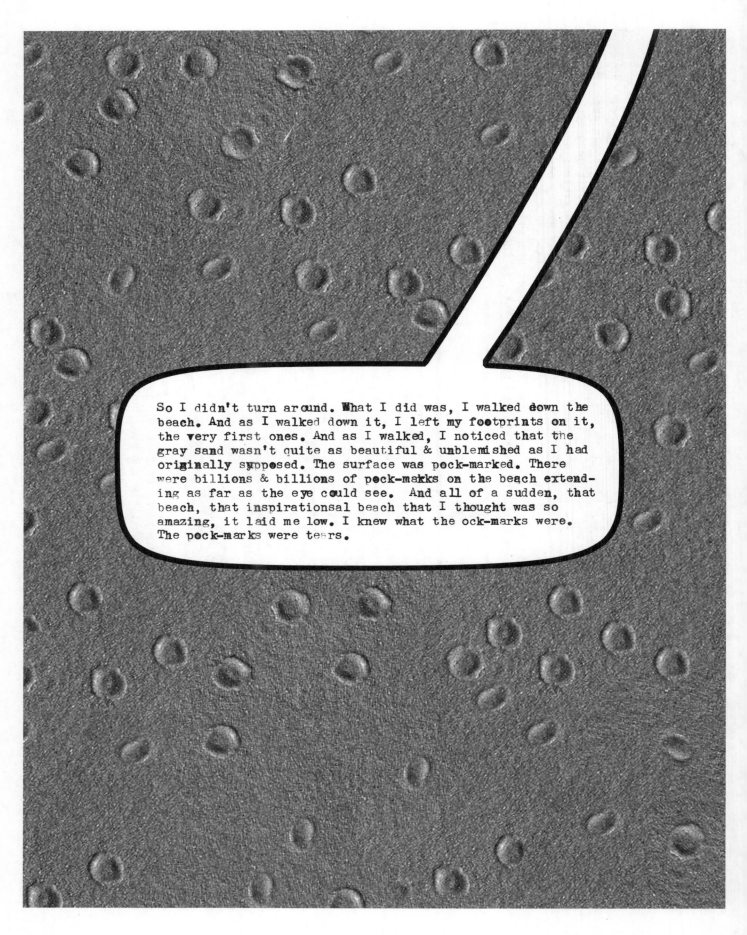

So I didn't turn around. What I did was, I walked down the beach. And as I walked down it, I left my footprints on it, the very first ones. And as I walked, I noticed that the gray sand wasn't quite as beautiful & unblemished as I had originally supposed. The surface was pock-marked. There were billions & billions of pock-marks on the beach extending as far as the eye could see. And all of a sudden, that beach, that inspirationsal beach that I thought was so amazing, it laid me low. I knew what the ock-marks were. The pock-marks were tears.

So, anyway, here I am on the radio, & thank you KBOO, thanks for giving me this half half-hour, it was very generous of you. I have to say something now that's personal & I'm sorry that I have to do it this way, but you see, I've made a mistake, we've all made a mistake, the whole country has made a mistake. We wake up every day, & we feel fresh & new, & we look at theworld, & we think, look, a fresh slate! I can do whatever I want today! But that isn't how theworld works. We don't have a fresh slate at all. What we have, here in America, is a pock-marked beach. And the closer we look, the more we will realize that we're walking on tears, & the more we think about this, the more we will realize that if we continue on, if we continue doing what we're doing, then that's all we're doing, is creating a moon   scape of tears.

Like I said, the couches at Mecca, it was like they had arms. Once they grabbed you they held you in. Listening to Booker on the radio was so different from seeing him live. On his crates, dressed in clothes too big for him, in that church full of spare bicycle parts, it never once occured to you that Booker might be serious, especially when the church was inhabited by post-apocalyptic bike punks. On the radio, however it was the opposite, it didn' occur to you that he could be otherwise. Stripped of everything but his words, Booker was the essence of sincerity. His brain patterns were a bit loopy, & that loopiness was full of humor, but overall you took what he said at face value.

So this is great, Booker, this depressing sentiment you're laying on us, but what are you really saying? What are you suggesting? How do we fix this? How do we keep from walking on aworld full of tears? I sat cross-legged on that beach wondering the same thing, & I have to confess that as I sat there, having received this revelation, I felt pretty despondent, & I wanted to add my own tears to the tear-stained beach.

What now? George W. Bush is going to be president for another four years. What do we do?

> I scoured my brain, & my brain, as it sometimes does, it fled
> to the gospels. It found nothing there. I was surprised, be-
> cause the ~~XXXXXXX~~ New Testament is chock-full of stuff, but
> there was nothing there that told me what to do. So my mind
> wandered a bit, & there was this pelican, & he landed on the
> beach & added his footprints to it, & I thought about how fine
> he was, the bird, & I thought about pelicans in general, & how
> it seemed to me that they were a rather ancient race of bird,
> that they had descended from pterodactyls or something. So I
> thought about that, about the anceint wisdom of pelicans, & my
> mind landed on this one thought: What about the Old Testament?
> What about those books that I avoided, with their antiquated
> rules & their obscurity, what would they have to say about
> America & George W. Bush & the evils of the times?
>
> It came to me then, what all the prophets were trying to tell
> us, what they always seemed to be leading the people towards.
> Repent! the Old Testament said to the people. Atone! it said
> to the people. Over and over again, these were the messages
> of the times. Repent & repair the damage done.

87

But anyway, I'm losing track of what I wanted to do today, because as I sat there thinking about sin & forgiveness, I realized that my own slate wasn't clean, that I'd left my own peck-marked beach. Here I am, lambasting my country for making mistakes & ignoring the consequences, while living in my own rat's nest.

You see, as I sat there on the beach everything came full-circle. What-ever I had told myself, I hadn't really taken that trip to the beach to think about this sermon, to figure out a way to enlighten the masses about the evils of the Bush administration, the real reason I was there was because I had betrayed a friend. I had done something despicable; I had done something that I felt was my right but that I knew in my heart was wrong. I was full of righteousness, I had excuse after excuse for what I had done, but in the end all that was left was the hurt I had caused, & the more I thought about it, the more I realized how erroneous my logic had been.

I can't tell you what I did, because that would only serve to humil-iate my friend more. But as I sat on the sand I knew that I needed to apologize, & I knew that I needed to make this apology public, that I needed to stand before my friend & all the people who knew him & say that I'd been wrong, that I'd been an asshole, that I... well... that I'm just like everybody else who's ever betrayed any-one, that I had my reasons, but I still fucking did it, & now, well, my friend's beautiful life is gone forever, & he can't get it back. I stole my friend's future.

Beale was squirming in the couch next to me, while I was the opposite, frozen, for the exact same reason. This was uncomfortable. Intellectually, I appreciated it, but emotionally I could do without public acknowledgement of getting screwed. I wished there was someone in the radio station to stop him. I envisioned Diogenes, with a pickax, breaking the glass windows in front of the station. His next line made things immeasurably worse.

"I blew it. I blew it for you and I blew it for Mercyx."

For starters, *blowing* was not a word I wanted Booker using in relation to Mercyx. I immediately got a visual of the side of her face, cheeks puffed out, sinking down on his cock. Worse, he'd actually mentioned her by name. I knew he was trying to apologize, but white-hot shame flooded in nonetheless.

"And worse yet, I made up some righteous bullshit about why it was okay for me to do. Free love is God's way, blah, blah, blah. You were my friend, you were loyal to me, you set me down on the path and you let me go. And what did I do? I took the power you granted me and threw it back in your face.

"Anyway, two months ago I gave a sermon about marriage, about how Jesus was actually an enemy of the institution of marriage, and I need to say, in front of everybody, that that speech was self-serving – it was designed to make me feel okay about something I'd done. Well, if ever there is a litmus test about whether or not something is divinely inspired or whether it is bullshit, that's all you need to look at: is what this supposed prophet said self-full or self-less? That, very quickly, will give you the answer."

I wasn't staring cross-eyed at the speakers anymore. I was watching the patrons of the café. They had all stopped what they were doing and were listening to Booker's radio address. Some were whispering to their companions at the café, asking them who Booker was. They made furtive glances towards the couch.

I wanted to run, of course, but I really was done with running. Besides that, the couch sort of had me. I didn't want to hear this out and yet I did want to hear this out. I sort of had to know; I sort of needed to hear what he was saying:

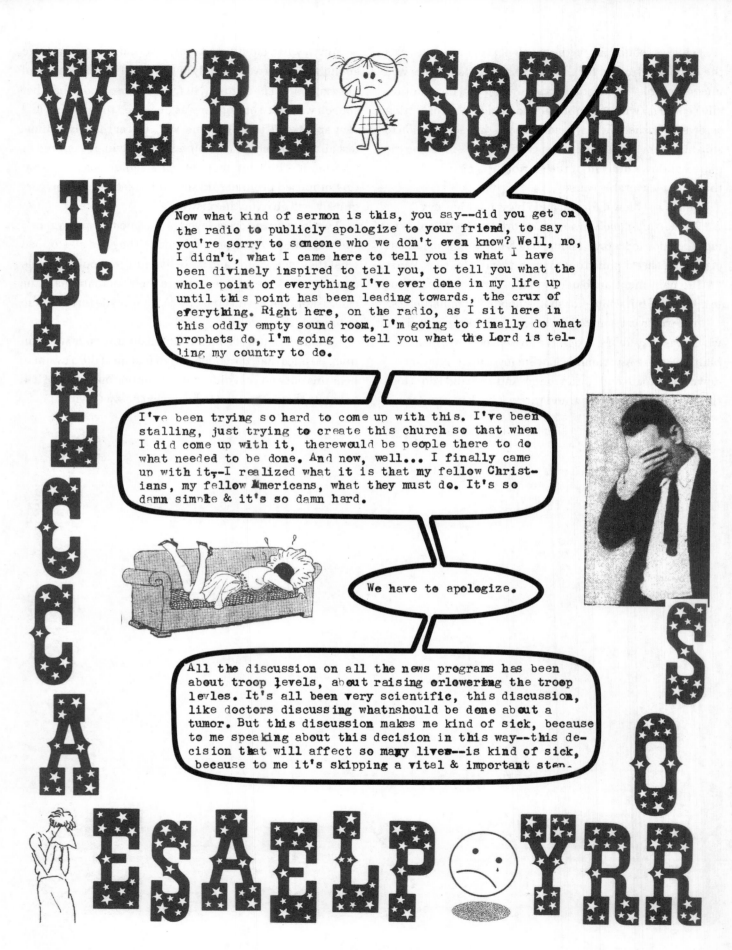

Imagine for a moment that America is a person instead of a country, & that Iraq is a person instead of a country. Now imagine that this person America sees this person Iraq & notices that this person Iraq has a gun in its hand, & imagine that this person America thinks the gun is loaded. Add to this the fact that this person America has his family members with him & that this gun--this ostensibly loaded gun--is pointed right at them. So what does this person America do? Well, this person America, he has a gun too, a huge semi-automatic actually, & as quickly as he can he whips it out & fires it, & the way this person America fires, his bullets are all scatter-shot, & one of t em takes out this person Iraq's daughter, (because, of course, this person Iraq has his family members with him as well) & one of them takes out this person Iraq's wife, & another one takes out his knee, & another one an eye, & so forth. So finally, this person America is done firing, but he's still pissed, because this person Iraq pointed a gun at his family, so he goes over & puts a bag over this person Iraq's head, & tells him to get down on his knees & bark like a dog, & then when this person America is done with that, it puts this person Iraq in a room filled with water, for days, so that this person Iraq can't sleep; & well... I could go on & on as this person America went on & on, piling the humiliations on this person Iraq who was going to kill him & his family & his loved ones.

Red Is The Blood Of Those We Kill. White Are Their Survivors' Faces. Blue Are The Bodies We Starved, God

There's No Way Like THE AMERICAN WAY!

So after this person America has done this, he takes a step back, his righteous anger having somewhat abated, & what this person America does is to pick up the gun that this person Iraq pointed at him, & when this person America picks up the gun, holy shit! he realizes that the gun isn't real--the gun that the person Iraq pointed at him is a fucking squirt gun;

THE BEST WAY OF LIFE IS THE AMERICAN WAY

Now let's get inside this person America's head & heart at this very moment, & let's assume that this person America is not a psychopath: what does this person America feel at this moment?

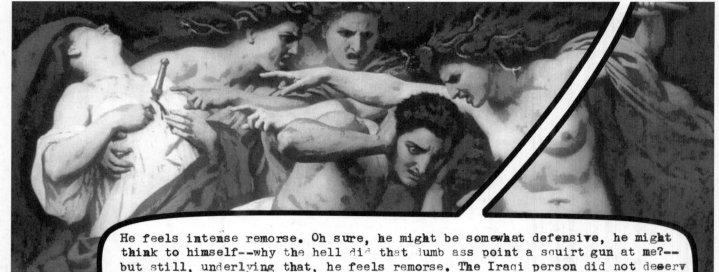

He feels intense remorse. Oh sure, he might be somewhat defensive, he might think to himself--why the hell did that dumb ass point a squirt gun at me?-- but still, underlying that, he feels remorse. The Iraqi person did not deserv serve what he got. He did not deserve a dead wife & a dead daughter. He did not deserve to lose an eye & a leg. He did not deserve the humiliations that were piled up on him.

And so this person America, if he were really a person--if he were a normal, healthy person--well, it's clear how this person would feel. This person America would be heartsick. This person America's face would be red. This per person America would cover his face with his hands. The horror of what this person America has just done fills him, blood rushing to all his extremities. This person falls to his knees & begins to weep. Tears rush out of this person's eyes onto stones beneath. And this person speaks. It is so hard for him, but he does it anyway, he does it anyway, he does it because it is obviously the right thing to do: 'I'm sorry' this person says, 'I'm so sorry.' 'What can I do to help you? My God, what can I do?'

Now some of us, we feel what this person America felt. We feel intense remorse morse, & every day when we wake up in the morning & read the news we are reminded of what our country has done; & every day because of this we feel a sort of low-level depression. But we don't think to apologize. It wasn't us that did it, we think, it was our president, it was our proxies. After all some of us, at least us liberals, we did what we could. We voted. We lost. Now, all we can do is go on; all we can do is to live our lives. Occasionally, we go to a protest, & we march in crowds that think as we do, & we shout at the empty weekend office buildings that line the streets, but that is about all we can do.

The truth is, though, that it is not all we can do. We can apologize. No one wants to hear what I am about to say, because what I am about to say implie cates each & every one of us, what I am about to say,puts each & every one of us in dire & extreme danger.

Well it didn't turn out all that well for the kid. He never got to do any Gonzo journalism. He couldn't speak any Farsi, so there weren't too many questions he could ask of the Iraqis, & before he could even get his bearings straight he got swept up by the Americans military & sent back home to be chastised by his parents, his teachers, the American pres, & pretty much the entire population of the country for his idiocy Of course, on the other hand, it didn't turn out all that badly either— I mean, considering what our country has done to their country, you wou think someone would have stuffed him in a bag & stoned him the minute he got off the plane.

But anyway, neitherwhat did nor what didn't happen to the boy is the point. The point is, in fact, Xd hidden in the middle of the story. Thepoint is, simply, that even a sixteen year-old boy can get on a plane & fly to Baghdad.

He we are sitting in our safe little homes. Here we are in rainy & miserable Portland, Oregon, discussing how horrible it is, whata crime it is, what we have done to the people of Iraq. Here we are saying, oh, but if only there was something we could do. But you see, there is something we can do. We can buy a ticket. We can get on a plane

Imagine it, Flynn. Imagine Nietzsche's vision of a planet full of Gods. Imagine a hundred young Jesuses, a thousand young Jesuses, taking planes to Baghdad. Imagine them getting off these planes, walking down the tarmac, unarmed, ready to die on a cross for the forgiveness of their country's sins.

You know, we live in these nihilistic times, we live in these times when people think that everything has been done before. Artists don't know what to paint, because everything has been painted before, so they paint abstracts. Writers don't know what to write, because everything has been written before, so they write for sheer entertainment. Everybody thinks that everything has been done before, so they conclude that the world must come to an end.

Well, maybe the world is coming to an end, but if it comes to an end it's not because we've reached a point where everything's been done before. You see, we haven't even scratched the surface. We've never attempted to do what Isiah suggested we do, what Jesus suggested we do. We've never walked into the lion's den and said do with me what you will. Jesus spoke of a Way, & what was this Way? Jesus's vision was the same vision Isaiah had, it was a vision of the wolf living with the lamb, the leopard lying down with the goat, the calf & the lion & the yearling all being yanked around by a little child, _that_ is what the Way is. It's an impossible-to-fathom vision of peace. When the Bible uses the word faith thatis exactly what it means: faith that laying down your weapons will yield goodness--even laying your weapons down, rather stupidly, beforethe viper's nest. There is no other faith, there is no other Way, but these. And there is no otherWay to the Jerusalem that Isaiah envisions, no other Way to the Kingdom of Heaven that Jesus talks about, no other Way to win over the hearts & the minds of the people of Baghdad. then this Way.

All the whispering between patrons about who Booker was, & who Beale & I were had stopped. Everyone now was staring where I'd been staring before,' up at the speakers. They looked so mindless, spoons dangling loosely between forefingers & thumbs, torn sugar packets trickling their contents onto the pharmacy tables.

BITCH SLAPPED

> If we want nations to stream to a place of peace, then this is the only Way to do it, only if swords are beaten into plowshares, spears into pruning hooks, semi-automatics into scrap metal, enriched uranium into deeply buried nuclear waste.

AMERICA?

> I mean, why not try something that's never been tried before? Why not actually follow the dictates of our religious leaders? The Israelites of the Old Testament, they did not listen to their prophet: they did not turn their swords to plowshares & peace did not come to Jerusalem. The Israelites of the New Testament, they did not listen to Jesus: the Kingdom of Heaven on Earth that he envisioned XXX never came to pass. What will happen to the Americans of today? What will happen to this one nation XXXXXXXXXX under God, indivisible, with liberty & justice for all? Will they, for once, try to do what their Bible tells them to do? Or are they just as deaf? The irony of all this religion in today's America, is that it doesn't pay a damn bit of attention to its own religion's history. What part of not worshipping the golden cow do American's not understand? What part of turn the other cheek is not clear? What part of love your enemy as yourself is confusing?

> Come on! How fucking hard is this religious stuff! It's not hard at all. A three-year-old understands the basics: befriend strangers; don't throw rocks. And yet echoes of Jesus's unfinished business still reverberate 2,000 years after his death. All we have to do to have a King-dom of Heaven on Earth—the unbearably simple & painless answer to all the world's problems—is a universal commitment to turn the other cheek.

You know what, Flynn, I'm just going to keep going, it's just me
in an empty room with a mike! I just don't care anymore: here it
is, the giant spew. Do you ever think XXXXXXX about how painfully
& devastatingly boring the history of the human race is? I mean,
does any kid enjoy studying history? No, history is like numero
uno on the list of subjects most likely to bore students. Did
you ever think about how depressing that is? The entire history
of the human race: boring. I mean, instead of handing out text
books to kids in elementary school, we could just give them a
sentence, a history of the human race in one sentence: a group
of humans usurped some land from someone else by force, obtained
more land by force, & then continued on like this until some
other group of humans, driven to madness by the cruelty of the
first group of humans, finally found some way to undermine this
group of humans' power, & then killed the first group of humans,
usurped its land, & then started the cycle again.

The history of homo sapiens on the planet Earth can be summed
up in that above sentence, & that above sentence is painfully
boring & depressing. What Isaiah was suggesting, & what Jesus
was suggesting, & what I am suggesting, is that for once, if
for no other reason than to add a different sentence to the
sentence that is the boring history of the human race, if for
no other reason than to make our nation, America, stand out,
we ought to try & break the cycle, we ought to try & be mag-
nanimous instead of rapacious, we ought to repent, when we
sin.

How historical, it would be! How unprecedented! Just imagine
it, the American apology. One day we all just wake up in the
morning & hop a plane--a giant fucking flash mob. And there
we all are, standing in the dusty heat of Baghdad, T-shirt
& blue jean apparitions. The Iraqi's wouldn't know what to
do. Would they shoot us? Maybe. Would they greet us? Maybe.
Would they do a little of both? Probably. Would the day be
historic? Absolutely.

The thing is, on matter what happened, whether all those
Americans became martyrs or whether the Iraqi's turned out
to be overwhelmingly amicable, either way the day would be
like none other in the history of the world. And America,
at least that one day in American history, it would stand
out. We would celebrate it. The Iraqis would celebrate it.
The whole world would celebrate it. An unusual day, a day
to XXXcelebrate that wasn't simply another independence day,
That wasn't just another day to elebrate the day that someone else's land became our land, the day America gave another
nation a break, the day America saw the error of her ways,
the day she realized she had done something wrong--that she
had started a war under false pretenses--& apologized.

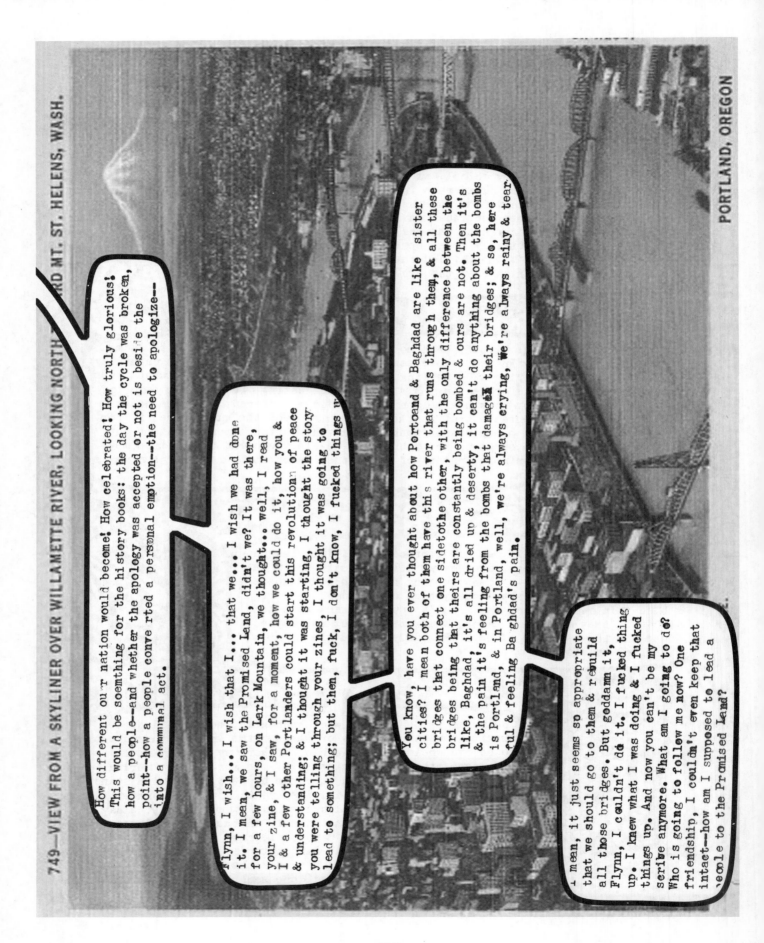

As you are probably aware, having read this whole thing, Booker had been talking a long time. I had reached an almost comatose state, so when the voice on the radio was no longer Booker, when the quivery, local voice of a KBOO broadcaster had given way to the calm voice of a national syndication, I didn't react, I just sat there, like you sit there after a movie that has deeply affected you, not wanting to move as the credits roll.

Now like I said, I had gone all inward while Booker's voice came through the speakers in the café, so up until this moment I hadn't realized what was happening around me. But now I did. And what I saw, well, it was quite amazing. People in the coffee shop were just standing there, still as statues. They were listening to the radio like some great and terrible event had just taken place: like Pearl Harbor was being bombed, or the Twin Towers taken down, or aliens invading the planet. Booker's voice, the words he spoke, to the people in this coffee shop, they carried that kind of weight.

When Booker had wrapped up, everyone in the café sat there in the same sort of watch the credits roll confusion that I'd been in. There was no script for this. There was no script for what you do when suddenly confronted by something that makes your hair stand on end. You remember the moment, later, in your head – you know, like when you first heard *Smells Like Teen Spirit* on the radio – but what do you actually do?

I don't know if you actually do anything. You feel this buzz, and maybe you roll down the windows and turn it up, but you don't actually do anything. That's sort of what happened in the coffee shop, for that moment, everyone just sort of looked electrified and big-eyed.

I knew, then, what Booker had wanted to be. If say, this radio program could be heard elsewhere, if it could be heard in Wausau, Wisconsin, and Manhattan, Kansas, and Lordsdale, New Mexico, people would drop whatever they were doing, turn up the radio, and listen to it. This guy, what's his name, Booker, he really was a prophet. And we really should, all of us really should wake up one morning and take a plane to Baghdad.

The moment, however long it was – the silent moment when everyone in that café thought these things – it ended. It was Beale who said it, and I knew he did it for my sake, despite having absorbed Booker's words, and found them true, and possibly wanting to go buy a ticket to Baghdad himself.

"Well, that was fucked up," Beale said.

The entire coffee shop turned to Beale when he said that, and small little smiles came to all of their lips, and all the emotion that had built up in their overcaffeinated souls, it

was drained. *Phew* everyone thought, inside their own skulls, this guy is crazy, just a crazy lunatic, we'd all get killed out there, and then they went back to whatever they were doing before they'd started listening and forgot about Baghdad and Booker forever. Or at least would have, if it weren't for certain other circumstances.

Chapter xxx

The Garden of Olives

LATER THAT SAME SUNDAY, THERE WAS a knock on the door. It was the time of day on a Sunday when I'd normally be on a bike riding with Mercyx, and because I neither had the bike nor Mercyx, it was a drag. I was near the end of *Don Quixote* where after all his fumblings he is finally heralded as a Don, and where he retires his dinner pan helmet and sheathes his lance.

I was not happy to hear the knock. It was either going to be a Jehovah's Witness, a Greenpeace volunteer, Mercyx, or Booker, none of whom I had the emotional energy to deal with.

I opened the door. It was the last person on the list. I wanted to be a movie Mafioso, and say "I have nothing to say to you," and slam the door, but even saying you have nothing to say is saying something. I didn't say anything.

He stood in the doorway. "I'm leaving town."

"Good," I wanted to say, but I kept my mouth shut. I was determined.

"Did you hear what I said on the radio?" Booker asked.

I tried to keep a poker face. To give him nothing. He deserved nothing.

"You deserved better," he said.

I couldn't look at him. I was looking at the floor. I knew that my poker face wasn't working and that my face held an angry expression. This pissed me off. I said something even though I didn't want to. "Wherever you're going, just go, man."

"Will you come with me?" he asked.

I looked at Booker oddly. His question was desperate. He was standing there like a drunk who couldn't stand to be alone. I didn't get it.

"No," I said.

"I mean, not with me with me, just to the airport, to wait for the plane," he said.

I wish that I'd been bigger. I knew everything really. I knew it without him having to tell me. He'd been drunk, they'd lost the election, and, well ... she was real, and he'd never had anyone real, all his girls were sex workers. I knew what he was doing, too. I knew where the plane was going. But I couldn't do it then.

I shut the door on him.

Or at least, I tried to – Booker shoved his foot in before I could twist shut the latch. We stood like that for a moment, both of us putting pressure on the door. I didn't have the emotional strength to keep it up, though. I let him reopen it. I looked back at the floor. We were both looking down at the floor.

Booker reached into his pocket and jangled something. "Take this," he said.

I didn't look up. I didn't reach out my hand. He dropped it on my welcome mat. It was a key.

"It's to the church," he said.

I scuffed my feet on the floor. Him standing outside, me standing inside, it was letting cold into the house.

"I loved somebody, too," he said. "I sold her out on a nightly basis, but I still loved her."

I regret this, of course. I regret that I didn't take his apology on the radio to heart. I know it was true and genuine and all that. But mending takes time and I wasn't ready.

"I have to try," he said.

My mind wasn't on him, it was on me. I was thinking of me and what had been done to me. And so I shut the door again. And locked it. And this time, Booker made no effort to stop me.

Chapter xxxi

Where I Deny Him Three Times

ABOUT THIRTY MINUTES LATER, THERE was a fresh knock on my door. I thought it was Booker again, not leaving well enough alone, but the thought that it could also be Mercyx occurred to me. Cursing the lack of a peephole, I opened it. There was a man I'd never seen before, dressed very smartly and crisply in a gray suit. Jehovah's Witness. Damn.

"My name is Roland Dial," he said. "I'm with the Federal Bureau of Investigation. Are you Bartholomew Flynn?"

I stood there for a moment trying to figure out whether I wanted to be Bartholomew Flynn. I decided that I didn't, but my long pause made it clear to Roland Dial that I was.

"No," I said.

Roland Dial squinted, making it clear he knew I was lying. Then he stepped into the apartment, and if ever there were two things more incompatible, it was Roland Dial and my apartment. Roland quickly scanned the room and chose to stand in the middle of it. I chose to lean up against the wall.

"Are you friends with a Joseph Patrick Booker?" Roland asked.

"No," I said. I wasn't friends with him, actually, so this didn't feel like lying.

"You don't know a Joseph Patrick Booker?" Roland asked.

"Nope," I said.

Now, I was lying. Why was I lying to an FBI agent? Was lying to an FBI agent a federal offense?

"You draw a comic book about his church, don't you?" Roland asked.

"No," I said. And now I could tell the truth. "My roommate does."

Roland was staring at me intently, as FBI agents, no doubt, are trained to do. I don't imagine I'm a very good liar, so I'm pretty sure he knew what I was up to. Still, he played along.

"So you do know who Booker is?" Roland asked.

Damn. I'd said I didn't know who I was, and then said I did know who he was. "No. I mean, not personally."

"Where would I find this roommate of yours?" Roland asked.

"He's probably at a strip club someplace," I said.

"And what's his name?" Roland asked.

"Flynn," I said.

"Barth Flynn?" Roland asked.

I tried not to cringe when he called me Barth. It was hard not to do. "Yes."

"And you are?" Roland asked.

"Chester Fields," I said.

Roland took out a Bic pen and a small notepad from the inside of his suit jacket. The pen was clipped onto the notepad. He twirled the pen around in his left hand while holding the pad with his right. Roland was a lefty. For some reason it struck me as odd that a lefty would become an FBI agent. I think Roland was standing there twirling his pen around to make me nervous, to see if I'd back off and give him any more information. Roland didn't know that long awkward silences were a specialty of mine.

"All right, look …" Roland finally finished twirling his pen and spoke up. "… when your roommate shows up give me a call." He reattached the pen to the notepad, slipped a card out it, handed it to me, then put the notepad back inside his suit jacket. I took the card and nodded to him stupidly.

Before leaving, Roland scanned the room a second time. His eyes alighted on an issue of *His Church That Sunday* lying on the floor.

I ALWAYS THOUGHT THE STORY IN THE BIBLE about how Peter denied Jesus three times was odd. I mean, if you had a friend who was potentially in trouble with the law, and strange people you didn't know started asking you questions about him, wasn't the right thing to do to say you didn't know him? I understand the point – the point in the Bible was that Peter was saving his own skin rather than standing up for what he believed in – but still, it seems a dumb thing to hold over someone's head: as cowardly as "denying" Jesus might have been, it also very well might have been the right thing to do. After all – who knows? – if Peter hadn't denied him three times maybe he and all eleven of the other apostles would have gotten strung up from a tree right beside Jesus, and then that would have been the end of it, no Christianity.

Anyway, this is a moot point. And to be honest, I only make it so that I'll feel better. It's not very productive to live your life wondering what you might have done.

COFFEE BREAK #7

ON DEATH

SHIT HAPPENS IN LIFE. THE WHOLE THREAD BECOMES UNRAVELED. THERE ISN'T SOME NICE STORY ARC: AN INITIAL SET-UP, RISING ACTION, A CLIMAX, A DENOUEMENT. INSTEAD WHAT HAPPENS IS THIS: YOU'RE BORN, THE SCENE IS SET UP, YOU SEE THE MOUNTAIN YOU HAVE TO CLIMB, YOU SET YOUR GOALS, YOU BEGIN THE CLIMB; AND THEN SOMEWHERE ALONG THE LINE, AS YOU'RE CLIMBING, YOU FALL THROUGH SOME ICE OR SOMETHING, AND YOU FREEZE TO DEATH; AND THE SADDEST PART OF IT IS THAT AS YOU'RE FREEZING TO DEATH, YOU CAN SEE THE TOP OF THE MOUNTAIN, THE CLIMAX, AND ALL YOU CAN THINK ABOUT IS HOW STUPID IT IS, HOW STUPID IT WAS THAT YOU SPENT YOU'RE WHOLE LIFE CLIMBING THIS MOUNTAIN; AND THEN OF COURSE YOU DIE AND YOU'RE FROZEN SOLID AND OTHER CLIMBERS, WELL, YOU DIED WAY UP THERE ON A MOUNTAIN, AND NO ONE HAS TIME TO BRING YOU DOWN AND BURY YOU PROPERLY, SO THEY SEE YOUR FACE FROZEN IN SOME LAKE, AND THEY SEE HOW IT'S LOOKING UP, AND THEY THINK THAT THE LOOK IS YOU YEARNING FOR THE TOP OF THAT MOUNTAIN, AND THEY THINK THAT YOU'RE SOME FUCKING SIGN OR SOMETHING THAT THEY SHOULD KEEP CLIMBING THEMSELVES, YEARNING FOR THE CLIMAX THAT YOU NEVER REACHED. THEY NEVER THINK WHAT YOU THOUGHT IN THE LAST MINUTE. THEY NEVER THINK ABOUT HOW STUPID IT IS. THEY NEVER THINK TO JUST QUIT, TO JUST STOP THERE IN THE MIDDLE, BEFORE THINGS GET TOO PRECARIOUS.

THE FIRST BOOK OF FLYNN
TO THE UNIVERSE

Chapter XXXII

Where Bartholomew Flynn Eats His Body and Drinks His Blood

J WALKED UP THE STAIRS. I WENT TO BED. I DIDN'T DO MUCH THE NEXT day. I laid around. I finished *Don Quixote*. It entranced me: this novel written some four hundred years ago about a man who lived in an alternate reality, a man who thought he was a knight in a world with no knights, and how in the final act the people around him find him so entertaining that they let him be a knight, and so in that way Don Quixote really is a knight, despite the fact that he is old and couldn't lift a sword to save his life. ¶ Another day passed. Another night passed. And I'm sorry about this,

I'm sorry that I'm writing about it in this cold, clipped way, but this is hard. I woke up. I took a shower. I brushed my teeth. I got dressed. It was Sunday.

I got on the Internet and there, on the front page of a news site, was that photo of him wearing a Roman collar, his hair parted to the side and that Tattoo smile on his face. In bold type was today's headline: RELIGIOUS FANATIC BEHEADED IN BAGHDAD. You would think that I'd react, that I would gasp or scream or cry, but I didn't do any of those things. I read the story, briefly, like I was some impartial observer:

Dwarf Preacher Beheaded in Iraq

Joseph Patrick Booker's head on a platter. Artist's rendition by Gern Blanston/Corbis

RAMADI (AP) -- Joseph Patrick Booker, 33, a self-proclaimed preacher from Portland, Oregon, was beheaded by youths in Iraq early this morning after crossing the Jordanian border in a taxi and entering a Sunni-controlled market alone and unarmed. Booker was a dwarf.

Booker flew into Jordan on Friday, accompanying a deported alien, then bribed a reluctant taxi driver $500US to drive him to Baghdad. The taxi driver, Pahenhm el Parma, stopped at a market in Ramadi to purchase food for himself and the passenger. Booker left the vehicle against the driver's advice.

El Parma said that Booker wished to "apologize to the Iraqi people."

Booker proceeded to the central square of the market, where he allegedly overturned a vendor's basket of eggplant, stood on it, disrobed, and began shouting. According to vendor, Ghaisel Fazi, 50, Booker was heckled by a growing crowd before he was brought down by sniper fire.

The Ramadi market is considered a "no go" zone by the United States military.

After the shooting, several youths surrounded the body. Ali Mohammad, 45, a merchant from the nearby Albu Bali region, claims that the youths chanted, "behead the midget," before he was decapitated. It is not known which of the youths beheaded the preacher.

According to several sources, Booker's head was paraded around the market for several minutes on a mezze platter before Ramadi police arrived to break up the riot. A battalion of U.S. troops arrived on the scene shortly after. No further violence was reported.

Lt. Col. Steve Bergencamp, commander of the 2nd battalion, 82nd Airborne, who secured the scene said, "the body sustained several bullet wounds to the chest and torso, and appeared to be decapitated with a sharp knife in accordance to Zabiha, the prescribed

After reading the article, I shut my laptop. I'd known him all this time, but I'd never known who his parents were, or how old he was, or any of the details you're supposed to know about your friends. I put on my cold weather gear, strapped on my messenger bag with the journal inside, put on my fanny pack, and headed outside.

Maybe other people who've experienced this sort of thing will understand my reaction. It was like when Booker had died, I had died too.

The day was cold. There was no wind. The sky was clear, but it was clear in a way that the sky at northern latitudes are clear, which is to say the sky is almost white, the sun hanging limply above the horizon, too weak to give the sky any color. It was a long walk to the church. By now, it was about an hour past when services were normally held, so there was no chance of me running into anyone who had come to hear a sermon. I rode, and as I approached and looked to the left I could see someone sitting on the steps. I knew who it was. I'd seen her many times off in the distance. I recognized her dot. It was Mercyx.

I didn't say anything as I approached. I could feel her gaze on me but I didn't meet it. I kept my eyes on the pavement. Each step I took seemed weighty and important, as if I'd forever remember the cracks in the sidewalk. (I do.) I arched up his walk, conscious of how measured my pace had become.

I walked past her. I pushed open the doors. I walked into his church.

———

IN AN INSTANT, I WAS JOLTED BACK TO LIFE. THE bike parts, the theater seats, the paint-splattered altar, the goddamn Big Six wheel, they were all still there, the way they'd been the last time I was there. I smelled sour coffee, first – that smell you get when you forget to turn off the burner on the automatic pot – and then I saw the doughnuts. Ten pink boxes there on the altar, all propped open, all full. I don't know how the coffee and doughnuts got there. Maybe Booker had someone else retrieving the doughnuts, and maybe that person didn't know what had happened. Or maybe, I don't know, maybe Booker had ordered them there as some sort of prize on the off-chance someone would come in expecting to hear a sermon but finding the church empty – finding the church empty except for the doughnuts.

I don't know why this particular detail disturbed me so much. The doughnuts, the way they were sitting there, so virginal, so exposed, they made me mad. I mean, these weren't just any doughnuts, they were Voodoo Doughnuts,

you know, magic-is-in-the-hole doughnuts, they were after-you've-seen-the-band-and-don't-want-to-go-home doughnuts. They were night doughnuts. They were cop and street walker doughnuts. They were only-in-Portland-Oregon doughnuts. And they were like, expensive, and they had toppings like Cocoa Puffs and Butterfingers and Oreos, and they were better than crack cocaine for keeping you buzzed all night. Fuck, here he was, getting on a plane to enter a war-zone, no army behind him, no weapon in his hand, and he still had the forethought to care for us, to feed his fucking sheep.

I'd just left him. He'd stood there, on my doorstep, and I'd just let him go. He'd asked me to stay up with him, he wanted, he wanted to tell me about it, he wanted to tell me about it and then he wanted me to stay and have me talk him out of it, and I … I hadn't even thought about him, all I'd thought about was me.

There they were, boxes and boxes of doughnuts and thermoses and thermoses of coffee, just sitting there. His doughnuts! His coffee! His body! His blood! Fuck! I mean, could you imagine that in another church, the little gold door unlocked and the little white wafers collecting flies?

I kind of went ape shit. When someone dies, especially like this, suddenly and unexpectedly, there's a tendency to go ape shit. I went ape shit. Incidentally, the first doughnut I picked up was a Grape Ape, a raised doughnut with vanilla frosting and grape Kool-Aid powder. I crushed it in my right hand. I grabbed another doughnut, a Dirty Snowball. It had some sort of dark gook filling and a pink marshmallow glaze and coconut sprinkles. I crushed that in my left. I threw them. Some of what I threw landed on the wall but most of it stayed in my hand: vanilla frosting and pink marshmallow and grape Kool-Aid mix and coconut. I kept going. I was on a roll. I crushed more doughnuts. I threw more doughnuts against the wall. I picked up the box of doughnuts. I dumped its contents on the floor. I stomped on the doughnuts. It was like hopscotch. Hopping from doughnut to doughnut to doughnut. It sounds funny, all of this, but it wasn't, it was horrible, it was tragic. I was crushing my dead best friend's doughnuts.

I got to the second box. I hadn't thought about that before. Best friend – it had never entered my head. It was a short best friendship but he was still my best friend. I knew it. He was, had been, my best friend. I stuck my head in the box. I put my nose into the hole of a Triple Chocolate Penetration. It was like bobbing for apples. I started eating. I started crying. Salt mixed with chocolate cake mixed with chocolate glaze mixed with goddamn Cocoa Puffs and I didn't care. I didn't care that no one else was there. I was going to do it all. I was going to single-handedly eat all his doughnuts. Two dozen doughnuts times the nine remaining boxes equals two-hundred something fucking doughnuts. That wasn't too many doughnuts. For Booker, that could be done. I, his scribe, was going to eat his doughnuts.

This sounds kind of homoerotic, what I was doing, and I suppose I should make it sound less so by saying "the doughnuts" instead of "his doughnuts," but in my mixed-up head at the moment, the doughnuts, they sort of did represent him, they were the closest thing to him that I had left, that I would ever have left, really. They were eccentric, like him. They were always buzzed, like him. Sometimes they were too much, like him.

It wasn't going as well as I hoped. I couldn't see. I had a large chunk of a Snickers bar in one eye and Strawberry Quik powder in the other. I started pecking like a chicken, eating whatever my mouth encountered, but it got kind of difficult, the Nyquil glazed doughnut not mixing too well with the Arnold Palmer lemon and tea powder; and my pace slowed, and I knew I couldn't maintain the fury that I felt, the fury that the situation demanded. I ran my vanilla-glazed, pink marshmallow, grape Kool-Aid, dark gook, coconut-sprinkled hands through my hair. I tasted devil's food, and banana, and Pepto-Bismol, and cream filling. Maybe I couldn't digest it in one sitting, maybe I'd need the rest of the day, and the night, and tomorrow. I pulled up. I was glaze and Boo Berry cereal and éclair from forehead to chin. I grabbed an apple fritter and I ate it like the Cookie Monster, letting most of it crumble and fall to the ground. I ate another topped with Rice Krispies.

He was dead. He was God and he was everything and he was dead. How could he be dead? How could he do that? How could he just go? He wasn't done yet. He'd just started. You don't just go to a place where they torture and behead people and get yourself tortured and beheaded. Why did he do that? He wasn't dead. I shouted it. I spitted it. I sputtered Rice Krispies it. I choked peanut butter it. "He's not dead!"

But he was dead. He'd started this church, he'd gathered together its people, and then he'd taken a plane to somewhere uninviting and died. June, July, August, September, October, November. Dead, dead, dead, dead, dead, dead. Six months like Jesus Christ.

There was too much peanut butter in my mouth. I was clogged. I was choking. I was going to die. I dug my finger in. There was peanut butter and there were banana chips and there were raisins. I pulled out a glop. I shook my finger and

some of the peanut butter and banana chips and raisins plopped onto the floor and some of it stuck to the pink marshmallow cream and coconuts already on my hand. I was every-flavored.

I wanted to see so I wiped my eyes with my sleeve but that only made my eyelids stick together. Fuck it. I put my hand back in the box.

That's when she slipped behind me. That's when Mercyx, the girl who'd been my friend, the girl who had almost been my girlfriend, the girl who I had stupidly asked to marry me, the girl who I hated and who had completely humiliated me, the girl who'd yes, fucked him, Booker, my dead best friend. She'd been behind me this whole time, saying things to me, trying to soothe me, trying to stop me. That *fucking* bitch.

I threw back my elbow. I threw it wild. My elbow, the corner of it, the edge of it, I could feel it go into her eye socket. I didn't care. Who the fuck cares? Joseph Patrick Booker was dead and there was no God. So who the fuck cared? Darwin was right and Jesus was wrong. Who the fuck cares?

She pushed me. I fell. I fell onto the boxes of doughnuts and the thermoses on the altar. It would have been more dramatic if we'd fallen onto the altar together and split it and landed in each other's arms, but that's not what happened, what happened was that the altar fell over from my weight, while I landed pretty solidly on the top of my head, then sort of just crumpled, my cheek sideways on the floor, my neck crooked, my knees against my head, sandwiched between a sideways altar and the wall.

It hurt really bad, but I didn't make any noise. I felt like this was what I deserved, having just elbowed Mercyx in the eye socket, and the pain in my neck and shooting up my spine, it was good, a good pain.

The altar was pulled aside, ostensibly by Mercyx, although I couldn't see anything, all that doughnut topping in my eye. I slid down along the wall and eventually came to rest on my back, expecting this to be the end of it, expecting some sort of sense to return.

It didn't. There were knees in my chest, and a hand on my shoulder, and then there was a fist, a very sharp and well-thrown fist, right in that self-same eye socket. Mercyx had made it an eye for an eye.

Excruciating is the word to describe it. All the wiring, retina and fovea and optic nerve, all of it jangling, an orchestra of pain. Black and blue light swirled, a Big Bang spontaneously forming galaxies. It was perfect, this, what Mercyx had just given me, this punch of punctuation, this answer to the question. I lay on the floor, sugar-shocked, and I could see everything, I understood what the light was at the end of the tunnel, all of us, we were all Jesus, we were all dying so that others might live. It was our power and our purpose, to die, and to die with the greatest explosion we could, to spatter our spores, to create sun and star and planet and life. It was going to be okay. This was the beginning of him, really. Not the end. Booker, we'd never let him die. He'd spread himself too far, too widely, to be completely forgotten. We would be together, for him; and our lives would be a commemoration of his memory.

The second punch came down on the side of my jaw. In my head, the first punch had balanced everything out, so the second punch, even though it was less damaging, even though all that cake doughnut, acting as insulation, softened the blow, it seemed a lot worse; my brain couldn't make sense of it, couldn't legitimize it by an eye for an eye, there not being a tooth before the tooth.

A third punch came down on my temple.

There might have been a fourth too, and a fifth and a sixth and a seventh. There's no telling how far Mercyx would have gone, but something animal took over. I needed to get her off me or she would knock me unconscious or worse. My hand, sticky and ghoul-like, shot up and grabbed her shoulder. My other hand, all that frosting and marshmallow cream, it grabbed her by the chin. I flipped her over. I couldn't see her, but I was on top of her. My hand it was around her throat, my other hand it held her wrist to the floor. I must have been quite the sight, hovering over her as I was, chocolate and tears and blood.

I could barely talk, my jaw creaky from flour and fist, but I said it anyway, I said "fuub." I was trying to say fuck you but I said "fuub."

And after I said "fuub," through the sugary eye blur, I got a look at her. She had been crying too. She had been crying and the soft spot above her hard cheekbone was already swelling from where I'd elbowed her. She was upset and I was upset and the two of us, locked like this, we reached a stalemate, we ceased to struggle.

And then it happened. Lodged deep in the Velcroed front pocket of my spare pair of cycling shorts, wedged behind a Clif Bar, it wriggled its way, like a Tolkien ring seeking a Hobbit, to the brink of its enclosure. And then it escaped. And then it fell. It fell and landed square on Mercyx's navel.

The Toys "R" Us ring.

She didn't say anything. I didn't say anything. We both saw it and knew what it was. And then I had my St. Peter at the gate moment. I saw myself riding over the bridge and I saw myself at the top of the ridge and I saw the deep dark green of the forest and the river reflecting that forest, and the heat of the embarrassment of being jilted, and the realization that two people, they really can't know each other, they really can't be as one, it came back to me and reddened me again, twofold, tenfold, a hundred-fold. And then I died as Booker had died and I was dead.

And Mercyx was below me, locked in my death embrace, not knowing that I'd been beheaded too, not knowing what I was thinking, because people can't possibly know what other people think. Not knowing that I wasn't thinking anything anymore because I was dead. She was below me and she was looking through the blur in her eyes into the blur of my eyes and then she said what she said:

She said, "I'll forgive you, if you'll forgive me."

I nodded.

And then, she took the ring, and put it on.

And from that day forward, "fuub" will forever mean, "Our best friend just died, will you marry me?"

Chapter XXXIII

Where Bartholomew Flynn and Annie Mercyx Exorcise Demons

"FLYNN," SHE WAS WHISPERING IN MY EAR. I'd pressed my body against hers, hugging her with all my might, caking her in an unspeakable mixture of refined sugar and blood. All that violence, followed by this, Mercyx's answer, it had produced a mighty hard-on. "Stop."

I pulled up off of her. As I did so, there was a splock, the sucking sound of glucose molecules detaching from glucose molecules. Horror filled her face. She was looking over my shoulder, as if ghosts hovered there.

I rolled off her, my dick tenting my cycling shorts. I looked up, my vision still blurry. They weren't ghosts; they were angels – ten, twenty, maybe thirty of them. One of the angels spread out a wing and extended a claw. Another angel held something heavy, an imp upon its shoulders.

Not angels – demons.

The demon held its claw inches from my mouth. The imp, with its glassy eye, stared. "Are you part of the cult?" the demon asked.

When confronted with a demon asking you if you're part of the cult, the smartest answer would seem to be yes. "Yes," I said.

Mercyx hopped to her feet. "Get out!" she shouted. "You … ants!"

Not angels, not demons, but ants. What else would be visiting the church right now, after Mercyx and I had dumped out and rolled around in ten boxes of Voodoo Doughnuts, but human-sized ants. The ants were clicking their mandibles. The ants were journalists. One of them was saying, "live from Portland, Oregon, in the meeting hall of the Thomas Sect, I'm Carver Cornlinn." One of them picked up a Fruit Loop-studded cruller, studied it, then nibbled.

"Out!" Mercyx shouted again.

She had her arms out as if she were trying to make herself look bigger in the presence of bears. Caked in doughnut, this looked pretty scary. Antennae quivered.

"Be gone!" It was I, Bartholomew Flynn, shouting now. After everything, after our little death picnic, this couldn't be spoiled by ants. We were blood and doughnut and unidentifiable goo. We were frightening. I stood up and faced them. I raised my arms like Mercyx had. I puffed out my chest.

The imps weren't imps they were cameras. The cameras turned my way. They were rolling. I was live from Portland, Oregon. I was a member of some dead midget's freaky death cult. They wanted a statement and I was here to give them one.

I stretched the elastic and dropped my cycling shorts.

After all this time you've spent with me, reading this story, after seeing me ride my bicycle away in fear at the mere thought of someone reading my zine, after watching the reverence and awe with which I put Mercyx on a pedestal, after observing me, at the moment of potential group acceptance, a beer bong in my throat, break into white-hot tears, after all this humiliation, shame piled upon shame piled upon shame, it seems so the opposite of what a mouse like Bartholomew Flynn would do.

But you see, I'd changed. In the presence of a witness, not Mercyx, although she'd certainly been an accomplice, but in the presence of Him or Her or It, of the Higher Power, of whatever you want to call that entity that some call God, I'd changed.

I'd eaten his doughnuts. I'd taken his body and made it mine. I wasn't a mouse anymore; I was a midget.

It's not really a mystery, you know, the mystery of Christ.

You find someone you admire, someone you'd sort of like to be, you invite them over for dinner, you break bread with them, and then, well, in little immeasurable increments, you become them. This, dear reader, is the mystery of Christ. This is how we live forever.

The shorts fell round my ankles.

Dirty with doughnut from the top of head to my waist, then again from just over the knee to the ends of my toes, but in that in-between space, that part of us we normally hide from the world, clean. I was some bizarre inversion of a man in a bathing suit.

It occurred to me as I stood in front of this swarm of ants, these reporters in need of a story, that I'd one-upped the both of them, that this was far more daring and brazen then anything Diogenes or Booker had ever done.

My left hand pointed to the door behind them. My right hand grabbed my erection. It came out of my mouth a croak, like the fuub before. "I banish you!" The power behind my words frightened even me, and I was the one who said them. All antennae fully extended. All bug eyes optimized.

And then live from Portland, Oregon, I pumped the shaft.

It was like they'd been sprayed with a can of Raid. They fell backwards over theater seats. They stumbled and tripped over bicycle parts. Their shoes came off in doughnut goo. They ran for the exit, leaving notepads and wires and sneakers behind.

I watched them in awe, still half-blind, little blurs running into everything as if a rainstorm had snuck up on them, in a frenzied panic to duck into their anthill.

And then they were gone.

It was funny, standing there like that. If someone were to make a statue of me after my death, I'd want it to be of that, me tarred and feathered in Voodoo Doughnut, my cycling shorts around my ankles, one hand pointing in anger at a church door, the other hand clutching my cock. It's my shining moment. Like Lewis & Clark gazing down the Columbia, flanked by the lovely Sacajawea.

In the end it was too weird, of course. Tape left on the cutting room floor. Live from Portland, Oregon, just what they say. They wanted us to be different – meek followers of a madman with a political agenda. This thing I was doing, it was too inexplicable for network television. It was never aired.

But even if this statement of mine never made it national, even if they told the story they wanted to tell about Booker, rather than the truth, my greatest expression did not go unappreciated. For Annie Mercyx, a Toys "R" Us engagement ring newly ensconced on her finger, cuddled up beside me, took my cock in her hand, and faced outward, the two of us side by side, towards the church doors.

The tears didn't come with sobs, or any other physical or verbal motion, they just sort of streamed, and with those streaming tears came clarity, literally visual clarity, all the dough in my eyes suddenly clearing away.

The ants had left the church doors open. From my vantage point I could see the traffic on Prescott Street, all the Port-landers with their Subaru Outbacks and bicycles, going about their business as if it were a normal day, as if it weren't a day in which someone great, someone amazing, had up and died. It wasn't completely normal, though. There was one thing that was unusual, something perhaps only a Portlander would find remarkable.

Through the doors of Booker's church came a ray of sunlight.

Chapter xxxiv

Where Much is Bequeathed

A FTER BARRING THE CHURCH DOORS WITH A chain of welded-together bicycle forks, Mercyx and I retreated to Booker's bedroom, unclear about what we would do when we got there. For one, it was clearly inappropriate to do anything in his bed. For two, we were sticky.

I opened the door. On the clothes lines that crisscrossed the ceiling, Booker's various costumes were draped in plas-tic, as if they'd just returned from the dry cleaners. His wall of stainless steel kitchen appliances were devoid of any stains or smudges – repair manuals and warranty cards had been thoughtfully placed on their tops. His bed had been made perfectly, the sheets tucked in at the corners. Overall, the room was impeccably clean – as if, well, as if Booker knew he'd never be here again.

We'd been holding hands as we'd walked through the church, but as we stood in the entranceway to his vestibule,

we were forced to release them. It was an awkward release, the doughnut mess having glued our hands together. Mercyx walked in first.

On his bed, lay his Scholar's Edition Bible. On top of the Bible, sat a scroll. On top of the scroll, was taped a sticky. We read the note at the same time:

TO BE OPENED UPON MY DEATH

It seemed like hours before either one of us spoke. The way those three objects lay there like that, it was like we'd discovered the Holy Grail.

"Shower," Mercyx said.

I nodded.

"Together," Mercyx said.

I nodded.

"Put them in the washer," Mercyx said.

She stripped while she barked out commands. She wad-ded together her clothes and tossed them into the washer. She did a U around Booker's bed and headed for Booker's bell tower-shaped shower. I stared. She was lovely, so little and hard and proportionate.

"For fucksake, I thought we were done with the deer-in-the-headlights shit," she said, disappearing into Booker's shower.

I took off my shoes, my socks, and my cycling jersey and shorts. I placed them in the washer. I shoveled out some detergent, poured it in. I twisted the dial to Heavy. I closed the lid and pushed On. I could hear the trickle of Booker's odd shower already, could imagine Mercyx's misted body inside it.

She was right about the staring thing, it was a little tacky, but while there's some things about us that we can change, there are some things that never will.

I walked into the shower and shut the door behind me, leaving the scroll, for the time being, unopened.

———

T OWELS WRAPPED AROUND US – HERS KNOTTED at her chest, mine knotted at the waist – we untied the gold ribbon with which he'd wrapped the scroll. The parch-ment unfurled itself on the cow print comforter of his bed. Inside the parchment were three much less fancy sheets of loose-leaf paper torn out of a spiral notebook. On the sheets, in thick pen, was Booker's scrawl:

I, Joseph Patrick Booker, of Portland, Oregon declare this to be my Last Will + Testament

Article 1:

FUNERAL RITES ARE TO BE HELD at C.H.V.R.C.H. 313 AND ADMINISTERED BY BARTHOLOMEW FLYNN, PASTOR, ALL funeral expenses to be paid from my estate.

Article II:

A: Specific Requests

1: I direct that my church the property at 414 Prescott St. be donated to C.H.V.R.C.H. 313 in the name of Bartholomew Flynn, pastor of 2955 Alberta Street.

2: I direct that my possessions associated with the church, including all theater seats, thirteen (13) chairs, seven (7) cassocks and stoles, and one (1) dining room table, be donated to C.H.V.R.C.H. 313 in the name of Bartholomew Flynn, pastor of 2955 Alberta Street.

3: I direct that one (1) Wisconsin Badgers cheerleaders uniform be donated to. C.H.V.R.C.H. 313 in the name of Bartholomew Flynn, pastor, for use as he sees fit.

4: I DIRECT THAT ONE-HUNDRED and THIRTY-NINE (139) UNVSED CONDOMS (OR LESS, SHOULD LESS BE FOUND) BE DONATED TO THE PORTLAND SEX WORKERS' UNION, 349 NW 13TH SUITE 392.

5: I DIRECT THAT all Bicycles, Bicycle parts anD BICYCLE TOOLS found at MY PROPERTY or ON THE GROUNDS OF MY PROPERTY, iNCLUDING ONE (1) TALL BIKE, ONE (1) CHOPPER Bike, and ONE (1) CARGO BIKE, be DONATED TO. C.H.V.C.K. 6969, IN THE NAME OF JOHN GUARDEROS, A.K.A. DiOGENES, PASTOR, OF UNDISCLosed COORDINATES, PORTLAND, OR

B: Residuary Estate. I DIRECT THAT $20,000 FROM MY RESiduARY ESTATE BE DONATED TO CH.U.R.C.H. 3B, TO BE Administered by Bartholomew Flynn, Pastor. AIE REMAINDER OF my residuary estate SHOULD be LIQUIDATed AND DONATED to the IRAQI ORPHAN FUND, PO BOX 3718, NY, NY

IN WITNESS WHEREOF, I have subscribed my name below, this 2nd day of December, 2004.

Joseph Patrick Booker

We, the undersigned, hereby certify that the above instrument, which consists of THREE (3) sheets of spiral notebook paper was signed in our sight by Joseph Patrick Booker, who declared this instrument to be his Last Will and Testament.

X _Juan Brunero_

3672 NE Condor Dr.
Gresham, OR 97352

X _Janet Six Reck_

539 NW 26th Ave #329
Portland, OR 97320

On top of this third sheet of loose leaf of paper was an-other sticky note. It read:

WHILE I SAT ON HIS BED, LETTING ALL THE implications of his will flood over me – the ownership of his residence, the twenty-thousand dollars, the directive to pastor his church – I recalled how this began, how I'd rid-den my bike through the rain that early fall morning, angst-ridden, unsure about what I was supposed to do with my life, how Booker had told me, on that day, how in asking, I would receive. I'd taken it all as schlock. Booker, this weird overzeal-ous midget pretending to be a preacher, he was an awesome fiction, but there wasn't anything real about him, anything that he could give.

I'd been wrong, of course. Six months after I'd met him the gifts I'd received were innumerable. He'd given me love, in the form of Mercyx. He'd given me fame, in the form of my comic. And now, he'd given me fortune, in the form of tan-gible property and twenty-thousand smackeroos.

If I'd any tears left in me, I'm sure I would have shed them now, but as it were the well was dry.

There was one other thing he'd given me as well. As I stood there gazing cross-eyed at the opening line of his odd legalese –

I, Joseph Patrick Booker, of Portland, Oregon declare this to be my Last Will and Testament – what my mind thought was different from what my eyes read – *I, Joseph Patrick Booker, of Portland, Oregon declare this to be* YOUR MISSION IN LIFE.

It was so clear to me what he had done, in this his last

gesture. I would never pick up that blue-linen journal again. My mission was written in thick ink in his scrawly hand:

Bartholomew Flynn, Pastor

And my first duty, as Bartholomew Flynn, not scribe, but pastor, was to preside at Joseph Patrick Booker's funeral.

Chapter xxxv

The Resurrection

THE BICYCLES, BICYCLE PARTS, BICYCLE tools, and all the welding equipment van-ished from the church one morning. Noth-ing else was missing. Not long after, bikes, tall and chopper and cargo, spray-painted entirely in white, began to show up on Portland street cor-ners, chained to stop signs and telephone poles, adorned with spring lilies and the photocopied image of Hervé Villechaize – Tattoo.

It began sporadically, but by the day of his funeral, they were everywhere.

The ghost bikes weren't the only things infesting Portland that week. It turned out that the ants who'd showed up at the church last Sunday were mere workers; by mid-week the city had been invaded by queens.

They came drycleaned and manicured and lip-sticked – color in Portland's grayscale. They came from Los Angeles and New York and London. They were pant-suited. It was an invasion of pretense, like the Disney Dreams Come True parade was marching down humble Alberta Street. They expected ululation. They beamed sunny smiles and jammed snow cones into your mouths.

It was why we all lived here, to escape them. And now they'd swarmed.

Meanwhile, in backrooms, drones did the dirty work, cut-ting and splicing to make the queens appear hard-nosed. They made us all look terrible. A whole city of David Koreshes.

Wacos.

On the networks, they flashed it hundreds of times, my face bloodied and full of doughnut. Mercyx's the same. They got footage of Diogenes, covered from head to foot in plaster from his entanglement at the Battle of the Bookers. Gassy's broken arm. Suddenly C.H.V.C.K. and C.H.V.R.C.H. were some kind of weird self-mutilation cult, and Booker had gone to Baghdad on a suicidal mission, his beheading religious fulfillment.

It was Grade A tabloid material.

And now, for the last act, they would film his funeral. They were ready for us. We were ready for them.

———

D ANTE'S BOUNCERS HAD BEEN POSTED IN front of the church. When I cracked open the door to his vestibule, I could tell they'd done their job. All the right people were there, the zinesters, the coffee baristas, the D&D nerds, the bike messengers, the sex workers, even the Voodoo Doughnut employees had materialized. There wasn't a single pant-suit.

I closed the door. Mercyx was sitting cross-legged and cross-armed on Booker's bed, looking ridiculous in a feather boa and a Vegas showgirl's bikini. Next to her were twelve boxes of Voodoo doughnuts. I looked equally ridiculous in my Wisconsin Badgers cheerleader get-up. Neither one of us was in our element. We both had goosebumps.

I'd spent the week hiding from the paparazzi in Beale's basement, writing out the eulogy under the light of a single bulb. I crinkled the pages in my hand. It had all seemed a good idea in the privacy of a basement, huddled away from the masses, but now that I was about to go out there, it dawned on me that what I was about to perform was the ultimate humiliation, and at a funeral no less.

I walked over to the mirror. I had a whore's wig on my head. I had black mascara freckles. I had pigtails. I was Raggedy Ann.

It was time. I exhaled. I walked out of the vestibule and into the church.

C.H.V.C.K. 6969 was in the front row, only they weren't C.H.V.C.K. 6969, they were just guys. Gassy had no gas mask. Mad Max, no bazooka. Diogenes was shaved and showered. They were dressed in black. They wore ties. If it weren't for all the crutches and plaster you would have thought they were normal. I could feel my face flush. Like a schoolgirl. Like Raggedy Ann.

The people from the funeral home were there, waiting in the wings. They had placed the body below the altar and propped it up on a table. It was an open casket. As I entered, their eyebrows raised.

The church was dead silent.

I strode, as Booker had so many times before, from the vestibule to the monolith. I stopped behind the milk crates, and when I do so, I was confronted with the same problem Booker had been confronted with the first time he had done this – there was no way to get on them.

I'd planned it out, all of it, but not once had I thought about the milk crates. I'd watched him do it a million times, that leapfrog thing he did, that thing where he splayed his legs out then landed, rump first, on the first of three crates. I paused for a long while. To the audience, it must have appeared to be for effect.

And then it occurred to me what this was, what it had always been – a leap of faith.

I put my hands together on the top crate and leapt. I splayed my legs.

Go Badgers!

I felt a pair of hands on my waist as I leapt. There wasn't a pair of hands there. I landed, just as he always had, rump-first and stable on the top crate. I looked at my audience. They were startled, just as I had been. I knew something that they would never know, standing on those milk crates.

Carefully, tentatively, I stood up. I was high. I felt vertigo. I felt sick. Below me, I could see his body, veins pumped full of formaldehyde. They'd brought him back. He had on a priest's formal wear, complete with a Roman collar to cover the stitching. It was time to start my eulogy, time to say all those things I'd spent the week writing out. But I couldn't. I'd left my entire speech in his vestibule.

"Fuck!" I said.

I was miked. Mercyx and I had decided to mike me.

"FUCK!" The church reverberated. We hadn't tested it. The volume was far too high.

It was terrible, starting this way, starting with fuck, now what was I going to do. I looked down. Diogenes was staring at me. I stared back. What I saw in his eyes wasn't what I expected. The eyes didn't say imbecile or faggot or asshole or anything like that. They said this:

I appreciate you. We're brothers. You forever have my respect.

And with that look I realized there'd been enough speeches, that how we felt and what needed to be said could be distilled into this one word, that when someone you love and respect dies, there is only one appropriate word, only one appropriate expression, and it's sort of a shame we don't hear that word at more funerals.

I shouted it with all my might, shouted it into the mike, with full knowledge of the ear-splitting repercussions:

FUCK!

Two things happened simultaneously with the shouting of that sacred word. The first involved the crucifix on the wall behind me. Knocked from its moorings from the reverb, it dropped from the wall and hit the floor, the base of the cross thumping the hardwood with a sickening pop, and then slowly, but gathering speed, it began to fall, Christ-forward, until it struck his altar, splitting it in two, splinters flying to the right and the left like fireworks. The second thing that happened involved Mercyx. Sensing that my speech had ended prematurely, or more likely, discovering the forgotten pages on top of Booker's washing machine and contriving a way to bring them to me, Mercyx walked out of the vestibule, in her arms, stacked tiltingly and cartoonishly, twelve pink boxes of Voodoo Doughnuts, all you could make of her being high heels, nude-hose-covered legs, and a gold-sequined bikini bottom.

The altar no longer in existence in its previous form, Mercyx halted, not knowing where to set the boxes. Where she stopped just happened to be next to the milk crates, the top doughnut box right next to me, at waist level. This certainly wasn't what we'd planned.

I opened the pink box. I took out a Mango Tango.

And then I looked down.

Booker was sitting up in his casket.

My jaw dropped. All the c.h.v.c.k. guys, their jaws dropped. Everyone in the church who could see, their jaws dropped. Even the funeral home attendants, so stoic and imperturbable, their jaws dropped. The tip of the crucifix, it had slid forward off the altar and onto his casket, in such a way that, yes, the face of Jesus lie in Booker's crotch, the weight of his wooden head, through some weird trick of rigor mortis, bending Booker's torso forward. Booker's head lolled back, and on his face, well, it was his smile, that huge all-encompassing smile.

Everything that happened up until this moment was plausible. Unlikely, certainly, but plausible. What happened next wasn't. Booker, and although it could have been some trick of the stained-glass windows, opened his eyes. I swear he opened him. And then, his face turned upwards towards me, that smile still on his face, he spoke:

"Feed my sheep."

I flung the Mango Tango. It spun like a Frisbee, its sunny innards raining down on the crowd. I grabbed a Strawberry Quik, did the same with that, powder falling from the sky like fairy dust. I daggered a Cock & Balls right at Diogenes. I kept going, tossing doughnut after doughnut, and then, real-izing they didn't get it what I was doing, I shouted at them from my perch atop the milk crates.

"Take this, his body, and eat of it, for it shall become the bread of life!"

And then they did. They took the doughnuts that I was tossing and ate them. And really, this all would have ended peaceably. We would have eaten some doughnuts and drank some coffee (it was still waiting there, in the back) and then the funeral attendants would have escorted us all out to the West Hills, where Mercyx and I had purchased a little plot in "the cemetery" we liked to cycle through, and we would have laid him to rest.

But peace was not to be. Just at the moment when things had settled down, when the chef paramedics had gone up to the altar, taken the boxes out of Mercyx's hands, and begun passing the doughnuts out in a sensible manner, the front doors of the church burst open, and in poured the ants.

It was unclear how they'd gotten past Dante's bouncers, I suspect that several of them had gone down first, but they had. The cameras were rolling instantly. All tuned to me.

I suppose I shouldn't have done it, given the symbolism, but I was so tired of them. I'd eaten half of it already by then, my personal Voodoo favorite, the Dirty Bastard. I threw it anyway.

That was all it took.

It was mob on mob.

The doughnuts flew at them from everywhere. Long-range, short-range, in your face. A coconut snowball got shoved into a $50,000 camera. A couple of applesauce vegans got stuffed into a pant-suit. A pretzel went up an anchor-woman's nose. It was a massacre, and one I really didn't care to watch.

Mercyx was next to the milk crate on which I stood. I held out a hand so she could help me down. We walked over to the casket, hand-in-hand, me in my cheerleader's uniform, Mercyx in her Vegas showgirl outfit, both of us having changed so much from knowing him.

His head, somehow, had shifted from lolling backward to lolling forward, his chin resting on his chest. Mercyx and I lifted the crucifix from his crotch, and placed it beside the casket, his body falling instantly back, his arms resting naturally over his stomach, his hands palms up. It was kind of gross to do what I did, but it sort of seemed befitting, the way those hands lie.

I placed a Voodoo doll there. And then together, Mercyx and I shut the lid.

Chapter XXXVI

Where Annie Mercyx and Bartholomew Flynn
and Their Child Pass a Day at Cathedral Park
and Where This Gospel Finally Ends

J AM SITTING IN CATHEDRAL PARK IN NORTH Portland. It is March. We've had an unusual dry spell, and the air temperature is such that I can just lie here on the grass, with a jacket and hat and gloves on, and not feel all that cold.

Time has passed, and Mercyx and I are lying next to each other under a blanket in Cathedral Park, body pressed against body for warmth. Meanwhile, a boy is running at top speed down the hill. We are both watching him. Subconsciously, we are playing a game of chicken, waiting to see which one of us will blink first, waiting to see who will leap out of the blanket and brave the cold to catch the boy before he drowns in the river.

It is Mercyx who blinks. She groans before she does it, a bit frustrated with my laziness. I watch her run down the slope, with the boy far ahead, and what I see is beautiful. There is our child, Booker Flynn, his red wool cap has a fluffy ball on the top, and the ball is bobbing in rhythm to the churning of his little legs. There is Mercyx in black tight pants and a blue sweater, taking long strides, sure-footed and strong. There is spring grass, a shamrock green. And there are gray arches. The pillars of the St. John's Bridge are decorative, in each of them is carved a high, Gothic arch.

I am watching this blur of color and I am thinking about this gospel. Before she ran to chase down the child, Mercyx and I had been discussing it. I had been trying to decide how to end it. I didn't want to leave you with a mundane ending: my attempt to maintain Booker's church; the trivial details of Mercyx and my married life. I wanted, well, I wanted Booker to finish the story. I wanted the title to mean something, for Booker to really be some sort of prophet, albeit a minor one.

But in order to be a prophet, a person's prophecies must come to pass.

The flash of blue has caught up with the bobbing red and they both have stopped. The drama over, I turn and face the sky. I close my eyes. It doesn't seem right. I had to give Booker the last word. But how? He wouldn't want me to lie; he wouldn't want me to make up some bullshit about his spirit ascending up into heaven; and yet I needed something from him.

What would you say Booker? If you had the last word what would you say?

I am thinking this and lamenting it, how badly we need Joseph Patrick Bookers and C.H.V.R.C.H 313s in this world, and I am thinking about this gospel and the years I've spent on it, and how I'm just a guy who sits in a room on a computer, day in and day out, when there is such a need for me to be out there like Booker, doing crazy things to show people how to change.

There is a clang. Three clangs actually. Clang. Clang. Clang. An object falls from the sky, heading straight for me. It is clear to me that something has fallen from a truck, bounced over the railing, pinballed against the scaffolding, and is now accelerating towards the earth to crush my head in, and yet I can't move. I am glued in place. I feel like Chicken Little.

The object misses my head by inches. It hits the ground. It bounces. It springs over me. It flips and twists and does a full rainbow, leaping from its landing-point and resting near my toes. What it has done seems impossible, as if the object were a yo-yo being controlled by an invisible hand.

I look down. When I look down my eyes do not immediately come into focus. Instead, they see my son running towards me, yelling something; and my wife running as well. In their eyes, is the question, *are you okay*? They saw the object fall, too.

Finally, I focus my eyes on the object in front of me. What has fallen from the sky and nearly killed me is an Alpenrose milk crate.